Something Borrowed

Series Starters by

Rebecca Connolly

The Arrangements:

An Arrangement of Sorts

The London League:

The Lady and the Gent

The Spinster Chronicles:

The Merry Lives of Spinsters

Agents of the Convent:

Fortune Favors the Sparrow

Cornwall Brides:

Something Old

Something Borrowed

Cornwall Brides
Book Three

REBECCA CONNOLLY

Phase Publishing, LLC
Seattle

Phase Publishing, LLC first paperback edition
December 2023

ISBN 978-1-952103-66-7
Library of Congress Control Number 2023921220
Cataloging-in-Publication Data on file.

Acknowledgements

To the city of Truro for being the most adorable, quaint, delightful, nostalgic place I've ever been. The place that could have been home for me within five minutes of arriving. The place with the cathedral that took my breath away. The place I was needing out about and was so much better than I imagined. Can't wait to go back.

And to British scones. The Cornish method really is the best one. Look it up.

Want to hear about future releases and upcoming events for Rebecca Connolly?

Sign up for the monthly Wit and Whimsy at:

www.rebeccaconnolly.com

Chapter One
England, 1829

"Will you marry me?"

There. That was simple enough, straightforward and to the point. No complications, no excesses, no puffed-up flattery, and no feigned declarations of feelings that were not there.

What more could a sensible woman want in a proposal?

Gage Trembath frowned to himself as he rode his horse headlong towards the Berkeley family estate on the outskirts of Bath. It was not a hasty decision, despite his present haste, but neither had it been extensively discussed with anyone.

Not even the woman involved.

Hence his present recitations on horseback.

Would she require more than the simple and honest question he was about to pose? She did not seem to be a particularly sentimental young woman, but he would not pretend that he understood the ways and means of the fairer sex. He had no sisters, but he had been blessed with a prodigious number of female cousins, and he knew enough to be fully aware that contradictions ran rampant in the feminine persuasion.

Dash it, what if he was going to do this poorly?

"It would be an honor," he said, clearing his throat, "if you would consent…"

Well, that was simply sounding pompous and overinflated. He definitely knew enough to know she would not appreciate a spectacle.

He might not know Miss Honora Berkeley enough to know what

sort of a wedding she might prefer, what activities might hold her interest, or how involved she might wish to be in the rearing of children, but he did know she was a woman of sense, reserve, and dignity.

Which was all he needed, really.

He'd had the great love of his life, and it had brought him nothing but a broken heart and a sour temper. And a solid fortress of carefully constructed internal defenses against ever succumbing to such reckless feelings ever again.

The love of his life, Margaret Teague, had chosen to wed the older and profoundly wealthy Lord Hastings from Devon before Gage had plucked up the courage to propose, though they had discussed their future in such terms that she had known of his intentions. Yet she had opted to marry elsewhere when the offer was made rather than give Gage the opportunity to try for her himself. It had been a crushing blow, to say the least, and he had been only too glad when all of the wedding festivities had taken place in Devon so he would have to neither hear about nor participate in them. He had rooted the woman out of his heart and scrubbed all memory of her from his mind, desperate to reclaim something of himself from the shambles.

Whether he had been successful or not in doing so would be for someone else to decide. He had not the insight nor the patience to examine himself to such an extent.

But it was time he stopped avoiding the noose of matrimony once and for all, which was what had him riding towards Bath at this time. No more was some pathetic wound from his past going to keep him from fulfilling his duty, let alone proceeding into the life he wanted for himself.

And no woman who had deliberately chosen against him deserved to stand in the way of his path to do so.

It had surprised Gage, when he had turned his thoughts seriously to matrimony, that the first person to come to mind was Honora Berkeley. They had met a handful of times, only when she had come to Cornwall to visit her cousin, Gage's lifelong friend Julia Roskelley, and those instances could hardly be described as being overtures for courtship. Indeed, it had been particularly casual, warm enough to render them fond acquaintances, and comfortable enough to allow them future interactions without awkwardness.

Further than that, he could not admit to, especially if he wished to consider himself an honest man, which he usually did.

Usually.

But the idea of Honora becoming his wife had not left his mind from the moment it had entered, no matter how many rational conversations he'd had with himself. So here he was, on his way to propose the idea, and the union, and praying she was just as sensible and sane as he had previously found her to be. If there was one thing his life did not need, it was dramatic and overly emotional engagements.

Gage sputtered to himself, shaking his head. Was there any way to pose the question in a way that would not shock the poor girl? He had never expressed particular interest in her as a prospect, let alone as a woman at all. They had danced a few times when she was in Cornwall, had shared meals at the homes of mutual friends, had conversed politely at various social engagements, but that was the extent of their relationship.

Would she even want to marry at all, let alone marry him?

She was the cousin of his oldest friend, which meant he knew more about her than he actually knew her, for better or worse. He knew she was the youngest of four children, three of whom were daughters, and he knew that her family had little enough to do with her. There was strife between the parents, who were basically leading completely separate lives now that their children were grown, and the other siblings were perfectly content to cling to their personal families rather than their extended relations.

All of which meant Honora was left alone more often than not and abandoned in truth. Caught between relations who were not fighting over her but wanting to be rid of her.

Gage was convinced that Julia was exaggerating some of the things she had shared with him, as any true and loyal cousin would in defense of one they loved. No family could be so dysfunctional and distant, though he had certainly seen some dysfunction and distance in enough families to know it existed. It was simply the extent to which his friend described her cousin's life that he doubted. Honora was a lovely, competent, charming woman, and she had the voice of an angel when she sang. Who would not be proud of and take pains with such a daughter?

But if she were not accustomed to affection, let alone attention, she would likely not take kindly to an overly attentive attempt at a proposal. It might overwhelm and confuse her, being so foreign a thing. Julia would have given her some of both, as a warm and caring relation, but it would certainly not be within the usual nature of Honora's life.

So what, then, would be the best way to pose the question?

"Might you be interested in marriage, Miss Berkeley?" he tried as he turned onto the main road towards Bath, reining in his horse just enough to bring his speed to a more gentlemanly trot.

Hmm. Those words felt almost patronizing on his tongue. No one wished to be patronized, and he suspected Miss Berkeley was smart enough to know when that was occurring. If there was one thing he had learned over the weeks she had been in his company, it was that she observed a great deal. Though she had never said so, he suspected she also had opinions to match them.

He could only hope she would grow comfortable with him enough to share those opinions, whatever they might be. There was nothing he loved so much as secret opinions from unexpected quarters.

"I need to marry," he said plainly, straightening in his saddle, "and of all eligible women of my acquaintance, I believe that you…"

He trailed off, making a face. He was starting to sound like his friend, Lord Harrison Basset, who had all the charm of a cantankerous coal miner and the forthrightness of a judge. He had married for duty to a woman of fortune and connection, and though things had started off with the promise of a storm at sea, they were now rather gushing with bliss.

How they had managed to avoid complete shipwreck with their vastly opposite natures and the manner in which their marriage unfolded, Gage would never know.

And then there were the Grangers. They split their time between London, Hampshire, and Cornwall, and had been married for several years. But they had only found love and harmony in their marriage recently, mostly because Granger had chosen to pursue the marriage for financial gains rather than emphasizing the longstanding affection and love he'd had for his wife prior to their marriage. Thus, neither of them had expressed themselves properly, and it had landed them in a shell of a marriage that could have been blissful from the start.

Gage was going to avoid both of those situations with his choice of wife. Honora was not sharp-tempered, as far as he knew, nor was she haughty. He was an open man himself and had no trouble with expressing the truth of his situation and feelings. There would be no risk of disappointment in the nature of their marriage when it would all be made perfectly plain from the very beginning. She would know he did not love her, that he had not been secretly pining for her, and that he had no expectations other than that they would be comfortable together and content to raise a family with friendly affection and mutual respect between them, as well as a dedication to the happiness of their future children.

It would be, in many respects, the ideal marriage.

If she consented, of course.

That was the ultimate question.

Would she choose to accept his proposal and marry him? Would she consent to being the mother of his children? Was she interested in being the mistress of Helwithin? Was Gage the sort of man to whom she would mind attaching herself?

What sort of marriage had she envisioned for herself prior to this?

He really should have talked this through with someone before he had left his home to proceed with the proposal. And, he hoped, the wedding. He had no interest in having a wedding at Helwithin church, nor of inviting his tenants and workers and friends to attend, though he would certainly host a gathering of all sorts to welcome his new bride to her home. He had no family in England, and a quick and quiet wedding was all he wanted.

He had the promise of a special license if he wanted one, and if he could convince Honora it would be worth the effort…

He was getting ahead of himself. He needed to figure out what he would say to the woman in his proposal, then actually propose, and then, pending her answer, move forward.

He could not plan further without an answer. It would be a waste of thought and energy.

He hated wasting either, let alone both.

"Miss Berkeley," he murmured to himself, keeping his voice down as there began to be more traffic on the roads, "I've a notion to marry."

He shook his head, snorting to himself. A notion. As though the idea had only just occurred to him, and he'd figured a jaunt to Bath would be no trouble at all.

No, this was not a notion, and he'd thought about it so long, he'd finally just determined that Honora Berkeley was as good an idea as any, stopped fighting the idea of her, and settled matters enough to be gone for a month or so, should she wish to marry in the traditional manner, banns and all.

The only real question was how long it would take to convince her of him.

He was fully prepared for a battle of sorts. He knew he was not a perfect candidate for matrimony, but he was a decent prospect, all things considered. Fortune, property, and connection, and, he flattered himself, he was not a bad-looking chap.

And he had it on good authority that he was amiable.

So, she ought to have no real complaints about him.

"Oh, to hell with it," Gage muttered, digging his heels into the horse's sides a little more. He was anxious to get the conversation underway and out of his mind, and ruminating on the topic over and over again was not going to assist him with that.

It did not matter how he presented the idea as long as he was honest about it. She would either accept him or reject him, and there was very little he could do about that until he asked.

Just a few miles farther, and he found himself riding towards the rather plain stone façade of Horsend Manor. There were several windows along the north face, all of which seemed to be clean enough, and the stone was free of ivy or vines, which was more than he could say for other houses in this part of the country. The gravel drive was well kept, the lawns tidy, and the parapets rather stately, though free of statues or embellishments. All in all, a clean presentation of an estate, though not as large a building as he would have expected, given the apparent wealth and status of the Berkeley family in the area.

Perhaps there was more to the place beyond what he could presently see.

A footman appeared in the entrance just as Gage dismounted, with the same unnerving sense of timing his own servants had managed to perfect, and moved with the horse towards the stables without a word to him.

Odd. He didn't think he was expected. He hadn't sent word on ahead, and he was absolutely certain Honora did not anticipate him or what he would ask.

He presented himself at the entrance to the house, looking around for any sign of a butler or housekeeper, given the precision of the footman. Sure enough, the butler stood just inside the door, chin aloft, eyes fixed on Gage, slight curve to the mouth in a show of welcome that was sure to puzzle anyone who saw it.

Butlers were strange creatures.

"Good day," Gage greeted, sweeping off his hat. "Gage Trembath to see Miss Honora Berkeley, if she is at home." He presented his card, smiling as pleasantly as he knew how with someone he did not know.

The butler took the card and eyed it, then flicked his gaze back to Gage. "Does Miss Berkeley know you, sir?"

"She does," Gage assured him, fighting the urge to reply to the question in a far more sarcastic manner. "I am friends with her cousin Julia Roskelley in Cornwall, and we have met several times on her visits."

A brisk nod was the butler's only response, and he turned slightly. "If you will follow me, sir, I will have you wait for Miss Berkeley in the drawing room. It should not be much more than a few moments, but if there is a delay, I will have some tea brought in to you. Does this sound acceptable?"

This sounded like a lesson in formality or a treatise on manners, but it was certainly acceptable enough.

Gage nodded, though the man would not see it. "It does, yes. She is not expecting me, so I anticipated a wait."

To this, there was no reply at all.

A butler's typical response to unnecessary conversation.

That was one black mark against Gage's name, he was sure of it.

The drawing room was as unremarkable as any other drawing room he had ever been in, and he made a show of nodding politely to the butler as he left the room to fetch Honora.

Then Gage paced.

He was not usually one who paced, but there was something about an impending proposal that made him unconscionably nervous. It was ridiculous, given that his hopes and dreams were not exactly pinned upon this particular woman for his choice of wife, but he did feel comfortable with the idea, and that surely ought to mean something significant. And while pacing did not change anything about his situation, it enabled him to do something, so it felt like progress.

Which seemed enough to settle something or other within him.

"Mr. Trembath?"

Gage turned halfway through a pace of his pacing. "Yes?"

Honora Berkeley stood in the doorway to the room, giving him a bewildered, but not displeased, look.

Right. He was not being summoned or about to be questioned. She was greeting him amidst confusion.

He was an idiot.

"Miss Berkeley," he recovered belatedly, fully facing her and bowing.

She gave him a hurried curtsey. "Delighted to see you, though I must admit to being surprised."

"I imagined you would be," he replied, somehow managing to chuckle in spite of his rising anxieties.

Honora bit her lip ever so slightly, giving her youthful appearance an even younger countenance, with her deep auburn hair plaited and pinned loosely back, her wide eyes staring at him. She cocked her head slightly. "What in the world are you doing here?"

All that Gage had thought he would say, or might say, or could say, flew out of his head, and only one simple statement remained.

It was honest, clear, and direct, and that was as good as it was going to get.

He shrugged a little. "I've come to ask you to marry me."

Chapter Two

Time. She had asked for time.

A handsome, eligible, friendly, respectful man had asked her to marry him, and she had asked for time to consider.

Honora Berkeley bit down softly on the inside of her lip, careful to avoid showing any outward signs of her nerves or distress. Her mother was sharp-eyed for such things, and she would not hesitate in calling out swift corrections for Honora.

Having Gage at the table enjoying the meal with them would not stop her.

What was there to think about, really? She was miserable at home most of the time, somehow always in the way even when she avoided both parents at any given time. It was unfortunate that both were in Horsend at the same time, as the tension that prevailed and the arguments that followed were brutal, cutting, and particularly shrill. Even in the silence that inevitably echoed throughout the house after the fighting, there was a defiant and consuming coldness that somehow shared the volume of the argument.

It was undoubtedly better to have one of her parents absent from the estate. Silence still reigned in the house, but it was an emotionless silence that did not wound nearly as much.

It simply bore loneliness.

That was life at Horsend to Honora. Lonely. Empty. A gaping, cavernous void in which she had no purpose.

And she needed to think about leaving it forever?

She had written to each of her three siblings, all of whom had experienced the tumultuous life of Horsend, to beg them to let her stay with them and their families. She had gone so far as to offer herself as a governess to her nieces and nephews, without the expectations of payment.

All of them had refused her. Each and every time.

They pitied her, that was always made plain, but they had no interest in giving her a reprieve from her situation. They did not want her to join them. Not even for short holidays.

Neither did her parents want her. They were always jaunting here and there with their social connections, if not their amorous ones, and usually without informing Honora of their plans. They never invited her on trips with them, and the mention of any such idea was enough to earn Honora a near perfectly scripted speech designed to manipulate and shame her for daring to think her life lacked something. The number of birthdays and holidays she had spent alone at Horsend were innumerable, and only recently had her beloved cousin Julia begun to realize just how dreadful life at the estate was for Honora. She had invited her to Cornwall several times, always to the apparent delight of Honora's parents, and it was on those visits that she had met Gage.

But she'd never gone so far as to imagine marrying him.

She'd never really thought about marrying anyone. She met almost no one socially, as she had no companion to escort her to events in Bath, and no one came to call at Horsend. She had been firmly placed on the path to spinsterhood by the age of eighteen, and there were no tools at her disposal to amend the course.

Until now.

Marriage. What did she even think about marriage? She was not a fanciful girl, never had been, and her personal experience with marriage had been practically disastrous. Her siblings had comfortable matches that were suitable enough, and without the disdain her parents cultivated for each other, which seemed monumental. She had seen happy marriages among Julia's friends in Cornwall, ones that seemed to include true affection, if not outright love.

She knew that pleasant marriages were possible and that some people married for love. She simply did not think that any such connection would happen for her. If she married, which had been a rather significant if, she'd always presumed it would be to some quiet, middle-aged curate who might want a rather unremarkable wife to bear him a few children to help him appear more respectable to his parish.

She'd like to be a mother, that much she knew about herself. She had seen how her own had chosen to mother and knew she could improve upon that simply by caring about her children for more than how they would reflect upon herself. She would pay attention to them and be an active part of their lives. She would raise the children with her husband rather than in spite of her husband.

If her husband wished to take part in the raising of the children.

Would Gage want to be involved in the raising of children?

She glanced across the table at him, a rise of sympathy settling in her chest as she noted his being trapped in conversation with her father. To Gage's credit, his expression held no hint of boredom or desperation, but that of polite interest. Honora could barely manage the same, and the man was her father.

But that was part of the pure magic of Gage. He was affable under any circumstances and had the tolerance, if not patience, of a saint. Yet he was no saint, as his natural naughtiness made plain, but it was so delightful, so witty and charming, that there was never any offense in his words or his antics.

He had never been anything less than familiar and comfortable with Honora, and that made her comfortable and relatively familiar as well, when she was usually a fairly shy creature. Unless she was singing. Of all strange things, she could not converse without much effort and thought, and considerable regrets upon reflection, but she could sing without remotely growing nervous.

Singing had never given her perspiring palms or a pounding heart, had never made her knees shake or her head swim. It was, perhaps, the only thing that truly felt natural to her.

Considering the fact that her own skin hardly felt natural to her most of the time, that was miraculous indeed.

One might think her parents would find pleasure in her accomplishment there.

One would be wrong.

"Honora, do not cut your potatoes with so much noise," her

mother hissed, not bothering to keep her voice down. "I shall send you to eat in the nursery like the child you are if you do not cease."

Honora looked down at her plate, her neck warming at being so blatantly called out, especially when her father was cutting his meat at a much louder volume than was strictly necessary.

He cut a shockingly loud slice at that moment, making her mother cringe. Had he done so on purpose? Honora flicked her glance towards him, but he seemed perfectly at ease in conversation with their guest.

"One needs no guessing as to where you picked up that dreadful habit," her mother grumbled, spearing her own piece of potato with too much gusto. "It's a wonder I ever come to Horsend at all. Nothing to sustain me here."

"No one invited you back, dearest," her husband interjected between bites, his attention still focused on Gage. "Don't blame Honora for your dislike of me."

She watched her mother's eyes narrow, the grip on her silverware tightening as she glared darkly down the length of the table.

They were always like this, which was why they never dined as a family. Her mother took trays in her rooms, her father ate in his study, and Honora ate alone in the dining room. It was a lonely hour or so, but no more than any hour of her day, and it was preferable to her parents picking at each other, or at her.

Or worse, fully having it out at the tops of their lungs.

"Eat your meat, Honora, or you'll never get pretty," her father scolded, rapping his knuckles on the table twice. "Go on, be a good girl."

To get him to stop talking to her like a child, Honora took a pointed bite of meat and avoided looking at Gage, whose attention seemed to be on her for the moment.

She wished it wouldn't be. It felt as though she was being watched to see if meat would have an immediate impact on her constitution.

It was the phrase her father had always used to make Honora eat, and she'd never liked it. Her sisters had never been told such things, and they were as fastidious with their eating as she was.

More so, in fact.

But they were born pretty, so no encouragement to become so would ever have done well there.

"Mr. Trembath," her mother broke in loudly, knowing full well that her husband had the man in conversation. "Pray tell me of my niece in Cornwall. She is my sister's daughter, you know, and she was once a frequent visitor here. But we see her so infrequently now."

Gage turned towards her in surprise, missing the dark glare Honora's father was casting down the table at his wife. "Mrs. Roskelley, ma'am? She is well, I believe. I dined at Ayrgoose before I came to Bath, and they were as happy and jovial as ever."

"How jovial could she be while with child?" Honora's mother sputtered loudly and took her glass of Madeira, sipping deeply. "Miserable condition."

"Some women find pleasure in childbearing and rearing," Honora's father answered with a hefty dose of spite. "And please, temper your imbibing before our guest."

In response, she toasted her husband with her glass and downed the remnants, then held the empty glass over her shoulder for a footman to refill.

Honora could have buried her face in her hands out of shame, but that would have been corrected.

"Honora, sit up straight, for heaven's sake!" her mother barked. "Why must you slump so? Truly, Mr. Trembath will regret his calling on you."

Honora sat up, straightening to an almost awkward degree, having not slumped in the slightest. But the appearance of correction was always important, even if there was nothing to correct.

"And how would you know women enjoy bearing and rearing children, hmm?" her mother went on, returning her attention down the table. "You were never involved with any of it."

"Hardly true," her father corrected with a loud scoff. "I was there for the most important part." He grinned, chuckling to himself and toasting her with his wine.

Honora thought her cheeks would burst into flames, and focused on the plate in front of her, though eating was beyond possibility.

"I'll not thank you for that, if that was your hope," Honora's mother shot back. "Worst times of my life, each and every time."

Oh heavens, would this torment never end? Gage was going to rescind his offer and flee the house, telling all of Cornwall what horrid people the Berkeleys were. Julia would never be able to invite Honora to visit again, and she would be trapped in this endless misery.

She didn't want Gage to rescind his offer. She wanted to accept it and run. She wanted to take anything he would offer if it got her away from this. Why hadn't she just said yes and been done with it?

Had she really thought anything else might be better?

"And how many children did you have, ma'am?" Gage said in a loud but pleasant voice, turning his attention almost entirely to Honora's mother, no strain appearing in his features at all. "Julia has always said she could never remember each of her cousins."

That made Honora's mother sniff with some poor attempt at a laugh. "Hardly surprising, the girl has the mind of a butterfly net, and there are children positively coming out of the rafters in the family. I had four myself, though if we'd had two boys, that would have been it."

"On that, we can agree," Honora's father concurred, his tone as bland as the potatoes. "It's the only reason Honora exists, trying for a second son. Pity." He gave his wife a dark look while moodily taking another sip of his drink.

"I don't decide the gender of the baby, you daft donkey," Honora's mother spat. "I was just as upset as you, if you'll recall."

He nodded at the recollection, glancing at Gage. "She wouldn't hold the baby for three days. Alice, our oldest, did that. She didn't understand why we weren't pleased. Daughters don't understand the strain that they are upon their parents. They simply see a chubby face they find adorable, and that is all they care about." He sniffed, eyeing his wine before glancing at Honora. "Weren't even that pleasant to look at, daughter. Such a pity."

Her mother actually snorted once. "She's not much to look at now, Berkeley, all things considered." Her severe, icy blue eyes surveyed Honora without pleasure or pride from top to bottom. "Scrawny, pale, silent little thing. Not even a beauty like her sisters. If she did not have a decent dowry, we'd never be rid of her."

"Mama, please," Honora whispered, gripping the fabric at her knees beneath the table. The criticism, she was perfectly accustomed to. But in front of a guest…

That was a new low, and Honora hadn't thought lower was possible.

"Still might not be," her father grunted. "No one's asking. Never has. Not sure what's wrong with her. Even the most particular of gents likes a fortune well enough."

Honora's throat tightened. "Papa…"

"What do you think, Trembath?" her father overrode, either not hearing or not caring about Honora's protest. "Do you know of any single men who might have a penchant for a skinny, mousy, strange little wife who won't be a bother?"

That was too much to bear, and before Honora knew what she was about, she was up from the table and rushing from the room. There were no tears, no hysterics, no panicking breaths that she would need to calm. The only thing she felt was shame.

Burning, crippling, soul-shriveling shame.

She couldn't face it, not with someone else in the room to bear witness. She knew full well what her parents thought of her; she had heard it time and time again almost from the day she was born. She was rather accustomed to the list by now. But it was quite another thing to have someone else hear it.

To hear any of it.

To have someone else know just how much her parents hated her. How much they wanted to be rid of her. How little they thought of her. How little they cared about her.

How very little she was worth to them.

She did not stop moving until she reached the end of the corridor where one of the tall windows on the north face of the house sat, the slivers of moonlight shining through onto the rug below. This always seemed to be the place Honora went when she'd had too much loneliness or been at the receiving end of her mother's rather cruel barbs—leaning against the glass, letting her brow touch the cool panes and looking out into the darkness of the landscape of Horsend's estate.

She knew each rise and fall of the terrain, almost down to the blade of grass. She knew where the wildflowers would grow and in what colors. She knew where puddles were likely to form and where the holes from small animals already existed. She knew everything about the land she could see.

Except where she fit in it.

This was home, and had always been home, but she had never belonged here. It had simply been the only place she could call home.

There was no other name for it.

Her parents would not come in search of her, nor would they apologize. There was nothing to apologize for, in their eyes, and they would believe Honora overreacted by leaving the room in the manner she had. Apology would be required from Honora to her parents for the embarrassment they would feel on behalf of their guest, and like any dutiful daughter, she would give it.

She always did.

And so things would go, on and on, again and again, until someone told her where to go or what to do or who to be, as none of those things were in her control or power.

She was trapped, and now that Gage knew just what her parents were like, what her life was like, and might see her as they do, he would rescind his offer and go on his way.

Her visits to Julia in Cornwall would be something he avoided, and she would have to hope that someday someone else might wish to marry her, thus setting her free from the monotony of loneliness, criticism, and an utterly empty life.

"Honora…"

She closed her eyes, exhaling a pained breath as she heard Gage's footsteps coming towards her. Now she would have to hear the pity in his voice and the weak apology as he took his leave. And she would have to hear the only united speech her parents ever gave: how Honora failed them.

"I am sorry you had to witness that," she whispered, folding her arms and wishing she could actually become the wallpaper beside the window. "Please don't feel that you have to stay."

Perhaps if she offered him the way out first, he wouldn't have to give her the awkward speech she anticipated. It would save them both the additional mortification.

"Honora."

Her name. He wasn't using the polite formality of earlier—he was using her name, as he had started to do with the rest in Cornwall. She hadn't noticed at first, she was so ashamed of herself and her family. But something about the gentle sound of her name in his voice in this moment was the most comforting, consoling, perfect thing she had ever heard.

She turned towards him, still leaning against the glass, and opened her eyes, her folded arms a shield between him and her shame.

Gage's expression was full of concern and goodness, nothing resembling disdain, disgust, or dismay in any facet, and that made the absent tears begin to form in Honora's eyes.

His keen eyes caught that rise, and he stepped forward, taking her hand from where it rested on her folded arms, his hands feeling positively fiery against her freezing one.

"Let me take you away from this, Honora," he murmured, rubbing her fingers gently. "Please, let me marry you, if for no other reason than because I can get you out of here. You'll never have to endure being treated like that again."

Honora bit her lip, a hitch in her breathing betraying her further tears. "You don't have to."

Gage took her hand more firmly and brought it to his lips, something more sweet than romantic about the gesture. "I was here asking the same before I knew things were like that, remember? Why wouldn't I renew the address when your parents made it very clear what you deserve?"

"They made it very clear what they think I deserve," Honora muttered as she glanced down the corridor towards the dining room. "They always do when they're together."

"That's not what I said," Gage insisted, sliding himself to block her view of the corridor. "They made it very clear to me what you do deserve, and it has nothing to do with what they think. You deserve to be valued, respected, liked, and cared for. I may not be able to promise you love, Honora, but I can damn well promise you that. Will you marry me and see if I'm not right?"

"I believe you," she told him in a small voice, finally pushing off of the glass and covering his hands with her spare one. "That isn't the problem."

Gage cocked his head at her, his brow wrinkling slightly. "What is, then? What makes you pause when you've been enduring this?"

Honora almost cried at the pained note in his voice, as though he couldn't believe she would refuse him.

But she wasn't refusing him.

He simply needed to understand.

"You," she murmured, rubbing his hands now. "You deserve more than me, Gage. More than a marriage out of kindness. More than a marriage of convenience, even. You deserve a marriage that you want with all your heart. I seem to recall you had a great love once. Don't you want to find such again? And marry then?"

Gage smiled, the first smile she had seen on him that reminded her of the man from Cornwall she'd always admired. "No, I do not. And it's got nothing to do with kindness or convenience—I've had to come all the way from Cornwall to do the asking."

Honora managed a laugh at that, her tears fading entirely. She sobered and gave him a searching look. "Are you certain, Gage? You could have anyone."

"I am certain," he assured her with a nod. "I want to marry you, Honora Berkeley. If you'll have me."

There was no doubting his sincerity, in his touch or his gaze, and Honora supposed she must believe him, then. Which meant there was only one thing to do.

"Then I am certain as well. Yes, Gage. I will marry you."

Chapter Three

Waiting wasn't usually something Gage enjoyed, but he could honestly say he was enjoying the weeklong delay between his proposal to Honora and the wedding.

It was the only break he was going to receive.

The Berkeleys had been so surprised by the engagement, so delighted by the prospect of being free of the shackles of their daughter, that Lord Berkeley had gone to get a special license for the occasion. His wife was in complete agreement on that subject, which seemed to be a miraculous thing, given the depth of their incompatibility and mutual spite. But the days following the engagement had been almost entirely that of bliss when the two were together.

Honora wore a look of near-constant bewilderment that only eased when they were left alone, and it was utterly adorable.

He hadn't thought he'd find something about her to be adorable, let alone so soon. Granted, he was perfectly fond of her, knew what a good heart and spirit she bore, and knew that she would be an excellent wife, mother, and mistress of Helwithin, but he'd never quite looked at her for appearances' sake.

There wasn't anything wrong in her looks, and he wouldn't have called her plain, let alone anything worse. It was just that her pale complexion, large green eyes, and dark auburn hair seemed to somehow blend in with the surroundings and become unremarkable. Something that one saw but never noticed, and even upon forced recollection, Gage could not have called to mind what exactly Honora looked like when she smiled.

That was getting better now, as he was spending more time with her, and concentrated time at that. Her parents had no issue with their being alone and took no trouble to play chaperone for them, not that there would be particular concerns between the pair of them. In the kindest sense, Honora might have been Gage's sister for the existing relationship between them.

That would need to change if he ever wanted children.

But there was something undeniably adorable about Honora's expression regarding her parents' present unity; he was honest enough to admit that.

Downright adorable and amusing.

In truth, though, it ought to have made anyone with understanding rather disheartened to see such surprise. There ought to have been delight on the face of a new bride that matched that of her parents, or at least her mother. A shared enjoyment of the prospect before them both.

Honora was content, she had made that very clear to Gage. She was happy to marry him and be free of the torrent of abuse that they unleashed upon her constantly. But she was torn by the alteration of her parents' treatment of her and had told Gage she was wavering between wanting the wedding over so her parents would resume their usual behavior and wanting to stretch time out so they liked her this much a bit longer.

Gage hadn't relayed the thought to Honora yet, but he was ready to have done with her parents altogether so his wife-to-be might have consistency in how she was treated. And treasured.

He would treasure her, in his way. He was not ignorant of how life would proceed between them. He knew they would likely disagree about one thing or another, depending on how much of a temper Honora could work up once she was used to him. But he would not fight with her in the company of others. Would take care that their disagreements would be carried out with the same dignity and respect that the rest of their married life would. No belittling, no spite, no anger, if he could help it.

And she would never ever doubt that he valued her.

She was a sweet woman, and it was a miracle her parents hadn't managed to rot that out of her with their behavior.

Gage would need a sweet woman to be his wife. He was rascally on his best days and unbearable on his worst, but he had no enemies, his servants liked him, his miners respected him, and his friends trusted him.

Surely that was enough to recommend him as a husband.

"Gage Trembath, what, in the name of all that is good and holy, have you gone and done now?"

There was only one woman in the world who would talk to him like that, and he would be grateful to the end of his days that she was in his life.

And that she spoke to him the way she did.

Gage lowered the news sheet, grinning at the sight of his oldest friend—and his intended's cousin—Julia Roskelley.

Who was technically the first woman Gage had ever proposed to.

But he'd released her from their engagement when she'd wanted to get married in truth, not that it was necessary. A proposal from a lad of ten wasn't contractually legal, as it happened.

"Good morning, Jules," Gage chirped, leaning back slightly in his chair. "You got Honora's note, then?"

Julia Roskelley, more of a brunette than her cousin, of a healthier complexion, and bearing bluer eyes, folded her arms and raised a brow, looking more severe than Gage had seen her, possibly in his life. "Do you see a smile on my face? Do you want to know how much pacing I have done since receiving that letter, which neither my husband nor my unborn child will thank you for? Do you really want to tease me right now, Gage?"

He really shouldn't continue to press her when she was already so agitated, let alone when she was in such an interesting condition, but his fears about facing her like this had been very real, and his fears had always hidden behind his humor.

"Not really," he replied with a scrunched-up face. "I was hoping you could tell me what I need to know before marrying your cousin."

Julia's expression shifted from angry to dubious. "Are you serious? Don't you think you should have thought about that before you waltzed up here to ask her?"

"I did think about that," he shot back. He winced as he realized he'd need to backtrack there. "Well, not about asking you, but about Honora. I thought about any number of young ladies, once I'd decided it was time and I couldn't put it off further. But I kept coming back to Honora, for whatever reason. I don't want you getting any fancy notions in your head, Jules. I'm not in love with her."

"I'd have been surprised if you were," Julia scoffed, brushing off a chair and sitting herself down into it with a slight flounce to her yellow muslin. "The pair of you have spent perhaps five hours in each other's company, all things considered, and none of that in a courtship setting. She's a timid little thing, and you're louder than a mine captain about to blast."

Gage ignored that. "And Honora is not in love with me," he went on. "This is a marriage of convenience, and a sensible one. I think very highly of Honora, and she has both sweetness and sense, which is becoming rarer and rarer in young ladies, I find."

"I wish that weren't true, but I agree." Julia made a face, shaking her head. "And you know I adore Honora. I have wished and wished that she might find a good match for herself one day, though I had hoped for love."

"Julia..." Gage began, grimacing as he sat forward.

She held up a hand to silence him. "I doubt she would ever have been able to find it on her own, Gage. Between her parents' obscene behaviors and opinions of her, and her own timidity and insecurity, it was highly unlikely she would ever have found much of a kinship, let alone a romance. I am not about to object to the wedding in the hopes that she may yet be swept off her feet by some heir to an earldom."

"Thank you, I think," Gage muttered, smiling wryly. "Though now I may have to watch out for one of those coming to Helwithin and riding away with my wife."

"Honora's not the sort," Julia assured him with a laugh. "You know that, don't you?"

Gage nodded and smiled easily. "I may not know her favorite flower, but I do know she's not the sort to run away."

"Yellow roses." Julia grinned, shrugging her shoulders. "Now you know."

"I'll tuck that away for safekeeping." He tapped his brow as though storing the information with the action.

Julia looked at him for a long moment, then heaved a sigh, her hands rubbing the swelling of her abdomen gently. "Gage, are you certain about this? You know I love Honora, and you know how I feel about you."

Gage felt his mouth curve to one side. "Honora asked me the same thing. Yes, I am certain. I want a comfortable marriage, Jules. You know what I thought I had with Margaret, and how that ended for me. I know how deeply I am capable of feeling things, and I cannot afford to lose myself again if anything goes wrong. I may not have the strength to come back next time."

"Of course you have the strength," his friend retorted with more sharpness than he expected. "Don't be so ridiculous or so demeaning."

There would be no reasoning with her about the subject, so he waved that off. "Regardless, this is what I have planned for since I resigned myself to marriage when I came back to myself. And when I looked at it with real intent, only Honora felt right. So do you object to me as a husband for your favorite cousin?"

Julia's smile turned rather tender, all things considered. "No, I don't object, Gage. I have concerns, but who wouldn't, under the circumstances? I daresay you have some concerns yourself."

He exhaled a breath, not quite of relief, but of resignation. "I do. None that stop me from proceeding, but they are certainly there." He leaned forward and rubbed at his eyes, suddenly weary. "What am I doing, Julia?"

"Marrying the sweetest girl on the planet."

"Yes, thank you, that one I knew." He lowered his hands just long enough to glare at her, then returned them. "I realize that I have to marry eventually. The continuation of the family line and the estate and the traditional duties of a man in my position… But I am not a husband."

"Not until you marry, no."

Gage chose to ignore that comment. After all, Julia would know what he meant, and her impudence was not going to help or change anything. "Honora deserves a good marriage, Julia. How do I give that to her?"

His friend cleared her throat, and he splayed his fingers to look at her in expectation. She was staring at him with wide eyes.

"What?" he demanded, unsure if she thought he was stupid or profound.

"You…" Julia began, blinking quickly. "You *live* a good marriage, Gage. It's not that complicated. If you want to give her a good marriage, you decide to have one. All that is required for that is for you to continue to be the good person you are and for you to treat Honora as the good person she is. Respect and honor, Gage. You can do that."

It sounded so simple when she said it like that, but Gage knew full well there was nothing in life that was as simple as it sounded. He just had this sinking feeling that he was going to muck this up, and that he should have chosen a less vulnerable bride.

And yet…

Honora was still right. He felt that to his core. He wanted to marry Honora. She fit every aspect of his general requirements for a wife, but also had the benefits of being pretty, being musically accomplished, having a sweet temperament, and having nothing obviously annoying about her person or manner. He could not imagine any person of his acquaintance disliking her, and while that was not a requisite, it was certainly a boon he was grateful for.

He tried his best to be a gentleman but did not always succeed. With a wife of her caliber, he would appear all the more gentlemanly and refined. She would bring so much goodness to Helwithin, both the house and the estate, and he looked forward to her being involved with the mining families. He already knew full well that she would be their favorite.

He wanted that for her. After a lifetime of abuse, disdain, and neglect from her family, she would now be practically worshipped by the village children, if not their parents as well, and she would have power and authority as mistress of Helwithin. As much as she wanted, in fact.

And she would never be mistreated by Gage. Never.

Would that be enough for her to be happy?

"I think she might deserve love, Julia," he admitted in a low voice, dropping his hands, "and I can't give that to her."

Julia smiled at him very softly, rather like the sister she had always seemed to be. "You deserve love, too, Gage. And I think the two of you will find that eventually. Not in the mindless, romantic sense that you seem to be thinking, and not perhaps in the way you loved Margaret, but a different kind of love. Something even more enduring. As you live together, as you learn from each other, as children eventually come… I think you will find love between you, if you'll allow room for it."

It was on the tip of Gage's tongue to refute that claim, but he bit it back. There was no point in arguing with Julia about anything, but especially over something she believed in so fiercely. Gage would never love again; he knew that down to his core. He had spent too long building up his defenses against such a thing and had rooted out any sort of sentimentality that might lead to love.

But the mention of a different kind of love… After all, he did love his cousins. He had loved his parents. He loved Julia, in a way. Why could he not hold space for possibly loving Honora for who she would be as his wife and the mother of his children? Respect and affection could easily become something deeper.

Not in a romantic sense, but in a familial one.

Surely that was more enduring anyway.

"Gage," Julia finally said with a sigh, "stop overthinking this. You are not making a love match, and you both know it. Yes?"

He nodded, crossing one leg over the other as he looked at Julia. "Yes. I've made sure she understands that, and she seems to."

"I am quite certain she is well aware of it," Julia replied with a small snort. "And you have likely seen how her parents are with her."

The reminder was enough to make Gage growl and give a very clipped nod, his jaw tightening.

Julia's tight smile settled him. "Quite. So, Honora also knows that marrying you allows her freedom from them, at last. She might love you for that alone, but she's not a silly girl, Gage. You are both coming into this arrangement with a full and clear understanding of what it entails. There is no reason it will not be a marvelous marriage, even if it is not one of ardent romance."

It would not be one of any romance, let alone ardent, but that was neither here nor there. It would at least be a marriage that started off better than the Bassets', he could say that for certain. An agreeable marriage would be well and good. He did not need a marriage of love, given how the feelings of love he'd once had for Margaret had turned so abruptly and so coldly.

He would always be honest with Honora. She did not know that yet, but he would be. A full and clear understanding, Julia had said. That was what he wanted in their marriage.

Gage suddenly winced as a particular aspect of marriage came to mind. "Julia…"

"Yes?" came the hesitant reply.

"About that full and clear understanding?" He cracked open an eye and gave her a grimacing look.

Julia returned it in bewilderment. "What about it? Why are you giving me that…?" She broke off, her eyes going perfectly round. "Oh!"

Gage tried to smile, though he feared it was just an extended grimace. "Yes. That."

"Right…" Julia coughed once, her cheeks going red. "Well, I won't leave that discussion to her mother."

A snort of outright derision, mixed with humor, escaped Gage. "Please don't. I've heard enough from that woman to have a fair idea of how that would go, and she would be utterly horrified, if not scared."

Julia held up a hand. "Now you, please don't. I am trying not to be sick. I will take care of it, Gage. She will know more than I did going into matters, but it will be up to the pair of you to settle on your… particular arrangement."

"Thank you, Julia!" he said loudly, now growing red himself and averting his eyes.

It was a deuced awkward conversation, even between friends as close as they were, but it had to be done. Honora would never have been able to make it through any sort of discussion on the subject, and it was crucial that she not be ignorant as to the details. Especially as it was not a marriage of romance, and he did not want it to be a marriage of strict responsibility and tasteless duties either.

"Tell her I will never force her," Gage murmured, keeping his gaze averted. "I will never demand. She has a voice, and I want her to use it. And please explain that… that it doesn't mean…"

"Consummation does not equal love, yes, I quite understand your meaning," Julia overrode with impatience. She pushed herself to her feet with a huff, drawing his attention back to her, her cheeks still pink. "If you keep insisting on not loving her, or you worry so much that she will fall in love with you, you're going to wind up like the Grangers for the first few years of their marriage. Just live life, Gage, but live it with Honora, not in spite of her. Now, if you'll excuse me, it appears I have much to speak with my cousin about before the wedding."

Without another word, Julia left the room, leaving Gage to his own thoughts.

He sank further into his chair, sputtering his lips on an exhale, unsure if he was relieved or perturbed or resigned. But at least facing Julia was done.

And she would see to the only true remaining concern that Gage had.

Which meant, in all honesty, that he could marry Honora today, if they wanted.

They wouldn't do so, of course. Her mother was rather enjoying planning a wedding. And the other siblings had to arrive, which was ridiculous, as they didn't care enough to take Honora in, but they wanted to celebrate her marriage. In Gage's mind, if you would not sacrifice for a person, you did not deserve to celebrate them.

At least Honora had clear sight where her family was concerned. She knew full well who they were and how they treated her, if not the reason for it. She expected nothing from them and held no particular fondness for them.

That would save Gage the trouble of asking her if they ought to consider any family names for their children, he expected.

Another heavy, less troubled sigh escaped him, but this time, he smiled.

He was getting married. Two days from now, he would take Honora Berkeley to be his wife, and would remove her from this poisonous place she had learned to endure. He would show her a world of freedom, if not sunshine, and would do his best to make her smile every day. Not because he loved her, but because he valued her and cared about her. He respected her. He wanted her to be happy.

And to be happy she married him.

Perhaps that could be love, in a philosophical way.

Steps in the corridor drew his gaze to the door, and he saw Honora passing, which made him smile. She stopped and peered into the room at him, her own small smile in place.

Gage waved at her, not entirely certain why.

"My cousin wants to speak with me," Honora said without preamble. "Any notion why?"

It was all Gage could do not to grin like a child or laugh hysterically. He shook his head from side to side. "I haven't the faintest idea. It's Julia. Although, she may want to warn you off of marrying me. She does know a great many secrets."

Honora's trim brows rows just a little. "Unless she tells me you've buried a body somewhere, it's not likely to change my mind. Anything that gets me out of here is worth it."

"Only burying the body?" Gage asked, feeling a trifle impish. "Not killing someone?"

Honora's smile spread. "If you killed someone, you'd have a good enough reason. It's the burying one I'd struggle with. That would make you an accomplice to someone else's crime, and I'd have to pause."

Gage laughed now, tossing his head back. "Honora…" He looked at her again, sobering just a little as he asked, "Pause? Not stop?"

She shrugged. "Like I said, if it gets me out of here…" She waved a little and left the room, her steps soon heard on the stairs nearby.

Gage closed his eyes, grinning to himself. What in the world was he so concerned about? Life with Honora was going to be absolutely delightful, and no one would convince him otherwise.

Chapter Four

She was a bride.

Well, technically, she had been a bride last week, but she had it on good authority that, until the novelty wore off, she was still a bride.

Honora could hardly believe it. She was a bride. A wife. Mrs. Trembath, and Mistress of Helwithin.

And they would be arriving at Helwithin shortly to begin that new life.

What a dreadfully imposing thought.

It would be the perfect opportunity to hide under a blanket in a carriage and pretend she did not exist.

Unfortunately, her new husband had a strange sense of humor and had rented a curricle for the last part of their journey, so they were seated side by side in open air and in plain view of everyone in Cornwall.

Or at least, those in the vicinity of Porthtowan, which as she understood it, they were now approaching.

Julia had taken her to Porthtowan before, Honora was certain of it. And St. Agnes, Blackwater, Camborne, and Redruth, but presently, Honora could not remember anything about them. Not one single thing.

Because she was now approaching it as someone who would live nearby as a woman of status. And as such, she knew absolutely nothing. About anything.

Gage was going to regret marrying her in roughly eleven minutes, she was certain of it.

He might already regret it, and it had only been a few days.

Granted, he didn't appear so. He was just as congenial as ever, an amusing combination of silly and sweet, and seemed shockingly aware of her presence at any given time.

She was not used to having this sort of attention without criticism being attached to it.

And as for the wedding night...

Well, it had been pretty aligned with what Julia had told her, but she had still not been prepared for the sensations it had conjured in her. Consummation was an interesting word for something so transcendent and sublime. And it had an oddly binding effect to it. Honora could not fathom engaging in any such activity with anyone but Gage, not only because she was legally his wife, but she somehow felt as though her body had been branded as his.

Not in a confining or controlling sense, and not even in a possessive sense. It was far more complicated than that. She was free with Gage, perfectly so, but linked to him in every sense. She had learned more about him in that single night than she had in their entire engagement and association, and she had every expectation that any future occasions of such things would open him even more to her awareness.

She would never have anticipated his being so tender, so attentive, or so affectionate, and yet...

Well, it would not do for her to sigh whimsically while seated beside him in a rented curricle shortly before making a grand entrance in the nearest village to their home, but her recollection of his attentions gave her that impulse.

As she understood things, that was his way of taking consideration for her due to the potentially unpleasant nature of such an experience from the woman's perspective. Nothing to do with true affection, but a sort of laying groundwork to make the experience pleasant. Julia had emphasized that not all men would do that, and Honora could certainly understand how that could be the case.

She was almost certain her parents had never enjoyed any part of the act with each other.

But Gage doing such a thing, especially considering it was not a love match, made her appreciate and respect him all the more. They could truly care for each other without having to worry about romance. If nothing else had indicated to her that this would be a good marriage, that had.

There was plenty that assured her of the rightness of this marriage, of course. His offer, for one. His willingness to continue with the proposal when it was clear that it was a rescue, for another. His even thinking of her was astonishing, but his commitment to the idea of her even more so. And he seemed to actually care about her as a human being as well.

She was a rather simple woman, she thought. She did not expect much and, she knew firsthand, she did not need much. Honora knew her husband did not love her, which saved her the trouble of wondering, and she knew he was a good man, which gave her nothing to fear. She knew he would take care of her and would value their children, should they have any. Anything more than that would be extraordinary.

Certainly welcome, but extraordinary.

She did not need extraordinary. Comfortable, happy, and simple would be enough. More than enough.

More than she had ever expected.

It would take her some time to be comfortable in a place like Helwithin, particularly as its mistress, but Gage had assured her repeatedly that his staff were not intimidating, that she would have all the time, grace, and education she needed, and that she never had to do anything she did not want to.

Honora knew that wasn't exactly true, but she also knew that if she did make a complaint about any certain thing, Gage would almost certainly intervene. Because he found her to be sensible and knew her to be dutiful, even if she wasn't perfectly at ease. If he'd thought her a ninny, he wouldn't have made her that offer.

He might not have made her any offer at all, come to think of it.

Honora's fingers began to tingle with new awareness as the buildings of the town started to appear, along with the townspeople. Eyes moved in their direction and hovered upon them, followed by whispers to others. Speculation would now run rampant until the news was made public, and even when it was, Honora would be very carefully analyzed and scrutinized by everyone.

Absolutely everyone.

"I think I can hear you panicking, Honora," Gage quipped, a grin evident in his voice. He flicked the reins with the slightest motion of his wrist, before switching them to his right hand alone. He then offered her his newly freed left hand, palm up.

Needing no encouragement, Honora placed her gloved hand in his, feeling her breath come just a little easier when his fingers gripped gently against hers. "I'm all right. Just a trifle nervous."

"I'd be surprised if you were not." He rested their joined hands against his knee, his thumb brushing over her hand in smooth, even patterns. "Our marriage has been announced in the papers, so if they've read it, they'll know exactly who you are."

Honora nodded and exhaled, startled by how shaky that exhale turned out to be. "And do you anticipate inviting people to Helwithin for some sort of celebration? Or to introduce me?"

The pressure on her hand increased markedly. "I don't know, Honora. You're the mistress of Helwithin. Would you like to have people invited to meet you or to celebrate?"

How had she not suspected that he would turn this on her immediately? He was so determined to give her the freedom to choose for herself and to trust her with responsibilities that she really ought to have felt the pressure of the thing from the moment they had been pronounced man and wife.

They were all crashing down on her now, there was no question.

"What I would like," Honora grumbled, reaching up to brush discreetly at her brow, which she feared was perspiring, "and what is polite and acceptable are not always in neat alignment."

Gage barked a loud laugh, startling her. "Now that is the statement by which I could define my life."

Honora took very little comfort from that, but managed a smile all the same. "It would probably be wise to entertain guests at some point to signify our marriage, but I think we may give ourselves time to settle into our new life before we rush into it."

"I quite agree," Gage affirmed with a nod. "And when you do feel ready, we would also be wise to have you come out to the mines and meet everyone there."

"I have a feeling that will be less intimidating," Honora murmured.

Gage brought their hands up and kissed her glove quickly. "Undoubtedly. But I am sure that everyone from every station, high and low, will adore you. If you would like, we can have a small dinner first with our friends. Very informal, and you can invite any of the ladies over at any time. It is your home now. I want you to feel that."

Honora leaned against him, more for comfort and strength than in adoration or affection. "I know. I am sure I will, eventually. The anticipation is always worse than the thing itself."

"Was the anticipation of marrying me worse than actually marrying me?" he teased, grinning down at her.

She shook her head, now smiling in earnest. "No. I was so desperate to marry you and get away from Horsend that none of it was anxiety-inducing at all."

"Desperate to marry me," Gage repeated with a chuckle. "I'll keep that line in my mind for a very long time. I think it will make me quite happy."

"I am glad to entertain, then." She hid a smile against his shoulder before straightening, though she noted with some fondness that he did not release her hand.

It was impressive that he could drive so adeptly with just the one hand. Of course, the streets were not teeming, and they had not yet had to slow or turn, so perhaps it was not all that impressive in the scheme of things. But Honora was a touch sheltered compared to other girls of her age and situation, so she had no doubt she would be impressed by a few things that others might find perfectly mundane.

Another carriage was crossing the road ahead of them, so Gage slid his hand from hers to take the reins in both hands and guide the horses appropriately. A very fine barouche crossed in front of them, an older woman in a beautifully adorned bonnet sitting on one side, while a stunning younger woman wreathed in black and wearing a black velvet bonnet sat within it. The younger woman looked over at them as they crossed, and Honora noted the pristine nature of her complexion, smoother than silk and as pure as china.

The young woman's eyes widened as she saw them, and her narrow throat tightened visibly.

Gage reached up to his hat and tipped the brim, but said nothing.

Honora looked at him, searching his expression for any sort of indication of who she might have been or how he might have felt. But she did not know him well enough yet to decipher emotions, and his face was completely blank. Neither pleased nor displeased. Completely unaffected.

Except she had felt the air between them change, and though he had not stiffened in his seat, something about him had altered just enough.

She hastily looked back at the woman before they disappeared and noted the quick dip of her chin. Then they were gone, and Gage flicked the reins and continued on ahead.

Honora waited for them to cross another two streets and turn onto the third before she ventured to say anything at all. "Did you know those ladies in the barouche? Or was that your natural politeness?"

"I knew them," he replied, his voice holding no emotion one way or the other. "That was Lady Teague and her daughter, Lady Hastings. The Teagues have property some seven miles from Helwithin. Our families have naturally been acquainted for years."

"I see," Honora said softly, doing her best to inject little to no emotion into her words as well. "And Lady Hastings? She seems to be in mourning."

Gage nodded again. "She is. Her husband passed three months ago or so." He was silent for a long moment, then exhaled roughly. "You may already know, but she and I had an understanding years ago. Or I believed we did, at any rate. But she chose to marry Lord Hastings before I made an official offer, and we've had no contact since then."

Honora's heart seemed to begin a slow descent from its place in her chest to the very pit of her stomach, and it was an icy, agonizing fall. "But now…" she managed, her mouth feeling dry. "She is a widow."

"Yes."

Biting her lip, Honora looked away, watching the buildings of the town pass. "Did you know of her widowhood when you came to see me at Horsend?"

"I did."

"Why did you ask me, then? Why not wait for her mourning to end?"

"She did not choose me the first time," Gage told her easily, shrugging as he turned the curricle at a mews and began moving them away from the town. "Why would she choose me a second?"

Honora looked up at the trees that were now almost above them. "Change in situation, security of her future, realization of a mistake…"

"I saw no need to pursue her," Gage overrode firmly, but without heat or temper.

Honora chanced a look at him. "Because your pride could not risk a second refusal?"

Gage returned her look, doing her the credit of not appearing surprised. "Because I had already made my decision."

"A decision that was not binding until we made the vows," she reminded him. "You could have waited for her. Or anyone. But you went through with it."

"I did." He pulled the horses to a gentle stop and turned in his seat to face her fully. "Ask me why."

Honora did not shrink from his direct invitation. "Why?" she whispered.

Gage plucked up her hand and squeezed it. "Because in spite of what you might now think, I wanted to marry you."

"Because it was easier?" she dared to ask.

His expression turned scolding. "Now you flatter neither of us, yourself least of all. I married you because it was right and good. It felt right then, and it still does. I don't know why Lady Hastings is here, and it makes no difference to me that she is. You are my wife."

"And I would hate to see you sorry for that," Honora said in a soft voice, hating herself for the almost petulant tone her voice had taken on.

Gage cocked his head, his brow creasing a little. "Why would I be?"

She lifted a shoulder. "I am not her."

"Thank God for that." He kissed her hand and grinned, but she was not sure she believed it. "We'll be at Helwithin soon. I'm taking you the long way so you can see the house from the best view." He flicked the reins and started the horses again, whistling as though all was perfectly well.

Honora did not feel his same sense of optimism. He had every opportunity to marry Lady Hastings if he wished to, but he had chosen her. No matter how right and good he seemed to think it was, Honora was no fool. Deep feelings between young people were not so easily replaced by coolness and detachment. And based on the expression on Lady Hastings's face, the woman was not nearly as cool towards Gage as he seemed to be towards her.

Right and good might not have been reason enough for his marriage. She'd known it was comfortable and convenient at the time and had not been bothered by that one bit. She still wasn't, by all accounts. But given what she now suspected he was avoiding with this "right and good marriage," it did not seem reason enough to have done it.

Not that anything could be done about it now. The marriage had been made and consummated, and, if Gage was to be believed, he had made those vows with a full understanding of Lady Hastings's widowhood. He, at least, had known what he was getting into.

Honora hadn't, but did he have a duty to tell her of his past connections before they wed? Had she had a right to know such things?

Did it actually matter?

Of that she could not be sure. The only thing she knew was that she, Honora, was certainly no escape, not from a woman of that kind of beauty and a history of such deep affection. She was a pittance by comparison in so many respects.

Surely, Gage could see that. Surely, he knew that.

Why, then, would he knowingly choose her when he could have had what he had once wanted so dearly?

She had no reason to suspect Gage of anything untoward or insincere, and she did not know him well enough to be certain of his ability to distance himself from his past. But she was suddenly uneasy about that woman being in the same vicinity as her.

And especially about the woman being in the same vicinity as her husband.

She chanced a look at Gage again, wondering if she could believe in his present carefreeness and take it for herself. If she could ignore the sudden doubts and fears that she would lose the husband she had only so recently gained. If she could be brave enough to believe that her husband was not like either of her parents, who carried on with whomever they wished at any given time.

That was it. Her husband was not her parents. He would not treat her so abominably. He was a man of honor and respectability. Julia adored him and had known him almost her entire life and had been nothing but encouraging about the match before the wedding. Her cousin would not have stood by silently if Honora were marrying a man without morals or feeling.

Or a man who would not respect her.

She was being childish and naive, then, in fearing so much from him so fast.

He deserved the chance to prove himself to be the man he claimed and the man she hoped he was.

"How old is Helwithin?" Honora asked, not particularly caring, but doing her best to improve her enthusiasm.

"Not as old as others," Gage answered with another flick of his hands, urging the horses faster up the slight incline. "Seventeenth century. But it has the distinction of being one of the few buildings in the area to have been built entirely from Pentewan stone, which is fairly rare. And it gives the house a most particular sheen in sunlight and a distinct color at all times. My grandfathers were quite proud of its design for that reason, if nothing else."

Honora smiled in true amusement. "Why 'if nothing else,' Gage?"

He chuckled softly and directed the horses to the left hand of a fork in the road and passed a few trees. "Well, there is the view..." he mused, gesturing his fingers towards the right as the last tree swept by them.

Honora looked where he indicated and felt her breath catch somewhere between her throat and lungs without actually being within either.

The house was the most gorgeous building she had ever seen in her life. The sunlight on the stone made it almost glow with a shimmering, ethereal light of silver, and the glint on the perfectly aligned rows of windows only added to the heavenly light. A simple, refined portico with pristine columns led to the main entrance, and dormers dotted the roof of the front façade, the Pentewan stone in them imbuing them with a sort of halo. Stretching out to the sides of the main house were colonnaded wings of brick, and the entrance itself was encased in what appeared to be more brick of the same, forming a courtyard contained by a wrought-iron gate.

She could not even see beyond the house as yet, for the trees and grandeur of it, and already she was rather violently in love with the place.

"Breathe, my dear," Gage reminded her from her right, laughter rife in his voice.

Honora forced herself to do so, fearing it sounded more like a pant and a gasp than anything natural.

"I take it the lady is pleased with her new home?"

She tried to nod, but could not feel anything but the corners of her mouth spreading against her cheeks, stretching until her face positively ached with the motion.

"My word," her husband said softly. "And I thought the house was a stirring sight."

Honora blinked and forced her eyes to flick to Gage, confused by the note of awe in his voice.

His gaze was still on her, eyes wide and dark, seeming almost unsettled by her, though he bore a smile. Small, gentle, but it was there.

Did he have to be so very handsome? He was her husband, after all, and it would not do for her to fancy him after all of this.

Her cheeks began to heat, and she dropped her eyes.

"No, don't look away," Gage urged, reaching for her chin and trying to lift her eyes back to him.

She obeyed instinctively, though her smile turned small and bashful.

His, on the other hand, grew. "That blush, Mrs. Trembath, after how you just looked... Well, it could very well get you in trouble one day."

Honora wasn't entirely certain what that meant, but judging by the way he seemed to be laughing privately at her, she trusted that understanding would only heighten her blush.

"Come on," he suggested, tapping the underside of her jaw. "Let's go see the place. I have a feeling you're going to enjoy it."

Chapter Five

Being married wasn't all that hard. What was all the fuss about?

Gage had been married for two weeks now, and it was the simplest thing he had ever done. Certainly the best, and unquestionably the wisest as well, but it was also remarkably easy.

Why the devil had he waited so long?

Or perhaps it was just the wonder that was Honora.

And what a wonder she was!

He had fully anticipated that his delicate little wife would be terrified of Helwithin when they arrived and would do nothing but cower for the first few weeks, if not months. He would have to take her by the hand and guide her along, show her the way of things and how to not be afraid of taking charge. Then, little by little, her confidence would blossom, and she would find herself growing into the position of mistress of the house.

And she would be his wife all the while, though he had no expectations of regular relations or anything of the sort. Simple companionship as friends, as either of them might have need, and acting as advisor when the time arose.

But while his wife might be delicate in frame, she was certainly not delicate in spirit.

He had not known how educated or prepared any young woman was in running a house before marriage, but it would seem that was the crux of a proper education and the mark of true accomplishment. While Honora might not speak her mind freely, she most certainly knew it. Within three days of taking up residence, she had started the refurbishment of the same number of rooms with the sort of detail and expertise he would not have expected. She and their housekeeper, Mrs. Crane, had become the closest of allies and seemed to be of one mind as they moved about the house and reordered whatever they pleased.

Gage had not thought the place so beyond taste and function, but with the two of them at the helm of things, he felt quite tasteless and utterly superfluous.

And then there was the running of the house in general.

He had never had complaints about Helwithin and never thought anything amiss, but now… Everything was prompt and orderly, the place was spotless, and the windows seemed to let in more light than he had ever noticed before. It was not that the windows had been dirty before and were especially clean now, but there was simply more light shining through them. As though the sun had gained an added measure of its glow.

That was perhaps the most whimsical thought he'd ever had in his entire life, but it was the truth, in his eyes.

How else could he explain his wife's smiles at supper? The color in her complexion that was so beautifully heightened? The general air of contentment that followed her into whatever room she entered?

Honora made him smile. He was a relatively pleasant man any given day of the week, if not one for optimism, but she was like the sun itself, and he had not expected that when he'd asked her to marry him. Honora had always been the quaint little mouse with the beautiful voice and the slow but pleasing smile he'd try to tease out. The favorite cousin of his oldest friend, and thus a girl he would hold in high esteem without knowing well, but barely visible for her own sake.

Had that been of her own volition or purely from the life she had been crushed into living?

Was this the true Honora? This content, petite creature who carried heaven in her palm and had become this flower in the wilds of Cornwall, of all places, when she had not managed to do so in a place like Bath. Who had been considered a weed by those who ought to have tended her well, and only here, with him, was she allowed to be anything else.

He did not flatter himself that he was the cause of any of it. He was nothing special and had not given her anything but a new name and a position.

The rest of it was all down to her.

Honora was allowed to be Honora, and perhaps that was all she had ever needed.

Gage hadn't asked her if she was happy, mostly because he hadn't thought it necessary when she smiled almost constantly, but perhaps that was the secret to a marriage being content and such.

A happy wife.

Surely this could not be a surprise to anyone. Any man with a wife had to know that life was easier when she was happy. Gage did not even have a demanding wife, as others complained to, and he knew this.

Perhaps he ought to write a treatise on the secrets to a good marriage. He felt rather wise and satisfied with his own, so perhaps others were simply ignorant about the way it could be managed and clueless when it came to women.

Or perhaps he had just married well.

That was undoubtedly the more likely scenario.

Why praise himself when there was so very little to praise?

"Is there a reason you look so smug, Gage? Or is that simply the arrangement of your face?"

Gage turned to one of his oldest friends, Lord Harrison Basset, and allowed himself to grin with all the pride in the world. "I feel rather smug, Basset. Is that so wrong?"

The dark-haired, finely dressed man scoffed softly and sipped his brandy. "Not usually, no. But why are you entitled to feeling smug?"

"Isn't it obvious?" Gage gestured towards Honora, who sat among Basset's wife Adelaide, as well as her cousin Julia and Basset's sister Emblyn. "I have a most excellent wife."

"And that is somehow a credit to you?"

Gage gave his friend a bewildered look. "Is it not? I am the one who thought of her and asked her."

Basset hissed in indecision. "Well, my wife did think of it last Christmas when Honora was visiting, and we had you all over for supper and music. She and Julia discussed the idea, I believe. Did nobody mention the subject to you?"

"They what?" Gage set down his glass and folded his arms, glaring at Basset darkly. "I thought Julia was simply fond of her cousin and was concerned about her, since she was speaking of her so often. And your wife knew nobody here, so of course she would be fond of a sweet girl like Honora after meeting her. You mean to tell me they were trying to sway my mind towards her?"

Holding up his hands in a gesture of surrender, Basset shook his head, though his smile seemed more sincere than anything else. "I don't know how they played out their idea. I am only telling you what I know. Roskelley, help me out, here."

John Roskelley, Julia's husband, had been standing nearby and now came closer. "How can I help, gentlemen?"

"Did your wife scheme to have me marry her cousin?" Gage demanded, bypassing politeness on his way to indignation.

John blinked and looked at Basset. "What did you have to tell him that for? We were all getting along so well."

Basset chortled and downed his drink in one gulp.

Gage frowned and did his best not to slump against the wall. "So it's true. The idea was not my own."

"Of course it was your own idea, don't be an idiot," Basset told him with a derisive snort. "Even if the thought of Honora was planted in your mind, or wherever such things grow, you still had to decide upon it and consider it best for yourself. If you'd had enough doubts about Honora as a wife, you'd never have done so."

"That's true," Gage mused, glancing back over at his wife, almost in speculation. "I do have a mind of my own."

She was sitting among the other ladies, chatting happily and without any notion of the discussion across the room. The sight of her still gave him satisfaction, so he supposed that was something. He did not think he had been coerced into marrying her, given how indignant Julia had been when he'd actually done it. And there was no way Honora would have known anything about it, or she would have been mortified.

"And I doubt either of them expected you to just up and decide to marry her without courtship," Basset pointed out with a nudge to his side.

Gage had to laugh a little at that and eyed his friend ruefully.

"That might have been a trifle hasty on my part, but I had no taste for courting. I've tried that before and it got me nowhere. And I had thought that Honora would be a sensible enough woman to value honesty and the offer for what it was."

"You've made a business arrangement," John told Gage, his expression completely blank. "That's all. With a canny partner, I'll grant you, but it is not marriage you've entered into."

"I can assure you," Gage protested, "this is a marriage. Officially. In all matters."

Basset coughed in surprise. "Thank you for clearing up what we were clearly wondering, as it is a matter of our business how married you are."

Gage only shrugged and pointed at John. "He started it. Said my marriage was a business arrangement."

"Come off it, man, so was mine." Basset turned to pour himself another drink from the sideboard. "Most marriages are entered into that way. You simply did it with more haste and zeal. I, at least, was in conversations with my wife's father before it was official."

"That's what I don't understand, Basset." Gage looked at him through narrowed eyes. "You had time to evaluate your choice of wife and you still chose Adelaide. Did you care so little about the woman you married that her willfulness didn't matter?"

To his surprise, Basset nodded without reservation. "I cared about pedigree more than anything. And beauty, if I could manage it. Fortune, preferably, but not required. I planned to spend little enough time with her that her personality would not matter." He chuckled wryly and looked over at the women, the soft turn of his mouth indicating only too well which one had his attention. "You can see how well that turned out."

Gage whistled low, remembering clearly how stubborn, high-spirited, fussy, and puffed-up Adelaide was when she had first come to Cornwall. He had never met a worse match for his friend, but it had already been done, so there had been no point in saying any such thing. He had done his best to try and like her, for Basset's sake, and had been surprised to find her warming and gentling more and more with every passing visit.

And then, miraculously, she was the woman who was perfect for

44

Harrison Basset. Without actually changing herself all that much, she was his perfect match, and they were in love.

How exactly that had transpired, Gage was not sure and had never asked. That was certainly not his concern, but he could see it and knew it.

How had Basset been so deuced lucky to marry for everything but affection and wind up with love?

Gage had at least married for convenience and been conscious of his selection. Honora was not like Adelaide had been at first and could never be.

Comfortable marriages were probably as rare as love matches, in truth. Ones of true comfort, anyway. Not ones of impatient tolerance, but actual comfort.

He'd take the marriage he had over the emotional waves of a deep and fathomless sea that were others.

"I commend your choice," Basset announced, breaking into Gage's thoughts on the subject.

Gage shook himself and looked at his friend quickly. "Do you?"

Basset rolled his eyes and gave him the sort of look he had grown up perfecting. "Must you have my approval even for that?"

"I do so crave any attention you can give me," he quipped with a bat of his lashes.

"My commendation," Basset went on, ignoring his impertinence, as usual, "has nothing to do with you other than that you made it. But you made it because of who she is, and that is what I commend." He nodded his head in Honora's direction. "She is the commendation. I've been impressed by her from almost the moment I made her acquaintance, and my favor improves with every meeting. Now that she is Mrs. Trembath, I must give her condolences, I expect. And be on hand for when she despairs of her husband."

Gage sniffed dismissively. "I very much beg your pardon."

"I'm with him," John offered, gesturing to Basset. "She is far better than I thought you'd manage for a wife. More sophisticated and refined, of a softer demeanor and quieter air, a sweeter disposition and finer heart, and of a more fragile appearance. All in all, a rather impressive choice."

John's opinion was mostly irrelevant, as Honora was his wife's cousin, and he was therefore more inclined to like her, but Gage could not help but be confused by the nature of his praise of her.

"So you thought I would marry a coarse, loud, rude, cold, statuesque woman?" Gage inquired, wondering just how low an opinion of him his friends truly had. "Hell and the devil, this gets worse and worse."

"I didn't think you would ever marry," John corrected without shame or defensiveness. "Despite all your claims to the contrary, you never did anything about it. Not after what's-her-name."

Gage gave him a dark look. "She has a name, and there is no issue with anybody saying it."

"Doesn't do any good to bring her into things, does it?" Basset shook his head firmly. "Honora could not be more different."

"Is that a good thing or a bad thing?"

The group of them fell silent at Gage's rather offhand comment, and he wasn't certain even he had an answer for it.

He hadn't meant to compare anyone to Margaret when he had decided it was time to find a wife. He hadn't thought of anything except moving forward in his life and doing what was expected. He hadn't felt any gaping wound that needed to be healed by a wife, or some loneliness that only a wife would cure. He hadn't dreamed of marriage, or even thought about it much, which was probably why he hadn't proposed to Margaret before she had accepted Hastings's proposal. Perhaps she had tired of waiting for him, though she had never shied away from speaking her mind with him before.

If he had known what she was thinking...

If he had known...

But he hadn't known, and that was the point. He had not known, and choices had been made that he had never considered. He could not know what any other person was thinking or wanted, and he would not try.

It was his duty to marry and to sire an heir so that Helwithin would not have to be entailed away. So that the work he had done in his life would carry on. So that the respect he had cultivated upon his father's incomparable foundation would continue. So that the mines would continue to succeed and the lives that depended upon them would survive.

And if he was going to marry, he might as well marry someone he could bear to be married to.

That was all that had gone into his decision.

Could he really expect to be commended for such a callous motivation? He'd even congratulated himself on rescuing Honora from her situation with her parents, but he hadn't intended that when he'd thought of her. It had only solidified his decision and made him more determined to go through with it.

He was glad he'd chosen Honora. It was better for him to have her, and it was almost certainly better for her.

But that wasn't why he'd chosen her. He was no hero. Honora knew he was no hero, which helped. She wasn't showering him with gratitude at every moment of the day or looking upon him like some divinely sent creature. She barely noted him at all except for their shared supper. They hadn't entertained before this evening, and they had not attended events together as man and wife, so they had very little interaction with each other throughout the day.

It was a mutually independent existence, even if they were bound together by law.

It was what he'd expected marriage to be when he'd taken up the idea. Nothing more and nothing less. He would need to be married for longer than a fortnight to truly get a taste of the matter and to appreciate the wife he had for the woman she was rather than for any wife he could have had.

Margaret or not.

Perhaps he did not need to write a book on the subject after all.

"Just different," Basset finally said from beside him.

It took Gage several moments to recollect what they had been speaking about, and then he looked at his friend curiously. "You're not going to stand there and declare that Honora is better because she accepted me?"

Basset met his eyes squarely. "You never offered for the other one. Not really. And as I understand it, you didn't argue the situation when she made her choice. I never minded the other one when she was among us, so I won't pretend I do now that she isn't."

"Always the fair-minded one," Gage grumbled, shaking his head and taking a drink.

"Do you want me to take a side?" Basset countered. "I know where my sword falls, even if you don't."

Gage brushed that away. "I know, I know." He pressed his tongue to the front of his teeth, letting a tsking sound eventually escape. "I saw her today, you know."

"Who?"

Gage flicked his eyes away and took another slow drink.

"The other one? No…"

Gage nodded, swallowing without any further reaction.

Basset softly swore under his breath. "And she's a widow now. That's awkward."

"Gage had word of that before the marriage," John offered as though it was helpful. "Julia told him herself."

"Didn't matter," Gage told them both without waiting for the invitation to do so. "She made her choice. I made mine."

"No regrets?"

He thought Basset had been the one to ask the question, but he really could not have been sure. He was too busy looking at Honora. Or trying to look at Honora. If he was looking at Honora, he could not possibly think of Margaret. Of how Margaret had wounded him in a way that he had only thought death capable of. Of how disinclined he was to ever look upon Margaret again, and yet… seeing her that day…

The sting of his past had lashed across his chest with a swift burning while his wife had sat beside him.

He didn't want her again. It wasn't that simple.

The sight of her had merely brought back years of memories in an instant, all flashing through his mind, until the day he had learned of her engagement. She had faced him one further time, her face set and without the sweetness he had always known in her. And she had told him that it had been her decision, and he had not given her any reason to refuse. She would not wait for him any longer, in spite of all the plans they had talked of for years.

Gage hadn't understood that at the time. She had never expressed impatience with him and his lack of offer. She had never given him any indication that she was entertaining any other suitors. She had not warned him of any impending offers or hinted that her parents were pressing her to move on, and their relationship until that point had been open enough for such discussions.

Her parents had always liked Gage and been in favor of their suit. He knew this for certain, as her father had told him so in no uncertain terms.

Yet Margaret had married elsewhere without giving him a chance to ask for himself.

The years had rid him of the depth of his pain, but the memory of it was perfectly clear. And the medley of emotions regarding Margaret were what the sight of her had brought up.

The thrill of wanting her. The pain of losing her. The dejection of her abandonment. The coldness of his defenses. The satisfaction of moving on. All memories now, dredged up together.

"No regrets," Gage replied firmly, if a trifle delayed.

And he meant that. He had no regrets about his choice to marry before encountering the widowed Lady Hastings.

The only regrets he did have were that a single woman could have such an impact on his thoughts and feelings, then and now, even if the reactions to each could not be more different.

"I think I must tell you something," John said softly, turning to face Gage fully, his back to the ladies. "And Julia cannot know that I am doing so."

Basset immediately turned inwards as well, closing off their group entirely. "I think I know what it is."

Gage looked at his friend in surprise. "That makes one of us."

Basset ignored him. "Go on, Roskelley."

John lowered his eyes for just a brief moment, then raised them to meet Gage's gaze rather squarely. "If you take the other one as a mistress while married to Honora, I'll have the coat off your back."

All of the air rushed out of Gage's lungs, more in shock than with any real sense of feeling. "Are you serious?"

"Oh, I believe he is deadly serious," Basset replied without any hint of surprise. "And I wouldn't stop him, either."

Gage looked at both friends as though he had never seen them before. "You honestly think I could do that?"

"At this moment, no," John answered. "But I've seen good men sink low when tempted with the right sin. And while I wouldn't dare tell you how to manage your marriage, I would put my foot down there and avenge family honor."

"No, that isn't what I mean." Gage set his glass aside and cleared his throat before folding his arms and glaring. "You truly think that I would take a mistress? Any mistress at all?" He looked at Basset in disbelief. "I saw what your father's behavior did to your mother. You think I'd do the same?"

Basset did him the courtesy of nodding in acknowledgement before turning his attention to John for a final word.

"I don't believe you would," John told him, his voice dipping lower. "But it needed to be said, Gage. Just in case temptation arises."

Gage was torn between offense and outrage, wondering how Julia would take it if he throttled her husband. But then he heard something that took the wind out of his sails.

His wife laughed.

He knew it was her because he knew it was not Adelaide, Emblyn, or Julia, all of whom he had heard laugh more often. And there was something undeniably sweet about the sound of her laughter, something raw and unpracticed that gripped at the base of his throat.

That sound broke through his fury and drew his attention to her.

She was laughing among friends there, open and engaging and without the polite reserve she had always seemed to bear when in their company on her previous visits. She was comfortable at the moment, but how fragile was that new comfort? How long before confidence would begin to form and the novelty of her position wore off?

Her parents had affairs openly, and it had created a grotesque festering in their family. She knew all too well the hurt that could turn to spite, and she had chosen to marry for comfort and convenience instead of for affection, as so many others would have the pleasure of doing.

A betrayal of the vows and the implied trust between them might tamp down this freshly blossoming version of Honora and crush her into some milder shadow of her mother.

He sighed and let his eyes move back to John, a new realization dawning. John wasn't casting aspersions against Gage and his character; he was firmly planting his stake in protecting Honora from any possible damage.

What's more, he was right to be doing so.

Especially where Margaret was concerned.

"I promise you," Gage told him, with Basset as witness, "that I will not take a mistress, let alone the woman you mentioned. And should the temptation arise, however unlikely, I will remove myself and my wife to any other part of the world to save us both."

"You'd leave Cornwall?" Basset grunted a soft sound of disbelief at the claim.

Gage kept his attention on John. "I am a man of my word. You know this. I consider it the duty and responsibility of my life to see to my wife's health, happiness, and security. Should I ever act in a way that betrays those responsibilities, I hope the Almighty will strike me dead."

"Which wouldn't do much for her health and security," Basset replied before John could do so, "but it may just improve her happiness."

"Would you shut up and shove off?" Gage asked his friend, throwing him a look of frank exasperation.

Basset was unmoved. "I think Roskelley gets the point."

"I do, thank you," John agreed. "We understand each other now. I thought we should get this out of the way now, because I would be the tamer one of us, should the worst arise." He nudged his head towards his wife, and Gage blanched at the thought.

Julia would have him flayed alive without a second thought.

He suddenly felt as though he ought to take a vow of complete celibacy, just in case. "Should we go in to supper?" he asked in a slightly higher voice. "I think it must be ready by now."

Chapter Six

It was too soon to be headed to a ball. Why had she agreed to this? It was complete and utter madness, and she ought to have known better.

The carriage jolted over a bump in the road, and words began tumbling from Honora's mouth. "Why did I not go to the mines first? Why in the world did I let you talk me into this?"

"I haven't even been to the mines since we've returned, how could you possibly have gone?"

"I know I am going to embarrass you. I just know it."

"How's that? You aren't an embarrassing figure."

Honora fanned herself, the stiff fabric moving rapidly in her trembling hold, her face absolutely flaming with heat as her chest tightened and squeezed around each panicking breath. "This is a mistake. This is such a mistake."

"It is not a mistake," her husband soothed without much sympathy. "It is the way of things. You've been in company plenty of times before this. You sang in company while you were visiting, for heaven's sake. You aren't any different now than you were then."

She looked at him in utter disbelief. "Aren't any different? I am now your wife. One of them. It didn't matter who I was before, or even what I was like, so long as I behaved myself. I was just a relation of someone, and no one need have bothered even noticing me. But now that I am the wife of Gage Trembath and Mistress of Helwithin—and newly both at that—I will be worthy of all the attention for curiosity's sake. I will be talked about and examined and gossiped about for weeks, and everything about me, from the gown

I have chosen to the style of my hair to the manner in which I eat my soup, will be noted. And unlike my mother, they will keep their criticisms to themselves. Which ought to make me feel better, but when one is used to knowing exactly what irks and chafes against another's tastes, the silence about them leaves only my imaginations of what they could be. Knowing that they exist, but in complete ignorance of what they are. That will be torment."

Gage did not respond, staring at her in silence, his eyes dark and wide in the dim light of the carriage.

Honora swallowed and let the pace of her fanning slow. "What?"

Her husband shook his head slightly. "I've never heard you say so much all at once. I am trying to take it in."

"That is not exactly helpful," Honora grumbled, turning her attention to the window and picking up the pace of her fanning. "We must surely almost be to Trevadden, and Adelaide is going to know something is wrong when she sees my face, which will distract her from the business of hosting…"

"World devastation wouldn't distract Adelaide from hosting," Gage quipped with a low chuckle. "The woman has an uncanny eye for such a thing."

Before Honora could retort anything in response, Gage sat forward and stilled her fan.

She looked at him impatiently, but found his eyes wholly serious, even if there was a small smile on his lips.

"Honora," he said softly, moving his hand down from her fan to her fingers, curling them into his hold. "You don't have to be anything for anyone other than yourself. You are not going to embarrass me. You are not capable of embarrassing me because I have no expectations of you. And you are not responsible for anyone's expectations of you other than yourself. And unfortunately, it seems to me that you are expecting rather a lot of yourself unnecessarily. Is all of this going on in your mind all the time? Or just tonight?"

"Always," Honora whispered, wishing her breath didn't hitch as she made that admission. "But it's worse tonight because I'll be on display."

Gage brought her hand to his lips for a quick kiss, though the glove stifled most of the feel of it. "Well, we'll have to address what is going on in your head constantly another time, but for now, just know that you can be whomever and whatever you want. I don't care what anyone else may think or may say or may presume based on their first encounter with you as my wife. They don't know you."

"And you do?" Honora asked before she could stop herself.

It was a terrible question. Her husband did not truly know her, could not truly know her, after such a short time of being married, let alone the paltry excuses for association they had before that.

But did he know enough?

That was the question she ought to have asked, but in her panicked state, sanity and sense had not prevailed.

"Not really, but I know you better than they do, I think," Gage admitted with a bemused chuckle. "Nobody else knows about the freckle on the back of your left shoulder blade, do they?"

Honora's eyes went wide, and she wished she could fan herself, but it still dangled helplessly from her wrist, her fingers secure in her husband's hold. And so her cheeks began to burn... and burn furiously.

"There it is," Gage murmured, his voice almost a purr. "There's my pretty wife's perfect blush."

"Please," Honora whispered as she averted her eyes, wishing she were anywhere else, and yet dying to be in his arms.

It had seemed so long since that one and only night, though it had only been weeks, and her skin yearned for his touch as though it had known him for years.

She swallowed hard, then cleared her throat. "You are just trying to shock me, Gage. To keep me from being nervous."

"Less than three weeks wed, and already you know me so well." His smile spread and he squeezed her fingers gently. "You don't need to please anybody, Honora. Tonight or any night. Just please yourself."

"My duty as a wife is to please you, isn't it?" Honora felt small to even ask such a question, but she knew full well how this worked. She had heard the arguments of her parents for years.

"Depends on who you talk to," Gage hedged, "but if that's how you feel about marriage, then know it pleases me most for you to be pleased with yourself. I really don't require anything else."

Honora blinked at him, finding that hard to believe. Not from Gage—he was a unique enough individual to surprise her every day for the rest of their lives, and a good man above all—but for any man to expect nothing more of his wife than that she be pleased with herself? That seemed too much to hope for, let alone too much to be true. Surely, he had ideas for what he wanted in a wife and the type of woman she would be among others. Surely, he would wish for his wife to be considered impressive and beautiful and accomplished and captivating.

But then, if he expected all of those things, he could not have truly considered Honora a decent candidate for his wife.

"Really?" she asked him dubiously, pleased that this time she sounded more like herself than the small mouse she was always taken for.

Her husband nodded firmly. "Really." He released her hand and sat back against his seat, folding his arms. "I don't know if you know this, Honora, but I'm not altogether that concerned with people and their opinions. I like people well enough, but only in the most cursory sense. Be whomever you like."

"I wish I liked people," Honora murmured more to herself than to him, opening her fan once more to gently wave it before her. "I don't dislike them, I just… don't know many."

"Fortunate girl," Gage said, surprising her. "It's exhausting, liking people. And pretending to like them when you know enough to not like them. Someday, I fully intend to dislike them openly. Would you still be married to me if I opted to receive nobody and go nowhere just for my own peace of mind?"

Honora smiled at that, her panic finally seeming to dissipate completely. "Of course. Helwithin is full of books, and we could read all of them."

"You'll stay indoors with me? For the rest of our lives?" He raised a brow, the question one of teasing, but somehow also seeming to be a dare.

She shrugged. "Why not? You're good company."

His smile was slower than she expected and more delicious than she could have anticipated. "So are you, dear wife. So are you."

Somehow, she held his gaze and kept her smile, wondering if she would ever adjust to the feeling of a handsome man smiling at her.

Especially when that man knew about the freckle on the back of her left shoulder.

"I should warn you, though," Gage went on as the moment of quiet, content companionship slipped from them. "I am a terrible reader. Always have to sound things out. It will get quite annoying for you."

Honora found herself laughing at the image of himself Gage presented, and those last edges of her nerves finally settled in full. "I, on the other hand, am an excellent reader, having had little else to do at Horsend. But never fear, with all of the years ahead of us in the library, I am sure I can teach you a thing or two."

Gage laughed to himself, looking positively delighted. "The cheek of my wife! Who would have thought such a thing?"

"You would," she pointed out. "You're the only one who can pry that out of me."

"Excellent. It shall be our little secret." He winked and looked out the window. "Ah, we are arriving."

The peace of the last few moments blackened and curled in the sudden flames of anxiety, disintegrating before her very eyes as the looming edifice of Trevadden grew closer. It did not matter that the host and hostess were now friends of hers. It did not matter that she was comfortable in their company. It did not matter that her cousin would be in attendance or that she would have her husband's arm for however long she wished. It did not even matter that he had given her all the freedom she could ever hope for.

She did care what people thought of her. She had been raised to care about it. To adapt to it. To guise herself to fit whatever mold was thought necessary. That was not broken so easily.

And despite what Gage had said, she knew full well she was capable of embarrassing him.

Perhaps not on a large and dramatic scale, and perhaps not in a shocking way, but over time, word of the unremarkable wife of Gage Trembath would spread. He would be pitied for having a wife who did not impress anyone and could only sing for her supper. All would say that they expected better of him, and what a shame it was that he had been saddled, for whatever reason, with the most boring creature in womanly form that had ever existed.

And he would grow so tired of the pity.

Which would create resentment between them.

She could not bear that.

The carriage pulled to a stop, and it was all Honora could do to keep her expression from showing the tension that was rather rapidly taking over her body. If Gage saw her distress, he would take pains to comfort her again, and she did not need him to think she was such a ninny.

He would know that soon enough anyway.

Gage climbed from the carriage and turned to offer her a hand, which she took in the hopes that it would steady her for more than just her descent. But as he led her towards the house, she could feel the slight trembling in each and every step, from her ankles to her knees.

"I can feel how you shake, you know," Gage murmured, perfectly reading her thoughts. "I can only tell you not to worry so many times and in so many ways. Just be yourself."

"Is there anyone important I need to dance with or make conversation with?" Honora asked, ignoring his advice. "For politeness and propriety."

Thankfully, Gage was content to go along with her fears. "Basset, naturally. He'll likely be first in line, so you don't need to worry there. Grangers aren't in town, so he's out…"

He rattled off some names, but Honora only half heard him, nodding with each name he gave. She trusted he would make the most important introductions, and she could remember those easily enough. The anticipation of the thing was always worse than the thing itself. She would almost certainly feel better once she was within. Once she had seen Adelaide and felt the certainty in her smile. Once her cousin was by her side and could make conversation that would distract Honora from everything else. Once she had danced with Gage.

"Will you dance with me tonight?" Honora inquired quickly. "That is… I am not asking you to. Only if I should expect it."

Gage gave her a surprised look. "Why shouldn't you ask me to?

You can ask me anytime you like. I hope I can ask you anytime I like, but I won't presume, given how popular you are destined to be."

"Hardly," Honora grumbled. "And I'll give you any dance you want, taken or not."

"We'll see," he replied, patting the hand that was now looped through his arm. "Sweet to offer, though."

Honora exhaled a short breath. "Well, I am nothing if not sweet. So, should I expect to dance with you?"

"You should," he confirmed. "At least twice. One of them will take place throughout the night, but I am afraid I must insist upon the last dance of the night to be mine. Wherever we are. Call it a tradition, shall we? Then we can be certain the night will end on a redeeming note."

That made her smile, more for the wryness in his tone than the offer itself. "For a man who claims to like people, you don't seem to have much faith in them."

"Faith in people is entirely different than liking them," he insisted with a faint sniff. "Now, will you reserve your final dance of this and every night for me, Mrs. Trembath?"

"Oh, why not?" she sighed, pretending it was some matter of concern. "At least then we'll know where to find each other so we can leave."

"Now you see my ulterior motive." He patted her hand again. "Clever girl."

Honora managed a smile, only moderately soothed by the plan. They ascended the steps to Trevadden, and something about the weight of the skirts in her hand as she did so made her reconsider her ensemble with irritation.

"I should have asked Adelaide what she wanted me to wear," she muttered with a shake of her head. "I don't even know if Adelaide likes green, and it's not a particularly fine gown."

"My word, are you going to criticize everything about yourself tonight?" Gage stopped them and made a show of looking her over. "The gown is very pretty. It suits your coloring, and it is fine enough for Lady Adelaide Basset, who is your friend, and who would have let you know if she had any particular requests or expectations as to what her guests should wear. Now, to stop you from fearing your tastes in fashion in the future, I am ordering you to go with her to the finest modiste in the region and run up a bill so exorbitant, Adelaide is giddy with it."

"This is not the time for exaggeration," Honora said with exasperation. "Nor of jest."

Gage took her jaw in hand and held her gaze firmly. "I neither exaggerate nor jest. Your mother did not assemble you a trousseau, and considering her tastes, we must both be grateful for that. Adelaide will now be in charge of your trousseau, and I most certainly have the funds enough to set my wife up in proper fashion so she cannot criticize anything she chooses to wear ever again. And if you find anything else lacking in yourself tonight, I will take equally drastic measures to clear those up as well. Is that clear, wife?"

It ought to have been a laughable moment, but she saw nothing of humor in her husband's countenance. He was not angry either, which was a relief. He was firm, determined, and entirely serious.

"Honora," he said softly, one finger running almost absently under her chin. "Is that clear?"

"Yes," she whispered in response, a trail of ticklish fire following the path of his finger on her skin.

His mouth curved, though she could not call it a smile as such. "Good. Then let us go and greet the Bassets so you might be a little less terrified of the ordeal."

He released her jaw, and they moved the rest of the way up the stairs and into the grand house, the path to the ballroom clear by the line of servants standing at attention. She was grateful for the display, even if it was a trifle excessive. It had been nearly a year since Honora had visited Cornwall, and her memories of Trevadden were not particularly clear. She might have wandered helplessly for ages before finding the right direction to the ballroom.

Timid little mouse that she was, she would never have asked for help.

No, she told herself harshly. She was not a mouse. Her mother and father thought she was a mouse, and she had no doubt that members of the public thought so, too, considering how little she spoke in company. But that was due to the criticism of her parents throughout her life, not her own nature. She might not know how to properly express her nature yet, but she would soon learn. Gage wanted her to be herself, and so she would be.

Once she discovered who that was and what she liked.

The Bassets were just up ahead of them now, and already Honora was in awe of them. Even knowing them and being comfortable with them, she was now intimidated by their resplendence. They were such a contrast in looks, the pair of them. Lord Basset was dark haired and dark eyed, tanned from the sun, all stark angles and relative somberness. His wife was fair haired and blue eyed, pale where she ought to be and perfectly rosy where it suited, and a smile that could welcome and shun without a single shift of its shape. They were dressed to brilliance tonight, Adelaide in a shimmering silvery blue and Basset in a deeper blue that could have been black had he not been standing beside his wife.

No one would ever look at her and Gage the way they looked at the Bassets. Gage was handsome and refined when he wished it, but Honora...

There was nothing for anyone to be awestruck about.

"Well, they look rather godlike, don't they?" Gage said in a low tone. "Did I miss some grand transfiguration ceremony for them?"

Honora released a surprised snicker, covering her mouth and nose with one hand.

"This might reach entirely new levels of ridiculousness for them. I knew Adelaide was fanciful, but truly, are we starting a new religion?"

It was all Honora could do to keep silent, her hand pressing even harder against her mouth and nose.

"It is most unfair to don such ethereal attire when the rest of us have not," Gage went on, either ignoring her state or entirely unaware of it. "The superiority of our friends, Honora. I must question our friendship entirely for being made to feel so low."

"I am quite certain you will rally," she managed between giggles as they neared the couple. "Stop it now!"

"Yes, wife," he replied with utmost obedience.

Was this another attempt of his to lighten her spirits and distract her nerves? Or was he truly just this ridiculous? It was difficult to say, as Gage was so generally pleasant and amusing. If he was trying to set her at ease, that was particularly sweet of him. If he was simply being himself, then she had been wiser than she'd anticipated in accepting his hand. Simply by being himself, he could set her at ease.

So long as she never went anywhere without her husband, she'd likely be fine.

But they almost never went anywhere together. Or they hadn't yet, at any rate. Perhaps he would be willing to change that.

Unless he'd prefer not to have his wife hanging about him like some poor pantomime of a desperate puppy.

The only comfort he'd have in that would be that his wife was only terrified and not lovesick.

What a pitiful scene it would be.

Honora felt herself breathe a trifle more easily as her smile felt less forced and the distance between them and the Bassets closed. Adelaide's perfect complexion seemed to brighten when she saw Honora, though it could easily have only been the light of recognition stretching her smile further.

"At last," Adelaide said through her smile, "someone I do not have to feign interest in."

"Is that for my wife or for me?" Gage asked, bowing with all due politeness for Adelaide before shaking Lord Basset's hand.

"Your wife, of course," she shot back without hesitation. "I had my fill of you in my first three months in Cornwall." She leaned in to kiss Honora's cheek, smiling. "Darling Honora, you look so lovely."

"It is kind of you to say so, Adelaide," she said softly, feeling her cheeks heat, "though it is clear I pale in comparison to you."

Adelaide rolled her eyes and took Honora by the arms. "Do not say so. It is monstrously unfair to compare any two women in looks alone. My husband cannot contradict you without offending his vow to me, and your husband cannot argue with us while we are hosting. It is no competition, and I will not have it. I say you look lovely, and I must be believed."

"She truly must," Basset insisted, leaning towards them with a small smile. "She does not flatter. If someone does not look well in her eyes, she says it is lovely to see them and makes no comment on appearance."

"Tush!" Adelaide flicked a hand at his chest, landing a blow with resonating sound. "Do not give away my secrets. Gage would sing like a canary with them, if given the right incentive."

Gage coughed and clasped a hand to his chest. "The indignity, my lady! Honora, we must go, I have been grossly insulted."

"No, you're not taking my friend away from me," Adelaide scolded as she winked at Honora. "You will simply have to get over it, Gage. And kindly lend me your wife the moment I finish this intolerable line of guests."

Basset heaved a small but mighty sigh, though his dark eyes were filled with amusement. "You know it is bad when she calls it intolerable and not I." He put his hand at his wife's back, then raised a brow at Honora. "Save a dance for me, will you, Mrs. Trembath? Supper set, perhaps?"

Honora blinked at the flattering but wholly unexpected offer. "What? My lord, you should save that for a woman of status here."

"I have," he said simply. "You're mistress of one of the oldest and finest families around. Who else should I escort to supper?"

"But... but..." Honora fumbled for words and looked at Gage.

He shook his head. "Don't look at me, he did not ask me to dance the supper set."

Impossible husband of hers. He was supposed to tell her what to do, not put the responsibility of a reply on her own shoulders.

She looked back at Basset, who seemed bemused by her reluctance and hesitancy.

Adelaide cleared her throat and leaned forward. "This is the part," she whispered, "where you say yes."

Well, if Adelaide did not think it improper as hostess, then Honora could not argue the point. She had done her best as far as modesty was concerned, and to continue demurring would be unseemly.

Why was she reciting rules of etiquette to herself as though she had just come out of a lesson with her governess?

"Yes, my lord," Honora finally replied with a smile for Basset. "I would be delighted to reserve the supper set for you."

Basset nodded as though it had not taken Honora an age to answer his request. "Thank you, my dear. It will be a relief to know there is good company awaiting me at some point." He straightened and nodded, which seemed to signal an end to the encounter.

Gage took her hand and held it before him as he led her away from the Bassets and towards the ballroom. For a long moment, nothing was said, but then he seemed to hum with soft laughter.

"Did I do it horribly wrong?" Honora whispered. "Is that why you're laughing?"

"Wrong?" Gage repeated with another laugh. "I don't think it could have gone more right. Basset is proclaiming your status in his eyes without saying a word. It's perfection."

Honora shook her head quickly. "He is being kind, and it is unnecessary. As your wife, surely I have all the status I need."

"Social status, darling," Gage told her, his thumb rubbing over her knuckles. "His approval, if you will. Not that anybody should doubt it, given the friendship between he and I, but it is an important mark for your entry, and he is stamping it."

It was impossible to escape the feeling of utter smallness in that moment. It was exactly what she had feared her situation would be. Judged by everyone and everything, needing powerful influence to even be worthy of her presence anywhere. Gage was enough, but she couldn't be.

Cornwall might as well have been London.

"The magnificent thing about that is that now you don't have to meet anyone unless you want to," Gage went on as they entered the ballroom. "Basset choosing you will make everyone want to come to you, not the other way around."

"Does he really hold such power?" Honora asked softly, smiling for those staring at them, though she would have thought gawking a better word for what they were doing. "To take insignificant little me and put me on a pedestal?"

Gage exhaled shortly and brought her hand to his lips. "This has nothing to do with you, Honora. It is for them. You belong wherever the hell you please, pedestal or not, and need no one to put you anywhere. Not me, not Basset, not even the King. None of this, none of them, are real. Our life in Helwithin is the only real thing. You and me, Honora."

"And that is enough for you?" she whispered even as the warmth of his words lit up her chest. "Am I?"

"Pardon?" He squeezed her hand gently. "Are you all right?"

Honora sniffed once. "Nervous. I still think we should have gone to the mines first."

"I prefer the mines myself," her husband quipped. "Not to worry, though. You'll do fine." He turned his head and brought his mouth closer to her ear. "And if I ever hear you call yourself insignificant again, you'll be in trouble. You are enough."

Blanching, Honora managed a soft, embarrassed giggle. "I didn't think you heard that."

His laughter so close to her ear sent ripples of heat down her neck. "The only things you are allowed to mutter under your breath are the exasperating remarks you have regarding that idiot of a husband you married, Mrs. Trembath. Now, what say we open tonight with a dance together, hmm?"

Chapter Seven

Honora was remarkably pretty.

He'd known she was an attractive girl, of course. He was not blind. But something about the way she looked tonight made the fact of her attractiveness stand out even more starkly.

No one would compare her to the startling vision that was Adelaide or the more obvious beauty of some of the other ladies in attendance, but there was something about Honora that drew his attention in a new way. Perhaps it was because she was his wife, and so he was now more attuned to her, but his eyes always seemed to find her whenever they looked about the room. And when they did find her, something peculiar happened.

He found her pretty. Each and every time. But in a way that surprised him. How could he be surprised by the appearance of his wife when they had been married for three weeks and he had seen her every day?

They had shared a wedding night, for heaven's sake! And, he prided himself, he had done his utmost to make it an experience she would enjoy rather than something to try and forget. She had been stunning that night, but his nerves and desire to take care of her had distracted him fairly well from focusing too much on the subject. He remembered a few things, such as the freckle on the back of her left shoulder and how she relaxed in an instant when his fingers ran through her hair, but he could honestly say she had not been on his mind much since that night.

Yet now he was being surprised by her beauty? Catching every degree of her smile and every hint of strain in her features, marveling at the way her eyes seemed to change shade depending on her proximity to candles. Her gown brought out the purity of her complexion, and while it was not as fine as others present, it suited her. And there was a natural grace and majesty to her air and bearing that could not be taught or even practiced.

How could she be so timid when she was so magnificent? He'd had no idea before tonight just how insecure and anxious she was, and it baffled him. More than that, he had little idea what to do about it. He was conscious of the fact that she was in a new place, with new circles to acquaint herself with, but she had visited this area several times and had never seemed to be ill at ease within them.

But then, he had not especially noticed her on those occasions. Perhaps she had been. Or perhaps she hid it well. Perhaps she had not felt the same sort of pressure then as she did now. Being a visitor to the area was very different than being a member of it. But how could she think so little of herself?

She was not prone to making scenes or blunders, she never called attention to herself apart from when she was invited to sing, and she was sweetness and politeness itself at all times. Yet she saw herself as a mistake waiting to happen, as though bad luck followed her everywhere, and as though she could not be trusted to behave or act or think. And she reacted to praise as though it ought never be given to her.

What sort of hell had she been raised in? He'd thought he'd had enough of an idea from the time he had spent at Horsend before the wedding, but this…

This was clearly far worse.

"Why in the world do you look so troubled?"

Of all the voices he anticipated asking him such a question, that of Adelaide Basset was not one of them. The woman was their hostess for the evening, and rarely spared a moment for Gage in public settings due to the more fashionable demands on her time.

But perhaps the expression on his face presently did not match her ideas of the décor.

Gage did his friend's wife the courtesy of turning to face her and bowing in greeting before resuming his surveyal of the room. "My lady. One could never be troubled in your presence."

"Clearly you don't speak with my husband or my son very often," Adelaide said with a short laugh, hiding her words behind her slowly moving fan. "Now, what is it?"

Trust Adelaide not to let the thing go, and to see through his bald-faced flattery.

Gage slid his gaze to her briefly. "My wife."

Adelaide immediately began looking for her. "What about her? Is she in distress?" She paused a moment, then hummed. "No, she seems perfectly well. Smiling, even. Why are you troubled about your wife?"

"She thinks she's small," he said in as low a voice as he could, not wanting anyone in the area to overhear.

"She is small," Adelaide retorted with a soft snort. "She's as petite as a china doll."

"Not that kind of small, Adelaide." Gage swallowed back his impatience, knowing she would never mean to impugn his wife, even in misunderstanding. "She thinks she means nothing and is worth nothing. She was terrified to come tonight. Was afraid she'd embarrass me. Or you."

"What?" Adelaide yelped before covering her mouth and turning her back on the dancing, her fan going up to cover the side of her face onlookers would see. "What?" she demanded again, this time keeping her voice tight and small.

Gage managed a slight smile for the genuine distress Adelaide was showing. "She called herself insignificant. I think she actually believes she is insignificant. And because of that, she is terrified of what everyone will think about her. I spent almost the entire carriage ride either listening to her nerves, trying to soothe her nerves, or distracting her from her nerves. Perhaps I should have taken her home, but she did not seem in distress or swooning... I don't know what I should have done, if anything. Perhaps I should have asked what she can tolerate with her nerves. Perhaps it's fine. Perhaps—"

"You are making my head spin. Stop." Adelaide exhaled slowly through her nose, a tiny muscle in her jaw ticking. "Why does she believe this about herself?"

Gage shook his head, looking at his wife with sympathy and concern, despite her seeming to be fine where she stood. "Her parents. Her home life. She's always been unwanted and unappreciated. Criticized and demeaned, from the way she walks to the way she breathes. I am convinced that only Julia has shown her genuine affection in her life. Perhaps other cousins, but certainly not her parents or siblings. And we believe what we hear most."

Adelaide's fan began to slowly move again. "And what do you tell her, Gage?"

"That she is enough," he replied, feeling as though it were possible to tell Honora the same again from across the room. "That she does not have to impress anyone or live up to any expectations. That she does not have to please anyone but herself. That I never want to hear her call herself insignificant again. What else can I do?"

Adelaide surprised him by putting a hand on his arm and turning towards him with a rather lovely smile. "That is perfect for now. Everything else will take time. You've said the words, now you must show her with action."

Gage nodded at that. "Speaking of action, I must ask a favor of you. She was criticizing her gown earlier."

"Why?" Adelaide demanded turning to look at Honora herself now. "It's lovely and perfect for her complexion."

"She did not think it was fine enough for an event at your home and did not want you to be embarrassed by her. Or for me to be embarrassed of my wife."

Adelaide growled softly. "I may have to shake that darling wife of yours. Very gently, of course."

Gage laughed and patted the hand that still rested on his arm. "I've a better idea, if you'll agree. I told Honora that you are in charge of assembling a ridiculously expensive and flattering trousseau for her, so she will feel comfortable, confident, and worthy of any amount of money."

"Done," Adelaide ground out, patting his arm back before dropping her hand entirely. "I've been dying to take Emblyn shopping lately, so perhaps I'll get her to come along for this. She'll be just as determined to raise Honora's spirits and opinion of herself and will be able to offer a more sensible opinion than me, which your wife will appreciate."

"I knew you would know just what to do." Gage smiled at

Adelaide rather fondly. "I knew Honora was a sensible, soft-spoken woman with a beautiful voice, and I knew that, according to Julia, she was never particularly wanted at home. But I never knew she thought so little of herself. I thought she simply…."

"Thought little about herself?" Adelaide nodded knowingly. "Sometimes there is little distinction between the two for outside eyes, but it is a very different thing for the one feeling it."

There was such certainty in this woman's tone, on a subject in such contrast to her evident confidence, that Gage looked at her with some concern.

She caught it and laughed once. "Oh, not me, Gage. Heavens, I could use a touch of either in my life, but I have neither. I'm talking about Emblyn. She and I have discussed the subject a time or two. And I think your little wife could use some instruction on the distinction. But that may have to wait for her to grow more settled."

Slightly appeased, Gage returned his attention to Honora, now talking with Julia and her husband and looking more animated and delighted than she had all evening. And the rise in her looks was something that could not go unnoticed.

"My wife is really rather pretty," he said before he could stop himself.

"Well spotted," came the wry reply from his left.

He had to chuckle at that, knowing what an oaf he had just made himself out to be. "Yes, I know. I knew that well enough already; she was pretty when I first met her. But I seem to notice it more and more now. Is that normal?"

Adelaide sighed. "Best not to ask me what is normal in a marriage. However, I did come to find Harrison more attractive with every passing day. Long before I ever felt true fondness for him. I seemed to notice him all the time, even if I had no wish to. But I did not like it for a long time afterwards. Then it became quite useful, as I actually wanted to see him frequently."

"So either this is normal, or I am becoming more like you?"

She barked a laugh and rapped his arm with the fan she held. "You would only be so fortunate, dear. The supper set will be soon, and your pretty wife will dance with my handsome husband, and I will make certain that Honora knows how much Harrison hates the supper set just so she knows how highly he thinks of her."

"She'll think he's just being kind," Gage countered softly, shaking his head. "It's all she's said all night. I'm not even sure she believes that I actually wanted to marry her at this point."

Adelaide tsked rather loudly and tossed her brilliantly coifed fair hair. "We shall see about that." She strode away from him before he could make any further comment, barely avoiding causing an interruption in the dancing as she made a near direct line to Honora.

Gage probably should have looked away, as it would be all too clear where Adelaide had come from, but he was far too interested in what his friend's wife would do.

In true Adelaide form, she was perfectly behaved for the guests and the gathering, and kissed Honora's cheeks with a familiarity that no one else in the room had received. People looked and fans were raised for the sharing of gossip. Adelaide made a show of praising Honora's hairstyle and what it did for the shape of her face. She begged her to make time for them to go into Redruth soon and visit Adelaide's favorite modiste, and then, oddly enough, asked Honora to take a turn about the ballroom with her.

Honora looked as though she had been invited to visit royalty, though her confusion was clear to Gage.

Would others notice that as well?

"Why is my wife making a show over yours?" Basset asked, somehow appearing at Gage's side without his knowledge.

He chuckled and took a fresh glass of punch from a passing footman. "I have yet to understand the way your wife's mind works, Basset. I can only guess she wants to make sure my wife feels important."

His friend grunted softly. "Does your wife need to feel important?"

"You offered to dance the supper set and lead her into dinner," Gage reminded him, giving Basset a sidelong look. "You are also making her feel important."

Basset smiled just a little. "So I am. Honestly, that is for everyone else. Honora surely knows we are her friends, yes?"

Gage sobered and shrugged. "I don't know what Honora knows and does not know. She is... Well, she lacks your wife's exuberant confidence."

"Not necessarily a bad thing," Basset laughed. "But then, my sister is defiantly confident in her lowly state, which drives me mental. I am surrounded by extremely confident women who could not be more different in their confidence."

"And I simply have a woman without confidence and a desperation to find her place," Gage murmured, trying now to see where Adelaide had taken her. "I didn't expect this as part of marriage, I will admit."

"What, problems?"

Gage shook his head at once. "No, this isn't a problem. At least, I don't think it is. Honora isn't a problem at all. I didn't expect... to care so much."

"About...?"

"Anything." He took a quick drink of punch. "Her mood, for example. She was so nervous on the way over, and it really had nothing to do with me, except that she is my wife. And I cared. I wanted to fix it. I wanted her to be at ease, and..." He sputtered and took another drink when no other words came.

Basset patted him rather patronizingly on the arm. "You're already a better husband than I was when I married Adelaide," his friend offered, as though that could somehow be helpful. "I didn't care two figs about Adelaide's mood. I intentionally provoked her."

Gage snorted softly at the memory. "Yes, so I recall."

"But you have always been more sensitive to that sort of thing than I," Basset went on, ignoring the jab. "Better with people and putting them at ease, more aware of their thoughts and feelings and the like."

"You make me sound rather soft," Gage grumbled, shifting his weight uncomfortably at the idea of being pegged as an emotional sort.

Basset raised a brow. "Do I? I rather thought of it as you being perceptive and particularly observant, and of a disposition capable of caring a great deal. And acting upon what you see."

Now Gage looked at his friend with some mild concern and suspicion. "Are you quite well, Basset? That is, without a doubt, the nicest thing you have said to me in our entire lives. What is wrong?

Or are you simply anticipating the end of days and wishing to make amends everywhere?"

As he'd suspected, Basset rolled his eyes. "I am capable of genuine expression without provocation."

"For your wife, perhaps," Gage allowed. "Your sister, when it suits. Me? Never." He shook his head with firm solemnity. "So explain, please."

Basset's moment of silence, followed by a short exhale, told Gage he was right, though there was no anticipating what his friend might answer.

"She's here."

Gage frowned. "Sounds ominous. Who is?"

Basset cleared his throat. "Lady Hastings."

Even that was not clear enough, and Gage looked at Basset, utterly confused.

Then it struck him. Like one of the church bells ringing on a holiday.

And with just as much reverberation.

"Lady Hastings," Gage repeated slowly. "As in…"

Basset nodded slowly. "Indeed."

He swallowed, finding his throat oddly tight. "I see."

"It was unavoidable," Basset explained, though Gage demanded no explanation. "She is staying with her mother, and we could not invite Mrs. Teague while ignoring her…"

"No, of course not," Gage murmured. He felt his brow crease, which was a strange sensation, as he believed such a thing usually took place without much sensation.

Why should he feel those muscles working in that particular manner now?

"You don't have to see her," Basset pointed out. "There is nothing that says you must maintain contact or communication with someone who… well, with someone…"

"I quite understand," Gage overrode, not particularly feeling the need to elaborate on what Margaret had done or had not done, what she was or was not, and ultimately, what he did or did not need to do where she was concerned.

He would not pretend that seeing her back in Cornwall the other day had not unnerved him, but he would also not pretend that it meant something. He was married now, and he was not about to forget how the woman had thrown away everything he had thought they had planned for their lives. If he had meant so little to her, why should she mean anything to him?

And yet…

"I have no reason to be anything but polite towards Lady Hastings," Gage said stiffly, clearing his throat. "She has nothing to fear from me."

Basset made a soft sound of indifference. "Good to know, though I wasn't concerned about you making a scene. Just didn't want you to be taken by surprise. Should there still be dark feelings there."

Gage was of half a mind to laugh his friend off, to make the entire situation lighthearted and turn to reveling in his state of newly wedded bliss, or whatever it was called. To tell Basset he could invite whomever he wished to any event he hosted, regardless of Gage's history with them. To plaster his usual jovial smile upon his face and resume the act of polite and affable guest.

But Basset knew too much about the past, and Gage felt the need to be honest.

"There are no dark feelings," he admitted, keeping his voice low. "Only a heaviness of memory. She made her choices, and I have made mine. I refuse to hold on to bitterness as though I still wish to change circumstances where she and I are concerned. That being said, I cannot say with any certainty what it is I do feel at the prospect of renewing any sort of connection."

"Fair enough." Basset clapped Gage on the back, smiling slightly. "I must now find both of our wives so I might claim my dance with yours. Do try to keep out of trouble, won't you?" He raised a warning brow that did not quite seem to match his smile and left him.

Gage watched his friend go, wondering at the gesture. Basset had already said he hadn't thought he would create a scene, so what sort of trouble did he expect? Gage was not the sort to yell at a woman, especially in public, and enough years had passed that yelling would not solve anything. The worst he could do, in all honesty, was ignore the woman. Or perhaps give her the cut direct, if he were feeling particularly peeved.

Nobody would blame him for either, of that he was certain. The amount of sympathy Gage had received in the days following the engagement announcement of Margaret Teague to Lord Hastings, and of the wedding itself, had proven to him that he was not the only one who had presumed certain things of their relationship. Of the expectations everyone had held of the two of them, and the shock of such a seemingly rash decision on Margaret's part.

It would likely be more difficult for Margaret to permanently return to Cornwall at all than for Gage to have to endure such a return.

Not that such a thing was fair, so to speak. In the distance from his heartbreak, Gage could admit that Margaret had been free to make her own choices at her will, and without any real consideration of him, should she wish. It was not jilting, as there had been no plan in place. Public perception was rarely fair, however, and though Cornwall was not London, it could be just as harsh.

If not more so.

The hum of conversation around him, none of which had been particularly noticed, suddenly dipped in volume, and the change was palpable in the air around him. He turned to survey what had caught the attention of those nearby, only mildly interested.

Lady Margaret Hastings was walking in his general direction, fair hair swept into a similar elegance to anyone else, her gown a muted mauve, and those she passed fell almost silent as she approached and gave her a wide berth as though to avoid some kind of contagion that she might pass on to them. It was a blatant combination, the sort of treatment one might give a pariah, and somehow Margaret continued to walk with her head held high, complexion mostly unchanged. Her color was high, but her jaw was set, and her eyes determined.

Gage knew that expression well; he had seen it frequently from childhood.

For a faint moment, he almost smiled. It might as well have been Julia coming towards him with that determination. That was how close he and Margaret had been before they had found love. Or what he thought was love. They had been friends long before anything else, and somehow, some shade of that familiarity still existed within him.

Only a few years ago, he would have beaten that part of him

down until it was lost again.

But tonight…

He weighed his options, and decided that, ultimately, no one deserved to be condemned for exercising their right to choose their own manner of happiness, particularly where only one person's feelings had been wounded and no promises were broken.

No scandal truly existed.

Exhaling shortly, Gage turned towards Margaret rather than away from her, keeping his own head high.

He did not miss the light of relief in her expression as she reached him.

"Lady Hastings," Gage greeted, keeping his voice polite and bowing as neatly as he might have done with anyone else.

"Mr. Trembath," came her soft reply as she curtseyed.

All eyes were on them now, and Gage knew it well.

He kept his attention on the woman before him. "My condolences, my lady, on the recent loss of your husband."

Margaret's throat moved on a swallow. "Thank you. It was rather sudden, though his health had not been robust of late. My boys do miss him."

"You have sons?" Gage found himself smiling just a little. "My felicitations. What ages are they?"

Margaret smiled in return, though not at him. "Five and two. Perfect little tyrants, when they are of a mind." As though seeming to realize with whom she was speaking, and on what subject, her smile vanished in an instant. "We have come to Cornwall to visit my parents for a time and to make happier memories than what currently exist for us at Hastings Park."

"I am sure your family is pleased to have you back," Gage offered. "And if I recall, Chyandour has some excellent grounds for young boys to scamper about."

"It does, and they do." Margaret lowered her eyes for a moment, and he noted her throat working again. "I hear that you have recently been married, Mr. Trembath. Was that your wife in the curricle with you when we passed in town the other day?"

Gage allowed his smile to spread, as much for effect as for genuine fondness for the woman she spoke of. "It was indeed. Mrs.

Trembath is dancing with Lord Basset at the moment, or I would introduce you." He turned slightly to scan the dancing, then indicated Honora when he spotted the pair.

Margaret watched them, her expression unreadable, though she smiled. "She is lovely, Mr. Trembath. I congratulate you."

"Thank you." Gage smiled as Basset made Honora laugh about something, then turned back to Margaret. "She's a cousin of Mrs. Roskelley, you know."

That made her eyes light up. "Is she? What a fortunate connection! Now I must meet her, if you'll permit me to."

Sensing there was a marked importance to this moment, Gage took a brief pause before nodding. "Of course, my lady. It would be my pleasure to introduce you while you are visiting."

Margaret's smile was soft, and there was an almost shimmering light in her eyes as she looked at him. "Thank you. I would like that very much. If you will now excuse me, sir, I must seek out my mother before supper."

Gage inclined his head in a slight bow. "Lady Hastings."

"Mr. Trembath," she returned, dipping her chin. "Good evening." She turned and walked away without haste, without looking back, and without attracting the same shock and gossip as before.

Gage, on the other hand, was now being intensely studied and wondered if he might have just opened Pandora's box in this moment when all he had intended was to extend cordial politeness and to not participate in shunning the woman.

He would have to take very careful steps for the rest of the evening, if not for the next few days.

Chapter Eight

"You're certain you want to come with me this morning? I'll be going fairly regularly now that we're back, so any other day would do as well."

Honora looked at her husband with an almost rueful smile. "You have been trying to talk me out of accompanying you all morning. Is there something you want to tell me about why today is not as good a day as any to visit the mine?"

Gage grinned at her, not appearing even remotely sheepish. "No, not at all. We were just out so late at Trevadden, I thought you might like to sleep later. Or have a restful morning."

It was a sweet thought, but it also showed just how little Gage really knew her. "I have never been very good at sleeping, no matter how late I am out, and being restful is not in my particular skillset. When you said you were going to visit Wheal Stout, it seemed the best opportunity for me to do the same. Especially for my first time."

"I am not very good at sleep either," Gage admitted with a laugh, "though it does not keep me from having an aching head from late nights. But I have put off going to the mine for too long, so today it is."

"Today it is," Honora echoed with a quick smile. She sighed as she looked out over the path before him. She took a moment to breathe in the fresh Cornish air, delighted to be going to the mine on horseback rather than by carriage or wagon or some other transportation. There was something so delightful about being on horseback, and the Cornish landscape positively begged to be ridden across with some sort of abandon, though Honora had never been an especially reckless rider. Just a passionate one.

Riding at Horsend had been something that saved her, and when her parents were not about, she was free to ride whenever she chose and however she chose. Even now, she was not wearing a riding habit, in the technical sense. She wore the military-style coat that came with her one good riding habit, its rich green color perfect for the setting and the gold detailing minimal and faded enough to not express overt finery. Other than that, she wore her most simple cotton dress and boots that had plenty of scuffs on them, her hair in a basic pinned plait.

She had wondered what Gage would say about her appearance, but if he had noticed anything out of sorts, he had said nothing about it. He himself was dressed more as one to work in the mine than one who owned the mine. His coat was simple and worn in places, his cravat was minimally done, his linen shirt something coarser than she had seen yet, and it was clear that his breeches had been worked in a time or two. As they had been at a ball the night before, he was perfectly shaved still, but Honora had the sense that he would not have shaved for this occasion.

He was more handsome when dressed this way than he had been the night before, if she did say so herself.

"Tell me about Wheal Stout," Honora asked as they rode. "Is it your only mine?"

"Our only mine," Gage corrected with a pointed look.

Honora had to smile at that. "Noted," she replied softly, trying to hide just how much it meant to hear. Would he always be reminding her that he considered her an equal partner in this marriage?

"And yes," Gage went on, "it is the only one. Wheal Stout is one of the oldest mines in the region and has been in my family for four generations. It continues to produce copper and tin rather steadily, and we employ around two hundred men and women there alone. We've prospected out space for a second mine, but as yet, haven't found anything worth exploring. Certainly nothing that is worth risking what Stout offers."

"Is Wheal Stout the main source of income for the estate?" Honora asked, her brow furrowing as she thought. "If it is that old, surely there is a risk of it petering out before long."

"Which is why we continue to prospect," Gage said with a nod, his smile rather encouraging. "But we do have several tenant farms that also give us a decent income. And then there is our cove, which opens to Polmiskin Beach, and some of our tenants are also fisher folk. A portion of the profits of each catch goes to the estate, which keeps the taxes on each house and farm low. It's really rather complicated, but it still works for all involved."

Honora shook her head. "So it would seem. And are you—that is, are we very involved with our tenants?"

Gage flashed her a quick grin and a wink at her correction. "We are, yes. I've never seen a need for great distance between us. It is as much my responsibility to provide for them as it is for them to provide for the estate. If one part fails, so does the whole. And I am not a very great gentleman, after all. Why shouldn't I toil alongside the men in the mine or on a roof or in a field? I'm a terrible fisherman, but I try to go out with them at least once a season, if they'll have me."

"And what may I do?" Honora asked with an eagerness she had not known she was feeling.

There was a sudden energy at the prospect of being useful and active for perhaps the first time in her life. She had married a man of action, and there was something captivating and contagious about it. She wanted to be his match in any way she could, purely for the satisfaction of making the marriage work well, but in this…

This was something she also wanted for herself.

"What may you do?" Gage repeated, looking up at the sky with a thoughtful expression. "Hmm."

Was he teasing her, or was it truly something that required thought? She did not know him well enough to always decipher his meaning, but there was something consistently amusing about his manner.

A slight inkling prickled at the back of her mind, and taking a leap of faith, she gave her husband a scolding look. "Don't you dare tell me whatever I decide."

Gage barked a surprised laugh. "How the devil did you know that was where I was going?"

"Fortunate guess," she quipped. "My decision is that I want to be involved with our tenants and help where I am able. Now I need you to advise me as to the specifics of what is available, conceivable, and within my capabilities."

"I have no idea what you might be capable of, Honora," Gage replied, still grinning in that wild, almost windswept way. "You are constantly surprising me. However, I do believe there are a few options before you."

Her cheeks had begun to burn at his obvious praise, and against her inclination to shy away in embarrassment, she managed to maintain eye contact with him. If he noticed the change, he gave no indication.

But Honora noticed. Could she possibly grow more accepting of praise and compliments from him and be able to be less retreating? She had no desire to be a mouse, however much her parents called her one, and if she could avoid turning Mrs. Trembath into a mouselike figure, it would almost certainly go well for Gage in all social matters. She might never be a paragon worthy of societal praise, but she would very much like to avoid its derision.

"The most obvious option at the moment," Gage went on, looking off into the distance ahead of them, "is to assist the bal maidens."

Honora frowned at the term. "The what maidens?"

He smiled. "Bal. It comes from the Cornish word for mine. It's a role that women and older girls working at the mine take on. They pick and sort the ore from the rock, sometimes crush the ore into small grain to get it ready for smelting, and they transport ore to different parts of the mine and the various apparatuses we use. There's some machinery to do the work as well, but machines don't have the eyes that the bal maidens do." He glanced at her. "I have no doubt you'll catch on very quickly."

"I'll admit, I have no idea what you're talking about," Honora said, biting her lip quickly. "But I am willing to work however I can. If nothing else, perhaps I can fetch water and tend children so others can work."

"That is a very kind offer. And likely one people will take up. But Honora…" Gage turned a little in his saddle and pulled his horse to a stop.

She stopped as well. "What? What is it?"

He seemed to be weighing his words or his thoughts, hesitating as his brow furrowed.

Or perhaps he was weighing her.

"What?" Honora asked again, this time more softly.

"You could be nothing more or less than the lady of the estate and the mine," Gage told her, his expression utterly serious. "Bringing baskets to those in need, comforting the widows and the ailing, that sort of thing. I don't want you to feel pressured into doing something simply because I am a very active land and mine owner. These are rough people. Good, hardworking, salt of the earth people, but most certainly rough. They are uneducated, for the most part, and probably going to remain that way. Some of them struggle from season to season, even when we have a good year. I know you want to help, but really, you can determine how you do that."

Honora found herself smiling at the concern she heard in his tone, at the picture he painted of the people they were about to see, at the opportunities he was giving her in every single possible direction. He knew of her nature to please, and he was doing everything in his power to keep her from doing that here. He did not want to influence her, knowing how susceptible she could be to such a thing.

Gage was a far better man than he gave himself credit for.

Honora did him the courtesy of waiting before responding, exhaling softly. "I do not feel pressure because of you. Quite the opposite. I feel freedom to act as I choose and to be whom I choose, possibly for the first time in my life. You move outside of the constraints of your social station, and I want to do the same. I don't mind if the workers at the mine or on the farms or who fish are poor and rough and illiterate. That matters so very little to me. I may be small in frame and timid in nature, so I may not know what use I may be, but I am determined to be of some use somehow. If that is wiping the noses of little children of miners or kneeling in the dirt with the women themselves, so be it."

She hadn't meant for it to sound like a speech or some grand monologue, and she certainly did not believe she was saying anything of real importance. She was simply speaking her mind, not that she had much practice in doing so. But he was giving her this newfound freedom, and slowly she would learn to use it.

All she wanted was that freedom he offered her. To be herself, once she discovered who that woman was. To feel pride in what she accomplished in her day rather than simply existing from one day to the next and feeling as though there was nothing offered. To her or to the day from her. To the world from her.

She wanted to feel like something of substance. A person of consequence, even if that consequence were only to her husband or her future children. To feel as though it mattered that she was here.

She had never felt that with her family.

Perhaps she could feel it with Gage. Or if not with him, in the life he provided.

He was staring at her still, his expression not changing. Then, gradually, the somber demeanor shifted and a soft, beautiful smile burst forth like the dawn on the horizon. "Incredible. As I said, you are constantly surprising me, Honora. I don't think I've ever been prouder of anyone than I am right now of you. And that sounds so deuced condescending, I am so sorry." He put a hand to his brow, sighing and laughing at himself.

Honora managed a laugh herself. "That's all right. I don't mind, and I don't think you're condescending."

"I am very condescending," he corrected with a quick look, "but it is not intended. And I don't think you're all that timid, to be frank."

"You don't?" she asked in surprise.

Gage winked. "Not anymore, I don't. Come on, the mine is just this way." He nudged his head and his horse moved in that direction, leaving Honora to follow.

Not timid? She had spent her entire life being timid. How could he not find her so now?

But perhaps he did not think timid people shared their opinions when they had them. That timid only meant silent, shy, and retreating, which she certainly was.

But that was not all that timid meant, nor all that timid was. Timid was not a habit nor a whim, but a nature. It was something that defined her, though she did not need to be restrained by it. She could be open with Gage while still being a timid woman, but she supposed he was not aware of that.

Perhaps timid only meant weak to some.

Still, she knew what he meant by his words, and felt the approval in them. He wanted her to speak her mind and be comfortable, and the more she did that, the happier he would be.

By being herself, she would make him happy? That was as foreign a concept as any she had ever known, something she had never witnessed or even heard of. Her parents had only ever wanted each other to be completely and entirely different and had never shared a single moment of appreciation for each other. There was no praise, no comfort, no pride, no gratitude, no selflessness of any kind.

Yet here was a man who had married Honora not for love, but for comfort. His own, almost certainly, but he also intended for it to be a comfortable match for her, in more than just fortune and situation.

How many women who married for comfort could truly say they had comfort within the marriage?

Shaking her head at her own good fortune, Honora pressed her horse a touch harder to catch up to Gage and smiled as the ground opened up around the bend to reveal the very busy and active scene of Wheal Stout. It was a stirring sight, in a way. A vista of industry and progress set into the rough, rugged, beautiful Cornish landscape.

The energy of the place almost throbbed in its intensity, and Honora loved it.

It took a few more minutes for the two of them to make their way down the hill along the dirt road, but eventually, they reached a small stone building with its door ajar.

Gage hopped down from his horse and came over to Honora, hands outstretched. She frowned a little, grateful she'd ridden sidesaddle on this occasion, but unhooked her feet and leaned over to rest her hands on his shoulders and slide down, his hands finding her waist and steadying her descent. He nodded when she was on the ground and moved to tie the reins of their horses together.

Honora was grateful for his departure. She'd not be alive if she didn't find the feeling of strong hands at her waist something to blush over.

She pushed her hair back from her brow and smiled over at him as the heat in her cheeks began to fade. "I don't look too windswept, do I?"

He glanced at her, smiling broadly. "You look delightfully windswept, and altogether rather pretty." He rubbed both horses on the nose before coming back to Honora. "Ready?"

She shrugged, her smile impossible to remove after he called her pretty. "As I'll ever be, I suppose."

He gave her a curious look. "You're not nervous."

It wasn't a question, which meant Honora did not technically need to answer. Still, she cocked her head. "Should I be?"

"You were last night," he pointed out, his smile turning impish.

Honora made a face. "That was different. That was finery and being on display and people being false to your face and having to perform in some regard. This is far more comfortable."

"Because it's not fine?"

"No," she said quickly. "Because I can be me. And I have feeling there's a great deal of honesty in the people here, and that will be positively refreshing."

Gage began to chuckle, shaking his head and holding out a hand for her to take. "You're a curious creature, Honora Trembath."

"Is that a good thing?" she asked, the warmth of his hand spreading into her arm.

He laced their fingers as he nodded. "Oh yes. It's a very good thing." He shook their joined hands slightly, winking before leading her towards the building, where a middle-aged man in work clothes stood, grinning openly.

"Well, well," the man called out, "if it ain't his lordship come 'ome again. And 'e's brought himself a maid, to boot." He let out an ear-splitting whistle, undoubtedly some sort of signal, as Honora heard some of the bustle of the place quiet.

Gage heaved a rather dramatic groan of irritation. "Lovely, Rowe. Thank you for such a warm welcome, and for embarrassing me in front of my bride. His lordship, indeed. As though I have ever been called that anywhere."

Rowe laughed loudly and strode forward, hand outstretched. "On'y jokin', Gage. 'Ow be knackin' fore?"

Taking his hand, Gage shook it firmly, grinning. "Very well, indeed, as I am sure you can see." He turned to Honora and indicated the man. "Honora, this is Captain Rowe, our mine captain. We've known each other since we were boys, though his brother was my age and got me into more than my share of trouble."

"I did me bes' to save 'em both the trouble, ma'am," Rowe told Honora with as much apology in his tone as possible. "But age did me no favor in their eyes. I was not quite old enough to be either's father, an' they paid me no heed." He belatedly bowed in greeting, an impish light of good humor in his eyes.

Honora smiled at him and inclined her head. "I am learning, Captain Rowe, that there is no one who can make my husband do something he does not wish to, and no steering him from something he has set his own mind upon."

Captain Rowe grinned, his teeth flashing in neat, almost aligned rows. "Clever as ee be fair, I see, mistress. Well spotted."

"I have certainly married above my station in many ways," Gage replied with a sage nod, looking almost bemused by Honora's response. "My wife would like to see the place, Rowe. Get a feel for its workings, meet some of the people..." He looked at Honora, gesturing for her to continue, if she wished.

She only shrugged. "I've never seen a mine, Captain Rowe. Nor met anyone who has been inside one."

"Not true," Gage protested. "I've been in many."

Honora ignored him, as did Rowe. "How can I be a fair mistress of the mine or any place without understanding what occurs here or meeting any of the people? And I am willing and able to help where I may, provided I do not get in anybody's way."

Rowe scratched at the stubble at his jaw and neck. "Well, ee be small as a croggan, so ee'd not likely be in any way a'tall. Lemme see thy hands, mistress."

Curious, Honora pulled her gloves from her hands and held them out, palms up, giving Gage a look.

He shrugged in confusion but smiled easily.

Rowe made a show of examining her hands, feeling the tip of each finger. "They be fine, soft hands, mistress, though not so fine and soft as some. If ee intend to toil alongside, we must be gradual like so as not to cause ee injury."

Honora nodded obediently, then offered the mine captain a small smile. "You won't tell me this is not my place? Or tell my husband not to let me do so?"

Gage laughed out loud as Rowe grinned at her, his eyes crinkling. "I like a woman who can give 'er husband somethin' to itch about, and ee'll hear he's no' complaining against ee." He gave Gage a shrewd look. "Do ee think she's like to fail, Gage? Is tha' wha' keeps ee silent?"

"My wife has her own mind," Gage told him, holding up his hands in defense. "I want her to learn to speak it and act on it. And how can I expect her to keep her hands soft and fine when mine are not?"

"You're not a lady," Honora pointed out. "It is not expected of you."

Gage returned her look with one of his own. "And I don't expect it of you. They're your own hands, use them how you will. And I'll never object to you doing good in the world." His smile turned unbearably fond. "Which, I have a sense, is all you ever do."

Well, now her heart was positively skipping and dancing a reel, and she did not even fancy her husband.

Not that she did not fancy him...

He was attractive and kind and amusing and good. She was delighted to be married to him, and at this moment, she would have loved to kiss him.

Having only done it the one night, she had little enough practice, but what she recalled was rather lovely...

Dash it, this was all confusing.

"When ee be finished flittin' about each other like a pair of overheated pixies," Rowe mused ruefully, "there be people waitin' to make the lady's acquaintance. And thump Gage for good measure."

Honora averted her gaze with a quick clearing of her throat, startled that her husband's sweet praise should be mistaken for flirtation. But Captain Rowe was quite right, they should truly start as they meant to go on, and that would require them to greet the workers and for Honora, for one, to learn the lay of the land and the way of things.

They did not need to stand here chatting about nothing.

Gage made no sign or sound of discomfort or awkwardness and simply turned towards the mine, and towards the workers who were now gathering, all of whom bore smiles.

That alone was indication enough to Honora as to the sort of man Gage was. To see him so adored by those who worked for him, those who could so easily have been oppressed by a man in his position, and likely often were, but who instead welcomed him almost as one of their own and were delighted by even the sight of him. And seeing how he greeted each and every one, the feeling was entirely mutual.

What was this magical place where classes mingled and mixed, and a man was as welcomed as he might have been at home with family?

But then, perhaps this was his family, as he had lost what there had been of his.

Apart from her.

Not that they were family yet, but soon, she could hope.

Gage turned once more, this time towards Honora, smiling and gesturing for her to join him. "And this, my friends, is my wife."

"Felicitations, mistress!" a woman called from somewhere. "Thy 'usband be a good'un!"

Honora managed a smile and looked around as she neared, wondering who might have offered her such rousing words of comfort. "Thank you. I have found that to be the case myself, but it is most pleasing to hear it from others as well. I have no doubt you will tell me all sorts of things about him, as you've known him longer."

Gage groaned on cue, bringing a laugh from the gathered group. "Don't tell her anything. I cannot have her disillusioned so soon!"

"Mistress, thy 'usband do knaw the bes' drinkin' songs," one of the men shouted. "An' sings 'em with t'others at gatherin's!"

Honora blinked at this revelation, looking at her husband. "You sing?"

"If you can call it that," he said, shaking his head. "It's always when I've had too much to drink and they encourage me."

"Lies!" another man bellowed, laughing. "The man sings like a canary, mistress. We'll have 'im singing for ee one o' these days."

Gage continued to shake his head steadily, but Honora suspected there was something to the words of the others, that his refusal was the lie, not the statement.

But she would not pressure him, nor would she press the issue.

Perhaps someday he would share that part of himself with her, perhaps not. But she would eventually know some things, and for now, that would be enough.

Honora forced her smile to spread and turned back to the group, seizing upon the boldest, most impish part of her that had ever existed even for a moment. "And where does my husband do his best work here?"

"The tables in the office every other Friday!" someone called out. "When he pays us our wages!"

More laughter sounded from the group, and Gage dropped his head, snorting a laugh. "For that, Paul Wyatt, you're losing half a day's pay."

"I'll take it, sir!" the man replied at the top of his voice.

Gage gave Honora a longsuffering look. "Can we go home now?"

She laughed at that, finding the stroke of boldness within her lingering just a bit longer than she expected. "Nonsense. We must see the mine, mustn't we?" She smiled at the workers. "Who will show me the mine? I've never seen one before, let alone gone in."

At least a dozen hands shot into the air, and it was rather touching to see.

Gage stepped closer to Honora and offered his arm. "I don't trust more'n half o' ee," he announced in a perfect mimicry of their accent. "Cap'n Rowe and Tom Drake will take us down."

A bell rang from somewhere in the yard, and it seemed to give a signal to the gathering. They dispersed without much haste, but with a familiarity that spoke of routine.

Honora and Gage followed, and he surprised her by taking her hand in his, even as their arms were linked. "I knew you'd be marvelous with them," he whispered, squeezing her hand. "I just knew it."

"Let's hope I won't disappoint," Honora whispered back,

exhaling heavily.

"Don't worry," came his wry reply. "I disappoint them all the time."

Rolling her eyes, she nudged him hard, gratified to hear the slight wheezing in his laughter.

Chapter Nine

Honora was a natural. So natural, in fact, that Gage wasn't entirely sure he belonged at the mine any longer, and it was a place he had been routinely visiting since the age of seven.

But he did not mind that she had charmed everyone and made him almost superfluous to the entirety of Wheal Stout.

Well, not the entirety. Honora could not actually take a pick to the mine herself, so at least Gage would be useful there.

Which was where he preferred to be anyway.

But today, he would not venture to work in such a way. He was showing his wife this place that was so important to him, not simply because he owned it, but because he had grown up here. He had learned who he was while working in its depths. He had decided on the man he would be while working alongside men who would never have his opportunities. He had learned the ways of the world in this place and had vowed to do all he could to correct those ways.

It was as much a home to him as Helwithin was.

Only slightly less comfortable.

Though he had slept here a time or two in his life.

Not well, but that was entirely the point.

It was a home away from home, and he was just as much himself here as he was anywhere else.

How could he hope to explain that to Honora upon introduction to it?

He smiled to himself now as she listened to one of their oldest miners, Ted Pengarth, explain what they looked for in the rock. The lamps had been lit, but it was not as though that meant much down here. If Honora could actually tell the difference between the quartz, the rock, and the actual ore, Gage would be astonished. He could barely see a difference, and he knew what he was looking for.

Still, she was attentive and seemed to actually appear interested. She might truly be so—he could not say. She was a curious one, his little wife. He had meant what he had told her; she was constantly surprising him. His expectations of her had been minimal, entirely based on their previous and polite encounters, and without any real knowledge of the woman she was beneath that façade of a quiet, composed, angelic singer. He could not have known that there was a quick mind eager to be taught and a will that was trying to find its footing.

She lacked confidence in most things, but as in all things, she would learn. He would encourage where he could, insist where he must, and hopefully, be able to stand back someday and see her shine forth in all the glory he suspected she was capable of. It was all he wanted in the world, to be frank, and he was struggling with the weight of that wish. He did not want her to be like Adelaide or Lily Granger or even Emblyn Moyle, Basset's half-sister, who was so unapologetically herself at any given moment that it was impossible to mistake her for anyone else.

He just wanted Honora to be Honora. Proudly and unreservedly.

Surely, at that point, he could stop worrying about her. He did not even know that he did worry about her until recently, but there it was.

On days like today, however, he did not have to worry much.

"We'd best have ee above ground now, mistress," Captain Rowe suggested as Ted was finishing his latest instruction. "Some o' the women be able to show ee wha' they do. And we may show thy hands how t'work 'em less soft."

"Cap'n Rowe not like to think o' ee workin' a pick yerself, mistress," Ted laughed, wheezing with his usual roughness. "Thinks ee might find a liking fer it and be rather fitty."

Gage snorted softly. "She'd find a new lode forthwith, I have no doubt."

Honora glanced over her shoulder at him with a shy little smirk. "I don't think there's any danger of that. Though there might be danger for those standing nearby if I try to wield the pickax."

The men chuckled, and Gage smiled at his quietly witty wife before indicating that she follow them out. She did so, without the slightest hint of trepidation or trembling, no fuss over the dark, dank tunnel, no trouble with the ladder leading upwards and out of the mine…

What other fine lady could navigate a place like this without qualms?

Up on the surface, Honora paused to tilt her face back into the sun. "It must be blinding for those who have been below ground all day to step into such light."

"It can be," Gage agreed as he came up behind her, setting a hand to her back. "But for the most part, they don't come up while the sun is at its full, so it is not so glaring. There are exceptions, of course, such as when we are blasting and the like, but the work is what it is, and we all know it."

They started walking towards some of the women working nearby, Captain Rowe chatting amiably with Tom Drake ahead of them.

"Have you worked a full day down there?" Honora asked softly. "I can tell that you've done some work, but how…?"

"I have," he replied easily. "Many times. My father preferred working in the mine to being the gentleman, so I was brought up the same. I was to have a proper education and to speak with a more cultured tongue, but that was not to elevate me unnecessarily. I was no better than they, and if I did not work as they worked, I would be worse than they."

Honora hummed at this, her fingers knitting loosely together in front of her. "Such a dangerous occupation. I am surprised he allowed you to do it, given you were the heir."

"What was that danger for me compared to them?" he returned with a slight shrug. "Why should my position protect me from the danger we expect others to take up on our behalf?"

"An excellent point," Honora allowed, nodding in thought. "And one against which I cannot argue."

Gage smiled at her. "Do you argue? At all?"

His wife returned his smile, just a little. "Not aloud, but there are plenty of arguments in my mind at any given time."

"Glad to hear it!" Gage laughed and gestured towards the women just up ahead, one of whom had a bucket of water in hand. "You'll like this bunch. The one with the bucket, that's Nellie Spargo. She is the fifth generation of her family to work here. Three brothers and a husband below and herself above. Her son is destined to work here when he's old enough, and her daughter…" He frowned. "Hmm."

"What?" Honora asked. "Her daughter what?"

Gage ignored the question as they reached the group. "Good day, ladies. Nellie, where's Grace today?"

Nellie set the bucket down and wiped her brow, smiling. "She be about her readin' and writin' today, sir. Two 'alf days a week, and it be makin' all the difference."

"I forgot about the school!" Gage laughed and nodded. "Good for Grace. She's already a clever girl, but with a little education, the world will be hers for the conquering!"

"An' don't she know it, sir." Nellie wiped her hands on her apron and offered a warm, if teeth-stained, smile to Honora. "An' be this thy wife, sir?"

Gage nodded, smiling as he looked at his wife. "It is. Honora, this is Nellie Spargo. If you have any questions about the mine, the people, the land, or the sea, she is your woman."

"Go on wi' ee, sir," Nellie scolded, laughing in her usual croaking way. "I knows no more than anyone else." She curtseyed awkwardly to Honora. "Pleasure to meet ee, mistress. Will we be seein' ee here often?"

"I hope so," Honora said. "If I can be of use. Would you be willing to show me around, Mrs. Spargo? If it will not get in the way of your tasks." She looked at Gage quickly. "Is it all right if she does that?"

The almost childlike question made his smile turn softer, the genuine concern about what was permissible evident. She was a very careful woman, he decided. Always seeking permission and wanting to please, always considering the effects of actions on others and more than willing to alter her course if it would inconvenience too many…

With the parents she had, who could find the most miniscule fault in any given moment, how could she be any other way?

"I am certain it is," he told her, looking to Captain Rowe, who nodded.

Honora managed a smile and returned her attention to Nellie. "If you wish it, Mrs. Spargo. Please do not feel that you have to."

Truly, if Honora continued to bend in every which way to be so accommodating to everyone, she would wind up breaking her back, her neck, or her ankles.

Nellie gave her what could only be called a motherly look. "Bless ee, mistress, but ee are a sweet wee critter. Come 'ere, I'll show ee wha's wha' around 'ere." She held out a dirty, callused hand, which Honora took at once, allowing herself to be tugged away.

Captain Rowe chuckled and came over to stand by him. "Are ee going to follow 'em, Gage?"

He folded his arms, shaking his head as he watched them go. "I don't think so. Honora likes to defer to anyone she thinks has more authority and ask for permission and the like. If she and Nellie go on their own, she might feel freedom to speak and act without restraint. And it would be good for her to make her own friends here, not only the ones I bring about."

"Friends?" Rowe repeated. "Is tha' wha' ee be lookin' for 'ere? For thy wife?"

"Why not?" Gage glanced at him, still smiling. "I have friends here, do I not?"

Rowe returned the smile. "That ee do, Gage. That ee do." He looked after Nellie and Honora, exhaling. "Still, ee grew up here. In Cornwall and in the mine. Thy wife did not. She be a fine lady, be she not?"

"Yes, very genteel," Gage affirmed, noting the difference between the manner in which Honora and Nellie walked, in both gait and bearing. "Raised by a proper lord and lady, a fine house, a good fortune, the picture of respectability... But she is not a fine lady in the traditional sense of the word. She does not care for the details that set a body apart from another in Society. Her parents treated her poorly, but they did provide for her, I suppose. She does not know what it is to starve, but she does know what it is to be starved of love

94

and affection. She does not know what it is to struggle, but she knows what it is to be part of a struggle. She may not know what it is to be poor, but I have never seen someone so poor in spirit. She…"

"Sounds to me like ee rescued her, Gage," Rowe murmured when he trailed off.

Gage hesitated before nodding. "I did not intend to. Not at first. I simply sought a convenient match with someone who would not disrupt my life too much and would not annoy me. My equal in status, but not so concerned with status as to lord it over anyone."

"Already aiming high there," Rowe said with a snort.

"But then I saw how she was treated," Gage went on, acknowledging his comment with a raise of a brow. "Witnessed it and suffered through a supper of watching her shrink more and more, willing herself into nonexistence in front of the people who should have loved her best… And yes, I pressed my suit further still after that. I wanted to marry her more than I could have planned in seeing that. I wanted to rescue her from that, knowing that even a loveless life with me would be better than that."

Rowe grunted softly. "T'aint seem all that loveless to me, Gage. Mayhap not romantic and all, but ee have a care for 'er and she for ee. And is tha' not also love?"

Gage found himself nodding in spite of his usual inclination to twitch at the word. "I suppose it is. But I didn't marry her out of pity. At least, I don't think I did. I hope I did not."

His friend and mine captain clapped him on the back. "Good intentions be all we can claim in life, for truth. And I thank ee, Gage."

"For what?" he asked with a laugh. "For rambling like a schoolboy because I'm not certain of my own mind?"

"Nay," Rowe returned, shaking his head almost gravely. "For remindin' me wha' truly matters. We may not have much here, though others have it worse, but our children have love in their homes and ne'er feel unwanted. Mistress knows loss as keenly as the rest o' us, just in different ways. An' in a way, that be a blessin'."

Gage frowned, tugging at his cravat a little in the rising heat of the day. "You're going to have to explain that one to me."

Rowe inclined his head in the direction the women had gone. "She'll not see herself as a grand lady if she always felt herself as lackin'. She'll not be better than any o' us in her own mind, an' be more inclined to see us straight. As ee do. As yer father did."

"That is an excellent point." Gage laughed softly to himself. "I tried to tell her that she didn't have to come, but she was persistent. And I've yet to see any sort of true discomfort from her here."

"Did ee expect discomfort?" Rowe inquired. "Mistress does not seem to be aught but serene and patient."

Thinking back to last evening, Gage sighed. "I thought the same, before I knew her better. But I have since learned that underneath that serene, patient exterior is a vault of insecurity and uncertainty, born of never pleasing those who should have loved her best. A fear of never measuring up to expectation and a reality of only ever disappointing them."

"Then 'tis no wonder she like it here," Rowe said, propping his hands on his hips. "We 'ave no expectations of her. She may be as ever she pleases with us. We are as we are, and she be as she be."

"I can see that." Gage smiled a little and looked around. "Well, if we're not going to follow my wife, shall we go below?"

Rowe surprised him by shaking his head. "Nay, we've some matters to discuss with ee first, if ee don't mind."

Gage turned towards him, his interest piqued. "Who is 'we'?"

"Tom and myself." Rowe nodded at Tom, who started back for the office. "In thy absence, we've noticed a thing or two that might be o' some concern. Might be nothin', but we thought 'twould be best to discuss it with ee before moving further."

It was not often that Rowe felt Gage needed to be fully debriefed before action was taken. It was customary that he do so, but far more often than not, Gage's opinion was perfectly in line with Rowe's and superfluous to the situation. He had given the captain full permission to do as he saw fit, and time and again he did so, but always keeping Gage fully informed.

Gage was present as often as he could be, working as well as directing, but his other duties required him to divide his attention more than he liked. He would have solely focused on the mine if he were able, as it was his clear favorite, but needs must. The responsibilities of his position were nearly as great as the opportunities, which kept him sufficiently busy, but the mine had his thoughts, if not his heart. He could not have left it alone as often as he must if he did not have a captain he trusted so implicitly as Rowe.

The fact that he was determined to talk to Gage before acting on something he had concerns about was unnerving, to say the least.

They moved to the office without a word, but also without haste, which was a little encouraging. Surely anything truly emergent would have required haste.

Then again, a true emergency would have had him talking to Gage immediately when they arrived, or writing to him while he was away.

But that did not mean that the situation could not become emergent if he had pursued the issue without consulting Gage.

Maps of the mine and its tunnels were on the table, spread out as though the captain had been looking them over before Gage had arrived. One quick look told him there hadn't been any significant changes since he had left to ask Honora to marry him. There was some relief in that, but also some confusion.

If nothing significant had changed, what could be such a cause for concern?

"Before ee left ta fetch a wife," Rowe began, his smile a trifle impish for just a moment, "we talked about explorin' tha options on tha west side o' the twenty level. Settin' aside a small group ta do exploratory extensions towards tha rumored Polpenna lode."

Gage nodded in recollection, eyeing the map to familiarize himself with the layout, though he likely could have drawn it from memory. "Yes, heading eventually towards the coast."

"Aye," Rowe confirmed. "An' tha work has been goin' well. No clear sign o' it yet, but thar's no indication it may not lay ahead, neither."

"Tha problem," Tom Drake broke in before Gage could ask, "is that tha stone is growin' weaker tha farther we be goin' in that direction."

That didn't sound good. Gage frowned and looked at them both. "How so?"

Captain Rowe gestured for Tom to explain. "Tha rock crumbles as ee hit it in places. Crumbles instead o' cracks, like it be drier almost, but it shouldn't be. Thar's still a dampness to it like everywhere else.

I've seen nothing quite like it."

"Anything curious on the surface in that part of the mine?" Gage asked. "Weakness in the soil, poor consistency, too much water… Anything?"

The other two shook their heads. "No sign o' anything," Tom said. No drippin' water ta indicate a flood, neither. Just a strange consistency of rock."

Gage twisted his lips, considering the information carefully. "And we have never seen something like this in Stout before?"

"Never," Rowe affirmed. "I seen nothing like this ever. 'Twould be one thing if tha signs of a lode petered out or tha rock grew more damp, or one of 'tother signs that we should discontinue. 'Tis just strange, Gage."

The three of them looked at the maps intently and in silence, and Gage, for one, was weighing possibilities. It was no trouble to stop work in that area of the mine, but if the Polpenna lode was really at hand, it would keep the mine flourishing for years and provide a surplus that would allow him to pay his workers more. The mine did not necessarily need the excess to stay in operation, but it would do much good if it were found.

"Tom," Gage said slowly, "you're the most experienced miner in the room. Do you see any danger in continuing to explore this portion?"

Tom was already frowning at the maps, his arms tightly folded. He waited a long moment, then exhaled a rough sound. "Not if we proceed with caution. 'Tis a mite unpredictable but doesn't seem to be unstable. We might need ta use smaller tools 'til we see what 'appens. 'Twill be slower goin', but it should keep the men safer than if we'd go in as we are."

Gage nodded and looked at Rowe. "Do you agree, Rowe?"

"Aye," he stated with his own exhale. "If there's 'nother bad sign, we can stop and move tha men back down ta thirty level for tha new tunnels. Right now, tis just tha consistency of that rock that concerns me. 'Tother option…" He trailed off, grimacing a touch.

"What?" Gage pressed, knowing it was not like Rowe to hesitate in his opinions.

He looked at Gage and Tom in turn, then back at the map. "We could take a mornin' one o' these days an' blast tha new portion. See what 'appens with tha rock then. Mayhap 'tis just a strange portion and getting' past it 'twould return tha tunnel to its usual consistency."

"Now there be a thought, Cap'n." Tom murmured, leaning on the table and surveying the map with new interest. "I hadna thought of blastin' to get through it."

"Could that provide greater risk?" Gage asked them. "If the consistency of rock is questionable…"

Rowe shook his head. "We'd have tha men out o' tha mine but for those necessary ta set tha blast. Worst than could happen is tha new part caves in, and then we'd know not ta chase it further. We'd lose 'alf a day for tha blast, but that's about it."

Gage looked around at the others, then took a moment before stating, "Then I think that is what we should do."

"I be inclined to agree, Gage," Tom concurred. "We 'ave enough for an exploratory blast, and 'twould give us more answers faster than the gentler touch."

Rowe was nodding, but he still did not look as convinced. "Aye. There's no telling what 'twill do, but as it be just tha new portion, we can keep tha charge contained. Shouldn't endanger anyone, if we take care."

"We will. 'Tis tha surest way, Cap'n. We've got to see what's behind tha crumbly rock to know if we keep goin' or not."

"Aye, ee be right," Rowe said, swallowing and nodding more firmly. "'Twill do tha trick without fuss." He looked at them now with more resolution. "Next week, then?"

They agreed on that and began making plans for the exploratory blast to take place, then moved on to the progress being made in other tunnels, the recent auctions, and the prospect for any other new additions to be made in the coming weeks and months.

It was astonishing how productive Gage felt when he was at the mine, even if he was not actively working down in its depths. There was a satisfaction he felt here that he could not find anywhere else, and it filled him.

He hoped Honora liked her time at Wheal Stout. It would make it easier for him to spend an extended amount of time at the mine if his wife also enjoyed it.

Chapter Ten

Honora was shaking again.

She was going to earn herself the reputation of being unstable if she continued to react in such a way to things, but she could not help herself today.

She was being blatantly and pointedly stared at and examined from every single angle humanly possible, and her complexion could only go so red. There was no other option but for her limbs to shake in response.

"Honora, sweet, breathe."

She immediately released a breath, though she hadn't exactly been holding one. She was simply not breathing much or well under so much scrutiny.

And this was supposed to be what ladies did for amusement?

"It really is a lovely gown," Jane was saying from her seat, absently rubbing the gentle swell of her stomach. "I had no idea you could look so ravishing in cream, cousin."

"I'm not certain I wish to look ravishing," Honora mumbled, looking down at the lace embellishments and gold-sprigged fabric currently encircling her. "But it does not seem over-trimmed."

"It isn't," Adelaide assured her with a hand on her arm. She patted her gently, then circled around, hands clasped behind her back as though she were the modiste herself. "Your figure is positively envy-inducing, Honora. What a delight that fashions are trending towards emphasizing those things."

Honora shook her head. "I'm only small. There's nothing of a figure to mention."

Adelaide looked up at her in some irritation, but also a note of concern. "Who in the world told you that?"

It was greatly to Adelaide's credit that she did not declare it immediate nonsense and was intuitive enough to understand where Honora's perspective came from.

"My mother's modiste," she said softly, ducking her chin. "Every time I saw her."

Adelaide sputtered and looked at their modiste, the kindly and barely graying Mrs. Treneglos. "Have you ever heard such nonsense, Mrs. Treneglos?"

"Not in my life, my lady," she returned with a touch of spite. She huffed and came to Honora with a shimmering gold ribbon. "I am going to sew a weaving pattern of this ribbon along the entire length of the bodice and downwards, madam. Dropping to a deep vee at your hips to elongate your torso. You will appear extraordinarily regal, and it will show the entire world just how perfect your figure happens to be."

Honora glanced at her in surprise. "But I wear the smallest stays of anyone. I've always been told that."

Mrs. Treneglos looked up at her with knowing brown eyes. "A woman's figure is far more than her bust, my lamb. Anyone who says differently is depraved, to my mind. And I have ways of improving that aspect, if you should wish it."

Honora's cheeks flushed, and she heard someone clear their throat softly, but wasn't sure if it was Julia, Adelaide, or Emblyn. It could have been any of them, but she was not sure it mattered.

She might take the woman up on the offer. She had always been insecure about that part of her body and its lack of substance compared to other girls her age. But ladies did not speak of such things, unless it was her mother and her modiste disparaging her.

"How many gowns is this, Mrs. Treneglos?" Adelaide asked as she moved back over to Julia and Emblyn. "Six or seven?"

"Six, my lady," the modiste replied as she fixed the ribbons in place around Honora's middle, a few additional pins in her mouth.

Adelaide nodded. "We'll need at least a dozen more."

Honora looked at Emblyn for some sort of help, as the young woman had been mostly silent this entire appointment. The common, low-born, half-sister of Lord Basset was outspoken in the extreme, but bore the sweetest and most loyal heart of anyone Honora had ever met. She was also supposed to be Honora's link to restraint and simpler tastes, and thus far, she had not been so.

The dark-haired beauty looked at Honora with her pale blue eyes, and her mouth curved into a small, knowing smile. She dipped her chin ever so slightly, then cleared her throat. "Addie, be 'ee sure ta give Honora dresses fer regular wear, naw jus' fer yer parties. She be goin' down ta Wheal Stout with Gage atimes, an' ee've naw given 'er any dresses she could wear there."

Adelaide stared at her sister-in-law for a moment, then looked at Honora in confusion. "You don't have dresses now that could be your mine-venturing gowns?"

Honora blanched at that, her mind suddenly unable to conjure up a single dress currently in her bureau. "Yes, a few. I think Emblyn might mean some morning dresses or day dresses, yes?" She looked at Emblyn for confirmation.

She smirked a little, quirking a brow at Honora's hasty correction. "Aye, tha' be it. Sommat less extravagant and just simple. Common folk won't listen well ta a fancy, fligged up, 'igh an' mighty mistress."

Understanding seemed to dawn on Adelaide's fair features, and she immediately began nodding. "Yes, of course. Visiting dresses. For calling upon tenants and the like. Yes, quite right. You will need several well-made, sturdy gowns for such things, though if you ever wear one of these new creations to the mine, Honora, I will personally throttle you."

She nodded quickly. "But could I, perhaps, request a coat and stays and boots that would be suitable for helping at the mine? What I have is simply old and worn, which means it will not be ruined, but does not necessarily mean it will be suitable."

Adelaide smiled at her rather fondly and took her hand. "Of course! You are a sweet thing for wanting to help there. I have no stamina for such things, so I stay well away apart from celebrations and annual visits, but if you truly wish to venture, we will give you the necessary ensembles to see you safe, hardy, and hale while you do so."

"Honora speaking her mind," Julia murmured as she sipped a cup of tea brought by an assistant. "What will she think of next?" She winked at Honora, her affection plain to see, and it warmed Honora's heart.

"I do not have much practice," she replied softly, feeling her cheeks tinge a little. "But my husband wishes me to try."

Emblyn sat up a little. "Surely ee wish ta try as well, Honora. Naw only Gage."

She shrugged. "I was never permitted to speak my mind before, so I grew accustomed to not having a mind on many things. It was easier to be told what to do when I did not care one way or the other."

Emblyn blinked, then looked at Julia with an almost accusatory scowl. "Ee knowed about this?"

Julia nodded and made no attempt to grow defensive. "None of their children could do much right, but they seemed to despise Honora the most. It boggles the mind, as she is the best of the lot."

"I don't know about that," she whispered, shrugging out of the gown with assistance from Mrs. Treneglos.

Julia only gestured at her as though it illustrated something of her point, though Honora did not believe it would suggest any such thing. "When I was able, I invited Honora to visit us here, and after my marriage, it was easier to convince her parents to allow her to come. I trust I am not much of an improvement to their children in their eyes, but all they have ever wanted was to be rid of Honora."

It ought to have mortified Honora to hear herself spoken of in such a way, or to hear her parents described thusly, but she was well aware of her past and the nature of those who had raised her, and there was no mortification left to be found. Julia was putting the situation mildly for the benefit of their friends, and it would do no good to have any point refuted or defended, even for the sake of politeness.

Julia's parents had always been the sort of relations that Honora had wished could have been her parents, and it was only from exposure to them that she recognized how it was possible to grow up without harshness and criticism. It had not given Honora opinions or a backbone, but it had given her scope enough to know that there was another way to live.

A way she intended to provide for any children she and Gage might have.

"So you see," Julia went on, "Honora is only used to doing what will please others. It will take some practice for her to truly express herself for her own sake."

Emblyn returned her attention to Honora, a deep sadness in her lovely eyes. "I knowed ee'd not been well treated, Honora, but naw tha' full scope. I'm tha' grieved for ee."

Honora smiled for her. "Thank you, Emblyn. Truth be told, I am looking forward to discovering myself, now that I am at liberty to do so. The only real thing I have learned so far is that I love riding in Cornwall."

"Then we shall have four riding habits made!" Adelaide announced with delight. "A masterful horsewoman must always be appreciated."

Honora and Emblyn groaned in unison, while Julia only laughed.

"Get used to it, cousin," Julia suggested. "Gage has given Adelaide all power over your trousseau and unlimited funds. If you do not have strong opinions, rest assured, she will."

"I simply don't wish to be overly extravagant," Honora protested weakly. "I don't know how to be... that."

Adelaide patted her hand gently. "Not everyone does. And you bear a natural elegance and grace that outstrips anything that can be worn."

"Flatterer," Honora told her, snorting faintly as she stepped into the form of a skirt for Mrs. Treneglos.

"I rarely flatter," Adelaide argued with a faint sniff. "Particularly in private and among friends. Flattery only works when it serves a greater purpose, and it would be entirely lost on you. Rest assured, any praise for you is sincere. And to prove that, I will only insist on three extravagant dresses, which will still not be as extravagant as mine, as my tastes differ from yours. The rest of the finer dresses will have the elegant restraint that I think you prefer. Are we agreed?"

It was still more than Honora would have wished, but considering the prospect was so much worse, she supposed it was better than she could have gotten otherwise. And if she did have the more elaborate gowns at hand, she might not feel so ill-equipped for the next grand ball at Trevadden.

"Agreed," she told Adelaide with a small smile. "Thank you."

Adelaide gave her a prim nod, then turned to Mrs. Treneglos, hard at work securing the skirts. "We will need three walking dresses in addition to the visiting dresses, seven morning dresses, four opera dresses, and six suitable for fine dining."

Honora's throat tightened and she wondered if her stays had been cinched too tightly without her knowledge. "Will we really?"

"The opera dresses are not for attending the opera, dear," Adelaide assured her, as though that would help. "They are for when you know you are going to sing. I realize that you may often be asked at the last moment, and that is one thing, but when you know you will perform, you may now dress accordingly. If all eyes are going to be on you, your appearance ought to match the glorious sounds of your voice."

She wouldn't argue that, but she thought she might grow ill at the number of gowns being created just for her.

"Adelaide," Julia broke in, her eyes fixed on Honora, "I think she is overwhelmed. I have several fine dining and walking dresses that I don't wear anymore that could easily be made over into the latest fashions and suited to Honora's tastes. Would you greatly object to that?"

Honora exhaled a short sigh of relief and smiled at her cousin, all of which Adelaide caught.

"Oh, sweet girl," Adelaide hummed, reaching up to pat her cheek. "You hate this, don't you? Would you want secondhand clothing? I've no objection to it, as I trust Julia would not give you worn things, but I want your voice to tell me so."

"Yes, please," Honora told her in as firm a voice as she could manage. "That would make me much more comfortable."

"Of course." Adelaide nodded, then took on a distinctly impish light. "But will you let me shower you with coats and cloaks and chemises and stockings?"

Honora bit her lip, giggling with a touch of embarrassment. "Yes, if you must."

"And nightdresses," Adelaide said as an afterthought. "Perhaps five. Julia?" She turned to look at her, her expression rather quizzical.

Julia's expression was more thoughtful. "Five sounds fair. She may not need them yet, but eventually, I think it would serve."

"I have nightdresses," Honora said slowly, looking between the two in confusion.

Emblyn seemed just as confused but said nothing.

"That's what we're saying," Adelaide told Honora, returning her attention to her. "You will not need them yet, but it is always good to have more than you need." She cleared her throat and clapped her hands once. "And stays. All sorts of stays for all sorts of gowns. And some that you can be active at the mine in, should you desire." She winked and flashed a quick smile, which almost erased the thoughts of excessive nightdresses from Honora's mind.

Honora returned her smile almost shyly as she slid her arms into the small sleeves of fabric Mrs. Treneglos was holding out. "Thank you, Adelaide."

Adelaide laughed merrily as she ran her fingers over a bolt of nearby fabric. "Oh, don't thank me, darling. Your husband is paying for this, I am simply picking things out." She adjusted the fabric to move it between her thumb and forefinger, a softer smile appearing on her lips. "This is lovely, Mrs. Treneglos. And the shade is utterly perfect for Mrs. Trembath. What if we build two other gowns that could match it? Vary them enough that they could never be mistaken for one another, but draw from this fabric as inspiration for both. When a shade flatters a lady this well, we must make the most of it."

"Oh, but—" Honora began, cutting herself off before the full protest could form.

"Yes?" Adelaide asked, glancing over her shoulder, almost daring her to speak.

It seemed rather like a test of some sort, this moment. Would Honora speak her mind and express her concerns? Would Adelaide listen if she did? Was Honora fully aware of what she was protesting and why? Or was she simply going to complain about the excesses again, knowing that Adelaide was only acting upon the instructions of Gage?

Honora paused, allowed herself a swallow, and did her best to look at Adelaide steadily. "That seems excessive, given the amount already planned."

Her face flamed the moment she said it, and it was on the tip of her tongue to immediately apologize and shrink. More than that, the very words of the apology seemed to be making their way up her throat, and her lips tingled in anticipation of saying them. Her fingers began to feel warm, her palms slightly damp, and the hair at the top of her head was suddenly painfully sensitive. Mrs. Treneglos was securing fabric around her torso, but it now seemed as though the pins were being stuck into her skin rather than the material.

Adelaide did not seem to move at all, but Honora caught the faintest twitch of her lips. "Excellent point, my dear. So we shall alter the plans for some of the others. From this fabric, or inspired by it, let us create… one classic ballgown, one elegant evening gown, and one utterly exquisite creation that will captivate anyone who sees her. And be sure that the same slippers and ribbons and accoutrements might be used for all three, to spare our friend's blushes about extravagance." She turned and quirked her brows with a rather smug smile. "You see? I can be accommodating, too."

Laughter positively erupted from Honora, followed quickly by Julia and Emblyn, immediately releasing the tension she had been feeling in her chest and stomach almost from the moment they had entered the modiste's shop. Laughter when she was feeling exposed and indecisive. Laughter when she was torn between wanting to please and wanting to stand up for herself. Laughter when laughter ought to have been impossible.

Where it would have been impossible only weeks before.

But this was the life of Honora Trembath now. Not the life of Honora Berkeley.

And she was going to hold on with both hands.

"Oh! Lady Basset, what a pleasure to see you here!"

Honora tried to twist and see who had spoken to Adelaide, but Mrs. Treneglos had a firm hold on the fabric at her back, making motion in general difficult. The remnants of laughter were still in Honora's heart and lungs, and she could feel the relaxed smile on her face, which probably meant her color was high. Being full of pins and looking positively giddy was not precisely the state in which she wished to greet someone.

"Lady Hastings," Adelaide greeted pleasantly. "What a surprise!"

Ice latched on to Honora's heart and began to pump steadily into her veins, keeping her frozen in place and unable to move, even if she had wished to.

She did not want to meet this woman. Did not want to see her. Did not want to be reminded that she even existed.

And she could not look at Adelaide or at Julia while she was feeling this way.

Adelaide was too polite and of too great a status to be cold to someone she had only recently met, and she had not known Gage long enough to have much of an opinion one way or the other. Julia had been friends with the woman for years before what had happened, and Honora did not want to know what she now felt towards her.

Emblyn was the only one who might be safe to look at, and Honora could not even manage to raise her eyes enough to do that. She kept them lowered, focused on the rug on the ground in front of the small platform on which she stood. It was a habit born from years of trying to become small enough to disappear. It had not worked yet, but it would not keep her from trying.

A motion just above her eyeline drew her attention, and she saw, to her dismay, Julia rising to her feet, albeit awkwardly. She was smiling a little, though Honora could tell that it was a touch strained. There was some comfort in that. She supposed that Julia could not be impolite, and to be fair, Lady Hastings ought to be able to visit her family without being shunned by those who had grown up with her.

But it was the most awkward situation Honora had ever experienced, knowing that her husband had loved this woman, and quite possibly, she had loved him.

That perhaps they could have been together now if Honora had not agreed to his proposal.

His proposal. He had chosen her, she reminded herself. Knowing that Lady Hastings was a widow, Gage had still chosen Honora.

That had to mean something, and she had to remember that it meant something.

"Lady Hastings," Julia greeted, her tone particularly stiff.

"Oh please, Julia!" Lady Hastings replied. "Don't get up! You should be resting in your condition. I remember it all too well. You are probably feeling uncomfortable all the time."

Julia exhaled heavily, the sound that of the weight of the world. "Yes. It is a miserable state of things, and I can only be grateful that this is not an eternally progressing condition."

"How much longer until your confinement?" Lady Hastings asked, her voice as sweet as honey and as natural as the Cornish landscape.

Honora forced herself to swallow, though it was difficult to do so, the conversation of the others fading to her ears. The woman sounded like the most wonderful, genuine person in the world, and every word she spoke had an almost musical quality to it. Honora's voice sounded like she was in a constant state of sickness and as though it hadn't been used enough to know the way of it. She rarely varied from one tone to another and had to force herself to speak above that of a faint humming sound. She would never stand out in a crowd by her voice, and there was nothing pleasant about its sound or its bearing.

"Lady Hastings, you won't have met her at the ball the other evening, but this is Lord Basset's sister, Miss Emblyn Moyle."

Honora stiffened as Lady Hastings came into her line of sight to greet Emblyn.

Golden curls peeked out from a lovely hat of navy blue, perfectly coordinating with her gown and creating an impression of elegance that Honora could not feel while half-dressed and held together with pins.

"Sister?" Lady Hastings repeated with a slight squeal in her voice. "Harrison has a sister? How marvelous!"

She could call his lordship by his given name? After all this time? What would Emblyn and Adelaide make of that?

"Half-sister," Emblyn said with some emphasis, curtseying to Lady Hastings. "An' 'e only knowed of me recent-like. My mother was a maid at Trevadden, and our father sent her away when she knowed a me. Basset found me and brung me into his life. I keep to my own mostly, but 'e and Addie still claim me."

"When she lets us," Adelaide added, her fond exasperation clear. If either were uncomfortable with the discussion, they were not showing it.

Truly, was Honora the only one doomed to die from this encounter?

Lady Hastings took Emblyn's hands without hesitation. "There is no one who deserves a sister more than Harrison. I cannot wait to know you better, Miss Moyle, and believe me, I know plenty of stories about a young Harrison Basset, should you ever need them."

Julia cleared her throat very softly. "And this, Lady Hastings, is Gage's wife, Mrs. Honora Trembath."

It might have been Honora alone, but it suddenly felt as though the entire room had lost its air. The only thing she was certain she could feel was Mrs. Treneglos's gentle hand resting at the small of her back. There was no logical reason for it to be placed there with her work, so it must have been a gesture of comfort.

Honora was grateful for that.

Lady Hastings turned to face her, and there was a trace of uncertainty in her eyes that she was certain must have only been a reflection of her own. Lady Hastings was the most beautiful woman she had ever seen, including Adelaide. Her complexion was like porcelain, her eyes that of the morning sky, and her hair bore the sheen of pure gold and seemed to hold the curls with the sort of exactness only an artist could have painted. Her lips were perfectly full and spread into a small but perfect smile.

And there was no strain in her features at this meeting. But why would there be? Lady Hastings did not need to feel strained about anything. She had married her choice, gained a fortune, borne children, and was now a wealthy widow with the freedom to do whatever she pleased. She had returned to the home of her childhood and found herself welcome. But above all, she had once known the love of a heart as pure and true as Gage.

Which she had thrown away.

Did she now regret that? Would she hate Honora for existing? Had she planned on reclaiming Gage for herself and atoning for her egregious error?

Would this perfect friendliness extend to Honora in the least?

"Mrs. Trembath," Lady Hastings greeted, curtseying rather needlessly. "I saw you dancing at the Bassets' ball but found no good moment for an introduction. It is such a delight to meet you."

Honora blinked and inclined her head, as the state of her present attire would not allow for a return curtsey. "Lady Hastings, you are too kind."

Lady Hastings's perfect smile grew even more perfect as it spread. "I doubt that. I am quite certain you are someone very special. But I wanted to meet you as soon as I could to try and defuse as much awkwardness as possible. I know full well that you probably had no intention of ever meeting me."

That was an understatement, but at least Honora did not have to be the one expressing it.

"I am just so pleased that Gage has found someone," she went on. "He is such a good man and would never give his heart fleetingly. I could see his feelings for you when he pointed you out to me."

Oh, heavens. Did she think they had made a love match? What had Gage said? What had his expression shown that made her think this was love?

Why did she think she was in any position to discuss Gage's heart?

Then again, why did Honora?

Lady Hastings smiled up at her as though they were old friends. "I will not detain you from your appointment any longer, Mrs. Trembath. I do hope we'll see each other soon. And I must say, that shade of purple is so very becoming on you. My goodness, I cannot wait to see you wear it. Good day."

She curtseyed and moved away, smiling for the others, and Honora barely felt her lips moving in some form of a polite farewell.

Alone again, Julia returned to her seat, groaning as she sat down. "Well, that was less awkward than I thought it would be."

Honora kept silent on that score, swallowed the burning sensation in her throat, and focused on the fabric before her, now unsure if she liked the color at all.

Chapter Eleven

The day of the harvest celebration was always one of Gage's favorite days of the year. It held most of the excitement of Christmas, but without the chill or the expectation of gifts. There was dancing and music, there was food and drink, there was symbolism and tradition…

It was one of those days where Gage felt less like the master and more like one of the people. When he was allowed to be that. When the celebration was on his property, but not filled with finery or exclusivity. It was simply a celebration of what they had accomplished together over the course of a season, and the fruitfulness of whatever had been managed.

He had been as eager as a child all week leading up to this day, and poor Honora had been trying to grasp what he had been telling her, but ultimately, he had failed to properly express any of it. She would see soon enough, and he was fairly certain she would love it.

He hadn't seen her much in the last day or so, what with him working in the fields to ensure they would accomplish enough and her working with Mrs. Crane and the Helwithin staff on preparation for the celebration. Then there were the preparations at the mine with the blasting in the coming days, which had occupied Gage's mind completely when he wasn't anticipating the harvest celebration, so he had probably been a fairly lackluster sort of husband recently. He would make it up to her somehow, if he saw any sign that she was displeased with him.

If Honora was even capable of being displeased.

He was not under the impression that he had married an angel, but he also had never met anyone that made him occasionally wonder about such a thing.

Ever since his parents had renovated Helwithin during Gage's adolescence, rendering the ballroom a touch too grand for the rustic harvest celebration, they had begun hosting the event in the old grain barn on the estate. It was only used for storing equipment in the off months by then, so it only required a bit of reinforcement, clearing out, and cleaning prior to the day of the event.

Gage had ordered all such preparations to be done ahead of time and had let Honora know that the staff would know exactly what to do and she need not overthink or worry herself about any of those aspects. If she was relieved by that attempt at reassurance, she gave no indication. A simple nod and her thanks was all that he received, and he had to remind himself that she did not know how enjoyable this event would be. She had no scope for it, and therefore, could not react in a way that he found most appropriate.

But she would see, and she would learn, and next year, she would be just as excited.

An excited Honora.

What in the world would that look like?

Gage smiled to himself, allowing the image to form in his mind of his little wife grinning and all but skipping about in anticipation of the celebration. Greenish eyes sparkling like spring and the color in her cheeks high, her hair streaming long and loose behind her... In his mind, he took her hand and they raced to the barn like children, laughing together without shame.

Was that something he wanted? Was Honora even capable of being that carefree and open? Would he be able to lead her there?

Why was he suddenly curious about the future possibilities with his wife? There was far too much else to be considering at this moment, and someone was going to discover that he was not focused on finishing the task that would announce the start of the evening.

The last small piece of land to be harvested.

The workers were beginning to gather around, seeing the remaining tiny square of wheat, and some of the other tenants and villagers gathered for the tradition. Gage waved as he saw them, then found himself waving again when he caught sight of Honora standing nearby. She looked like a perfect member of the group in a red dress, with a shawl neatly fastened about her shoulders, her hair half loose and streaming in the wind. One would have to look closely to notice that her gown was of a better quality than the others, and he was glad for it.

Honora waved back, though her hand never raised above the level of her waist.

There was something adorable about that.

"Here ee be, sir," one of the workers said, handing Gage a fresh scythe with which to complete the final strokes.

Gage nodded, switching the scythe he had been using for the new one, and turned to the square of wheat. There was a touch of pressure to try and get the thing in one sweep, but ultimately, it would not matter. It would not change the celebration a jot, and there would be no ribbing of him if he should require a few.

There was a great sense of joy in the air, and Gage felt himself smiling at it. He adjusted his grip on the scythe and swung it, just as he had been doing for the last few hours.

He'd almost cleared the whole square, but not entirely.

Laughing to himself, he made a quick second sweep to get the rest.

Two of the workers sprang forward and bundled the wheat up, tying the bunch together with straw, then propped it up on its end. They stepped back and looked at Gage expectantly.

He was already grinning as he handed off the scythe to the man beside him. He stepped to the bunch, stooped, and picked it up, holding it high above his head.

"I 'ave 'un," he called, smiling at the gathering. "I 'ave 'un! I 'ave 'un!"

"What 'ave ee? What 'ave ee? What 'ave ee?" they yelled back.

Gage turned a little, looking for Honora in the group. "A neck! A neck! A neck!"

He found her and saw the brilliance of her smile as she joined the others in calling, "Hurrah! Hurrah! Hurrah for Mr. Trembath!"

Applause filled the space, and Gage lowered the token neck from over his head, tucking it under an arm and smiling as he moved towards the edge of the makeshift circle. Without ceremony, everyone started moving in the same direction, all heading for the barn.

Honora, however, waited for him, smiling brightly. "That was even better than you described!" she whispered.

Gage chuckled and held out his free hand for her. "And what was so much better about it?"

She took his hand without hesitation and laced their fingers as though they'd been holding hands for years. "The sheer excitement! It is one thing to hear about a tradition and another to be part of it. I've never cared much about harvest before, but suddenly, I'm entirely caught up in it!"

"That is the point," he told her, more pleased than he would ever let on. "The Crying of the Neck is only the beginning of the celebration of harvest, but there is a sort of thrill to it."

"And relief, I'd imagine," Honora said with some soberness. "For years when the harvest is not substantial enough for all."

Gage's smile softened a touch, though the feeling towards his wife did not soften a jot. "True enough. The pilchards coming in help to alleviate a great deal, particularly when the harvest is weak. This year is a good harvest, but the pilchards do tend to dictate how the winter will go."

Honora made a very soft tsking sound. "It must be maddening to have such a significant aspect be so out of one's control. It is not as though we can call the pilchards into our cove."

"If only we could." He squeezed her hand firmly. "But tonight, we celebrate a good harvest and a bounteous feast ahead of us."

"Yes," she said quickly, nodding fervently enough to make her hair ribbons bob. "Mrs. Crane and Mrs. Reed have been absolute dervishes over it and refused to let me help with a single part."

Gage chuckled at that. "Yes, I probably should have warned you about how they can be. They mean well."

"Oh, I was not offended," Honora assured him. "Not in the least. I only felt useless and restless. At least I was able to oversee the music for tonight."

"Were you, indeed?" Gage rubbed his thumb over her hand fondly. "That's rather perfect. I have no doubt you found some good Cornish music?"

She nodded, her smile threatening to break her cheeks. "Emblyn helped me. I know she's not one of our tenants, but I invited her anyway. And the Bassets, of course. And John and Julia."

"Good. I hope they all come. I hope everyone comes. There is plenty of room, and this is a celebration! It should feel like it!" He exhaled deeply, loving the feeling of a job well done, the post-harvest ambiance about them, the slight chill that was just beginning to nip at the air...

He loved all of it.

It took a moment for him to realize that Honora was giggling softly, and he gave her a wry look. "What's so funny, wife?"

"You," she said between giggles. "You love this so much. Is it the tradition, the harvest, the party, or just some natural enthusiasm?"

Gage grinned openly. "Probably all of it. I love a good party. Not all parties, mind you. Just good ones. But as for the rest..." He shrugged, never having given it all that much thought. "It is just who I am, I suppose. This has always been part of my life, and I cannot imagine ever going without it."

"Then I hope tonight does not disappoint." Honora put a hand to her cheek, her eyes fixed ahead of them to the old grain barn, all lit from within like the grandest estate for a ball. "I've never been to anything like this, Gage. We never associated with tenants or neighbors at Horsend, and I was only permitted to be social if it was high society. I have... nothing to compare this to. I don't know what to expect, and there is something rather freeing about that."

"You get anxious when you know what to expect and excited when you don't?" he asked with some gentle teasing, shaking the hand he held just a little.

She tossed her head back on a laugh, momentarily transfixing him with the loveliness and completely natural manner of it all. "No, it's nothing so simple as that. I know the people in high society, and don't much care for disappointing them. I am far more comfortable with people who are not trying to impress and do not expect anyone else to impress. And as is the case tonight, when it is an occasion that someone else knows well, I don't fear anything at all. Especially since you're so thrilled about it, and I'll be with you."

Gage reared back just a little in surprise. "You're more

comfortable because I'm here?"

A touch of color raced into her cheeks, and he felt a delicious knot of heat twist in his stomach, as he always seemed to.

"Well," she murmured softly, tucking a long strand of her hair behind one ear, "I can hardly expect to be uncomfortable at an event that is your favorite of the year, can I?"

"That's not what you said, Honora," Gage replied slowly, stepping just a little closer. "You said you would be with me."

"Should that not make me comfortable?" she returned, doing everything in her power to avoid looking anywhere near him.

He found himself laughing at these antics of his suddenly shy, adorable wife. "I suppose it should. And I now find myself hoping that someday, the very sight of me will bring you comfort."

As he'd hoped, her cheeks continued to flame, and he watched her delicate throat work on a swallow.

Privately, he made a vow that someday he would also test this most interesting experience of saying genuine thoughts of warmth and fondness to his wife, just to see what was possible from it.

"I trust that I may count on you for our new dancing tradition this evening?" Gage asked in a lighter tone, knowing Honora would appreciate the shift to a less sensitive topic.

"Of course," she murmured, her voice barely audible, even to him. "Though is the dancing not expected to go on quite late?"

"Quite early, depending on your persuasion," Gage said with a quick laugh. "Are you one who also retires for the night rather early?"

He received a jolt of surprise shrieking down his left leg as he felt her thumb brush absently against his fingers. "Not always. And I would never do so when we are the hosts." Her chin rose from its demure position, and he caught sight of a corner of a smile. "I may not be particularly coordinated in the last dance of the night, particularly if it is taking place rather early tomorrow, but it will be your dance nevertheless."

Was she joking with him? That was somehow the most adorable thing he had seen yet, more for its unexpectedness than its level of humor.

"Then we will be delirious and giddy and uncoordinated together," he vowed with all of the faux gallantry he could muster.

Honora looked at him then, full smile, the color of embarrassment completely gone. "Done," she replied simply.

He had to smile back; there was nothing else to do when faced with something so fetching. His throat tightened with some new shade of joy, and he struggled against a swallow. "Did you happen to prepare a song for tonight? I trust you were informed that there will be singing as well as dancing."

"Yes, that was made very clear." She giggled just a hint, the sound something of a hum and a hiccup and rather endearing. "I wasn't certain what the mood would be, so I've prepared three. If you will only signal me when the moment is right for me to perform, I'll happily comply."

"Thank you," he said, squeezing her hand, "but you are the mistress of the land and hostess. There is not a right or wrong moment according to anyone's dictates. When you sense a good time for singing, and should you wish to do so, you may decide yourself."

Her eyes lowered somewhere to the level of his cravat, her smooth brow gaining the faintest of creases. "Very well, but if it is something that requires directing attention, I think it still must be you. My voice does not carry, and I have not yet learned the way to command attention."

"I love that you said 'yet,' Honora," Gage told her in a low voice. "Not that commanding attention is an essential in life, but that you mean to learn and grow and develop in ways that you feel important. And I think you will find that you know more than you think, and you attract more attention and respect than you might believe. Our tenants and workers may not yet know just how well you sing, but after tonight, I believe any room they are in will fall silent when they see you intend to."

Impossibly, that did not seem to embarrass Honora a jot. "I'd much rather command respect than attention, but commanding anything is not really my way. I doubt it ever will be. But if I may earn respect tonight by singing, and singing songs of their culture and tradition, I might make a start."

She had prepared Cornish songs for the night? They would not only respect her for that, they would fall at her feet. And quite honestly, Gage just might join them.

He drew the back of her hand to his lips for just a moment, not sure he trusted himself to say anything more.

They were reaching the barn, and the music within was already lively and bright. No dancing had started yet, but the tables were set with the plates and cutlery for the meal, and the goblets set out, with plenty of ale prepared to be dispersed. If Gage was not mistaken, there were also a few casks of brandy somewhere abouts, more than likely from a recent smuggling run. Officially, he, of course, condemned such action and the lack of duty paid to the necessary gaugers. Unofficially...

Well, tradition was tradition.

The barn looked splendid this year, with corn dollies hung about the entire space, paired with ribbons, and fresh straw had been strewn about the floor. Lanterns had been lit and hung all about, and in the space outside the far door, a bonfire was beginning. The evening would undoubtedly end with the last few stragglers gathered around it, wasted away drunk and hypnotized by the flames in a way that could only be comprehended when inebriated. Stories would be spun and retold, legends passed along, and boasts of great achievements declared, all before sleep overtook them all.

It would be a night to remember, for those who maintained the ability to recollect anything at all.

Entering the barn fully, Gage handed the neck of wheat to a footman, who took it to place at the head table.

Mrs. Crane came towards him, bobbing a quick curtsey of greeting. "We've a few minutes yet before the food will be out, sir," she told him, her tone that of mild apology. "We'd meant to greet you upon your entrance with the full feast, but..."

Gage put a hand to her arm. "It's fine, Mrs. Crane. We will simply open the dancing before the feast and enjoy ourselves shamelessly until the meal is set. No harm done."

The housekeeper gave him a grateful look and hurried away after a lightning-quick nod.

Exhaling, Gage turned to Honora. "Well, will you open the dance with me, Mrs. Trembath?"

Her eyes lit up and her smile matched it. "Of course!" She bit her lip, glancing down at herself. "Do I look all right? I wanted to

119

blend in with everyone as tastefully as I could."

Gage shook his head, reaching out to touch her chin and raise her eyes back to his. "You look perfect," he assured her, stroking the soft skin beneath her chin with his finger. "Positively lovely, and exactly as you should. But you'll never fully blend in, my dear. Not when you were made to stand out."

Her cheeks tinged with pink again, but she held his eyes. "I was made for no such thing," she whispered, no doubt trying to scold him.

"Could have fooled me." He winked and lowered his hand from her, leading her out to the center of the barn floor. He nodded at the musicians, and the jaunty sounds of the traditional "Harvest Home" began.

It was always the first song of the night, and it would not take long for others to join in.

Gage bowed as Honora curtseyed, and then they skipped in place a moment before proceeding to each other's left side, passing back-to-back, then retreating towards their lines. Then they moved forward once more, this time joining hands and spinning each other around in circles. Then they adjusted their hands and promenaded around some imaginary line of other dancers.

As they bowed and curtseyed again, other couples joined them and formed lines beside them, as well as two other groups of lines in the barn. The skipping commenced, followed by the progression of back-to-back, and the rest of the patterns that Gage and Honora had done.

Spinning with Honora this time, Gage heard someone elsewhere whoop, and she laughed at the sound.

That seemed to break the spell for everyone in the dance, and there immediately began to be cheers, whooping, whistles, and laughter aplenty among all of the groups dancing. The promenading allowed a moment for Honora to attempt to compose herself, if the expression on her face was anything to go by.

"Don't hold back," Gage whispered as they prepared to return to their lines. "I love to hear you laugh."

She looked at him in surprise, then moved with the rest of the ladies back to the line.

Gage watched her as soon as he could, loving the shade of her cheeks as she curtseyed, and was quite certain that her skipping was a touch lighter this time. She was grinning amidst the cheerful sounds of other dancers, and giggled when Gage quirked a brow at her right before their back-to-back.

He found himself chuckling as they backed up to their lines, and with the next movement of the dance, gave in to the impish impulse of swinging her around much faster than they had been doing, which made her squeal. Barking a loud laugh, Gage adjusted his hold for the promenade and mimicked a sort of rowing motion with their arms as they moved. His wife's giggling mixed beautifully with the music, and the whistles and yelps of other dancers filled his lungs and his legs with more energy than he'd had all day.

Gads, he loved this celebration.

They continued dancing round after round, the onlookers now clapping in time with the music and offering their own calls and whistles to the mix.

Honora was a wild vision, to Gage's mind. Her hair, already loose, was now the slightest bit unkempt about her brow and her ears, her color was high, and the smile on her lips was wide and grand as any he had ever seen. She laughed as musically as she sang, though in a lower, almost rough sort of way. A clearly unpracticed, rare sound that her throat and lungs and frame had to be unaccustomed to, and she bore a wide-eyed astonishment at her own entertainment.

He'd never forget the way she looked tonight, of that he was certain.

The last round of the motions was upon them, and Gage let loose a whistle that had Honora laughing almost uproariously as they passed each other back-to-back.

"You're a madman!" she told him over her shoulder.

"Aye, that I am," he replied, wagging his eyebrows at her as he proceeded back to his line.

As they moved forward to begin spinning, Gage dipped and scooped Honora into his arms, spinning around with her as she frantically clung to him, her startled yelp making him positively howl with laughter. He set her down in just enough time for them to promenade to the top of the line, and end with the final bows and curtseys.

Applause filled the room and Honora put a hand to her chest, still laughing as she came to him. "I have never danced like that in my entire life!" she told him breathlessly, beaming and shaking her head.

Gage took her free hand, rubbing it a little. "As long as you're married to me, Honora Trembath, we'll be dancing like that any chance we get."

Her smile remained and her eyes seemed to continue their dancing. "Good," she said simply. "I loved it."

He nodded at that. "So did I." His eyes flicked to Mrs. Crane, who was indicating to him that the meal was ready. "Now, my dear wife, I think we had better feast before everyone decides to dance the night away instead."

"Aren't we going to dance the night away anyway?" Honora quipped as they moved towards their table.

"Well, yes," Gage allowed with a tilt of his head. "But if we don't feast, Mrs. Crane and Mrs. Reed will be quite miffed, and we will all be starving when the dancing ends. Best to do the eating first and the dancing second, just to take care of those things."

Honora sighed, the sound so convincing, he had to look at her. "I suppose you must be right. But the moment the eating is done, I insist we dance again."

"Insist?" Gage repeated. "Why, Mrs. Trembath, I am rather flattered, and I will bow to your insistence. And if the beverages are as free flowing as they usually are at these events, there will be much dancing, indeed."

Chapter Twelve

This was turning into a night that Honora had never even dreamed could be possible. And she was the mistress of the entire gathering.

It was something out of a dream, really.

Not one of her dreams, but clearly, it was one of Gage's.

The first dance had been some sort of a release for Honora, a breaking free of the restraints that had been ingrained in her from almost the moment of her birth. The ability to be open in demeanor, if not in behavior, and to fully embrace the joy of her surroundings and the energy filling her soul. Something had happened to her natural reserve, and it had now been set aside, something she had never felt in her entire life. She knew full well she could replace it when all of this was over, much like a screen for the fire, but she hadn't realized that such a thing was even possible.

How could she suddenly feel unreserved and lively without also feeling exposed and coarse? It was the most unlike herself she had ever felt, and yet...

And yet she felt as though it was herself. Bright, shining, and new, somehow aglow with a fire she had never experienced or known, smiling and laughing as though she had not been silenced for her entire existence. As though she had only known laughter and light. As though loneliness had never touched her. As though these were her people, and this was her life.

If she took a moment or two to ponder too long on the subject, she might weep for the joy that she felt, if not in sheer gratitude for the experience. She might never know anything like this again, and, should that be the case, she would cling to the memories of being this alive for the rest of her days.

A reminder that she was capable of feeling deep and wondrous things, and that being relegated to the quiet corners of the world need not be her lot.

All of that from one dance. From the air of this space, the energy of these people, the thrill of a good harvest, the exhilaration of this tradition.

The feasting had been no less a thing, with toasts occurring every few minutes from any corner of the place to rousing applause, and the intoxicating aromas of well-prepared and well-seasoned food settled all into an ease of company that was quite rare indeed. It was impossible to tell how much would be left over, as there were so many about the room and all of them were eating to their fill, but none of that particularly mattered. Whatever was left would go to poorer tenants for their use and sustenance, and whatever had been consumed would nourish and strengthen all who had partaken.

Looking around, seeing the joy and satisfaction on every face present, Honora felt a thrill of pride at not only being part of this, but in being able to provide it, as hostess. That she had married into a place of such wholesome tradition and generosity, and to a man who valued people more than profit or position. That her husband was a rare sort of man who not only saw life, but lived it.

Pride and gratitude, all at once.

What a strange combination!

Gage had been up and dancing again since the bulk of the feast had completed, and she saw him now, dancing with Emblyn among the others, and she could only laugh at his childlike enthusiasm for every single aspect of this day. He was grinning and laughing like a madman, free of his jacket and uncaring about the increasing looseness of his cravat. One would never guess he was the master of this estate, if they saw him like this, and Honora suspected that was exactly as he would prefer it.

She took this moment to observe her husband with some appreciation, stepping back while the tables were cleared and the planks of those tables removed to allow for more celebration space. Gage was a handsome man at any given moment, but he certainly had moments where his attractiveness was on greater display and more poignant.

This was one of those moments.

His dark hair was growing more and more unkempt, as well as slightly damp, and his dark eyes sparkled more with every glint of lantern light. He was clean shaven, but the shadow of stubble was beginning, and her fingers itched to touch his face to see just how abrasive it might be. He had rolled his linen shirtsleeves to his elbow, and there was something impossibly and indescribably tempting about that. The way he moved was lithe and graceful for a man of his build and bearing, and the exuberance of the dance did nothing to minimize the impression of his strength and athleticism.

He was the finest figure of a man Honora had ever seen, not that she had seen many, and he was undoubtedly the most appealing, dashing, and striking man in the room.

Apologies to Lord Basset, who was very handsome in his own right, but it was true.

And to poor John, who had been so good to Honora since he had married her cousin. A very good man, but he could not compare to Gage in looks.

There was a strange delight she was now feeling in being married to the most handsome man she knew. Looks were not everything, and certainly no sign of character, but Gage seemed to match interior and exterior in being entirely favorable to anyone with eyes to see either. Theirs was not a love match, but it was on its way to being a good one, nevertheless.

Provided Honora did not do something to bungle it up.

The present dance finished, and applause filled the room. Gage turned to the musicians, applauding them in particular for the fine number. His eyes flicked to Honora, and his smile seemed to deepen, which had the unnerving effect of propelling her towards the musicians without being fully aware of it.

Apparently, it was time for her to sing.

As she had hoped, Gage moved towards her as soon as he saw her go. Once at her side, he murmured, "You wish to sing now?"

She nodded, though really, she could have waited. "If it will not bring the mood down. I fear I did not prepare something jaunty. I did not know that it would be like this."

He gave her a quick wink. "It's fine. We've had several raucous dances in a row, so it is the perfect time to enjoy something slower and to rest our feet. And get a drink, as it were."

Honora nodded, hoping he was right. She was rarely nervous to sing, but these were people who had never heard her before, and she had prepared something just for them. For her true introduction to them. And hopefully, to become one of them.

They reached the musicians and turned to face everyone else, who were already looking in that direction for the next song. They quieted at once, seeing Gage there.

"Once again," he called out, his smile just as prevalent in his voice as it was in his face, "we thank you all for joining us here tonight, and for all that you have done this harvest. For those of you who are unaware, my wife Honora is a very accomplished singer, and as part of her first harvest celebration, she would like to share a song with us all. And if you are anything like me, you will be positively transfixed from the very first note."

Honora flushed at once, trying desperately to swallow. He could not have meant that. He'd heard her sing a number of times when she had come to visit Cornwall, and he had never said anything astonishing about it. Complimentary, certainly, but he had never declared anything about it.

He turned to her, applauding with all the rest. His eyes darted over her cheeks, and his smile grew. "Whoops," he whispered for her alone.

"Wretch," she hissed back, wishing his impish nature did not make him that much more attractive to her.

He only shrugged and stepped back as people filled the dance space to listen to her.

Honora turned to the musicians for just a moment. "'*An Awhesyth*,'" she murmured, though they likely already knew, as she had informed the fiddler of her intention days ago.

They nodded and set their instruments while she turned back, hoping no one had heard her. This was intended to be a surprise for all of them, and the fact that she was singing the song in Cornish, and not the English that she had originally learned it in, was to be the even greater surprise.

She caught sight of Emblyn, who had been helping her with pronunciation, and she nodded in encouragement.

People did not get more Cornish than Emblyn Moyle, and if she thought Honora was ready, she supposed it must be true.

The musicians started, the song a touch faster than Honora had usually heard it, but not in a way that would complicate her task. It would only improve it, considering the environment.

Perfect.

"*Del en-vy ow kerdhes un myttyn yn mys me,*" she began, enjoying the play of expressions of those watching and listening as they realized she sung in Cornish. The shift from polite to startled to delighted on nearly every face was a drop of pure joy into her soul.

"*Y clewys moren yowynk, neb geryow yn-meth hy,*" Honora sang on, noting Emblyn seeming to translate for Adelaide beside her.

Adelaide might, of course, know the song in its English form, as "The Lark" was popular in other counties, but there was something about singing it here in their native tongue that made the song so much sweeter.

Honora continued to sing, taking great care not to focus her attention on her husband. He alone had the power to unsettle her, and she needed to get through this. She felt herself grow lighter with each passing line, as each verse came and went, and as she saw each smile bloom on those before her. People who did not know her and had no reason to like her, apart from her marriage to Gage, smiling with genuine warmth and delight at her. She knew well enough when someone was only being polite, and these people were not.

They knew nothing but the honesty of their emotions, and suddenly, she felt as welcome here as though she had been born among them.

As she moved into the final verse, Honora finally allowed herself to observe her husband as he watched her.

Transfixed, he had said. And at this moment, she might have believed him. His hands were behind his back, and his eyes were wide, dark, and captivating, and fixed upon her face. His smile was soft, almost tender, and there was a distinct air of breathlessness about him. How she could know that, how she could think that, was inexplicable, but it was there all the same.

Was she being fanciful now that she was growing more and more fond of her husband? Was she seeing what she wished to see where there was only warmth and familiar pride? Was she wishing for more than there was between them?

She felt herself soften and smile as she watched him, though smiling was not usually part of her singing performance. But for the first time in her life, she wondered if it ought to be. If she might smile while doing anything and everything. If it might become impossible to do anything but smile when her husband was about. If smiling while singing might pour more goodness and happiness into whatever it was that she sang.

For a sensible, unemotional creature such as Honora Trembath, née Berkeley, that was an illuminating thought.

The song finished, and for the space of a heartbeat, there was no sound. Then there was applause. Raucous, whistling, earsplitting applause that had her beaming beyond anything she could recall. Gage's shoulders dropped on an exhale, and he shook his head, grinning as he came to her. He plucked up both her hands and kissed each before pulling her into an embrace.

Embarrassed but delighted, Honora buried her face into his chest, her breathing suddenly feeling unsteady and shallow.

"*Mar deg*, Honora," he whispered in her ear.

She looked up at him with a smile as applause continued. "What does that mean?"

He cupped her cheek, his thumb stroking gently. "So beautiful."

Her throat tightened at once, and her cheeks flamed. Somehow, she managed to smile, even as his thumb touched the flushing surface of her skin. "Thank you."

He kissed her brow quickly, then turned to face the group with his arm around her waist. "I give you, my wife!"

The gathering roared again, and Honora ducked her chin, smiling still. They called out phrases in Cornish, but she would have Emblyn tell her about it later. She started inching away from the musicians, grateful when Gage came with her and loving the way his arm felt around her waist.

"Oy!" one of the guests shouted. "Play ee 'The Barley-Mow'!"

The fiddler nodded at the request and struck up a tune that Honora vaguely recognized. She frowned slightly when there was no move to form lines. "Are they going to dance again?"

He grinned at the gathering, shaking his head. "No, they intend to sing. It is one of our common songs, particularly at harvest." He glanced down at her, still grinning. "Look what you've started."

Honora nudged him a little, looking away even as she smiled.

Gage chuckled and moved his hand to hers. "Come on, let's get you something to drink. The best way to sing this one is with a drink in hand."

"I don't drink much," Honora told him, finding a bit of apology in her tone.

"Tell me something I don't know," he retorted with another laugh. He gestured to a table just ahead. "Cider will be just the thing for you. Not that strong, and rather refreshing. And you know you can request something from the house, should you need it."

Honora shook her head firmly. "I am not about to be a fine lady. Not tonight."

Gage opened his mouth to say something, when he was suddenly tugged away by one of the men singing. He shrugged an apology to Honora and went along, joining in.

She took some of the cider and turned to face the music, smiling at the variety of voices she could hear raised in joyous, boisterous song.

> "We'll drink it out of the half-a-pint, boys,
> Here's a health to the barley-mow!
> The half-a-pint, quarter-pint, the nipperkin,
> And the jolly brown bowl!
> Here's a health to the barley-mow, my brave boys,
> Here's a health to the barley-mow!"

There was laughter among the singing, and Honora laughed along with it. From what she could tell, the verses got longer as a new drinking vessel was added to the list, and some in the company struggled to remember each of them.

It was clear this was a particularly fond drinking song, and she wondered if it might have been too early in the evening for the most entertaining version of it.

"We'll drink it out of the pint, my brave boys,
Here's a health to the barley-mow!
The pint, half-a-pint, quarter-pint, the nipperkin,
And the jolly brown bowl!
Here's a health to the barley-mow, my brave boys,
Here's a health to the barley-mow!"

Honora sipped her cider, shaking her head in amusement as her husband sang along with the rest, his arm slung around the shoulder of the man next to him, who had thrust a tankard of some sort in his hand. But it was not the men alone who sang and sang in such a hearty fashion. There were just as many women in the chorus as men, and they laughed just as much.

It ought to have offended Honora, based upon her upbringing and the society with which she had been brought up. It ought to have made her ashamed and given her a sense of lowering herself to associating with farmhands, bal maidens, fisherfolk, servants, and the like. It ought to have dismayed her, quite honestly, and if her mother knew, she would have railed against Honora for lowering her standards.

Luckily, Honora felt none of these things, only contentment and satisfaction.

Things she never felt for a moment growing up.

"You look happy, cousin."

Honora blinked and smiled at the arrival of John and Julia, approaching her arm in arm, Julia's condition very evident and looking more and more uncomfortable. There was strain in her cousin's face, but she seemed truly pleased to be there, in spite of it.

"Do I?" Honora answered, offering a glass of cider to Julia. "I feel happy, for what that is worth."

She took the glass with a small nod of thanks. "It is worth a great deal."

"A very great," John emphasized. "Much as we like Gage, Honora, you must know how we worried about your being truly happy here."

"Not that Gage would not ensure your wellbeing," Julia added hastily. "He is very good, but you know so little of the world and of respect. I would have wished a love match for you, though I know your parents would never have allowed someone worthy of you to get close enough."

"That's true," Honora murmured with another sip. "I was fortunate to ever get to a ball or social occasion."

John nodded with fervency. "Exactly. We talked about this often, and marriage seemed so unlikely for you, given all of that."

"So to see you happy in your marriage," Julia said, one hand going to her stomach, "brings me the greatest comfort."

Honora gave them both warm smiles. "You are both so dear, truly. It is all still so very new, but Gage is the best husband I could have imagined. Encouraging, respectful, treats me with honor, gives me independence, allows me decisions… Even when I don't wish to make decisions, he will occasionally insist. He wishes me to know my own mind and to speak it. No one has ever wished that for me, apart from you. And I was never very good at it then."

John laughed and put a hand on Honora's arm, rubbing fondly. "You will learn how with practice, though I doubt you will ever grow bold or insistent."

"I doubt that very much, indeed," Honora agreed. She looked at Julia with more concern. "Are you feeling well? Should you even be here?"

"I would never miss a harvest celebration," Julia told her with some firmness, her smile almost convincing. "Indeed, we have ours next week. And after that, I believe I will start my confinement. A bit early, but moving is growing more and more uncomfortable."

"Yes, I thought you said it would be Christmas, or thereabouts," Honora replied. "Have you seen a doctor of late?"

Julia nodded, her smile turning positively reassuring. "Yes, and all appears well. I am only larger than expected, which accounts for the awkwardness and the discomfort. I will rest after the harvest and shall feel all the better for it."

Honora flicked her gaze to John. "I trust you will see to that."

"With great firmness," he told her, his smile showing not only his care for Julia, but his excitement about the forthcoming child. "She will be waited on hand and foot."

"She'll hate that," Honora warned him even as Julia groaned.

"I know." He put his arm about Julia's waist and kissed the side of her head. "But it will be worth it."

Honora nodded and looked back at the singing, which was, impossibly, still on the same song. "How many verses are there?" she asked in astonishment.

Julia laughed once. "This is the final one. Listen."

"We'll drink it out of the ocean, my boys,
Here's a health to the barley-mow!
The ocean, the river, the well, the pipe, the hogshead,
The half-hogshead, the anker, the half-anker,
The gallon, the pottle, the quart, the pint,
The half-a-pint, the quarter-pint, the nipperkin,
And the jolly brown bowl!
Here's a health to the barley-mow, my brave boys,
Here's a health to the barley-mow!"

A hearty whooping and hollering commenced after the grand finish, followed by uproarious laughter, clinks of tankards, and hugs all around.

"Why do I feel like I've stepped into a tavern?" Honora asked with a surprisingly fond smile.

"Oh, believe me," John told her wryly, "this is far more wholesome."

Julia scoffed loudly before shushing them both. "Oh, look! They're pushing Gage to the front! I wonder if he'll sing."

Honora watched his progress, her heart beating hard as though she had been asked to dance alone in the center of the room. "Would he?"

"Oh, yes," her cousin replied. "He's quite good, though he rarely shows it. This is one of the rare occasions, and now that he's danced and participated in other ways, he'll be more inclined."

Honora watched as Gage reached the musicians and said something quietly, then gestured for the gathering to quiet.

The music began, and suddenly the most beautiful, deep, pure voice began to sing. It was a folk song that Honora was unfamiliar with, but words were entirely lost upon her. All she knew, all she could feel, was the sensation of this velvety voice reaching into her body and coiling perfectly around her heart, and the unbearable heat from such an embrace that spread through her frame. It was as though she had bathed in drinking chocolate, and it left an almost shocking awareness of the very air against her skin.

Gage sang with such ease, just as he spoke, and there was a rough, unpolished quality that only improved the effect of its tone. She had never seen or heard anything like it. She had heard men sing before, and even sung duets with them, but this… This was raw, real, and refreshing, and it was singlehandedly changing her life yet again.

They had told her Gage could sing. No one had said that he could sing like this.

"This is a traditional song," John whispered, his voice sounding very far away indeed. "It's sung every year."

Honora tried to nod, but she wasn't sure if it actually occurred. She was intent upon Gage, afraid that if she looked away, the voice might stop, and she would discover it was all a dream.

Gage's dark eyes met hers then, and it was as though he could sense her soul-deep chaos, if his crooked smile was any indication. His voice dipped into the lovely valleys it had so easily been sweeping through, and soon after danced to the sweet higher notes, reminding her of an Irish singer she had heard once, whose singing lilted more than his speech had, and with a delightful wave of sound.

Gage's voice did the same, and this time, she was lost to it.

"So boys, will we drink? Or what do you think?
There is nothing like cutting down brooms, green brooms.
There's nothing like cutting down brooms, green brooms.
There's nothing like cutting down brooms."

His voice faded with the music, and applause thundered in the barn, as well as in Honora's ears. She joined in, wishing she could raise her voice to a volume that would match the exuberance she felt in her heart. But she was a small creature, and volume had never been her specialty.

It had never been an issue until now.

Gage waved at the group and stepped aside, gesturing for the musicians to play, and soon, another dance was forming.

"I think I may manage this dance, darling," Julia said to her husband, though it was rather distant in Honora's ears.

"Just the one, my love," John warned, leading her away.

Honora ignored them as they left her, her eyes fixed on Gage, who was now walking in her direction. Whether it was towards her, or it was simply a coincidence, she wasn't certain, but she hoped and prayed with all of her might that it might bring him to her.

Sure enough, he raised his eyes to hers, his smile a little sheepish. "Well, how did I do?"

Honora's mouth opened, but there were no words at first. She shook her head, then found herself laughing. "What in heaven's name, Gage? That was... how did you say it? *Mar deg*."

His smile broke into a wide grin, his eyes dancing. "Really? You think so?"

"I don't know how to lie," Honora assured him, still shaking her head in disbelief. "Or flatter. Gage, I've never heard anything like that. Ever."

For the first time ever, she saw his cheeks color. He averted his eyes and gripped the back of his neck. "Thank you. Coming from you, that is quite some praise."

Honora took his hand and squeezed tightly, waiting for him to look at her again. "I mean it," she insisted. "I wish I had better words for it, but... I mean it."

He looked at their hands, then smiled a little as he twisted his fingers to lace between hers. "I know you do. That's why it touches me."

A ticklish heat began to brew in Honora's stomach, and her hold on Gage's hand became almost clenching. She needed to say something more, something else, but what?

Movement behind Gage caught her eye, and Honora saw one of the families beginning to leave. "Wait, Gage. What's their name?"

He glanced behind them. "The Blighs."

Honora nodded and released his hand at once, moving past him at a fast clip. "Mr. Bligh! Mrs. Bligh!"

They stopped and looked back at her in surprise, their oldest children with them, also looking at Honora with interest.

She smiled at them and indicated they wait while she moved to an enclosed storage part of the barn, retrieving a basket laden with food, warm and sturdy fabric, stockings, and bottles of wine and cider. She brought it over to the family, who looked at her in shock.

"Thank you for coming," Honora said as she handed it to Mrs. Bligh, "and for all of your hard work this season. There are some preserves in there, as well as honey and salt for meat and fish."

Mrs. Bligh bobbed a curtsey, looking as though she might cry. "Thank you, mistress. It is very kind."

"Most generous," Mr. Bligh grunted, giving her a nod.

"You are most welcome," Honora told them. "Good night." She waved and turned to walk back to Gage, who had come forward a few paces, and looked at her as though he had seen a ghost.

Her warm feeling faded as soon as she saw his face. "What?" she asked him, hurrying over. "Should I not have done that?"

He blinked, saying nothing.

Honora bit her lip, wringing her fingers together. "It's my own fault. It was my idea. I wanted to do something for our workers and tenants, and all I could think of was baskets. I am so sorry; I'll do better next time."

A sound she couldn't quite make out came from Gage, who continued to stare at her. Then he shook his head slowly before closing the distance between them and pressing his lips to hers, his hands landing on her shoulders, then moving up to cradle her face.

Honora stiffened in surprise at the contact, then softened at once as he almost insistently foraged at her lips. Her fingers, which had been knotted before her, wedged their way up to his weskit and curled into the fabric for stability.

Gage broke off before she expected, but touched his brow to hers in almost the same moment. "Sometimes, Honora," he rasped, "I don't quite believe you are real."

Honora could only release an unsteady breath.

Blessedly, that seemed to be all Gage needed, and he brought his lips to hers again, this time gentle, tender, and wringing sanity, sense, and reserve out of Honora's every waking nerve. She tugged on his weskit just a little, yearning for more of this, more of him, more of everything. He wrapped one of his arms around her, the other tilting her face up to kiss her more deeply, more thoroughly, and yet with the same sweetness as before. Giving in to impulse, Honora snaked one hand up to his jaw and finally felt the tender abrasion of his stubble against her palm.

Gage hummed at the contact, his kiss momentarily intensifying. With surprise, it seemed, and with pleasure.

That made two of them.

Chapter Thirteen

There were days when being industrious was a thrill and days where it was utter drudgery.

This day was most assuredly the latter.

The blast had gone well at Wheat Stout, and now they were clearing it while the exploratory team continued in their attempts to make progress in the tunnel. The strange, soft rock had seemed to have gone with the blast, and they were back to the same sturdy rock as before.

What Gage wouldn't give to be working in that part of the mine. Clearing the results of the blast was never enjoyable for him. But until they had cleared it and ensured that all dead fuses had been properly snuffed, they could not divert anyone else to the new expansion. Other parts of the mine were being worked, as per usual, so it was only Gage and a few others relegated to the tedium.

They were almost through after this half-day of steady work, and thankfully, they would all be divided up afterwards to work in other, more productive areas of the mine.

Gage took his two buckets to the mine entrance, weaving his way around the other workers and gingerly making his way up the ladder to the next level, and the next, until he had reached the entrance. "Above," he called, signaling for whoever was picking up the buckets for sifting.

"Coming!" a clear voice rang out, though the volume wasn't much.

He knew that tone, and he knew that volume, and he paused on the ladder, quite certain his eyes would tell the truth when his ears clearly were not.

But no, there was Honora coming around the corner of the engine house, her plaited and pinned hair mostly hidden by a kerchief she had tied around it all, her skirts and boots stained with dust, dirt, and even mud. Her face shone with perspiration, and the apron she had donned upon their arrival was an entirely different series of shades than what it had been before. Unless one fully examined the quality of her clothing, they would not have known she was any sort of fine lady.

"Honora?" Gage half laughed as she approached.

She stuttered a step as she looked up in surprise, then smiled at the sight of him. "Gage," she greeted almost cheerily as she approached. "How goes it?"

He shook his head, grinning. "It goes. I am bored out of my mind, but it'll be done soon, and then I might take up a pick."

Honora nodded, still smiling as she came to get the buckets. "Lucky you."

"What are you doing fetching buckets?" he asked, folding his arms on the top of the ladder and pointing at them. "That wasn't what you said you were going to do today."

"No, but it needs to be done, and it is faster if more hands are at it." She shrugged and wiped at her brow. "And besides, the children have all gone to school for the day, so there is naught to do but actually work. I don't mind."

Gage set his chin upon his arms a moment. "I know you don't mind, but you also don't have to."

This earned him a pointed look. "Neither do you." She scanned him up and down to prove her point.

He looked down at himself and laughed at the sight. He looked no better than she did, and probably far worse. Sweat had dampened almost the entire front of his shirt, making the dust easier to stick and darken everything, and he was quite certain he had as much dust upon his face and hair as was on his clothes. Neither of them would look the part of their station today, and there was no observable reason why they ought to be here in the first place.

Except they wanted to be.

"Point taken," Gage admitted, straightening up. "Well, don't work too hard, Mrs. Trembath."

"I will work just hard enough, Mr. Trembath," she shot back. She bent and lifted the buckets without any hint of strain, which was, he would admit, impressive for her slight stature.

He smirked wryly at her quip, rather pleased she had done so. "Right then, give me a kiss before I go below again."

Her lips clamped together, as though she was restraining a laugh, her eyes dancing. But she came over and did so, lingering longer than he expected, her kiss doing rather funny things to the backs of his knees.

She broke off, snickering. "You taste of dust," she informed him as she stepped back, her color heightened, but her smile in place.

Gage cleared his throat, hoping it would strengthen his knees. "You're welcome," he said with a nod, starting back down the ladder. He waved before disappearing entirely and caught the raising of her chin in acknowledgement of it.

Taste. Why did she have to use that word? Now it would be all he could think of while he worked—the taste of his wife and how he tasted to her. He might taste of dust, but she tasted of honey and salt and something vaguely floral that was destined to linger in his consciousness for some time, maddeningly enough.

Ever since the harvest celebration the other day, kissing his wife was becoming routine. He couldn't help it; once he had done so there, it was nearly impossible to avoid continuing to do so. And despite what she had initially thought, the kiss at the celebration had nothing to do with how much he'd had to drink and everything to do with her. He had been growing more and more attracted to her since the wedding, it was true, but it was not until he had seen her appear with baskets for the tenants, something that had never before been done at harvest in its history, had he decided that kissing her was the only course of action.

Odd that it had been her generous heart that had put him over the edge, and not something physical.

But Honora was befuddling that way, and he had no regrets. Especially in discovering that she enjoyed kissing him and was getting better at it.

He actually might regret her getting better at it. There was something so invigorating about an untutored kiss. But he would only regret it a very little. He suspected Honora would always kiss with a little bit of innocent eagerness, if not disbelief, and that was not something he would take for granted.

Deuce take it, but there was something about her lips that distracted him. They were not the fullest lips he had ever seen, nor the most perfect. Yet the way they moved when she spoke, and when she sang, was absolutely captivating. He hadn't thought so before he married her, as far as he could recall, but since their marriage, it was growing more and more so. The more he kissed her, the more he wanted to kiss her, and the more distracting those lips became.

It did not help that there was a faint freckle just off the upper ridge of her lip on the left side that drove him mad, nor that her slightly pointed jaw fit absolutely perfectly against the curve of his hand.

She was perfectly built for kissing him.

Utter insanity, realizing that.

How would any red-blooded man survive such an idea?

Gage shook his head as he traipsed further down into the mine, returning to his position on the clearing team. Tedium would breed more thinking, which would mean more of Honora's mouth and more imagining the sort of kissing he might get when they were back home and clean. He was not going to be particularly productive with that on the horizon, unless he somehow could speed up time with working faster.

But that was not usually how things worked.

He sighed, stooping to begin clearing another small section, when he smelled something a trifle different from what he was used to in the mine. He sniffed more cautiously, the hairs on his arms standing on end as the scent sank in.

Sulfur.

"Rowe?" he called out, his eyes darting about the space, looking for some cause for the sulfur to be apparent in the air. The blast had been the day before; there should not have been any remaining gunpowder. But if he was smelling it, then not only would it have to be somewhere, but it would have to have been triggered somehow.

"Gage?" the call came back, at the other end of the mine, away from the exploratory end where the gunpowder could be.

Gage looked at the young man across from him and tapped him on the shoulder. "Ray, go tell Cap'n Rowe I need to speak with him. You can take his place in the line while he comes back."

Ray nodded, making no effort to hide his relief at being able to do something besides clearing. He darted down the tunnel with light steps and a bit of a whistle, leaving Gage to exhale with his own slight relief after him.

If there was a problem, at least the lad would be away from it.

He was only sixteen, which was more than old enough to work in the mine, but it seemed very young in the face of danger.

Gage glanced down the expansion tunnel, wishing he could call a warning down to them without raising panic in the entire mine. But until Rowe came and verified Gage's fear, he couldn't do anything more. He only prayed that Rowe would arrive before Jago Bray returned from delivering buckets above. It would be one more life certainly spared.

Heavy footfalls echoed in the tunnel, and Gage turned to face the approaching figure of Rowe. "Ee called?" he said as he entered the space, his grin almost shockingly pale in comparison to the rest of him and the darkness of their surroundings.

Rowe stopped a good ten feet from him, sniffing the air.

"That," Gage told him in a low voice. "I knew I hadn't imagined it."

Rowe's sharp eyes began moving over every surface, slowly approaching Gage's area. "They cleared it of fuses, aye?"

"So they said," he answered, nodding and setting his hands on his hips. "It did not smell of this when we started."

They started towards the expansion tunnel together, moving slowly while the now-ominous sounds of pick against rock echoed ahead of them. The scent of the sulfur grew as they moved, and that was exactly what Gage was afraid of.

Rowe put a hand to his arm sharply, stopping his progress.

"What?" Gage hissed, unsure if they were going to disturb the six working men ahead.

Rowe's eyes were wide, his jaw set. "Fuse must have been damp, but it's no' dead. We need to get them out. Now."

Gage looked at the workers, watching as Cary Tresize hammered hard on an iron bar in the rock.

A deafening explosion of sound and dust filled the small, cramped space, and Gage was unaware of anything at all for what felt like several minutes.

His ears rang, his head buzzed, and something cold and wet was digging into his back. He could feel himself coughing but heard nothing from it. He blinked, and blinked again, his eyes finally beginning to make sense of his vision. He was staring at dark, damp rock, but it wasn't what he had been looking at moments before.

He blinked a third time, and his mind caught up with his vision. He was lying flat on his back on the ground, staring up at the top of the tunnel. His ears still rang, though shouting and scraping was barely heard beneath the piercing din. That unsettling sound seemed to be connecting one ear to the other, filling the entire space between with its horrid resonance, making thought difficult and his head ache.

He coughed again, hearing it this time as well as feeling shooting pain in his left shoulder. He raised his head, which hurt, and looked at his shoulder, which sported a large gash, though it did not seem to be bleeding badly. He examined the rest of his body, which was dusty and coated in rock, but nothing large or immovable, and shifted what he could, testing his back and limbs.

All working well enough, though nothing felt comfortable.

Hands gripped beneath his arms and hauled him back, and Gage shook his head, trying to wave his hand. "I'm all right," he shouted, pleased he could make out his own voice above the noise. "Help me up."

He was hoisted to his feet and felt only a touch of dizziness as he oriented himself.

Then he looked around him in truth.

The expansion tunnel was more than halfway concealed with rock and grime, and he could already see the bodies of three men within not moving.

Faintly, he heard the bell clanging above and knew that the local doctor would be summoned to tend the wounded. Now they just needed to get the wounded up to him.

Gage started towards the tunnel but was stopped by someone at his feet. He looked down and saw a groaning Rowe, whose leg was badly cut and bleeding.

"Damn," Gage hissed, moving for him while others headed into the tunnel. "Rowe, hang on."

"Be ee careful, lads!" Tom Drake hollered. "Might be unstable from the blast! Ee feel something else shake, ee bolt like hares, aye?"

"Aye!" the others shouted.

Gage pulled his kerchief from his neck and thrust one end under Rowe's leg, the man almost writhing with the movement it caused his leg. "Stop, if you can," Gage ordered. "I've got to tie this, just in case. Might save your leg."

Rowe ground out some coarse Cornish words between his teeth.

"Don't let your wife hear you say that," Gage teased as he knotted the fabric as tightly as he could. "She'll send you out to sleep with the livestock." He tugged at the knot hard to be sure it would not move. "There. Come on, let's get you above."

"Get t'others," Rowe instructed, his voice tight and strained.

Gage shook his head. "You can order the others, my friend, but you cannot order me."

He moved around to heft Rowe upright as much possible, watching as the man struggled with his good leg to find purchase. Then he had it and balanced unsteadily on that leg.

Nodding, Gage came to his bad side and wrapped one arm around Rowe's waist as the man dropped his arm over Gage's shoulders.

"This be folly," Rowe told him. "T'others will be worse."

Gage grunted as the two of them started moving forward, Rowe awkwardly and painfully hopping while Gage kept him as balanced and upright as he was able. "Then you'd better help me get you above as quickly as possible so I can help them, too."

Rowe began mumbling incoherently, which was probably for the best.

They reached the ladder up to ten level, and Gage whistled. "Help me get him up!"

Three men appeared above them at once. One held the ladder steady and the other two reached down.

Rowe shook his head and reached up to them while Gage

stooped to hoist him up from below. It was an awkward maneuver, but the help from the others allowed it to be relatively quick. Gage clambered up the ladder and nodded his thanks as he took Rowe's weight again.

"Stay and help get others out, if you can," Gage ordered. "We need to clear quickly."

"Aye," they chorused.

Gage moved on with Rowe, noticing that the weight of him was getting heavier, and he glanced at his friend in concern.

He was growing pale, and his jaw was almost slack, where it had been tense and taut moments before.

"Rowe," Gage barked, doing his best to shake him as they moved. "Stay with me, I don't want to haul your deadweight out of this hole because you swooned."

Rowe chuckled in a drowsy, almost intoxicated sound. "Ee'd be dragging me carcass o'er the ladder like a slaughtered cow."

"Don't be ridiculous," he retorted. "Cows smell better."

Rowe continued to laugh, but Gage moved with more haste in his step. The loss of blood could put Rowe in great danger, even with his binding in place, and despite his jokes, he truly was afraid of his friend going unconscious. He didn't know what he'd do if that happened. Throw him on his back and do his best to get to the doctor? He should have brought someone with him to get Rowe out, but at the time...

"Gage, be tha' the cap'n?" a new voice shouted from ahead.

"Aye!" Gage called, gripping Rowe tightly as he felt the man begin to slack.

Quick steps reached him, and he felt part of the weight lifted as the newcomer took up Rowe's other side and helped Gage get him to the ladder. Waiting hands pulled Rowe from the hole and Gage climbed up after, more to make sure his friend wouldn't die that moment.

"Doctor Cox," Gage greeted as the man came to inspect Rowe.

He glanced at Gage with a nod, then looked at him more closely. "You need to get that arm looked at. And your leg."

Gage glanced down, noticing for the first time the cut on his leg as well. He waved both off. "I will later. We need to get the others out. Is he going to be all right?"

Cox listened to Rowe's chest, then looked at the leg. "Seems so. You did well to bind his leg, slowed the bleeding there. He's more in danger of raising a fever or infection than anything else, and that can be just as deadly. He'll be fine for now."

Gage nodded and kicked Rowe's boot on his good leg. "Hear that? You're being dramatic."

"Aye, I 'eard 'im," Rowe murmured, his smile weak.

"Gage!"

He whirled, knowing that voice, but never knowing it could make a sound like that.

Honora was bolting for him, her expression full of terror.

He thought his heart would snap in two just at seeing it. Immediately, he opened his arms and caught her, holding her tightly to him. Her arms wrapped around his neck like a vice, her strength more undeniable now than when he had seen her with the buckets earlier.

And she was shaking.

"I'm all right," he assured her, running a hand over her still-covered hair. "It's all right."

Honora exhaled against his ear, and it was only then he realized the ringing had stopped. "When I heard the blast, I thought…" She shook her head and buried her face. "I was so afraid."

Gage pulled back and kissed her gently. "I'm sorry," he whispered. "I promise, I am fine."

She touched her brow to his, nodding as she swallowed.

He cupped her cheek and brushed it with his thumb. "I need to help get the others out. I'll be out as soon as I can."

She did not respond except another nod, her hands still linked behind his neck tightly. And she was still shaking.

"Honora," he murmured, rubbing her back gently. "I need to go back down."

"I know," she told him in the smallest voice known to man. "Will you be safe?"

He smiled, though her eyes were still closed. "As safe as I can be. As safe as anyone else. Will you be all right up here?"

She swallowed again. "Of course. And I'll be even better once you don't have to go back down."

"Ever?" he asked, testing her feelings.

Blessedly, she shook her head and pulled back just enough, her eyes opening and a stray tear falling from one. "Of course not. Just until it's secure enough to resume work."

Gage kissed her quickly, but with fervency. "You are a queen among women," he assured her, pressing his palm into her cheek.

"I am not," she whispered back, finally smiling.

He laughed and brushed his lips over her brow. "Be right back," he vowed, finally feeling her hands release him.

He headed back for the mine, but glanced over his shoulder at her, and caught her watching him with an almost forlorn expression.

It was astonishing how close they had become without actually knowing each other all that well. They were familiar with each other, comfortable physically with each other, for the most part, and knew that they could rely on each other. But he didn't know what her favorite music to sing was. He didn't know what she enjoyed reading. He didn't know how she felt about her siblings, what her favorite color was, or if she liked dogs.

There were so many little things he did not know, and suddenly the little things seemed so important. But he was not entirely ignorant. He did know a few things.

He knew she enjoyed lively dancing, which had surprised them both. He knew she was an early riser. He knew she did not mind hard work or low company. He knew she liked to ride, knew she could play as well as sing, knew she liked yellow roses—thanks to Julia—and knew she was instinctively generous, which was a miracle after the upbringing she had.

But he did not know the names of her siblings. He did not know how she amused herself. He did not know if she liked pheasant. He did not know if she snored, if she picked her own flowers, if she enjoyed walking, if she might like to see their cove…

Heavens, he did not even know if she could swim, and that was something he should insist upon! They had a beach and a cove and a coastline, and she would be in great danger if she could not swim.

He would teach her, he vowed. Tomorrow, if they had the time.

He made his way down the ladder to the ten level, then down to the twenty once more, nodding at the men who were bringing out others. By his calculation, there should be two more down here, unless there had been problems in other tunnels. He had not heard any cries of utter dismay yet, but he supposed there was still time for it.

"Tom!" Gage called as he came near the expansion tunnel. "Tom, who is left?"

"Paul Kimbrel and Charlie Skuse!"

Gage climbed over the rubble and entered the space, coming over to the unmoving body of Charlie. "Are they alive?"

Tom shrugged as he and his son picked up Paul. "Hard to say, Gage. I ain't taken time to check 'ere."

Gage nodded and reached under Charlie's shoulders, wrapping his arms around his chest and pulling him towards the tunnel. "Makes sense to me. Trouble anywhere else?"

"Just 'ere," Tom replied as they moved ahead of him down the tunnel. "Someone'll be along soon to help ee, and then we're done."

"I'll just get him out of the expansion," Gage said with a nudge of his head. "I'll be just behind you. Go on."

They disappeared down the tunnel, and Gage continued to haul Charlie towards the safety on the other side of the rubble.

He might have missed the first pebble from above, though he did think something bounced off his head, but he certainly noticed the second one, as it pelted him directly on the bridge of his nose. His stomach dipped in apprehension as he looked up, just in time for a half dozen larger pebbles to drop at once.

He managed one last lunge with Charlie's body before the top of the tunnel fell directly above him, and all went black.

Chapter Fourteen

It had been two days, and Gage had not been awake for more than fifteen minutes at a time. And even when he had been, he was utterly incoherent. When he was asleep, he was restless, and his bandages had become detached so many times that Honora had actually changed the last one while half-asleep and done it perfectly well.

At this moment, he was calm and asleep, which was a relief.

Sitting in the chair just across from the bed in his rooms, Honora stared at him, watching his chest move up and down with each breath. The bandages on his shoulder were secured by ones around his chest, and they exaggerated the measure of his breathing in a way that was oddly comforting to her. There was nothing more comfortable, she decided, than hearing the smooth sounds of her husband's breath.

Particularly when she had once feared it was gone.

The day of the blast at Wheal Stout, she had been terrified to hear its deafening sound. The women she had been working with had run with sure legs and stout hearts, but Honora had been frozen in place. She had known the risks of a mine; it had been spelled out for her quite clearly her first day visiting. But she had never expected to be present for an accident.

When Nellie Spargo had first placed the disaster images in her mind, Honora imagined herself as jumping into the fray with the rest of the women, tending to the wounded and fetching water for those who were doing the rescuing. She vowed to herself that she would not be afraid, but be determined, comforting, and full of hope for those who would need it. She would be the very best version of herself.

Yet when faced with the disaster, and actually confronted with the fact that her husband was below, she had been entirely consumed with fear, dread, and panic.

Belatedly, she had been able to move, though each step had been tremulous and timid, and she had searched the mass of exiting men for her husband, dreading that she would never find him. Each breath had felt more like a hiccup, and everyone had been so concerned with the men around them, no one paid her any attention or tried to help her find Gage. Not that she had asked for any help.

Words had been beyond her, too.

Then, as though Fate had decided at the very last moment to keep her heart from breaking, she saw him. Her feet had propelled her forward, and his name had been torn from her throat with a shrillness she had never expected herself capable of.

Those moments in his arms had brought her back to life, she was certain of it. And she was nearly just as certain now that she was well on her way to falling in love with her husband. It was possibly a dreadful development, but time would tell. He wouldn't love her, she knew that, too, but perhaps he might come to like her enough to delude her at times into believing it was love.

He needed to recover from his injuries first, though.

Sending him back into the mine had been hard, but she had believed him when he'd said he would be safe.

She hadn't expected the second set of crashing sounds from the mine, and nor had anyone else. The hollering of the men had convinced her that she had not died at the sound, but her eyes refused to move from the mine entrance, where she fully expected to see her husband walking triumphantly out, covered in more dust, but unharmed. Perhaps even heroically carrying another miner over his back, having gotten out just in time.

When the sounds had silenced and no one walked out of the mine, she had collapsed to the ground, her eyes still fixed on it.

The women had instantly rallied around her, their own husbands and sons accounted for, for better or worse, while Honora waited in agony. One other woman, the intended of another miner, also waited, and it was not long before the two of them were holding hands while staring at the mine together.

The able-bodied men had raced into the mine, but it was all a blur to Honora. She only remembered the way her heart pounded, each and every painful beat, until the men came back out of the mine, carrying both Gage's body and that of the other miner, neither of whom were moving.

Honora had not grown hysterical or dissolved into tears upon seeing him like that, oddly enough. She had instead gone numb and sat down beside Gage while taking his hand in hers. The doctor had told her he was alive, and she had only nodded and laced their fingers together, just as he was always doing.

While they had waited for conveyance to take him back to Helwithin, Honora had set about cleaning his face, not that it would matter much. He would need to be fully bathed when they got him home, and his wounds carefully tended. Besides the shoulder wound she had seen, and the one on his leg, he had picked up a nasty-looking cut on his head as well as a number of bruises. She would not know the full extent until he had been properly examined, of course, but so long as there was life in him, there was hope in her.

Lord Basset had somehow heard about the incident and rode over, reaching them before the wagon had arrived. He'd insisted on sending word for their personal physician, Dr. Waite, and riding to Helwithin with Honora.

She remembered nothing of their conversation on the way, but somehow, she wound up leaning into Lord Basset with her head on his shoulder as though he were a brother. If he had minded this, he gave no inclination.

Emblyn, Adelaide, and John were waiting at Helwithin for them. Julia had stayed behind, given her condition, but she had threatened John with bodily harm if he did not go. It had been very kind of them all to come, but there was not much to do. She had tried to explain that, but they had all insisted they would stay until they knew everything and would help Honora however they could.

She had begun wondering if Gage actually had died and no one had told her.

Thankfully, the doctor had assured Honora that his heart was strong and his breathing unlabored. His unconsciousness could be the shock or from the impact to his head, but there were no signs that he was in mortal danger.

He had asked that they clean his body so he might examine the wounds better, and Honora had immediately removed her apron, rolled up her sleeves, and asked for everything necessary to be brought up. Basset and Adelaide had gone downstairs to make arrangements with Mrs. Crane, but John and Emblyn had helped Honora remove Gage's clothing and begin to wash him.

It had been an oddly intimate moment, even with others there, for Honora to wash her husband's body while he slept. Taking the damp cloth up and down his arm, along each finger, and each nail. Wincing when she had washed around his wound, and worrying when he showed no sign of pain that she did so. Running the cloth over his chest and sides, wondering how such a strong, fit man could be so helpless in this moment. Rinsing his hair into a bowl that Emblyn held, running her fingers through his dark, thick tresses in a way she had only ever imagined doing.

But not like this. Never like this.

The cut on his head had been deeper than Dr. Waite had originally thought, so he had opted to suture it, as he had done to the shoulder and to the leg. Gage had been perfectly immovable for all of it, with not even an involuntary reaction to the procedures.

Fever would be the main concern for now, the doctor had told Honora then. He would return the following day but invited her to send for him if she had need.

It was only then that Adelaide had returned to the room and demanded that Honora come with her while John and Basset sat with the still unconscious Gage. Once in her chambers, Adelaide had smiled and told Honora that a bath was being prepared for her, and there would be no arguments, and she and Emblyn would be tending her while she allowed herself some moments of being something less than brave, whatever that might be. Honora had tried to insist that she was well, and that tending Gage was what mattered, but there had been no arguing with Adelaide.

Under their care, Honora had silently sobbed over the events of the day, her current fears, her exhaustion, and the prospect before her. But she had not felt judged or alone for a single moment, as her friends had been there. Washing her hair and her body almost like she had just done with Gage, only she was aware of their ministrations. She had heard their sniffling at times, but no one had said anything on the subject. It had simply been a moment for reflection, love, and healing.

She had not known she would need it, but Adelaide had.

She had hugged her friend a little more tightly before they had left.

That first night, it had been Honora and Mrs. Crane tending to Gage, sleeping fitfully in turns. He had first regained some semblance of consciousness at around four in the morning, but it had been all nonsense and incoherence. Still, Dr. Waite had declared it a good sign when he returned.

The day had progressed the same, though Emblyn had come to give her a respite and then stayed the night to allow Mrs. Crane enough sleep to manage the household.

There had not been any real sign of Gage being aware of anything as yet, and that was what Honora now craved.

Some indication that her husband would return to her and not simply exist in some state of there and not there at the same time. She would give anything for him to tell her a joke, say something ridiculous, or make her blush. Or even for him to hold her hand when she held his. For his thumb to brush her knuckles as it always seemed to do when he forgot he was holding her hand.

For anything.

She sniffed once, only to find she'd begun crying again, as sometimes happened when she was alone with him, and she quickly dashed her tears away, clearing her throat to make sure any sign of emotion was gone before someone else entered.

A sound drew Honora's attention to the door, but it remained closed, and no knocking came. She looked out of the window, but the day was fair and the wind minimal, so nothing could have come from there. Where then…?

Her eyes flew to the bed, hardly able to hope.

"'Nora," Gage mumbled, his eyes blinking, but not fully opening.

She was up like a shot to the side of the bed. "Gage?"

He tried to wet his lips, but it did not seem to help, and his brow furrowed.

Honora reached for the willow bark tea beside his bed. It would be fairly cold now, but it would be better than nothing. "Here, darling. Let me help. Just a small sip."

His mouth barely opened when the teacup pressed his lips, but enough liquid entered that he swallowed, and then he successfully wet his lips. "'Nora. Why're you crying?"

The words were slurred, but they were the most beautiful words she'd ever heard. Sighing in a rush, Honora brought his hand up and kissed it once, then again, her tears collecting once more. "Because you've scared me to death, you wretch."

"Sorry," he rasped, one corner of his mouth quirking. His face scrunched up and he groaned. "Head."

Honora brushed his hair back gently, careful to avoid his cut. "What about it?"

He swallowed. "Hurts. Much."

She nodded, running her fingers through his hair in the hopes it might relax him. "Anything else?"

His chin moved up and down. "E'rything. All things. Hurts."

"I'm sorry, darling," she murmured, holding his hand to her cheek. "What can I do?"

He turned his head towards her, eyes still closed. "Sing."

She smiled at the word. "Sing what? You'll have to be specific."

Again, his mouth quirked, and it was the best sign of life she had seen yet. "Ae Fond Kiss," he said in a fairly clear voice. "Or 'Mo Ghile Mear.'"

Honora quirked a brow at the second one. "I don't know that one."

"'Tis Irish," he mumbled, turning his head back to face upward. "M'mother useta sing it."

"Well," Honora said softly, still running her fingers through his hair, "I'll have to learn it, then. Do you want me to sing the other now?"

He nodded, but just barely. "Softly," he slurred. "Head hurts."

"I know, love," she whispered. "I know." She cleared her throat, and began to sing quietly.

"Ae fond kiss, and then we sever
Ae fareweel, alas, forever!
Deep in heart-wrung tears I'll pledge thee
Warring sighs and groans I'll wage thee."

Gage's breathing seemed to ease as she sang, and his fingers moved against her cheek as though he was intending to brush against her. It would be impossible to know if he meant to, given his state, but Honora would cling to hope.

"Who shall say that Fortune grieves him
While the star of hope she leaves him?
Me, nae cheerfu' twinkle lights me,
Dark despair around benights me."

Gage mumbled something, sighing as he said whatever it was, and Honora waited for him to say it again, but he didn't. For a moment, she thought he might have fallen asleep once more, and she took the chance to watch him from her new position, knowing now that he was still there, even if he was weak, in pain, and unwell. He was there, and he would recover, and they would be able to resume this fun, flirtatious part of marriage they had just begun.

"'Nora," Gage mumbled, turning slightly towards her again.

Wondering if he was going to scold her for not singing more, she smiled. "Yes, Gage?"

A shiver rippled along his frame. "Cold," he whispered. "So c-cold."

Honora frowned at him, knowing the room was actually rather warm. "What?" She rose from her crouched position and touched his brow, but it was hard to tell much when she had been stroking his hair for the last few minutes. She leaned in and kissed his brow gently, then reared back in shock.

He was positively burning up.

"Dratted wretch," she muttered, giving his hand a quick kiss. "You couldn't have led with that?"

"S-s-sorr-y," Gage managed through now-chattering teeth.

Honora released his hand and ran over to the door, opening it

154

and hollering, "Mrs. Crane! Emblyn! Send for Dr. Waite!"

He was summoned and arrived within half an hour, and the first thing he did was check Gage's wounds. The one on his head looked well, but his arm and his leg were red and angry, in spite of Honora's attempts to keep them clean, dry, and covered.

"It is not alarming, ma'am," Dr. Waite assured her, though he was shrugging out of his coat and rolling up his sleeves. "Not yet. Many wounds raise inflammation like this. The trouble is that they may also raise a fever, which may make the whole situation worse."

Honora nodded, watching how Gage's entire body seemed to tremble with chills. "What do we do?"

"Cool him down," the doctor instructed with all patience. "I know he looks very cold, but I promise you, he is not. He will not thank us for this."

"Yesss, I w-will," Gage rasped through his dry-again lips. He cracked his eyes open, then immediately snapped them shut, grimacing. "Eyes. Hurt. Bright."

"Rest yourself, sir," Dr. Waite urged, putting a hand on his shoulder. "You've likely a head injury on top of everything else, but we will get you sorted."

Gage dipped his chin. "'Nora."

She came to the other side of the bed. "I'm here, Gage."

He moved his head just a little towards her. "Kiss? Jus' in case?"

She smiled, shaking her head. "Fine," she told him, leaning close. "But if you get any more demanding, I'll not think you ill at all."

Something that could have been a cough, a laugh, or a groan rumbled from him, but considering it came with a tick of his lips, she would count it a laugh. She brushed his hair back and gently laid her lips against his own, their parched surfaces doing absolutely nothing as far as kisses went, but she felt the faintest sigh from him.

She would take it.

"Thanks," he whispered when she broke off.

"It is a trial to appease you," Honora said with some teasing, though her voice hitched a little.

His brow creased briefly. "Liar."

She combed her fingers through his hair once more but said nothing.

"Mrs. Trembath?"

She looked across the bed at the doctor.

He smiled gently, but with firmness. "We need to get started. Have rags and cool water sent up. The sooner he gets cooled down, the better."

Honora nodded and left the room to order it done. To her surprise, both Mrs. Crane and Emblyn appeared with the requested items, not leaving the task to a single maid. It occurred to Honora faintly to object to both of them when there was so much else to be done, but one look at their faces told her that there would be arguments against such a thing, and it would only waste time.

Quietly, the four of them worked to cool down Gage's body with the cool, damp cloths. At some point, one of the footmen brought in buckets of ice that had been procured from the Bassets' icehouse, and they dumped that out on top of the blankets along Gage's body. He was shivering so violently by the time they were done that Honora had to restrain herself from fetching more blankets for him.

But Dr. Waite assured her that this was the best way to bring his temperature down.

Then he asked for a bowl of vinegar and water with some fresh linen to clean the wounds, just to try and reduce the infection there. Emblyn took this up, and actually asked the doctor to instruct her so that she might do the task in the days following.

Honora stood by Gage's bed and watched them tend the wounds while her husband shook, no longer seeming to be aware of anything at all.

"Madam?"

Honora blinked and looked at Mrs. Crane belatedly. "Yes?"

Mrs. Crane gave her a gentle smile. "I thought to go and brew some barley water to try and help the fever. Might I bring you up some tea? Or soup?"

"I am fine, Mrs. Crane," she said softly, shaking her head. "I don't need anything."

"I'll bring you some tea and biscuits," Mrs. Crane told her, as though Honora hadn't spoken. "And I'll have Cook prepare soup for tonight. If Mr. Trembath is alert enough to take some, so be it. If not, at least you will have a decent meal."

Honora managed a smile for the woman. "You won't allow me to argue against, will you?"

Mrs. Crane shook her head very firmly. "Not in the least, madam. You need your strength if you insist on tending to Mr. Trembath, and I'll make certain you have it." She nodded, then left the room, wiping her hands on her apron as she strode away.

Honora sighed to herself, watching Gage once more. He was either asleep or unconscious now, and there was something about how he appeared that made her suddenly fear he was dead. Something about being so still when he had been trembling so much had to indicate there was a problem. How could the doctor not see that Gage was dead or near death?

Yet she couldn't move, couldn't rush to her husband's side, couldn't take her eyes off of the slackness in her husband's face.

Because he was not dead, and she knew it. She could see his chest rise and fall, however faintly, and knew that Dr. Waite, and Emblyn, would know at once if the arm they worked on suddenly went entirely slack. She knew it was only her fears that were speaking to her now, and only the silence that fed those fears.

"Would it bother either of you if I sang to him?" Honora heard herself ask in a small voice, fearing that any sound at all might throw this uneasy balance entirely awry.

Dr. Waite looked over his shoulder, smiling in a way that made him look far younger than he was. "Of course not. Please do. I am certain your husband would take comfort from it."

That was exactly what Honora had been hoping for, and that Dr. Waite could see it so clearly spoke to her soul.

Her feet allowed her to move for this, for the action ahead of her rather than the dread from before. Action, not emotion. Work, not fear.

That was how she would get Gage through this, that was how she would get herself through this, and that was how every day would go until life could resume its new and tenuous normalcy.

Honora pulled a chair beside Gage's bed and took his good hand in her own, lacing their fingers and holding the back of it against her cheek. His hand was so cold now, but her fingers felt that steady pulse thrumming beneath the skin. That beat that would fill her own heart while she waited for his strength to return. Would be the only sound her ears wished to hear.

"Rest now, darling," Honora whispered, staring into Gage's face as her free hand stroked his shoulder. "Rest and heal. I'll be right here."

She kissed the back of his hand, then cleared her throat, deciding to pick up the song he'd requested where she had left off.

"I'll ne'er blame my partial fancy;
Nothing could resist my Nancy;
For to see her was to love her,
Love but her, and love for ever."

Chapter Fifteen

His head had never felt like this in his entire life. It was as though his mind were expanding and rolling like a cloud, filling the inside of his head with pressure that was unbearable. He half expected to open his eyes and see that his mind had leaked from his ears onto the pillow beneath him.

It didn't pound, per se, but Gage could feel every pulse of every vessel in his head, he was quite certain.

And also… thinking hurt. It was slow, and it hurt. Why did it hurt? Why was it difficult?

What had happened?

Slowly—very slowly—his mind played back what it could recall. The clearing of the mine, the fuse being live when they thought it was dead… but after that, there was nothing. It could have been yesterday, though he had a sense that he had been lying here a while. Flashes of faint and vague memories of being very cold, very hot, being wiped down with damp cloths, of liquid passing his lips… And then there were moments of singing, though he wasn't certain if he had dreamed that or not.

It was all so fuzzy in his mind. Time had little meaning, and nothing felt quite real. The combination of all of this was actually quite unsettling, if not alarming. But he had no energy for anything alarming, and even being awake seemed to hurt somehow.

What sort of hell had he survived, and would it have been better to have died?

Hesitantly, Gage cracked his eyes open, snapping them shut with a painful squeeze at the bright light and the agony it instantly created in his head.

But he needed to see. Needed to orient himself. Needed to live, not just lie here.

Again, with more awareness, he pried his eyes open and found the light less than he had previously thought. The curtains were drawn, though he could see light through the cracks. Daylight, then, in spite of their being closed. Why would they have kept the room dark during daylight?

Had he been lucid at some point and complained of it?

How could he not recall such an occasion?

He kept his attention on the window for a long moment, forcing his eyes to adjust to the light of the room and to bring what he was seeing into clearer focus. Then, and only then, did he begin a slow scan of the room. He was in his own chambers, that he could tell straightaway, and he had been here for some time. There were bowls and rags scattered about the room, linens on the floor, teacups and saucers on nightstands and tables, and a weak fire crackled and popped across the room.

His eyes fell on his wingback chair, which had been his father's and was probably older than Gage himself, and on the small figure curled into a ball within it.

Honora.

Her head was tucked against her knees, her arms slack in her lap. Her hair hung long in a plait, though the plait itself was messy and unkempt, and even from here, Gage could see the dark circles under her eyes. The pallor of her cheeks. The utter frailness of her frame.

She looked as unwell as he felt.

Honora was a delicate creature, by all appearances, but he knew full well how strong she was. How misleading her outward appearance was. How determined she could be, when she allowed herself that freedom. How little she thought of herself.

She had been tending him, he realized. It was a slower realization than he should have had, but he would blame whatever was wrong with him for the delay. She had been losing sleep and risking her own health to take care of him, for however long it was taking, and now he was lying here in his bed for whatever number of days, and she was sleeping curled up in a chair.

That was quite enough of that.

Gage tried to wet his lips and found his mouth as dry as they were. He swallowed a few times, tried again, and when that failed, just cleared his throat. "Honora."

The word was a struggle, and he was fairly certain a few syllables were unintelligible, but it was a start.

She didn't stir from her sleep.

Gage exhaled slowly, gathering his strength, and then said again, more loudly, "Honora."

His wife jerked from her curled-up position, her eyes wide and staring around frantically. It would have been comical had his head not begun filling with even more pressure than before. Her eyes fell on him, and somehow grew wider still.

He smiled at her. At least, he hoped he did. "Good morning. I think."

Honora blinked. "Gage?"

"I think so," he murmured, craning his neck on the pillow. "Could be wrong, though."

She smiled just a little. "That's the most you've said in three days."

Gage stared at her a long moment. "Three? How long have I been here?"

"Five days."

He groaned, closing his eyes again. "No wonder I feel like death warmed over." He swallowed and opened his eyes again, noting she hadn't moved. "Why are you sleeping in the chair?"

Honora looked about her, then shrugged. "I was tired of sleeping sitting by the bed."

Gage tried to raise a brow, but the action hurt too much. "Why not sleep in the bed?"

"Because you're in it?" Her smile turned quizzical as she wrapped her arms around her knees, her chin resting atop them. "And we've been tending you."

"We?" he repeated. "If there's a 'we' in this, you could sleep in your own bed."

Honora shook her head firmly. "I wasn't going to leave you."

Her words filled his chest with warmth, and Gage smiled.

"Clearly, I wasn't going anywhere. It would have been fine."

"You've been ill as well as injured," she said softly. "Very high fevers, chills, infections in your wounds... We've been very worried."

Gage tsked at that. "I'm sorry. If it helps, I don't remember any of that. Was I in a poor temper?"

Honora hummed the softest laugh he had ever heard. "Never. You were just as amusing and impudent as ever. A most accommodating patient."

"Glad to hear it." He swallowed, his throat feeling raw and scratchy. His aching mind tried to play back what had happened before he'd been in bed so long.

His heart jolted into his throat. "Charlie," he rasped. Clearing his throat, he tried again. "Charlie. Did he make it?"

Honora nodded, sitting up in her chair. "Shh. He did. You took most of the force with the rock fall. He has a broken arm, a few broken ribs, but he'll be fine."

Relaxing, Gage nodded, closing his eyes for a moment as he let his head stop ringing. "What time is it?"

"Early," she replied without looking at the window or a clock.

He nodded at this, then patted the place beside him. "Then come get some sleep here."

To his surprise, Honora got up from the chair and came over to him. But then she put her hand upon his brow, first her palm, then the back of her hand. "Good. No hint of a fever now. It's been lowering ever since yesterday, but this is the coolest you've been."

Gage looked up at her, her haggard and wan appearance telling him even more from this proximity. "Does that mean you'll let yourself rest now and lie here beside me? There's plenty of space."

Honora shook her head. "I need to change the bedsheets."

"I'd say you didn't, but I have a sense that you know better than I at this moment." He sniffed the air and made a face for show. "So get the help you need, do that, and then, when cleanliness is restored, you're going to lie here beside me while we both rest."

"I'm fine," she insisted.

"Good. Then you'll sleep perfectly well."

His wife gave him a rather exasperated look. "I have a bed of my own, Gage."

He tried to shrug where he lay, but it was difficult. "I know. But you won't sleep there because you'll be too worried about me. So lie here and save us both the trouble."

With a sigh that could have been irritated, longsuffering, or amused, Honora shook her head and began pulling at the sheets above his head, rolling them down. Then she moved to the far side of the room and brought over another set of linens, this one crisply folded. She unfolded it and began rolling it in a peculiar manner he could only watch. Once that was done, she set it at the top of the mattress and began stripping the one beneath him further down, then rolling the clean one down to replace it.

"I think I can move," Gage told her, shifting on the bed.

"No need," she said, putting a hand on his good shoulder. "Stay put."

He looked up at her in surprise. "Don't you need help?"

Her smile was small, but peculiarly confident. "I do not. We've been changing your linens daily, often multiple times, between your fever sweats, the ice, and the blood. I am quite used to this now." She proved this by moving the sheets beneath his pillows without jostling him too much, then replacing it with new linen in much the same manner.

It was a strange thing, having her lift one of his shoulders to move linens down and replace with new, then do the same with the other. Her nimble fingers worked along his entire body with expert motions, maneuvering not only around him, but in spite of him, and replacing the linens all the way down the mattress beneath him. It was as though he were not even in the bed, or that he were some inanimate object that had temporarily taken on consciousness. He didn't even manage embarrassment at being nearly without a stitch of clothing on, given the efficacy and almost complete detachment with which she worked.

No embarrassment from his little timid wife?

What sort of a turn of events was this?

Honora tossed the dirty linen to one side of the room, then picked up another new set, bringing it back over. With one hand, she tugged the quilt from Gage's body, sending it sprawling to the floor. Then she did the same with the top sheet, shocking him by exposing him entirely to the elements, but for the short pair of drawers he was wearing.

He didn't regularly wear these, and he definitely hadn't worn them to the mine.

Someone had put these on him.

That was embarrassing, and he didn't mind feeling that.

Entirely unaware of his emotional and mental state, Honora shook out the new linens and spread them over him, then did the same with a fresh quilt.

"Well," Gage said simply as she moved to replace the linens of his pillows beneath his head, "I feel rather superfluous now."

Honora scoffed quietly. "You've been superfluous for days, but it hasn't stopped me yet."

"Less of the cheek, you," Gage retorted, laughing at the quick jab from his usually sympathetic wife. "I've been unwell."

She stopped, pillow linens in her hands, and looked down at him. "I know. And it has scared me every minute."

Gage's laughter faded, and he took in the state of his wife with new eyes. She had been putting on an act in front of him, perhaps in front of all of them, and now her eyes shone with a new vulnerability that humbled him.

He could see everything in those eyes, suddenly understood far more than words would have allowed. She had exhausted herself to this extreme for him. Had likely been awake for unhealthy lengths of time in her efforts. Had stayed in this room with him, even when she slept, to care for him. Not because she was good, not because she was generous, not because she was selfless, but because she had been afraid of losing him. Because she was determined to keep him here and see him well again. Because she was his wife.

Because she cared that much.

He had never seen anything more beautiful than the drawn, weary, too-thin woman with messy hair and stained clothing before him in that moment. And he never would again.

He raised his right hand from the bed and held it out to her. "Come here, Honora. Come rest with me."

He saw her swallow, but she didn't move.

"Honora," he said again, as gently as he could, "you've done enough. Come here. Please."

She exhaled, and he could almost feel the weight of that breath. She dropped the pillow linens and climbed onto the bed, lying beside him and staring up at the ceiling.

Unaccountably emotional, and a trifle amused, Gage nudged her up with his hand. "I know for a fact you don't sleep like that, Honora. Come here."

He heard the faint giggle and swallowed a lump in his throat when she turned towards him, bringing her knees up a touch. "I don't want to hurt you," she whispered.

Gage moved the quilt to cover Honora as well, then slid over to allow her more space, pleased to not feel a single twinge of pain anywhere in his body. "You'd have to do a lot more than jab your knee into my thigh for me to even feel it." He slid his right arm beneath her, pulling her closer to his side and wrapping around her. "There, that's better. More comfortable for both of us."

"You don't have to do this, Gage," Honora murmured, the breath of each word rapping against the skin of his chest like waves on the shore.

There was a ticklish sensitivity to that, and he enjoyed it immensely.

"I am well aware," he told her, testing his bad arm by twisting it along his side. "But this is my good arm, so I might as well keep it in use."

Honora tucked her face into his shoulder, her laughter against his skin a tonic to his soul. "That isn't what I mean."

"I know, Honora," Gage told her, sighing a suddenly fatigued breath. "But I am much too tired now to explain more. And so are you. So why don't we just sleep for a while and take up this discussion again later?"

"Fine," she said on a yawn. "But will you do me a favor?"

Gage began rubbing her shoulder and back gently, almost absently, and very naturally. "If I can from this bed, yes."

Honora brought a hand tentatively up and laid it across his chest, resting her palm over his heart.

He might actually die in this bed now, he thought with the fastest speed yet. The connection was so pure, so powerful, so perfect... it was bound to kill him, he was sure of it.

"Will you call me Nora from now on?" she asked him in the smallest voice known to man.

Gage blinked amidst the turmoil her hand on his heart was causing and tried to look down at her, but she kept her face averted from his. "Nora? Why?"

"You don't remember?"

He shook his head, looking up at the canopy above them. "I don't remember much of anything right now."

"You've been calling me Nora for days," she told him. "Probably actually saying my name, but too fatigued or unwell to manage the whole thing. I've gotten used to being Nora to you. And I like it."

Gage grinned, though she wouldn't see it. "Are you actually telling me something you want?"

If she could feel how his heart pounded beneath her hand, she gave no sign. "Yes. It would seem I am."

He closed his eyes, a thrill of victory rippling through his entire body in a way she was certain to notice.

"Then yes, Nora," Gage said simply, turning to kiss the top of her head and pull her even closer. "I'll call you whatever you like. But only if it's just for me."

"Of course it's just for you," she said on another yawn, snuggling up against him. "Who else would I dare let be so familiar?"

Gage smiled at that. "She says as she curled up against a half-dressed man in bed."

"Only because he's my husband," Honora murmured sleepily. "And remarkably comfortable."

There was no need to respond to that, given that Honora was already more asleep than Gage could have predicted. That alone told the story of her care of him, the dedication with which she had tended to him, the sacrifices she'd made, the limits to which she had gone…

She was an incredible being, his wife, and he had only begun to know that.

Amazingly, lying there with her beside him, he found he was not as sleepy as he had thought. His head still felt as though it would explode, most likely through the front, and the actual processing of thought was a series of challenges that seemed rather stupid.

He felt rather exceptionally stupid, actually, for not even being able to think without trouble.

But with Honora beside him, it did not matter. That alone was enough to make things right. He might be stupid, which was hopefully a temporary state, and his head might explode, but this woman was beside him, fit perfectly against him, and fought tooth and nail to keep him safe, healthy, and even alive, if his life had been in jeopardy. She was exhausted, and he would need to spend the rest of his life making himself worth her efforts.

The door to his room opened, and Emblyn entered, looking confused at the empty chair. Her attention moved to the bed, and her brows shot up when she saw Gage looking back at her, and Honora beside him.

Gage raised his bad hand to wave her over very slightly.

Just as Honora had done, Emblyn touched his brow with the palm of her hand, then the back. "Ee be back to normal, then."

"I don't know about that," Gage murmured. "My head feels as though it might burst at any second."

"Ee were cracked mighty hard, they said," Emblyn replied with a shrug. "But so long as ee be free of fever, ee'll not be in much danger, Dr. Waite says."

Gage frowned, which hurt. "Dr. Waite. Do I know him?"

Emblyn's crooked smile appeared. "Nay, 'e be my brother's physician. But 'e ought to be yer closest friend, Gage, for all 'e be doin' fer ee."

"I will invite him to Christmas forthwith," Gage said easily. He glanced at the sleeping Honora, then back at Emblyn. "Tell me true, Em. My wife is dead on her feet, isn't she?"

"Honora," Emblyn said pointedly, raising a brow at him, "hasn't slept more'n an hour at a time, refuses to step away from yer care, and is all but starving herself. So if ee be quite through with fevers and the like, I'd be pleased to tend to the care of yer wife while yer head heals."

Gage chuckled and took her hand. "Please do. Please, please do. Until I am fit and able, I will need you and anyone else who is willing to take care of her the way she has taken care of me."

"Ee be more fortunate than ee know, Gage," Emblyn told him,

sitting on the bed, still letting him hold her hand. "Honora be a strong and fitty woman, though she be the size of a mite. I be in here tending yer wounds, and she be sitting beside ee jus' to sing to ee."

"Sing to me?" he repeated. "Why? Whatever for?"

Emblyn gave him a knowing look. "Ee asked her to. Often. Do ee not remember?"

"No," he breathed, shaking his head, even though it hurt to do so. "I don't remember that at all." He looked down at his sleeping wife, his fingers tracing up and down her arm still. "And yet... There is something about singing that remains in my mind. I can't explain it. I don't remember her singing, and somehow, I know she did."

"She learned a song for ee," Emblyn told him. "Sommat ee requested, she said. Some Irish tune yer mother used to sing."

"She did?" He kissed Honora's brow very softly, taking a moment to simply breathe against her. "She learned '*Mo Ghile Mear*' just to sing it for me. Em, have I actually married an angel?"

"Most like," came the easy quip. "I'd ne'er have done that."

Gage glanced over at her, grinning. "Believe me, I know. But I thank you for being here all the same. You're a good heart and a better soul."

"I'm a scamp and lowborn, so I be fitty to dirty my hands and scrub the sick," Emblyn said bluntly, just as averse as ever to accept praise. "But as I hate ee less than mos' folk, I mind a mite less."

"Refreshing as ever, imp," he said with a sigh. "Do you know of any remedies for the injured head that the estimable Dr. Waite might be unaware of, with all his book learning?"

Emblyn creased her brow in thought. "Naught I can call up quick like. Ma always said a body could do worse than sea air for what ails, but she'd no learnin'."

"I'm inclined to believe your mother where possible," Gage told her. "If you wouldn't mind asking around on the subject, I'll take any help. And if I forget we had this conversation, just remind me."

"I think ee might be beyond the forgettin' naw, Gage," Emblyn replied with a smile. "Ee already be better than when we last spoke."

Gage groaned, shutting his eyes. "Have we already had this conversation?"

"Nay, ee simply ain't asking me the same thing on end as afore."

She patted his hand, and he opened his eyes to see her rise. "Ee be stubborn enough to heal quick like. Get some proper rest, and ee'll be fitty right enough."

"Thank you, Em," he said as a yawn took him over. "I owe you."

"Aye, so ee do, and I'll see ee pay."

Gage nodded as he leaned his head against Honora's. "Good. Someone should hold me accountable." He inhaled deeply, then settled in with a sigh, letting his eyes close and the fatigue of his body seep into his mind as well.

Chapter Sixteen

"Would you sit down before you break something?"

It wasn't like Honora to screech under normal circumstances, but Gage was driving her to such extremes with such success, it was as though he intended to see her go mad.

He was really very good at it.

Gage looked at her with some amusement, though there was some strain in his features. "I have not broken anything yet, either in the house or on my person."

"Not for want of trying," she grumbled, going to his side and taking his arm as he made his way towards the door of his bedchamber, through which she had just entered. "You know you are not steady on your feet, and yet you still insist on trying."

"I am tired of being in bed constantly, Nora," he complained, doing his best not to lean on her. "The room might spin when I walk, but it spins less every single day. The more I am up, the faster I will recover."

"Unless," she told him as patiently as possible, "you overdo it and set yourself back in recovery. As Dr. Waite has said."

They'd had this conversation every day since he had first truly regained his health and some of his mental capacity. His health was almost fully restored, apart from his fatigue and well-healing wounds, but his head was another matter. He had to change positions slowly, be that moving from lying down to sitting up, sitting to standing, or standing to any other position. He walked slowly, as motion made him dizzy, and his ability to comprehend was diminished. He remembered poorly, had constant headaches, and got irritated rather quickly, all of which made him more frustrated than any human being alive.

Or so he claimed.

Honora was inclined to believe him, as he was very open with her about how and what he was feeling at any given time. She had asked him to be so, as she could not tell anything about his state of her own accord until it boiled over. There was an incredibly rewarding sense of being someone he trusted when he shared these more vulnerable thoughts and feelings with her, when he allowed himself to appear less than immortal or impervious. When he felt safe enough to express weakness.

He did not expect people to think him perfect, he was not nearly so arrogant. But Honora did very firmly believe that he tried very hard not to display obvious faults or weaknesses.

And this would certainly be something he would want to hide, even if it was temporary.

Being cooped up did not sit well with Gage, and the fact that he could not deny his need to restrain himself from activity sat even less well.

There was very little Honora could do but listen, console, and entertain, when he would let her. That and insist he rest when it was clear he had done too much.

But seeing him frustrated and upset was not sitting well with her either.

She sighed as they made their way out into the hall. "I will make you a compromise," she said slowly, knowing she needed to choose her words carefully, for he would take them at face value and head for the hills with them.

"I'm listening," he replied with interest, not looking at her, as he was keeping his focus wholly on the space before him.

"If we can get you downstairs to the drawing room, without incident, and you rest in there for the remainder of the morning, I will take you to walk along Polmiskin Beach in the afternoon." She looked up at him with some confidence, feeling certain there was no way he could weasel his way out of that arrangement.

Gage seemed to straighten as he walked, his fingers trailing the wall beside him rather than gripping on to it. "That seems manageable. How do you intend to get us to the beach? I hardly think I can ride a horse as yet."

Honora smiled at his admission. "Why, a carriage or wagon to the path, of course. And then we will walk down ourselves. It's an incline, so your head in this present state ought to feel quite at home with that."

Now he did look at her, trying to scowl in spite of his smile. "That is a low blow, Nora. Especially for you."

"Somebody has to tease you," she quipped with a shrug. "It might as well be me."

He tugged at her arm and pulled her to him, kissing her hard and effectively silencing her giggles. It was a quick kiss, but particularly emphatic, and that, she had to say, took her by surprise.

"There," Gage said triumphantly, tapping her warming cheek. "Now we're even."

He started to walk again, cautiously, and Honora cleared her throat as she hurried a step or two to hold his elbow.

"Any more flowers come in?" he asked mildly, as though he hadn't just kissed the actual breath out of her lungs.

Honora swallowed with some difficulty at the memory. "Seeking more admirers, are we, darling?"

"Always, my dear. So?" He raised a questioning brow, even as his focus remained ahead of them.

"As I understand it," Honora told him, shaking her head, "there have been flowers sent from Lord DeDunstaville, from the Grangers, from the Rowes, and from the Teagues. Oh, and a separate bunch from Lady Hastings."

Gage grunted softly. "Any messages?"

"From her?"

"From any of them."

Honora dipped her chin, hoping he would overlook her suggestion. "Lord DeDunstaville sends good wishes, and the Grangers said they owe you a basket? I am not sure what they mean by that."

Gage made a choking sort of a laugh but did not elaborate.

Biting her lip, Honora added, "And Lady Hastings asked if she might call when you are well enough."

"Did she?" he muttered. "Hmm."

She forced herself to say nothing at all and continued on their slow path to the stairs.

Only when they reached them did Gage look at her, his dark gaze all too knowing. "You don't like her," he said, no hint of a question in his voice.

"Don't be silly," Honora evaded. "I don't know her well enough to not like her."

"You don't want to like her."

She looked down. "Can you blame me?"

Gage reached out and took her chin gently, raising her eyes to his. "I don't blame you," he told her in a low voice, his finger brushing the underside of her jaw as always. "How could I? But let me assure you: There is no danger from her. You are my wife, and you have my loyalty and fidelity. There is nothing to fear, I think, on either part, but I know certainly from mine."

"Why did she come back?" Honora whispered, her eyes fixed on his with some unspeakable grip that had nothing to do with his hold on her chin and everything to do with his hold on her heart.

"I only know what she told me at the Basset ball," Gage murmured, cupping her cheek now. "It is the only time I have seen her. She said she was making happier memories for her boys with her parents, since the loss of Lord Hastings."

Honora nodded, leaning into his hand. "I cannot blame her for that. She was very kind at the modiste when I met her, but I am afraid I was not... sociable. I fear her, even though you say I shouldn't."

"Nora." Gage leaned in and kissed her brow very softly. "Take heart. When I had a choice, I chose you." He leaned back a little, making certain she could see him nod.

When she eventually nodded in return, he turned his attention to the stairs. "Now, I will leave it in your capable hands as to whether or not she may call and when. It makes no difference to me. The same with any other well-wishers, as I am certain there are many, many more in the village and surrounding area. Perhaps when I am at my full strength, you should throw a party for everyone to see just how well I am and to reassure them all of my renewed strength."

Honora had to laugh at the ridiculousness her husband was

currently reveling in, and at the blatant effort on his part to turn her attention away from unpleasantness.

Why couldn't she believe him? Why did she fear Lady Hastings so? Why should the former love of her husband be what haunted her thoughts and her dreams at times? Why did she doubt Gage, who had never given her reason to doubt in anything?

Honora had never been possessive of anything in her entire life, but suddenly she was very possessive of her husband. Determined to keep him in her presence whenever possible, obsessed with the sight of him, wanted to bind herself to him in every way, including physically, if it was possible…

It was an overwhelming feeling, her newfound devotion to owning her husband. Not that he was a possession or something she could actually claim, but she wanted, so badly, for him to be hers and hers alone. She would ask for nothing more in her entire life if she could ensure that Gage Trembath would tell the world he was hers. Not in the legal sense, as their marriage had declared, but in the truer sense of the heart.

The soul. The will. The desire.

The choice.

Mostly because Honora knew she was his, and for this love to only extend in one direction would be agony.

Her breath caught in her chest as she carefully made her way down the stairs beside him. Love? Was that certain now? She had never spent a single moment while tending to Gage thinking about how she loved him, or that she loved him, or about love at all. It had been entirely about caring for him and keeping him comfortable and alive, soothing whatever ailed him, making certain he knew he was not alone, needing to touch him for her own sake as well as his.

Heavens above, all of that was love, too.

She loved her husband.

She wasn't supposed to. They had agreed, in a way, that this would not be a marriage of love. Not that there would be actions against love, but not to expect it. She had not expected it, yet now she was standing here, directly beside him, and loving him so much, she hated a woman simply for existing. Loved him so much that she craved anything he could give her, anything in his power. He might never love her, but he had told her that from the beginning. But he treated her well. He had affection for her. He teased her when no one else had ever thought to.

He saw her.

And he kissed her.

Oh, how he kissed her! Every kiss was a rebirth for Honora, and she hadn't even known she had been dying.

How could she have fallen in love with him so fast? They had barely been acquaintances in the past. Naturally, she had thought well of him, as a friend of Julia and John. She had been complimented by him, been made to laugh by him, and of course, she had considered him to be remarkably handsome, but that had been all. His marriage proposal had been the greatest shock of her life, given their limited association.

She had viewed the marriage as something that saved her from the life she had been living up to that point. A freedom from criticism and darkness, a chance to actually enjoy existing, and perhaps a future that was worth looking forward to. She had never actually thought she would fall in love with the man rescuing her from that life and giving her those things. She had been grateful, of course, but what she felt now was certainly not gratitude.

It was devotion, love, and passion.

Was it the prospect of losing him that had driven her to this point so quickly after their marriage? Was it caring for him in his illness and injury? Was it the way he had first kissed her? Had it started from their tender wedding night? Was it possible the seed of love had been planted from the day he proposed?

She knew she had never considered loving him when she had met him. She had been certain her parents would arrange some polite, advantageous marriage for her somehow, but she knew she would never have a voice in it. She had never even looked at a man to consider him for herself, could not have said what she found attractive or what she looked for in a match.

Was this all some naivete on her part? Was she in love with him only because she had never known anything but him? Was it simply because he was here and showing her affection that she was latching on to him? Or was it truly because Gage was who he was, and she was simply fortunate enough to be his wife?

That would not be easy to tease apart, especially for someone as unfamiliar with positive emotion as she was. But she would need to figure that out before she let him in on this new secret of hers. Especially since it happened so quickly. How could she tell Gage that she loved him when she didn't even know what love was?

Poor little Honora, starved of love and now falling all over the man who had married her, all because he treated her nicely. And kissed like he enjoyed it. And made her feel important. And liked to make her blush. And...

She loved him. It was entirely different to what she felt for John, who was always so good and kind to her, or for Lord Basset, who respected her and looked out for her, or for any of the miners who bid her good morning or lightly teased her. It wasn't because he was a man who treated her well.

It was because he was Gage. Because of who he was and how he was. Because of who she was because of him. Gage saw Honora in a way that no one else had ever done. As a woman. As a wife. As a friend.

As a lover, if they ever got there.

That was why she feared losing him so desperately that day. He was the one who had brought meaning and beauty to her life. He was the one who was building her up and embracing her as she grew. He was the one who made her feel things and live her life fully. He was the one who made her want...

Well, the one who made her want.

She had never wanted anything in life before, but now...

What she truly wanted, it turned out, was him.

A wave of yearning rose up within her, from her toes to the coiled and pinned ends of her hair, and she bit her lip as she moved with Gage into the drawing room. Yearning to tell him how her heart was expanding at an alarming rate in her chest, how badly she wanted to kiss him in this moment, how overwhelmed she was by acknowledging that she loved him. Yearning for something she didn't understand. Yearning for a life she couldn't even imagine.

Yearning to apologize for loving him when it would be the last thing he wanted.

"How is your head?" Honora asked as Gage sat in a chair without her assistance, hoping her voice didn't sound as strained as it felt.

"Fine," he told her with a groan, leaning his head back. "It's my eyes that are the problem. They're making the room look like this." He held out his hands on a level with each other, then slanted them somewhat.

Honora smiled and brushed his hair back without thinking. "Always with the humor. Does anything actually rattle you?"

"Almost dying." He sighed as a smile curved one side of his mouth at her touch. "That feels nice."

She combed her fingers through his hair, leaning against the chair slightly. "I know. You told me a few times. It seemed to calm you."

"I wish I remembered that," he murmured. "You taking care of me. Singing to me. This. I wish I remembered any of it."

"Why? What good would it do?"

He opened his eyes and looked up at her, still smiling. "Because knowing about it isn't the same as experiencing it. I feel like I've lost something without knowing how important it was until now."

It was the most adorable thing she'd ever heard, and she tilted her head as her fingers continued her pattern. "I'm not going anywhere, and I am quite certain you would do the same."

"You'd let me run my fingers through your hair?" he pressed with a teasing brow. "Like you're doing now?"

"Any time," Honora told him, the raw honesty doing a fair bit to lessen the tension her emotions were creating in her chest. "You don't even have to ask."

It was a testament to how tired Gage was that he only smiled further and took her free hand, kissed the back, and closed his eyes once more to rest.

Honora took a few moments to enjoy showing her love to her husband in the only way she could as yet, then left the room when it was clear he was sleeping. She had promised that if he stayed in the room without trouble, she would take him to the beach, which sounded like a promise made to an unruly child, when she thought about it.

But it would do for now.

She walked to her parlor and sat down at her desk, putting her head in her hands for a moment. She didn't know whether to laugh or cry, but she was exhausted. Even now, knowing Gage was out of danger, she wasn't sleeping much. There was too much to consider, too much to feel, too many memories of the mine disaster for her to be confident that she wouldn't wake up to her husband dead or gone in some way, and all of her memories of caring for him some strange delusion or dream.

And now she loved him, on top of everything else.

Fear and love were ravaging her, and she didn't know what to do about it.

"Madam, can I get you anything?"

Honora looked up at the entrance to her parlor, smile in place for her housekeeper. "No, Mrs. Crane. Thank you, but I am fine."

The woman gave her as much of a scolding look as Honora had ever received from her mother. Only this one held no spite to it. "You are exhausted, madam. And it is no wonder, tending to Mr. Gage the way you have."

"Some tea, then," Honora allowed, sitting up and folding her hands in her lap. "I daresay I could use it."

Mrs. Crane's expression turned rather thoughtful, and she indicated a spare chair in the room. "May I, madam?"

Surprised, she nodded. "Of course."

Mrs. Crane brought the chair over and sat in it, exhaling a moment. "I have worked for the Trembath family since before Mr. Gage was born. His parents were loving and good, with each other and with others. They struggled for years to have more children, but none came. That was why he was so close with his friends. They were the siblings he never had. He had his Irish cousins, but when his mother died, it was more difficult for any of them to come to Cornwall."

"Cousins?" Honora repeated. "He never said. Well, he's never talked about his family. I've never asked. Why haven't I asked?"

Mrs. Crane reached out and put a hand on hers. "Madam, you had no reason to, and I do not tell you for guilt or shame. Only for context. Mr. Gage once knew a great deal about family and love and connections, and it has been years since I have seen that light in him again."

Honora exhaled, feeling her cheeks heat. "Since he lost Margaret."

"Lady Hastings?" Mrs. Crane sputtered and scoffed, waving that off. "She barely looked at him, no matter how he pined like a puppy. He was practically a child, and he sought the love he had seen in his parents. The love that had his father unable to visit Ireland once Mr. Gage's mother died, for the pain of her memory. Because of that, however, Gage did not spend another Christmas in Ireland with his cousins."

"It sounds like a loving family, Mrs. Crane," Honora murmured, shaking her head. "Something I've never known. My cousin Julia's family loved me more than any of my siblings or parents, but I was rarely permitted to visit, so I have no such memories."

Mrs. Crane patted her hands. "That is why I am telling you this, madam. You are Mr. Gage's family now, and the way he looks at you... Madam, I have never seen him look at anyone that way."

Honora smiled softly. "I am his family now. It makes sense. Family has always been important to him. Gage must have missed his cousins dreadfully when the visits stopped."

"I am certain he did," Mrs. Crane said, her brow creasing slightly. "But that isn't what I—"

"Did you say Christmas was spent in Ireland?" Honora overrode, an idea beginning to form in her mind.

Mrs. Crane nodded. "Every year. The Irish cousins would visit in the summer, and the Trembaths would go to Ireland for Christmas."

Honora bit her lip, nodding slowly. "Gage said his mother used to sing '*Mo Ghile Mear.*' He asked me to sing it when he was first unwell. Do his cousins sing as well? I trust you've heard him sing."

"Oh heavens, yes," Mrs. Crane confirmed, sitting back in her chair. "There was always music when the family got together. And the late Mr. Trembath had no family himself, so he adopted those cousins as though they were his own children. Even though he never saw them again, I know for a fact that he sent them money often."

"Are they poor?"

Mrs. Crane grimaced. "Not technically, I suppose. But they are Catholic, which, in Ireland, means they might as well be poor."

Honora shook her head sadly. "That is cruel." She looked at her desk a moment, her fingers tapping on the surface. "Mrs. Crane, when is Gage's birthday?"

"The twenty-ninth of November," she recited. "Why do you ask?"

A rather sly smile started across Honora's lips, which was a bizarre sensation. "Mrs. Crane, I think we may have a party to plan."

Chapter Seventeen

"Lady Hastings to see you, sir."

Gage lowered his news sheet in surprise, blinking at his butler. "Murray, did I hear that right? Did you say...?"

"Lady Hastings, sir," he said firmly, his eyes taking on a knowing look. "Yes."

Gage hissed through his teeth. "Where's Honora?"

"Coming, sir. As is Miss Moyle."

"Did she call in the entire village?" Gage shook his head, sitting up, wincing at the sudden shift in his position and what it did to his head. "Why is Emblyn coming?"

"As I understand it, Miss Moyle is leaving, but wishes to pay her respects to Lady Hastings." Murray clasped his hands behind his back. "If I may say, sir, that would be a mark of good breeding, which shows that Miss Moyle is learning."

Gage frowned at his butler, who knew entirely too much and expressed even more. "Thank you, Murray. Send Lady Hastings in, at her leisure."

Murray nodded and retreated from the library, leaving him alone again.

He pinched the bridge of his nose, wishing he had actually managed to read the news sheet without his head throbbing. It was a ridiculous thing, this injury to his head. He could now walk without too much jostling in his vision, but reading was still troublesome. Dr. Waite thought he would be back to full activity within the month, which was encouraging, but every day felt like a trial.

He felt trapped in Helwithin. Hemmed in by his own physical

restrictions. Limited by his inability to think, to move, to even function as a human being. Physically, his body was well. But his head...

It was the most aggravating situation he had ever been in. All he wanted to do was live, and these days, he felt like he was slowly dying more than anything else.

The only respite he had from the frustrations was when he and Honora walked Polmiskin Beach. They had begun doing so every day since he had been able to walk without much trouble, and now had reached the point of walking to the beach instead of being driven to it. He wasn't quite up to riding a horse yet, but he would start trying that next week, no matter what. His wounds were healing perfectly, without any lingering effects, as far as he could tell.

The beach represented freedom. Life. Vigor. Beauty. Everything he wanted to appreciate and couldn't at the moment. And Honora never said a word while they were there unless he spoke first. She was the gentlest, sweetest creature he had ever met, and she was keeping him from full insanity and rage. She never pressed him, never complained when he snapped, never did anything but treat him with kindness, with teasing, and with affection.

He'd have called it love, if he thought it possible. She was capable of great love, given her generous heart and spirit, and he knew that their children would be the most fortunate children on earth. And he, by all accounts, would be the most fortunate man.

Was the most fortunate man.

Someday, he'd tell her that. He'd give her something that testified to that. He'd spend a night just holding her in his arms. Not for love, but for comfort. For affection. For sheer appreciation and feeling ashamed that he'd ever thought her ordinary.

Once his head stopped hurting every day, he'd do all sorts of things with her and for her.

"Ee look like hell, Gage."

He looked up at the doorway, scowling. "That's not very nice, Em."

Emblyn shrugged and came in alone. "I be honest, Gage, not nice. Where's Lady Hastings?"

"Here," a more pristine, crisp voice answered.

Margaret entered the room, emphasizing her fortune versus Emblyn's lack thereof by the manner of her dress alone. A shimmering, silky mauve gown beneath a sleek, dark pelisse that nipped in neatly at her waist. Her bonnet was gone, leaving her dark blonde hair uncovered in its perfectly set coif, ringlets by her ears.

She looked far more refined than the young Margaret he had known. But, of course, now she was Lady Hastings.

Gage rose, smiling tightly when his head only vaguely ached. "Lady Hastings. You know Miss Moyle?"

Margaret smiled at Emblyn as she patted the back of her hair. "We have met, yes. It is lovely to see you again, Miss Moyle. My word, your eyes are extraordinary. How did Basset never get those?"

Emblyn raised a brow, her pale green gown of a coarser fabric highlighting her extraordinary eyes perfectly. "Different mothers, my lady. Plain and simple."

It took everything Gage had not to laugh at the statement, but that was quite simply Emblyn's way. He cleared his throat instead. "Emblyn, where's Honora? Didn't she come down with you?"

"Aye," Emblyn told him, flicking her eyes in his direction. "She be fetching a shawl she be sending with me. Fer Mrs. Spargo."

Gage smiled fondly, not entirely sure why his wife was getting a shawl for Nellie, but knowing it was entirely Honora's way to do so. "Of course she is."

"I be out of good reading," Emblyn told him, gesturing to the books behind him. "Can I borrow one o' yourn?"

"Of course." He waved at the shelves and moved to a set of chairs closer to the door, indicating that Margaret take one. "Lady Hastings, if you like."

"You didn't have to get up," Margaret told him, her smile warm, her brow wrinkled in concern. "I know you've not been well."

"I'm fine," Gage assured her, sitting when she did. "Just waiting for my head to finish healing. Everything else is fine."

Margaret gave him a look. "Gage, I know you. Your arm could be hanging off and you'd tell everyone you were fine, even if you were in agony."

She was calling him by his given name already? That was an interesting twist. Had he missed something else while he was incapacitated?

Her eyes widened at her blunder, and she lowered them quickly. "Sorry. Old habits. I never stopped thinking of you that way, so when I heard what had happened…"

"Lady Hastings…" Gage warned, looking towards Emblyn, who was intent on the books on the shelves.

"No, that's not what I mean." She turned towards him, her expression serious. "I never explained to you why I accepted Lord Hastings when he proposed. Even when you demanded it, I couldn't tell you. I didn't understand it then, but I do now."

Gage shook his head, more uncomfortable than his head had ever made him. "I don't need to hear this, my lady. It doesn't matter anymore."

"It does," she insisted loudly. She swallowed, looked down at her nails, then said again, "It does. Please, let me explain."

It was a bad idea for this to be taking place without his wife present, but he couldn't very well ask her to wait for her. Besides, Honora didn't understand how far back and how deep their connection had been. She might read something into this that ought not to be.

"Fine," Gage said softly, looking at her quickly. "But I don't need to hear it for my part. Just so you know."

She nodded and cleared her throat. "We were children together, Gage. You, me, Harrison, Julia… We were family. And when we got older… Gage, I didn't know what I wanted until Lord Hastings proposed. I felt something with him that I realized I had never felt with you. It was… exciting. New. A future I had never thought about."

"What was wrong with the future we had thought about?" Gage asked before he could stop himself. He winced, wishing the pang of irritation hadn't lashed across his tongue. How could he still be mad about something that no longer mattered?

"Nothing!" Margaret insisted. "I just didn't think there was another option, and when there was… Gage, you deserved someone who actually wanted to be with you, not somebody who just went along with it. I loved you, but not in the way you wanted me to. I didn't know there was a difference until I married Hastings."

There was a strange sensation taking place inside of Gage at this moment, and he was fairly certain it had nothing to do with his head. He felt… relief. A release. An understanding he never thought he would find, and the bizarre desire to laugh.

Laugh. In the presence of Margaret, Lady Hastings.

Because he didn't care that she hadn't married him. Not anymore.

And he understood exactly what she meant by not knowing something existed until it found her.

He was experiencing the same thing. Not love, per se. Not yet, but it could certainly lead there. He hadn't thought he could feel anything remotely like love again, but now…

Now there was a chance.

"Why are you here, Margaret?" Gage asked, smiling far more easily than he had in some time. "I am not dying. Never was. What do you really want?"

"Not what they're gossiping about, that's for certain," she retorted with a soft snort, looking more relaxed now. "I wanted to get back the friend that I lost and make up for the cruelty I put you through. But I have no interest in you romantically, Gage. Not anymore. I hope that doesn't offend."

He shook his head, grinning at her now. "Not even a little. I've held a grudge for far too long, and I apologize for that."

Margaret shrugged. "It is understandable. I broke your heart. Believe me, I had plenty of letters on the subject. I know what I did, and I apologize for that."

Looking at this woman now, seeing her as she was, feeling as Gage was, he no longer saw the woman who had captivated his heart, mind, and dreams for so long. He saw the girl he had grown up with, ran among the hills, moors, and cliffs with, hid in portions of abandoned mines with. He saw the pseudo-sister he had known for so long, the one who had laughed with his cousins on their visits, the one who had cried as hard as he did when his mother had died.

He'd always seen a future with her, but perhaps he hadn't allowed for alternative roles for her than wife. Perhaps she would always be a part of his life, but not in the way he had originally planned. Just as the childhood friend he had once known, and the fond memories that would always remain.

He need not always hate her. Need not hold himself aloof from feelings. Need not be held back by the resentment that had served nothing except to keep him from living.

He needed to embrace his life, especially now that he could really appreciate how precious it was. He could have died in that mine. Probably should have.

But he was here now, and he wanted to live.

Provided his head would let him.

"Besides," Margaret said, lowering her voice as Emblyn pulled a book from the shelf, "your wife is utterly adorable. Even if I did have intentions towards you, I am fairly certain I would be cursed for even thinking it."

Gage laughed and leaned his head back, his newfound freedom making him almost giddy. "That she is. It's supposed to be a marriage of convenience, but…"

Margaret laughed and put a hand on his arm. "Oh, dear. You know exactly what I was talking about, don't you?"

"Possibly," Gage hedged with a drumming of his fingers on the arms of his chair. "Too early to tell. But dash it, Margaret… I want to."

Before she could say anything else, Honora entered the room, shawl in hand. "Oh!" she gasped, eyes wide. "I am so sorry, my lady. I should have come in more haste!"

"No!" Margaret jumped to her feet, hands extended. "My dear Honora, you have certainly had enough to contend with on your own! I am only grateful you allowed me to visit. I tended Lord Hastings when he was unwell towards the end, so I know how exhausting it can be."

Honora smiled, though Gage still saw strain in her features. "I am so sorry for your loss. Your sons must be devastated."

"They are," Margaret said softly. "Hastings was a little older than one might have expected, but he was a devoted father to our boys, and a loving husband to me. I am only grateful we had the time with him we did before he slipped away."

Gage heard the emotion in her voice and lowered his head in respect for a moment.

He heard footsteps and glanced up to see Honora crossing over to Margaret and taking her hands, squeezing tightly. "Please forgive me, Lady Hastings. I should never have been so insensitive. Of course you miss him just as much. I made unjust assumptions, and I never should have."

She laughed softly. "Oh, Honora, please call me Margaret. And you have nothing to be forgiven for. I have made my peace with my husband's death and am only thinking of my sons now. Which brings me to one reason for coming." She looked at Gage again, then at Honora. "Would either of you mind if I brought them to Polmiskin Beach? I want to show it to them and let them swim in the waves."

"I don't mind," Gage said. "Honora?"

"Of course," she told Margaret firmly. "You are always welcome."

Always? That was an interesting change to the last conversation they'd had about Margaret. Honora was intimidated by the woman, there was no mistaking it, and possibly felt uncomfortable in her presence due to the past she had shared with Gage. And he suspected that she feared he would be susceptible to the temptation of a former love returned. That he would betray his vows and live the life of a rake, if a married one.

Given the example her parents had set for her, Gage could understand why she would think so, but he was not her parents. Never would be.

Time would prove it to her. Time and proof of fealty.

But perhaps his words last time had actually gone to some use in soothing her concerns.

"I trust Gage has been an accommodating patient?" Margaret asked Honora, turning to give him a dark look. "Or is he constantly complaining about being cooped up?"

He gaped in mock outrage. "I will have you know that I abide by every rule Honora gives."

Emblyn pointedly cleared her throat, looking at him.

He rolled his eyes. "Wonderful. Someone bring Julia over, and all of you can scold me in harmony."

They all laughed, and Honora gave him a dazzling smile. "He is a perfectly behaved version of himself, all things considered. And very rarely demanding."

There was something about that word that lit up Gage's mind, clearing a couple of cobwebs and kicking some new processing into gear. His lips tingled and his chest burned, and he suddenly wanted nothing more than to be alone with Honora. What in the world was this? She was telling the truth; he hadn't been demanding at all. He...

A fuzzy image began to form. He was looking up through thinly slitted eyes, seeing his wife's beautiful face above him, her fingers in his hair, and he had asked a question. What, he couldn't remember.

Fine, her voice echoed, *but if you get any more demanding, I'll not think you ill at all.*

Then she closed the distance between them and kissed him, gently and sweetly, and he had never felt more loved in his entire life.

Never.

Gage stared at his wife now, hoping his face did not show the shock that was scouring his soul inside and out. He might not remember much from his time abed, but he remembered that faint moment and feeling that hope she had given him. That love. That sweetness. That anchor to cling to.

She had pulled him through all of that, either by word or by deed, and he had known that, logically, but now he knew it. Felt it. Would swear by it on pain of death, damnation, or any other cruel fate.

Would he ever be a good enough man for the woman he had married? Would he ever hope to make her happy in the way she deserved? She did everything with her whole heart, and he hadn't even managed to really open his to her.

"How often does he just stare off like that?"

Gage blinked and shook his head, which didn't hurt. He looked at Honora and Margaret, then at Emblyn, who was coming over, book in hand, a wry smile on her face.

"What?" he asked, casting his attention among all three.

"Ee be off with the pixies, Gage," Emblyn said with a laugh. "Happens a'times with a knock on the head."

He grimaced. "Do I do it often?"

Emblyn shrugged her slender shoulders. "Ee be gettin' better." She came over and patted his cheek, but sharply, like a sister. "Ee don't have many smarts to restore, Gage. Shouldna be much longer."

He swatted at her arm, but she dodged out of the way, laughing. "You can go home now, imp," he said with a warning finger.

"I'll go with her," Margaret laughed. "If I were to send round an invitation for dinner at Chyandour, would you accept?"

Gage knew how he would answer but looked at Honora first. He had to.

"Of course," she said firmly. "We would be delighted." She winked at Gage. "He hasn't tried riding yet, and a carriage isn't comfortable, but I have a feeling he'll work on that."

She was winking at him now? Who was she and what had she done with his timid little wife?

He grinned at her, slowly, and as he hoped, her cheeks began to turn a particular shade of pink he was rather fond of.

Someday, he was going to do something about that blush.

In the meantime, he wanted to go to the beach. With his wife.

"I'll show you out," Honora said to Margaret and Emblyn, gesturing for the door. She started out after them, then popped her head back in the doorway and looked at Gage. "Polmiskin?"

"Please," he replied with a smile, delighted that she would know his mind so well.

Her smile in return told him exactly how she felt about the idea as well.

Was every marriage this delightful? Or was he just exceptionally fortunate?

It was only a few more minutes before they were walking away from Helwithin arm in arm, the autumn Cornish wind whipping at Honora's skirts and hair marvelously. She could have been a wildflower in the breeze, only made stronger and more beautiful for the harshness of the situation and surroundings. Appearing delicate to the untrained, but bearing roots that no one could get at.

No one would know what this flower could endure without losing a hint of bloom.

Honora sighed as she looked up at the cover of clouds above them. "Do you ever wish that you could fly? Soar above the clouds and see what they look like from such a view? Or what the sky looks like above the clouds?"

"No," Gage said slowly, the imagery of her statement taking him

189

by surprise. "I am afraid not. It has never occurred to me that I ought to wish for that."

His wife hummed a soft laugh. "I don't know that anyone ought to. But I do wonder what the sunrise is like above the clouds…"

He stared at her, trying to picture what she was wondering. "How curious your mind is, Nora. What do you think it looks like?"

"I don't think…"

"What do you imagine, then?" Gage pressed, enchanted by the childlike curiosity from someone who had never been permitted to be a child. "You cannot tell me you have not imagined it."

Her lips formed an almost dreamy smile, the breeze drawing a long tendril of her hair over her brow. "I imagine it is rather like a sunrise we might see, only grander. The sky is dark until a point begins to grow blue instead of black. It goes brighter and brighter, turns slightly green while the rest of the sky ripples into shades of blue. Then green becomes yellow, orange, then red. Even pink, and all of these colors reflect off the surface of the clouds hiding the rainbow from our vision. New colors are created in the reflections, beams of light going this way and that… Can you imagine what we miss when the clouds are in the way?"

Gage could honestly say he had never imagined anything of the sort. Truth be told, he had never seen a sunrise from start to finish, only portions of it from time to time. What Honora was describing spoke of experience in seeing such things, and then expanding them with a brilliance of imagination that he would never have suspected. Not only of her, but of any mind at all.

He had never met an artist, a poet, or a composer, but surely they must have a mind that could create visions such as this.

He shook his head, the path before him almost entirely ignored. "What an exquisite artist of the mind you are. How do you ever accomplish anything with such glorious visions to occupy your thoughts?"

Honora nudged him gently. "Not that glorious. I'm certain other people think such things."

"I am equally as certain that you are wrong," Gage assured her. "I know many, many people, and no one has ever described anything imaginary so beautifully." He took her hand from his arm and brought it to his lips for a moment before holding it to his jaw, stopping to peer out over the sea. "How many sunrises have you seen, Nora? I mean, really seen."

Her fingers brushed against his skin instinctively, rather like the motion of her fingers through his hair. "Four? Five? I don't know when I first did it, but I remember crying and not being able to sleep. Before I knew it, I was staring out of my window and watching the most extraordinary thing."

Gage shook his head and drew Honora into his arms, resting his head on hers. "I don't like the thought of you crying alone in your bedroom. Not at any age. Not under any conditions."

Honora wrapped her arms loosely about his waist. "Everybody cries, Gage. Tears happen, tears fall. They are not an evil."

"Your tears are an evil to me," he murmured. "Anything that hurts you is."

"I cried over you," she pointed out, leaning into him. "I cried several times while you were unwell."

He pressed his mouth against her hair, exhaling slowly. "Don't tell me that. It makes me feel worse."

"Stop." Honora looked up at him with a quizzical look. "You didn't blast the mine yourself. You didn't collapse the tunnel on your own head. You didn't give yourself a raging fever. You didn't scare me half to death on purpose."

"But I made you cry." He brushed the tendrils of hair from her face, traced the path a tear might have taken down her cheek, then cradled her face in one hand. "I promised you a marriage of many things, Nora. I didn't know what I was getting into. I didn't know what a wonder you are, or what a treasure I was gaining."

"Stop," she whispered softly, shaking her head.

He held her steady, his eyes locked on hers. "I didn't know," he continued, "that you would bring me back to life."

"The d-doctor did that," Honora insisted, her eyes widening. "I just did what I could."

"I'm not talking about taking care of me," Gage said, his thumb moving to gently touch her bottom lip, pulling it down ever so slightly. "I am talking about you. And what you do to me. For me. With me. You, Nora. I didn't know how much I was missing by pretending to be dead inside. I did not expect to start living again, and I certainly did not expect to love being alive."

Her breath rushed past his thumb, the light in her eyes something ethereal and captivating, drawing him in. He kissed her slowly, surely, lingering and showering as much adoration on her as the moment would allow, treasuring her sweet response to his attentions. She kissed the way she did everything else—with her whole heart and soul—and it was enough to weaken a man to his very core. Not to mention remove all feeling in his right knee.

He let her lips fall from his, a gentle parting more than a cessation, and nuzzled gently against her lips, her nose, her brow…

Honora's breathing was a shade below ragged, and Gage couldn't blame her.

He felt as though he had been doused in fire, and yet was unharmed.

"I want to know everything about you, Nora," he told her as his lips dusted across her brow. "Every single thing. It will take years and years and years. I hope you're prepared."

She laughed once, very breathlessly. "So long as you do the same and let me know you."

Gage chuckled and gave her a quicker, more emphatic kiss. "Done. But once you know my secrets, you'll have to keep them."

"I don't think that'll be a problem." She pulled back, grinning at him. "Julia already knows your secrets, and she's the only one I'd tell."

He made a rather impressed face, and looped her arm through his again, starting along the path from the cliff to the beach. "She's going to be confined imminently, yes? It might be a good time for you to find out what she knows and relay that back to me. It would be good to correct any misapprehensions she may give you now instead of waiting…"

Chapter Eighteen

The butterflies in her stomach were raging to such an extent, she thought for certain she would lose any portion of her meal she put in her mouth.

Honora knew that wasn't strictly true, but she could not deny that was the distinct impression she was getting.

She had been preparing for this night for weeks and weeks, keeping it from Gage as though her life depended on it. He was finally recovered in every way, much to his delight, and he wanted to do everything and anything available to him. It was all she could do to rein him in even a little.

She didn't really need him to be reined in, but she needed tonight to be a full celebration of his life and its renewal, not simply a birthday supper.

He knew they were having friends for the meal.

He had no idea about anything else.

If she lived through this night, Honora would consider herself fortunate. If she managed to surprise Gage, she would consider the event a success. If she managed to delight him by the surprises of the night, which was exactly what she hoped for, she would never ask for anything else in her entire life.

She had enlisted the help of Mrs. Crane, Lord Basset, Adelaide, Emblyn, Captain Rowe, and a few of the other miners and workers, all of them sworn to secrecy and all as eager to succeed in the venture. She hadn't known exactly why she was doing what she was doing early on, only that she thought Gage deserved the life party he had joked about in his recovery. But the closer they had become in the intervening weeks, the more she had realized the truth: She wanted to show Gage just how loved he was. How much family he had, even if they were not by blood. How valuable his life and his person were to so many.

Gage was not lonely, as far as she could tell, but he seemed to be collecting family about him to make up for the loss of his own. He had known a large and loving extended family, even if he only saw them occasionally, and loving, engaging parents. When that had started to break apart, through no one's fault and only fate, his friends—his local, self-adopted family—had become even more important, and he had never really stopped collecting people to his intimate circle. From high station to low, Gage had sought people with whom he could connect and kept them close, perhaps never identifying them as family, only calling himself a social creature and never even realizing what he was building.

Honora was going to show him what he had built. He was likely the most loved and respected person she had ever met, and she doubted he realized that. Since his accident and throughout his recovery, he had been talking about wanting to live his life, how he felt renewed by her, by this new chance, by the very feeling of Cornish air in his lungs. He was eager to take on his very existence with robust enthusiasm, and the energy was contagious.

Honora simply wanted him to see that the life he had already lived had not been wasted, and there should be no regrets about it as he took up the extension of his life so enthusiastically.

She would not lie; she hoped it might also encourage him to have no regrets about Margaret refusing him all those years ago.

Until she could know that, she would always wonder.

Yes, Gage had told her he had no regrets, but she had seen the two of them talking in the library. She saw the smiles and laughter between them. And Emblyn had told her of what she had observed of the two before Honora had arrived. She had said it was all very innocent, rather like two friends reconnecting. Friends, she was comfortable with. A friend who had once held the heart of her husband…

But she was willing to trust. Margaret was even at the supper tonight, just to extend that hope and friendship on her own.

But the focus of tonight would not be wasted on her.

It was all for Gage.

Sitting in the dining room now, Honora felt like a fraud at her end of the table, considering the fine and elegant people sitting there. The Bassets, Lady Hastings, John and Julia—who looked regal but miserable and probably should have stayed home—and even Emblyn, who had delighted her sister-in-law by adorning herself in finery. Honora had worn the green gown made from the fabric that Adelaide had been so inspired by, and she felt like the best version of herself that she could have been, by all appearances.

But she still felt small and insignificant. Undeserving of her position and her rank, of her perfectly flattering and expensively made gown, of the affection of the man sitting directly across from her at the other end of the table. He smiled at her as though he could not be more satisfied, as though this was exactly the life he had imagined for himself, as though everything he had ever wanted was here.

But how much of that had anything to do with her? His collected family was here at this table, and Honora was doing her utmost to be the best, most accommodating wife possible for him. How much of his affection for her was because of who she was and not what she was?

Honora took a small bite of her pheasant, Gage's favorite meal, and looked around the table at the plates of the rest. Until they were nearly finished, she could not start the next portion of the evening. Dessert would be part of the first surprise, and once everyone had settled into that one, thinking the evening was complete, the second surprise would take place, and there would be no recovering for anyone once it did.

The grand finale of the evening, while not the end of the night necessarily, might lead to an ending of anything else taking place. And she was fine with that. No one could convince her that the celebration had to extend into the small hours of the morning, as so many balls and parties did, if those involved in the event were content for it to end early.

She suspected it could be the case here but wouldn't maintain any expectations. Whatever Gage wanted from the night was exactly what would take place. So long as he was happy, she would also be content.

Lady Hastings said something that had Lord Basset, Julia, and Gage laughing uproariously, while everyone else merely smiled in various shades of confusion. Some private tale or joke that only the family could understand, which those who had joined later could only try to be amused by.

How many times would they be on the outer circles of that group, and how many times would Honora feel as though she were on the furthest circle from everyone else?

She watched calmly as Gage took the final bite of food on his plate, sitting back with a smile for Julia as she pointedly complained about her condition, and then brought her serviette to her mouth, dabbing one side, then the other, before laying it back in her lap and reaching for her Madeira, which she had not touched all evening.

It was the most obvious sign she had been able to think of that no one else would recognize as unusual.

If the footmen followed instructions as exactly as Murray and Mrs. Crane had trained them to do, they would have the door to the ballroom opened and instructed the musicians to begin playing. This would start the dancing and general revelry, and given the proximity of the ballroom to the dining room…

Honora suddenly felt like giggling in anticipation, but that would ruin everything. She needed to act as expertly as any woman of the stage for the next few minutes, and then she could be as real as she wanted for the rest of the night.

As real as she was.

All she had to do was wait.

Honora turned to engage in polite conversation with John beside her, even as the sounds of music and chatter began to waft into the dining room. The others would understand what was happening, but only Gage was supposed to react.

As though he could hear her thoughts, he cleared his throat. "What is that?"

Honora continued talking to John, who was struggling to avoid laughing himself.

"Music, I think," Lady Hastings replied with a convincing non-reaction. "Lovely to eat supper to music."

"Honora?"

She looked down the table at Gage, striving to keep her expression blank. "Yes?"

He raised a brow. "Do you hear that?"

Honora paused as though to listen. "Yes, I do. I wonder what that could be. I haven't arranged for musicians this evening."

Which was true. Adelaide had made the arrangements, knowing the best local musicians for hire.

Gage frowned, wiped at his mouth, and pushed back from the table. "Well, I'm going to find out who is using their instruments close enough to our house for us to hear it."

"Oh, Gage," Adelaide simpered, pushing back quickly. "Don't be sour about it. Surely, your local friends know of your birthday. Perhaps they are playing at a window to celebrate you."

It was an excellent point, and he smiled at the suggestion. "Do you know something I don't, Adelaide?"

She glared at him, as only Adelaide could, while the rest pushed back from the table to rise and follow. "You're the one with musical friends, Gage. I just don't like the idea of you ruining friendships because your dessert is delayed by their singing."

"What do you take me for?" he retorted. "I never lash out at anyone."

"I believe you will find at least three of us who can refute that," Basset added in from the back of the group.

Gage ignored him, looking at Honora. "Do you know of any of our friends' attempts to celebrate with me?"

She shook her head. "No one has mentioned anything to me."

Gage grunted softly. "Well, Honora doesn't lie, so she is the only one in this room I trust."

Now that was rich.

Honora determinedly did not look at anyone in the group as they walked together to investigate the musical sounds that were growing louder as they moved. Gage held his hand out to the side, palm facing back towards her. She immediately moved up and took it, lacing her fingers with his.

It was their unspoken cue for each other now, and Honora, for one, loved it. There was something about holding his hand that made her heart skip and rush and dance all at the same time. And when it was without gloves, it was even better.

Honora hadn't had a chance to replace her gloves after eating yet, and she knew Gage appreciated the bare hand against his, by the way his thumb brushed rather intently over her knuckle.

Fire was racing down Honora's left leg, but she couldn't afford to revel in that at the moment.

The first surprise was about to be revealed.

"Wait," Gage said slowly, "is that music coming from our ballroom?"

"It sounds that way," Honora agreed, trying to frown in some apparent concern. "You don't think Mrs. Crane might have…?"

"She just might," Gage finished with a shake of his head. "She likes to play the meddling aunt with me, so I wouldn't rule out anything where she is concerned."

The housekeeper as a scapegoat? Honora couldn't have planned this better if she had tried.

The ballroom was before them then, the doors open, but nothing could be seen immediately, which was exactly as they had planned. Gage would need to enter the room in order for the surprise to be complete.

He did so, his own confusion written in every single feature. Honora held her breath as she entered beside him, and as they turned to look across the room.

"*Penn-bloodh Lowen!*" the entire huddled mass of guests in the ballroom shouted, making Gage jerk so much he nearly stumbled.

Then the room was full of applause and laughter while he stared in shock.

Honora held his hand with both of hers, grinning at the guests. It was everyone she could think of from local society, plus those that Adelaide thought important, plus the input from Basset on anyone they had known in their younger years, plus those associated with the mines in any positive way. It was enough to create a massive invitation list of those who respected Gage, if not loved him.

And there was nothing Gage loved so well as a social occasion.

He started laughing beside her and looked at Honora with a wild grin. "What did you do?"

She shrugged. "Happy birthday," she offered by way of explanation.

He shook his head and surprised her by giving her a hard, fervent kiss, much to the delight of everyone in attendance.

Honora started laughing while her lips were still against his, and the vibration of the sound in the kiss was enough to set her chest on fire.

Gage broke off, touching his brow to hers as he cupped her cheek, still laughing. "You are really something, Honora Trembath."

"When you figure out what," she replied, wishing she was not quite so breathless, "do let me know."

He snickered and kissed her brow quickly, then stepped away to greet the guests on the other side of the room, spreading out his arms as though he could embrace each and every one.

Honora nodded to the musicians to strike up again, which they did immediately, and some of the guests began taking to the floor for dancing.

"Nicely done, cousin," Julia said as she came to stand beside Honora. "He never suspected a thing."

She nodded and looked at Julia fondly. "Now I can breathe, I suppose. It will be nice to not keep secrets from him."

"Secrets between spouses are the worst," Julia agreed. "I haven't told John about mine, and it's killing me."

"Yours?" Honora turned to face her cousin. "What's going on, Julia?"

She exhaled heavily, her hand going to her impossibly large abdomen. "I suspect there are two babies instead of one. And I suspect this is the last time I leave my house before the baby, or babies, arrive."

"Then why are you here?" Honora demanded, glancing around to find John's location so they could continue to talk without enlightening him. "You did not have to come! Gage and I would have understood!"

"Because it's Gage," Julia laughed, "and because it's you. Do you think I have it in me to resist either one of you, no matter how uncomfortable I am? I promise, I will be resting until I have regained control of my own body as soon as tonight is over, and I am not dancing, standing, or walking for long the entire evening. The doctor says I am as healthy as can be and that there is no reason why I should not have a perfect delivery."

Honora shook her head and took Julia's arm, leading her over to the chairs. "Neither Gage nor I would have felt any less loved by you if you had stayed home and kept to your confinement. Surely you know that."

"And if you think I am going to regret swollen ankles in the morning, you are quite wrong. I would take them any day over regretting witnessing my cousin showing her husband just how loved he is." She gave Honora a pointed look as she took the first seat.

Honora's face flamed. "Of course Gage is loved. I have yet to meet a single person who thinks anything less than that he is perfect."

Julia laughed, tossing her head back. "I can bring you a very long list of people who know full well that Gage is far from perfect."

"You know what I mean," Honora said, her cheeks still burning. "Everybody likes him immensely."

"Including you."

Honora looked across the room to find Gage, who was smiling and laughing with guests. "Of course I like him immensely. He is wonderful and kind and generous and full of life and sees no class divisions and…"

"You're in love with him, Honora."

"I know." She swallowed, then looked away from her husband, closing her eyes. "I didn't mean to," she whispered. "I am not supposed to love him."

"Says who?" Julia retorted with a snort. "Just because your marriage was not entered into for love does not mean either of you are forbidden from developing it. Some might say it would be inevitable, if both parties are even remotely open the idea."

Honora glanced at Gage once more, a feeling of yearning unlike anything she had ever known seeming to stretch out across the room, and she could only hope that feeling would tap her husband on the shoulder and force him to turn around and see her. Really see her. See her heart.

See that her heart was his.

"How can I know if he's open to it?" Honora asked, though she knew her cousin would have no response. "He loves easily, and he loves well, and he buries himself in the love surrounding him and tells himself that it is enough to sustain him. Does he even have enough of his own heart to give any of it to me?"

"Surely you don't think that heart is lodged elsewhere…"

Honora swallowed and looked at her cousin with a smile. "I only hope he will someday tell me where the key is to the lock he has placed on his heart."

Julia did not look convinced, and in fact looked a trifle worried.

This night could not be about the state of Honora's heart, not when she was trying to show her husband that he was the sun around which her tiny planet revolved.

And that he was not alone in the world, no matter how small his family tree looked.

She cleared her throat and took Julia's hand. "Let me fetch you something to drink. And please, don't feel that you must stay long." Julia nodded, squeezing her hand, then Honora left, her heart ricocheting off every rib.

If her cousin could see her love for Gage so clearly, it would only be a matter of time before others did as well. How would Gage react to knowing that his wife loved him when he'd married her without the promise of love, or likely, even the intention of it?

Once she had given refreshment to Julia, she began to make her rounds about the room, thanking people for coming, making superficial conversation as a good hostess should do, and seeing that everyone was enjoying themselves. The dancing was energetic, though not quite to the extent that the harvest celebration had been, and the music was lively. It was everything Honora had wanted for a celebration of Gage. It had everything he loved most about social occasions, and none of the formality he tended to despise.

On the dance floor, there were the Bassets, arguably the finest couple she had ever known in her life, and Captain Rowe with his wife, who, while respectable, were certainly not on a level with the Bassets. And every sort of person in between. She had not invited the miners and workers to this part of the evening, given the expectation of some sort of finery that they could not afford, but that was where the second portion of her surprise came in.

Arguably the largest part of her surprise.

She had asked a number of them about the arrangement of the evening, including inviting any of them to the ball, and every single one of them had said they would have felt out of place and uncomfortable at a fine ball. They loved Gage, but they were not about to rise above their station for him, even for a night.

Eventually, Honora found herself dancing with a few of the guests, all very polite and cordial, and she found none of the fluttery nerves or sense of being a fraud that she had felt that night of the Basset ball. She felt far more comfortable now, in her place and doing her duty, embracing the role of Honora Trembath, the lady of Helwithin and wife to the much-beloved, much-respected Gage Trembath.

This was what he had married her for.

Anything else was accidental. Or perhaps incidental.

Honora was just beginning to look for the time to consider initiating her second surprise of the night when she heard a throat clearing behind her.

She glanced over her shoulder out of curiosity and stopped still to see her husband there, looking at her with playful affection that made her knees shake. She turned fully and clasped her hands before her. "Yes? Can I help you with something?"

As he usually did when she was teasing, his smile turned crooked, his dark eyes crinkling. "I was only wondering, Mrs. Trembath, if your loveliness could withstand a dance with me."

"It is your birthday, Mr. Trembath," Honora said with a coy tilt of her head. "It is entirely up to you if you wish to risk it."

He barked a laugh and extended a hand to her, which she took, the glove on her hand keeping the friction between them minimal, unlike before.

It took Honora a moment before she recognized the music as being that of a waltz, and her throat tightened at the idea of being in such direct close quarters with her husband after feeling so much for him earlier. And now. And at all times.

How could she keep adoration off her face when she was spending the entire evening trying to show him just that? This was entirely different, this dance with him. She adored him on a very personal level, not only this public and community-wide level. She just adored him, and that was all there was to it.

He was going to know, and she wasn't sure how he would react to knowing. But he wouldn't hate her, that much she knew. He liked her. Valued her. Respected her. Saw her, in many respects.

He might simply establish some distance between them, if he did not want her to love him as she did.

Honora took up her position with Gage as the steps of the dance began, the feeling of dancing in such coordination one that surpassed graceful and ventured into ethereal. It was heavenly, being swept into motions by him and feeling carried in many ways. Yet she was there with him, her feet moving in time with his, and she was not weak and faltering in it.

A perfect pair in this, if nothing else.

"Nora," Gage murmured, smiling down at her. "Thank you for this. I don't even know how you managed it."

"I had a lot of assistance," she assured him with a laugh. "Everyone was quite helpful and willing. I simply put forth the idea."

"Well, no one has ever put forth an idea like this for me," he said softly, "and I am practically speechless about it."

Honora gave him a dubious look. "It is just a party, Gage."

He shook his head. "It is so much more than that, Nora. You don't think I know what this really is? That you are showering me with reminders of the care that is held for me by everyone here? By you? Do you have any idea how incredible this feels for me?"

"I'd hoped you would feel it," she admitted in a small voice. "I wanted today to feel special to you. After almost losing you, I wanted the chance to really celebrate you, and I knew you wouldn't condone anything extravagant or elaborate for yourself. You simply don't think it would be worth it. But it is."

He exhaled heavily, his smile growing softer. "How do you know me so well, Nora? How do you see me that clearly? And how, in heaven's name, do you make me want to be better in every single way just by the way you look at me?"

Heavens, she couldn't breathe. How did she look at him? She didn't know why it made a difference; she only knew that she loved him, and if that was injected into how she looked at him, perhaps that was it.

"I don't think you need to be better in any way," she heard herself admit, though her voice seemed barely audible to her own ears. "You are already the best man I have ever known. And the most handsome."

His eyes immediately turned darker and his hold on her tightened. "Nora," he breathed, her name doing more to increase the heat in her body than any other word she had ever heard. "I have never…"

She gasped at the deep, rasping nature of his voice, and only then realized that the music was over, and others were applauding.

She swallowed and tried to exhale, her lungs quivering beside her heart in the most peculiar way.

Gage was still intent on her, heat swirling in the deep darkness of his eyes.

The only thing that could have wrenched her away from this moment was her second surprise, which would show him just exactly what he meant and was worthy of, to her.

"Wait one moment," Honora heard herself whisper, her hand still secure in his hold. "I need to… do something…"

His smile curved and he kissed her hand, the fabric of her glove practically dissolving between them. "I'll wait two moments, if you'll be back."

Honora nodded, not daring to think further on the topic. She turned away and started to walk, noting that Gage took his time to release her hand. When he finally did, she allowed herself a very slow exhale and tried to focus on walking in a straight line as she moved towards the musicians, nodding at the footman at the ballroom door. He left the room, and Honora gave a second nod to the musicians, who shifted their music.

This was what Honora had been planning for weeks now, and it required just a few moments of vulnerability, bravery, and the confidence to be Mrs. Trembath in front of everyone here.

She turned to face the room, everyone now looking in her direction, as the music had not struck up for a new dance as yet.

It was time.

Chapter Nineteen

What in the world was Honora doing? He didn't mind her leaving him before he could tell her that he'd never felt this way about anyone—there would be plenty of time for that. He didn't even mind that she was standing up in the front of the room before all their guests and he had no idea what she was going to say.

He didn't mind any of this. He just didn't know how his wife, who hated attention, was presently at the center of it. On purpose.

He hadn't expected the party for him this evening and had every intention of questioning her at length about the extent of her secret-keeping. He was actually looking forward to the interrogation, especially as he intended to do so in a very convincing manner that she would like immensely.

They both would.

She was a vision this evening, and it was impossible to keep his eyes from her. Her hair now appeared as a rich brown shade that had been infused with ribbons of auburn, all coiled, plaited, and pinned into intricate folds, woven with gold and green. Whoever had developed or discovered the color she wore had clearly done so from the exact shade of her eyes, and draping her perfect figure in yards of such color illuminated her like some mystical woodland nymph. His very own muse, who had just told him that he was the best man she knew, as well as the most handsome. If she had been distracting him before, she was outright killing him now.

This entire night was unnecessary, but Honora had put her heart and soul into creating this experience for him, to celebrate him, to show him how valued he was. For a man whose life had recently been renewed, he felt ignited into living with enthusiasm, gratitude, and appreciation. And the very first thing he wanted to appreciate now was his wife.

His majestic, angelic, shy, insecure, underappreciated, remarkable, utterly delectable wife.

He wanted to shower her with affection and adoration. Wanted her to know just how badly he wanted her. Wanted her to feel how his heart stumbled over itself in her presence. Wanted her to see herself as he saw her.

Wanted her to want him, quite frankly.

Wanted to be worthy of her.

Wanted a family with her. Soon.

Gage forced himself to swallow against the startling realization. He'd thought of having children someday, of course, but he'd never given it a great deal of thought. Now, he was suddenly eager to see Honora glow with impending motherhood, to watch a child they had created together grow within her, to feel the kicks of that child as it developed, and to hold that child when it was born. He wanted to see the true majesty of Honora's strength as she delivered their child. He wanted...

Life with Honora. That was what he wanted.

More than anything.

"Ladies and gentlemen," Honora announced, her voice barely carrying over the sound of general conversation.

The relative din softened pointedly.

"Ladies and gentlemen," she said again, far more clearly to his ears. "Thank you very much for coming tonight to celebrate my husband, Gage Trembath."

The room applauded, everyone turning to look at or for Gage. He inclined his head ever so slightly and started moving forward just to get closer to his wife and whatever she was about to announce.

She smiled at him with a teasing light, the color in her cheeks still high in his favorite way. "When I first had the idea to arrange tonight for his birthday, it was really for one purpose: to remind Gage that his family is larger and more loving than he could possibly imagine. And that he is worth all of the effort and embracing possible. After almost losing him in the accident at Wheal Stout, I wanted him to know just how treasured he truly is."

Gage had never heard anything sweeter in his entire life, and he could not have spoken if he had tried. His throat was clogged and trying to close, his eyes burned, and the pit of his stomach seemed to be trying to lodge itself in his kneecaps. For all his jests and claims of confidence where he was concerned, he was rather sensitive to praise, and not always in a good way.

It was not that he was unused to it; he simply thought there was not all that much to praise. Just a regular gentleman trying to live his life in the best way he knew how. Why should that render praise from anyone?

But praise from Honora…

That was entirely different.

Was it possible to express oneself from across the room when in a deluge of emotion that was impossible to comprehend, let alone define? He hoped so; he needed her to know something of what he felt.

"With that in mind," Honora went on, "I would like to present a very special musical number that has been arranged particularly for him."

The guests made soft sounds of appreciation and awe, but Gage could not say or do anything but stare at his wife and smile. Smile because he could not help it. Because it was what one did with Honora. Because she was sunshine and joy. Because she even existed.

Smile because she was in his life.

She glanced behind her and nodded once.

The doors to the ballroom were thrust open and a single note was played by the musicians.

Then there were voices, all raised together on that exact note, followed by a few more. Men and women, perhaps even children, and none of them were presently seen. The words they sang were not quite clear, but there was something about the melody…

A drum played once.

The voices sang again and began making their way into the ballroom from the open door, still without any instruments accompanying them.

They were miners from Wheal Stout, villagers from the area,

tenants who worked on his farms, people he had sung with and among for years in the most joyous times, as well as some of the most somber. Now, they were singing for him.

The musicians joined in as the singers filed into position around them, standing behind Honora.

The words were finally registering in his mind, and his throat tightened. It was beautiful and familiar Irish, the language of his mother, and the words were that of the song she'd taught him as a child.

Honora was beaming at him, her hands clasped before her, then dropping to her sides as the singers softened.

"'Sé mo laoch mo Ghile Mear
'Sé mo Chaesar, Ghile Mear,
Suan ná séan ní bhfuaireas féin
Ó chuaigh i gcéin mo Ghile Mear."

Her voice was crystal clear, pure and vibrant, filled with sunshine, light, and the very waves of the sea. Her lilting, trilling tone perfectly fitted the Irish style, and it pierced his heart to hear it.

"Seal da rabhas im' mhaighdean shéimh,
'S anois im' bhaintreach chaite thréith,
Mo chéile ag treabhadh na dtonn go tréan
De bharr na gcnoc is imigéin."

The entire group joined her to sing the chorus, the Irish as perfect and crisp as though they had grown up their entire lives singing it.

"'Sé mo laoch mo ghile mear
'Sé mo Chaesar, ghile mear
Suan ná séan ní bhfuaireas féin
Ó chuaigh i gcéin mo ghile mear."

Memories swept across Gage's mind: Christmases with his cousins, quiet evenings by a fire with everyone singing, a blend of

Irish and English in both word and song and feeling, as though his entire world were right there with him. As though he would never want for anything. Even now, in this moment, it was as though his mother were alive again and standing beside him, her arm wrapped around his waist, smiling at this woman he had chosen to marry, who was bringing that world, that life, that home back to him.

There was a motion in the crowd, someone moving forward as the chorus was finishing, and the face that appeared was one he had not been prepared for.

His cousin Áine, singing the first line of the next verse. Then there was Máire taking the next, standing just a few feet from her sister. Grainne appeared next, followed by Roisin.

Gage couldn't breathe, his eyes filling with tears.

More appeared on the chorus, joining in those around them. Ciarán, who had only been a child when Gage had last seen him. Dónal, carrying a bodhrán in hand. Pádraig and Ailís, both carrying violins.

It was all of them. Every one of his cousins, singing the song they had sung for their parents as children, the one his mother had sung to him so often, he still heard it in his sleep. They were dressed only a touch better than the miners around them, though all of them were clearly in their best, and he loved that. He loved that they were just as much their proud selves as they had always been. Hardworking, a step above the poor, but hardly better than them in most respects, and all as filled with love and light as they had ever been.

Then the group changed their tempo, the song picking up, and Dónal began thumping the bodhrán in time with the musicians, everyone singing. The cousins seemed to be dividing harmonies and melodies between them now, the depth of sound resonating beautifully in the ballroom.

Dónal then turned to face the musicians, his bodhrán seeming to be having a contest with the timpani and the drums in the group. It was exactly the sort of energetic, competitive action that might have taken place around his uncle's campfire or within one of the pubs in their village, and it added to the poignancy of the moment with a lightness that made Gage grin outright.

The chorus began chanting musically, echoing the drums in a way.

Then Pádraig and Ailís took over on their violins, furiously playing in the fiddling way they had grown up hearing and learning, the bright and impressive speed of incomparable notes seeming to dance from the instruments. It was a jig in itself, but required no dancers, no guidance, no restraints. It was sound bursting into showers of light, but something only the ears and the mind could comprehend.

Heaven knew, he could not believe what his eyes saw as he tried to follow their fingers.

Just as the violins reached their pinnacle, the drums joined back in, and the song struck up again, more powerful than ever. Áine and Máire came forward and took Gage's hands, pulling him up to sing with them, their bright smiles driving away any resistance he might have felt to singing before this company.

"Ní labhrann cuach go suairc ar nóin
Is níl guth gadhair i gcoillte cnó,
Ná maidin shamhraidh i gcleanntaibh ceoigh
Ó d'imthigh sé uaim an buachaill beó."

He stood in a line now formed of his cousins and turned and faced the guests, raising his voice with theirs. He looked along the line of them, unable to believe this was real, that they were here, that they were once again singing together just as if their parents were still there watching them. This was his family, and he had never felt the bonds more strongly than now.

But where was Honora? She was no longer among them, had somehow stepped away without him noticing. He scanned the gathering before her, and saw her standing beside Adelaide, tears streaming down both of their faces.

His voice caught on part of the chorus, and he swallowed, then held out his hand to her.

"'Sé mo laoch mo ghile mear
'Sé mo Chaesar, ghile mear

Suan ná séan ní bhfuaireas féin
Ó chuaigh i gcéin mo ghile mear."

In the space of no heartbeats at all, she was walking up to him, placing her hand in his, their fingers lacing together as though they had done so for eternity.

There. Now his family was all together, and he could proudly finish this song with them.

"'Sé mo laoch mo ghile mear
'Sé mo Chaesar, ghile mear
Suan ná séan ní bhfuaireas féin
Ó chuaigh i gcéin mo ghile mear."

He shook his head to himself, the enormity and beauty of this night, this moment, dawning on him anew. It would never be matched by anything in his life.

"Ó chuaigh i gcéin mo ghile mear."

The applause in the room was thunderous. Rolling over heads and chandeliers and rafters, mingling with the artwork adorning the ceiling and beyond. It rattled the windows and rumbled the floor, and Gage could feel the love and warmth crashing over and through him, rippling down his arms and legs. More than that, he could feel his connection to Honora more powerfully than he ever had before. Their linked hands might as well have been linked hearts, beating in time with each other and sharing in the breath of their lungs to keep them alive.

He squeezed her hand gently, grinning at her, wondering if it were possible for one's face to shatter from smiling so hard and feeling so much.

She looked radiant, the sheen of tears on her cheeks and still swirling in her eyes, her smile the dawning of the sun. He saw relief, he saw joy, he saw hope, he saw...

He saw things he wasn't sure there were words for. But he saw her, and he knew in that instant that she saw him as well.

His other hand was squeezed, and he turned to Maíre on that side, laughing before he even saw her, and pulled her into his arms for a hug. Soon, all of the cousins were embracing, crying, and laughing together.

"How are you all here?" he asked between his laughter, looking around at each of them. "How did this happen?"

"Your wife," Áine told him, sniffing back tears. "She wrote us weeks ago with this plan. We've been staying with the Bassets for a few days to hide from you!"

Gage shook his head, swallowing hard. "Well, you're all staying here now. I insist."

"We know," Ciarán said with a laugh. "Honora already had our trunks sent over. We've been upstairs for hours."

That made all of them laugh more, and Gage made a mental note to hold his wife especially close after this. She, who had a family that barely resembled the name, had taken his as her own and done exactly as he would have done.

"How long can you stay?" he asked them, knowing he would have to get back to his guests soon.

Roisin beamed. "We're staying through Christmas, of course. Honora insisted."

Gage dropped his head, his eyes burning and his chest tightening. Someone squeezed his shoulder, and he nodded. "Good," he managed. "Good."

He exhaled, sniffled, and raised his head, smiling at them all. "Time to introduce you to those you don't know or don't remember." He stepped back and turned to wave at the others who had joined the singing, those he had worked alongside for years, those he had seen recently and those he had not, those who had helped him become the person he was. There was so much love and respect, in all of their wondrous shades, and he was touched.

He wandered around the room with at least two cousins at all times, introducing them to anyone he could, while the others mingled, danced, or took turns joining the musicians, in some cases. It was the best sort of chaos he could have imagined, and he wondered if he would ever wake from this dream.

He hoped not.

Between the magnificence of Honora and the reunion with his cousins, this was the best day of his entire life, there was no question.

He danced with each of his female cousins at least once throughout the night, then managed to snag a dance with his wife again when the final dance of the evening was announced, though it was a lively country dance, and allowed them almost no time to talk.

He needed to talk with her. Needed to find a way to explain what the night had meant to him. Needed to tell her how much he appreciated her. Needed her to know what she did to him.

Provided he could find a way to understand any of those things himself, and then express them.

The guests began to trickle out of the ballroom and into their carriages, and both Gage and Honora made their appropriate farewells and did their utmost duty as host and hostess. Many compliments were given, many felicitations for Gage on his birthday, many expressions of awe and delight at the spectacle Honora had arranged, and a few questioned what in the world would be planned for next year. Gage made some offhand comment about fireworks, but had made sure to laugh as though it was a ridiculous idea.

He knew where Honora had gotten the idea for a party and didn't dare press his luck by suggesting anything grand or spectacular anytime soon, at least while she was within earshot.

When everyone was gone, apart from his cousins, they all sat in the family drawing room, chatting aimlessly and a bit deliriously, laughing and reminiscing in a way that was destined to keep them all awake into the post-dawn hours. There was so much to talk about, and yet it seemed as though nothing had changed. Indeed, it felt as though the years apart had simply melted from existence. There would be plenty of time to talk with all of them, but there was also a drive to keep talking, to keep laughing, to continue to live in this day where magic had occurred, and his unspoken dreams had come to life.

Why had he never gone back to Ireland after his father had died? Why had he never extended an invitation for them to come see him in Cornwall? He had sent money, and regularly, but in all other ways, he had been just like his father had been in the end. Kept away by memories as he yearned for them all the while.

But that would all be mended now, thanks to Honora.

Gage glanced over at her and found her yawning behind a hand. She rose from her chair and said something to Grainne, who smiled and nodded. Her eyes moved to Gage, and she smiled softly before dipping her chin and turning from the room.

Gage was up at once, stopping by Grainne. "Where's she going?"

"To bed," she said with her own yawn. "I'd wager she's exhausted from planning and executing all of this."

Gage looked towards the door, wondering if he dared...

"You could walk her up," his cousin suggested, a smile in her voice. "It would be a polite and husbandly thing to do."

His feet were moving before he thought anything else, and he reached Honora's side in a moment, slipping his hand into hers, delighted that she had already removed her gloves.

His wife gave him a surprised look. "You don't have to escort me."

Gage only shrugged, smiling softly. "I know."

They didn't say a word as they moved up the stairs, but there was something new and different between them. Something in the connection of their hands that reached all the way into Gage's chest and encircled his heart with fingers of fire. Each breath that passed his lips, heated by his ignited heart, was counted and measured, slowly but steadily ridding him of sense, restraint, reserve, thought...

This was Honora. This was his wife. This was the most incredible, generous, incomparable, distracting... beautiful... vibrant...

Everything. She was everything.

Suddenly overcome, Gage took the hand he held and brought it to his lips. But not just once. That would never be enough, not anymore. He gently kissed each knuckle in turn, taking a slow moment for proper appreciation of each delicate joint. Then he moved his lips to the tip of each finger, unsure what he was doing or why, but certain that he had to shower affection however he could.

He felt the faint trembling in Honora's hand and experienced a similar sensation between his knees as they walked. Nothing to make him unsteady, just enough to let him know that he was not unmoved.

His lips lingered along the back of her hand, tracing absent patterns and memorizing every aspect of the sweet surface. The exact shape, scent, taste, every ridge and freckle, every curve and line. He would know this hand blindfolded by the time he was done, and then he would set about doing the same with the other.

Honora stopped walking then, and it took Gage a moment to realize they had reached her rooms.

He cleared his throat, his cheeks warm, and held Honora's hand in both of his at his chest. "I have no words, Nora," he said roughly, "for what tonight meant to me."

Her eyes raised to his, a light of hope swirling amidst the deep green shade the night was giving her exquisite eyes. "I wanted it to be special," she whispered, her perfect lips curving into a smile. "For you, I mean. I wanted it to be special for you."

"You succeeded," he assured her with a small laugh. "I have never... It was..." He shook his head, words utterly failing to adequately describe what he was feeling, what he had felt, how he had been affected, what she meant to him.

He swallowed and took the hand he held, pressing it firmly against his frantically and furiously pounding heart.

Honora stared at her hand, her eyes growing wide. "Oh, heavens! Are you all right?"

Gage chuckled and curled his fingers around hers where they rested on his chest. "Never better. This is what you have done to me. I can barely breathe, and words are nigh impossible."

Though it was dark in this corridor, he could see her cheeks turn pink, and it created a rather pleasant knot in his stomach. "A simple thank you would be more than enough," she murmured. "I don't need flattery."

"This isn't flattery, Nora," Gage told her firmly. "Nor is it gratitude."

"It's not?" Her voice was oddly clipped, soft but sharp, a raw edge to it that he had never heard.

Could it be possible that she just might be feeling some of the same gnawing heat as he was? As though their very skin was chafing against some inner need that seemed impossible to sate?

"It is not," Gage said softly. He shook his head, this time in utter disbelief. "Do you have any idea, Nora, how wonderful you are? No, not wonderful. Wondrous. There is no one like you, and no one could even remotely compare. Your thoughtfulness and kindness, your generosity and intuition, your angelic voice and somehow more angelic disposition…"

Honora whimpered softly. "Gage…"

"Your beauty," he went on, his voice now rasping against his throat. He reached out to stroke her cheek. "My beautiful girl, do you even see it? Do you even know your own loveliness?"

She nuzzled against his hand, her ragged breath scraping against his palm with the most delicious friction he had ever known, and his own breath caught. He kissed her out of sheer instinct and raw desire, intending to be gentle, but shifting at once when she arched into him with a fervor that unmanned him. His kisses turned deep and thorough, entwining with hers in a waltz unlike anything he had ever known, molding and caressing and shifting for more and more of each other. Seeking and finding, discovering and treasuring, declaring and defining, each kiss a confession and a surrender to utter bliss.

She matched him, each and every time. There were no questions, only answers. There were no walls, only welcoming, no greed, only giving. And yet…

And yet there was want. There was need. There was…

Them. There was them, and they were there.

She broke off with a shaking gasp, a soft keening sound catching Gage somewhere in the depth of his soul. Her fingers were twisted into his clothing, clutching at him and holding him close. She must have been on her tiptoes, for her brow met his without his leaning much at all. Their breath mingled between them like a cloud, tempting them for more.

And oh, how he was tempted!

He gently moved his fingers, now tangled in her hair, and scratched ever so softly against her scalp. His lips slowly dusted across her face, catching this surface and that, unable to keep from touching her in some way.

"Are you… going back downstairs?" Honora asked between breaths.

Gage shook his head, brushing his lips across hers with a sweet, tender pass.

"Are you tired?"

Again, he shook his head, this time kissing her jaw and starting a pointed path to her neck.

"Do you…?" she began, her fingers curling around his wrist. "Will you…?"

"I'll do whatever you want, Nora," he whispered as he kissed the place beneath her ear, his free hand cradling her face. "Give you anything you want."

Honora whimpered, buckling Gage's left knee. Her lips caught his palm in a way that sent his stomach plunging to the floor.

"What do you want, love?" he breathed against her skin. "Tell me."

Trembling from head to toe, Honora gripped his wrist hard. "I want you."

Gage groaned and took her mouth, kissing her passionately. "Then have me, Nora. Take me. However you want."

She kissed him then, hungrily and with an intensity that robbed him of breath. Her fingers moved to his cravat, and she hastily backed up to the door behind them. Gage fumbled for the handle and nudged her within when the door finally opened, his hands plucking at the pins and ribbons in her hair as she worked at his cravat.

Honora managed to get the knot free and slid the linen from his neck as her lips caught at his bottom one with a poignancy that sent him spinning.

He wrapped his arms around her and hauled her off of the ground, her hands gripping at his neck, her mouth perfectly distracting his own as he kicked the door shut behind them.

Chapter Twenty

Time had a way of moving rather rapidly when one was pleasantly occupied.

Christmas was upon them, and Honora felt as though she had barely left her chambers. Or perhaps she simply preferred remembering the nights and mornings spent with Gage in there than any of the delightful but ultimately less satisfying activities with his family. One might think that they would grow accustomed to such things, but if Honora or Gage were doing so, they made no sign of it. It seemed as though every time they were together, it was new and exhilarating and miraculous. But surely it would not always be that way. Surely it would change.

But as of now, it had not. Even if they barely spoke a word during the day, their kisses and caresses said volumes when they were alone.

Honora had never felt so worshipped, so adored, so alive as when she was with Gage. She could only hope that he felt the same with her, though she knew full well that she was inexperienced and unlearned in these things. Not as much as she had been on their wedding night, and she certainly was learning a few things, particularly the things that he liked best, but she still felt as though she could not give enough. Could not be enough.

He had never said or done anything that made her feel that way. In fact, his responses were just the opposite.

But Honora felt it all the same. That there had to be more she could give him. More that would please him. A body that would suit him better, as her own was so lacking in the feminine figure that seemed so appreciated by the male species.

Gage was very good at appreciating what Honora did have, but she always wondered if he might wish she possessed more.

They never spoke of their private interactions unless they were engaged in one, and Honora was fine with that. Her blush would be far too distracting otherwise.

Not that it wasn't distracting for Gage anyway. He seemed determined to make her entire body blush when they were together, and, as far as Honora could feel, he succeeded. Her skin caught fire with the merest touch of his now, knowing exactly what wonders he could perform and exactly what his lips felt like.

Giving gifts for Christmas felt wholly inadequate after such exquisite experiences, but she had to try.

First, however, she had to confer with her cousin, who had been delivered of a healthy pair of boys just a few days ago. The timing was a little fuzzy to Honora's mind, as her schedule had been a trifle occupied, but it seemed as though the babies came a week or so after Gage's party.

At least Julia's attendance at the event had not brought about the birth.

She was fortunate to be making this visit alone. Between Gage's warm and energetic cousins, their rambunctious and darling children, and her own particularly attentive husband, she'd barely had a moment to herself in the last few weeks. She hadn't minded any of that, but it was lovely to have a chance of breathing room at the moment. A chance to reflect. A chance to only smile if she wished to. A chance to allow herself to be something other than on display.

Not that she felt the need to be on display with Gage, but she still felt as though she needed to control her expressions and carefully conceal any nerves or distress. Any less-than-ideal emotions. Any imperfections.

With Julia, she need not do any of that.

Honora was shown into Julia's room at once and was pleased to see her cousin sitting up in bed, hair done, face fresh, and looking as well and whole as she had ever done. Two sleeping babies lay on the bed beside her, as angelic as anything, and Honora's attention was drawn to them for far longer than her cousin.

"Oh, Julia," she breathed, putting a hand to her heart. "They are so precious."

"Thank you," her cousin gushed with a fond smile. "They certainly gave me a time of it getting here, but they have been a joy ever since."

Honora shook her head and came to the bed, gently sitting and reaching for the fingers of one of the boys. "Have you thought of names for them?"

Julia nodded, touching the foot of the one closest to her. "Alexander John, and Gryffyn James."

"Lovely names." Honora looked at her cousin with a small smile. "May I hold one?"

"Please do!" Julia encouraged with a laugh. "They've just eaten, so they're not likely to wake."

Honora tenderly scooped up Gryffyn and felt her heart actually melt as he nuzzled into her at the change in position. "Oh, I need one of these," she said as she gently stroked his cheek with a finger.

"I am sure Gage would oblige in such efforts."

Heat raced into Honora's cheeks, and she focused intently on the baby in her arms as she thought of what she could say. How she could shift the topic.

"Ah-ha…" her cousin said slowly. "He already has, then."

There was no way Honora was going to talk further on that subject, so she began cooing softly to Gryffyn.

"Well, if your courses stop, you'll know," Julia quipped easily, sitting back against her pillows. "It may take a while, so don't worry if it doesn't happen right away."

Honora swallowed hard, her cheeks starting the warming process all over again. Her courses had been due last week, and nothing had happened. Still no sign of them. But she felt nothing. No fatigue, no sickness, no fullness, nothing she had ever heard in rumor of the first days of carrying a child. She might not know for some time, but it was certainly possible.

"I am glad you two get along so well," Julia went on, apparently ignorant as to Honora's thoughts and feelings at the moment. "There is no reason why you should not be perfectly happy together."

Perfectly happy. Yes, that was what Honora was, when she was in Gage's arms and the outside world did not seem to exist. Perfectly happy, content, and perfectly in love. But they never stayed in those embraces long enough for the feelings to sink deep into her heart and bring confidence to her soul. Even when Gage stayed the whole of the night, which was becoming more frequent, Honora still wondered…

"Do they always like it?" she blurted out without thinking, and without any sort of preamble. "Men, I mean. Do they always enjoy intimacy?"

Julia looked at her with wide eyes. "Well, I cannot say for certain, nor for all men, but I should think so. The advantage is all on their side, isn't it?"

That was not helpful.

"Why? Has Gage said anything?"

"No, of course not," Honora said in a rush. "He is wonderful. I only wondered if…"

"If the emotional attachment you now feel is on his side as well?"

Honora looked at her cousin quickly, startled at being so easily found out.

Julia bore a rather knowing smile. "That is how women work, is it not? It is perfectly natural to feel more for him because of such things. And the only way to really know his mind and heart is to ask him, quite frankly. Otherwise, it is all guesswork and insecurity."

Which was exactly where Honora was at the moment. Guesswork and insecurity.

Her husband wanted her physically, that much was clear. But would he have wanted any woman at all, and she was simply the one he was married to? He was such a good man, such a kind and generous one, and there was not a wicked bone in his body. He would never abandon her, as her parents did each other.

But would he wish he could? Would he someday wish to take back the vow to keep to her only? Would he want someone else more than he wanted Honora? She would not like to think so, but she only had her own parents for examples, and they had wanted a great many people who were not their spouses and had never had compunctions against avoiding such.

If Gage wanted something—someone—else now that he had

Honora... Well, that would break her. She would hate to see a man bound to a woman that he was unhappy with, but to know that bliss could exist with another...?

Why should he have to settle?

"Your thoughts are a long ways away," Julia murmured.

Honora shook herself and smiled. "Just thinking. I never thought about children before, not really. And now..." She shrugged, snuggling little Gryffyn close. "Now it feels perfect."

Julia laughed. "Well, I trust it will not be so perfect when they learn how to scream and speak their minds. I'm sending them to you and Gage when they get like that. As godparents, you'll be dealing with that."

"Godparents?" she gasped. "Julia, do you mean it?"

"Of course I mean it!" She sat up and reached for Honora's hand. "Who else would it be?"

Honora shook her head. "What about your sister?"

"Kate can have the next baby," Julia said with a shrug. "But Gryffyn will have you two and Alex will have the Bassets."

Honora looked down at the precious baby in her arms, his tiny nose and puffy cheeks tinged with rosiness that reminded her of her own blushes, his mouth open to allow his little breaths of sleep to pass through perfect lips... She adored him already, and her heart was stretching and expanding in ways she did not expect from merely holding the child of her cousin.

Her soon-to-be godson.

She wanted to be a mother. She had been speaking partially in jest when she had said that she needed a baby, but there was no jest in the idea now. She wanted to have Gage's baby, and she wanted to have it sooner rather than later.

Suddenly, her late courses were a cause for hope, not curiosity. A sign of something incredible, not something to watch. A secret to fill her heart with joy, not trepidation.

She couldn't say anything about it yet, of course. She needed time to make sure that her courses truly had been missed and not only late. She needed to know for certain before she told anyone, including Gage. It shouldn't be too much trouble, as the entire extended Dolan family was still in residence and tended to control or contribute to the entirety of conversations of late.

Christmas was only a week from now, and they would return to Ireland after Twelfth Night. Then Helwithin would belong to her and Gage once more, and she would be certain if there was a child growing within her.

What a way to begin a new year!

"We would be honored," Honora murmured, brushing a soft finger along the baby's cheek. "I believe I may safely speak for Gage in this."

"I thought so, too." Julia smiled warmly, sighing in a delighted way that Honora hadn't heard many times. "Tell me of your Christmas plans, cousin. Are you going to the Bassets' again this year?"

Honora shook her head, smiling at the mention of the holiday. "No, we've decided to have a Christmas *ceilidh* with the Dolans. You and John will be invited, of course, if you feel well enough. There will be dancing, singing, storytelling... I am told it will be quite the event."

Julia sat up, positively beaming now. "We used to have pretend *ceilidhs* when the Dolan cousins would visit! For such an occasion, I will make myself well enough."

Honora laughed and spent a few more minutes chatting with her cousin about this and that, avoiding discussion on the act of giving birth, as she was not certain she wanted to know while her heart was so filled with the desire for babies. Then she left her to rest and made the trip back to Helwithin.

She smiled the entire time in the carriage, her hand going to her abdomen in hopeful anticipation. If she were with child, would she hope it was a boy or a girl? It would not matter to her either way, but would she wish for one more than the other? Was that a natural thing to think or feel? Honora's mother had never talked about babies, children, or the process by which they came about. She never spoke of the experience of carrying them within her and had no description of fondness for anything to do with motherhood.

But Honora loved children. Had always loved children. Had always wanted children. Had known that her mother's way of doing things had not been the way by which she would do them.

She did not know much else about any of it. Nor did she know how Gage felt about any of it. She presumed he would one day wish to be a father, and given his open and engaging temperament, would likely be a fairly active one. He came from a loving family, so it would follow that he would be a loving father himself.

Could they build love for each other over a shared love of their child? Not that Honora needed the help in loving Gage, but perhaps it would be what he needed to love her. Not just want her, but love her. Not just be friends with her, but love her. Not just enjoy making her blush, but love her.

Really love her.

She would never have dreamed of getting herself with child to make him love her. But if she already was with child...

Surely it could bind them together. Keep them together. Make them a true family.

She needed to talk about this with someone. Share her feelings, her concerns, her hopes... She wanted to talk to her husband, but she could not discuss Gage with Gage, it was too much to bear. She could not talk to Julia, not when she was recovering from childbirth and glowing in new motherhood bliss. She could not talk to Adelaide, as she was far too confident by half and would not understand Honora's thoughts.

Which left Emblyn.

And Emblyn had never been a mother nor, as far as Honora knew, been in love. But she knew Gage and she knew people, and she was an excellent listener. She'd write to her and ask if they might take tea soon. Perhaps she could even help Honora with a present for Gage.

She had no time left to think of something complicated for him, and after what she'd managed for his birthday...

The best thing she could give him was a child. But she could not be certain of her condition that quickly, so something else would have to do. Something simple yet meaningful.

Absolutely nothing was coming to mind.

She was still thinking about gifts when she arrived back at Helwithin, and while she was walking up the stairs to her rooms. A brief lie-down before the evening meal would be just what she needed to face the rambunctious relations she had inherited and try to match their energy. She had no idea what anyone had done during the day, but she had given up playing hostess. None of them needed her to. They were more at home at Helwithin than she was.

She began tugging down her hair from its simple chignon as she moved to her rooms and was startled to see Gage sitting in a chair before her fire, looking pensive.

"Gage?" Honora asked, brushing out her hair with her fingers over a shoulder. "I am so sorry, were you waiting for me?"

Gage looked at her, smiling easily. "Yes and no. I knew you were with Julia, and this seemed as good a place as any to enjoy some peace and quiet."

Honora smiled at that. "You need peace and quiet?"

He shrugged and stood up. "What can I say? It's been years since I've been around my cousins, and I've forgotten the volume at which they live."

"So you wanted to hide in here?" She stepped in and gave him a wry look. "You have rooms, too, Gage."

"Are you kicking me out?" he asked with a pout.

She scoffed softly. "Of course not. I'm just surprised you chose here instead of your own." She walked over to her bureau and started removing her shoes. "But then, your cousins probably know which rooms are yours, so they could know you were in there?"

Gage laughed once. "I doubt they would barge into my rooms, though they do know them. I simply wanted your company, and no one else's."

Honora turned in surprise. "Mine? Really?"

Her husband exhaled with a sort of impatience. "The fact that you are still surprised by that tells me we have far more work to do, Mrs. Trembath. Yes, your company. And before you ask, it is because I enjoy your company. I enjoy your calmness. I enjoy your thoughts. I enjoy looking at you, talking with you, being with you. Hell, I even enjoy your silence, so long as it is a silence of contentment. Can we just be for a while? Together?"

It was the sweetest, most innocent request she had ever received from anyone. The fact that it came from the man who was occupying almost the entirety of her thoughts and feelings of late made it even sweeter.

"Of course we can," she assured him. "I am sorry I don't have a chaise or a sofa in here. I know how you enjoy running your fingers through my hair when quiet."

Gage's chin dipped as he gave her a more thorough look. "I know how you like me to run my fingers through your hair when we're quiet."

That was very, very true, and Honora's cheeks began to heat.

He would like that, and she would like that he would like that, and the entire idea of sitting quietly and enjoying each other's company would be null and void.

She needed to think.

Clearing her throat, Honora moved to the free chair and picked up the embroidery she had limply started a few days ago. "I'll never finish this before Christmas," she muttered, wishing her face would cool. "Roisin loves cornflowers, but I am dreadful with embroidery."

Gage chuckled, though it wasn't clear to Honora if he was laughing at her lame excuse or if he was laughing at her embroidery. "Roisin will love anything, Nora. She is easy to please. And it is thoughtful of you to embroider something if you are dreadful at it."

Honora made a sputtering noise and began to force the needle and thread through the fabric anyway. "If I botch this as much as I think I will, it won't be thoughtful at all to Roisin, and then I'll be frantic to think of something else."

Resuming his previous seat, Gage continued laughing and waved that off. "Don't worry too much about it. She would also love a shawl or a scarf or a book or a bottle of Cornish cider."

"From you, she probably would love anything," Honora told him, trying to make her cornflower look like a cornflower. "She doesn't know me well enough to love anything I give her."

He made a soft tsking sound. "You should hear what my cousins say about you, Nora. All of them. Each of them. They utterly adore you. They are already talking about me getting you to Ireland, and I can promise you, it isn't for my sake."

"I would love to see Ireland," Honora admitted almost whimsically, looking into the fire and leaning back into her chair. "The way they talk about it… I've never even imagined a place like that. But then, I never imagined Cornwall either and couldn't believe my eyes when I saw it."

"That is what you take away from what I said? That we should go to Ireland?"

Honora glanced at him, smiling just a little. "Why not? It's easier to talk about. So can we please talk about it?"

He shook his head, his smile small and peculiar. "Someday, Nora... Someday, I will have you seeing a glimpse of who you really are."

Her cheeks began their annoying warming pattern again, and she returned her attention to the dark blue thread in her hand. "Gage..."

"Yes, I will take you to Ireland," he said, his tone filled with amusement. "We can spend an entire summer there, if you like. Get a house somewhere. Ireland isn't so different from Cornwall in its appearance, but there are shades of green there that I have never seen anywhere else. So many of them, rich and rolling across the land, the scent of grass and salt and sweet flowers filling the air... It is the only place I know that feels like home to every person who has ever set foot on its shores."

The more he spoke, the more wondrous the place seemed in Honora's mind. Cornwall was a place of masterful beauties, and she had yet to fully explore their vastness, but Ireland... Ireland might as well have been heaven, in her mind. Just as ethereal, just as imagined, just as far away, just as desired.

She would give anything to go there, though it would only be so magical if Gage were with her. She could go to Ireland alone and enjoy its beauties and its music, but it would only be another place in the world that was beyond her reach. A place that might feel like home when she stepped on its shores but would never be a home she could call her own. Not one she could claim.

Life was only life with Gage. Without him, it was an existence. An expanse of awareness without significance, minimal points of pleasure and pain. A cold, calculating numbness that would never again suffice now that she had known the warmth and invigoration that life could be.

She bit her lip as she thought again on bringing a child into this world. Into this heart. Into this life she now treasured. Into this relationship she loved. She could almost feel the child in her arms, dozing just as Gryffyn had been, its precious weight strengthening her arms instead of wearing on them. The sensation of one's heart being outside the chest rather than within. A feeling of wholeness in the silence and comfort of three people in one space, encircled by a love beyond words. A lightness and hope for the future for all of them, and the first true happiness in a family she had ever known.

Would the child look like Gage or like her? Would he sing like his father? Would she have the shyness of her mother? There were so many possibilities, and all of them seemed to be running through her mind at once. Then there were the imagined scenarios: Gage cradling the baby in his arms and softly singing it to sleep, laying his head against her rounded belly to feel its movement, crawling on the floor with a toddler riding atop his back like a horse, Gage lying side by side in bed with Honora, his fingers running through her hair, asking when they could have another child...

Her cheeks slowly began to heat again as she lingered on that last scenario, almost feeling his fingers in her hair now. How many children would they have together? How many would he even want? How many did she want? Her parents had been trying for two boys to be done with the thing, but Gage wouldn't be like that. And Honora certainly wasn't. And if they enjoyed each other always the way they seemed to be now...

How many children would be a blatant testimony to such a thing?

"Nora, don't bite your lip."

She jerked at the almost harsh order, releasing her lip as though one of her parents had barked at her. She swallowed and looked at Gage, recollecting that she was not with her parents, nor was Gage prone to harshness. "Why?" she asked in surprise.

His eyes were dark, his jaw was set, and his attention was wholly and entirely fixed on her. "Because it makes me want to."

Honora's eyes widened and her jaw dropped. It was as though he could see exactly what she was imagining, exactly what she'd been feeling, and had his own ideas for such things. He wasn't prone to being descriptive or upfront about relations between them, in her experience, but there was something...

Gage shrugged a shoulder, his mouth curving into a slight smile.

"You asked."

He was right, she had asked. But that was not what she had been anticipating in response.

Honora wrenched her gaze away and focused on the fire, her embroidery entirely forgotten now. It was the middle of the afternoon, and her husband was thinking about... Well, to be fair, she had been thinking about it, too, but hardly...

Forget her cheeks, her entire body was growing warm, as well as ticklish. Her lips were buzzing, and her throat was dry, and she could not, for the life of her, imagine how her chair had suddenly become the most uncomfortable place she had ever sat in her entire life.

There was something heady and addictive about knowing that her husband desired her, especially when she felt the same about him. And if she was not with child at the moment, she certainly knew enough about herself now to know she wanted a child soon.

Might as well do something about that, if she could.

Pointedly, with a small smile, Honora pressed her teeth into her lower lip again, wondering how long it would take her very observant husband to notice.

"Nora," he said firmly, followed by a sigh, "you are biting..." He paused, and out of the corner of her eye, Honora saw him tilt his head ever so slightly. "And blushing. Now why would my Nora be blushing and biting her lip, especially when I've told her what that does to me?"

The impulse to giggle was suddenly hot and intense, but Honora bit it back and allowed her eyes to move to Gage. Heat and darkness swirled in his gaze, and his smile curled her stomach and her toes in the exact same manner.

"You little minx," Gage murmured as he slowly pushed out of his chair. "You know exactly what you're doing, don't you?"

Honora looked back at the flames, afraid she might mewl like a kitten if she watched him approach, and this wild streak of daring and confidence needed to last as long as possible.

"I've told you before that your blush will get you into trouble," he saw in a low, rough voice. "But biting your lip, Nora... now that I can perfectly appreciate the taste, the texture, the feeling of those lips... And you dare to blush while you do it? Nora, are you trying to kill me?"

She tried to swallow but couldn't manage it. Her throat was too tight, her mouth too dry, and her body refused to listen to her.

Gage was suddenly before her, lowering to his haunches and leaning close. "If you don't mind, love," he murmured, "I'm going to carry out my threat now. If I'm going to die, I might as well take you with me."

"Please do," Honora replied before she could stop herself, making him laugh.

Cupping her face, Gage leaned in and took her lips with his own, expertly devouring the last shreds of her sanity. She let her embroidery clatter to the floor and gripped the back of his neck hard, sighing into his mouth and deepening the kiss. One of his arms snaked around her back and hauled her in, a growl of satisfaction rumbling from his chest into Honora's mouth, rippling through her frame like the warmest wave of the sea.

"Cancel the evening," Gage managed as his mouth made his way along her jaw. "All of it. Whatever is planned, get rid of it."

Honora sighed a laugh, digging her fingers into Gage's hair as he trailed paths of fire along her skin. "They're your family."

"Then we can definitely cancel," he insisted, his teeth gently grazing the corner of her jaw in a way that made her shiver. "I don't care about anyone else. Just you." He groaned and pressed a featherlight kiss just below her ear. "Gads, Nora..."

She smiled as her toes curled of their own accord, and gently pressed Gage's face up towards her own, taking a moment to toy at his lips with hers before touching their brows and noses together. "You can have me," she said firmly, "anytime you want me."

"That's all the time," he whispered with a laugh.

Honora snorted softly, shaking her head, even as they were still touching. "I have no plans tonight. None. But we probably ought to have supper."

"We can have supper sent up from the kitchens," he retorted, his lips brushing against hers with each word. "In a basket. I've done that before. Not for myself, but for the Grangers. Ask them sometime."

"I could never," she protested, her back arching as his arm pressed her closer.

Gage chuckled and nudged Honora's nose with his own before kissing her slowly. "Still shy, Nora? Fascinating…"

"Not with you." Honora kissed him hard, knowing how he loved it when she took charge in any way.

"Pardon me, madam. Oh…" a voice said.

Honora broke from Gage's mouth and buried her face into his shoulder, her face flaming in mortification.

"Good day, Mrs. Crane," Gage replied for her, his hand on the back of Honora's head. "Do you need something?"

"Yes…" the housekeeper said slowly. "A thousand apologies, but I really do need to speak with the mistress."

Honora whimpered into Gage, torn between laughter and tears as her embarrassment increased.

He laughed softly and kissed Honora's hair, sighing. "Until later, love," he whispered at her ear. "My favorite freckle misses me, and I intend to give her every possible attention tonight."

Honora whacked him in the side. "Wretch."

"Yes, I am," Gage told her. "But I am your wretch. I'll see you later." He kissed her cheek, then rose from the floor and walked towards the door.

Somehow, even as her legs shook and her ears burned with his promise, Honora managed to sit upright, clear her throat, and form some semblance of decorum by the time her husband left the room. "Yes, Mrs. Crane, how can I help you?"

Chapter Twenty-One

Christmas was, without a doubt, Gage's favorite holiday.

An Irish Christmas *ceilidh* was destined to be his favorite Christmas ever.

Although there was last year, when Honora had sung his favorite Christmas song, which was probably when he had first thought of her as a possible wife…

If he had only known what he was getting into with her, he might have asked her to marry him then and there. More time with Honora would always be a good thing.

But regrets were not worth the thought or breath used to air them. They were here now, and the *ceilidh* was going to be incredible. Honora had been overseeing the decorations, with Adelaide Basset's help, and his cousins were taking care of the music for the occasion. It would be a fairly small gathering, compared to the birthday celebration and harvest supper they had hosted, but Christmas was different. Quieter, for the most part, and more intimate.

They could have held another large gathering, but Gage wasn't interested in that. There would be family, close and extended, and friends, of high standing and low. Those who were important enough to spend a holiday with them. Nothing for the sake of politeness, and nothing for the purpose of maintaining one's standing.

This way, he could be certain of enjoying himself. They all could.

"Nora!" he called as he left his rooms and headed for hers. "We need to go if we are to be at the barn before the others."

"I'm ready," his wife said calmly, stepping out of her rooms, looking as perfect as holly and ivy and twice as lovely. Her gown was green, his favorite shade of it on her, and wrapped about her body in a way that ought to be sinful, apart from the fact that it was entirely proper. Green and gold about her frame, ribbons of red, green, and gold in her hair, lips that were so perfectly red that he immediately kissed her. Thoroughly.

Honora hummed against his lips, giving him a bemused look when he pulled back. "What in the world was that for?"

"Couldn't help myself," he murmured, stroking her cheek that was now tinged with pink. "You are a gift, and it is Christmas."

"Stop that," Honora scolded as she nudged him without much pressure. "Besides, I do have a gift for you. It's downstairs."

"Are you sure?" Gage wrapped his arm around her waist, kissing the side of her head. "I am fairly certain it is here."

He heard the quiet laughter, knew how her cheeks would color, and pulled them to a stop, wrapping his arms around her and pulling her back against his front.

"Gage," Honora protested weakly, though she made no attempts to move away. "You just tried to hurry me along."

"Very short-sighted on my part," he insisted. He held her close, pressing his mouth to the top of her head, just breathing in the scent of her. "I miss our walks to the beach. Just you and me. I miss you."

She leaned her head back against him, her laughter a little louder now. "I am right here, and you've had no chance to miss me."

"Not true." He nuzzled against the perfectly coiled and set mass of her hair, then pressed his lips to the side of her neck, loving how she shivered against him. "I miss having only you here. Every minute of every day, just us. Before my accident, I had no idea how much... how badly... Ugh. Why are words difficult when I'm with you?"

"That should be my line," Honora whispered, bringing him back to the night before and making him hold her even closer, biting back a groan of need that there was no time to sate.

He'd never felt like this about anyone. The closer he grew to Honora, the closer he wanted to be. The more he knew her, the more he wanted to know. The more he wanted her...

It was a never-ending build, these feelings. Never enough.

How did anyone live like this? He was going to go mad, and yet he had never been so happy, so content, in his entire life. He couldn't even recognize the man he had been before her, let alone the life he had led.

There was only Honora.

How could he hope to explain that?

"Gage," she said on a sigh, patting his arms. "We have to go."

He nodded, pressing a quick kiss to her neck again. "I know, and my present for you will be downstairs as well."

That got her to turn, looking up at him in surprise. "Mine? You didn't have to give me anything!"

Gage returned her look with one of utter derision, apart from the hint of complete adoration that always adorned his looks for her. "Yes, I did. It's Christmas, and you are my wife, among the many greater things you are. What sort of heel would I be if I didn't get you something?"

She rolled her eyes, tsking at his statement. "Fine, let's get to them before we have to meet the others."

Reluctantly, he removed his arms from her and took her hand instead, moving down the corridor towards the stairs. Now he had to cope with his feelings for his wife superseding Christmas? What was this madness she stirred up in him? And why was he so delighted about it?

Once they were down the stairs, Honora began to lead, pulling him into the drawing room. Some papers had been rolled up and tied with ribbon, and she released his hand to fetch it. She turned back to him quickly, her skirts swirling about her petticoats with the force of her eager motions, her smile beaming.

"Someone is delighted with herself," Gage said with a laugh, folding his arms.

"It's really nothing," Honora assured him as she started towards him. "And it might be a present that is more for me than you, but I think… I hope…" She bit her lip, then released it quickly, giving him a quick warning look before holding it out to him. "Merry Christmas, Gage."

He took it from her with a smile, sliding the ribbon off and unrolling the pages. It was sheets of music, and as he looked through them, there were at least three different songs in there. He recognized two of the titles, but he had never sung any of them before. He'd never been given music before, as he rarely let anyone know he could sing, and most of his mining friends and coworkers didn't read music. They only learned it from others and handed it down.

But this…

"Your voice is so lovely, Gage," Honora told him quietly. "I want to hear it more often. Even if it is just for me. So I found a few songs that I thought would suit both your taste and your voice. They're all folk songs, Gage. This one? This is Irish and Scottish, depending on who you talk to. This one is from Cornwall, so Emblyn tells me. And this one… this one I adore. Robert Burns."

Gage only half heard her, looking through the notes and words, the melodies and the harmonies creating a beautiful symphony of sound in his mind. It was a simple gift, but personal, too. Intimate, even, knowing how little he sang. Encouraging, tasteful, thoughtful, and utterly sweet.

He swallowed, a wash of emotion rising within him. He took her hand and brought the back to his mouth, kissing it with feeling before holding it to his cheek. "Thank you, Nora. This is amazing."

"It really isn't," she hedged, even as one of her fingers traced against his cheek.

Her usual action when he held her hand like this. As though she refused to be left out of the show of affection, and her fingers couldn't help themselves. Did she know how much he adored her touch? How much he adored her? And this connection between them?

"It is," Gage insisted. "You see me, Nora. Like no one ever has. That's what this shows me. Thank you." He leaned in and kissed her, loving how she leaned into him when they kissed.

Honora sighed as he broke off, her small smile telling him as much as her blush. "You really like it?"

He lifted a brow. "You need more convincing?"

She immediately stepped back with a giggle, holding her hands out as though to restrain him. "Not right now, no."

"But… later?" he finished hopefully.

Honora barked a laugh, then covered her mouth, her brilliant green eyes dancing with light and, he flattered himself, desire.

"That is not a no," Gage pointed out with a nod. "Good. Now, for your present." Grinning at her, he reached into his trouser pocket and pulled out a small box.

Her eyes widened as she looked at it. "Expensive things come in small packages."

Gage laughed in surprise, closing the distance between them. "Who said that?"

"My mother." Honora swallowed, her skin going just the slightest bit pale. "Every time one of her friends sent something. It was an attack on my father, even if he never heard it."

"Well, this," Gage said slowly, trying to catch her eye, "is not nearly as expensive as your trousseau was."

As he'd hoped, she smiled, and color returned to her cheeks. She flicked her gaze to his eyes. "Nothing is as expensive as that was."

He nodded once. "So there's nothing to be afraid of in here." He opened the box and showed the contents to her.

He watched her face as her entire being softened, her lips parted, and her eyes began to shine. "Oh, Gage…"

"You already have my mother's ring," he murmured, taking the delicate band from its box. "She only ever wore the simple gold band. I thought that would be enough, but you deserve something that is just for you."

He took her right hand and slid the ring onto her fourth finger. "Rose gold is made with copper and gold, which I thought was apt. I cannot prove any of the copper came from our mine, but we can pretend. And the gems…" He shrugged, running his thumb over their surface. "I know that topaz and garnet are popular and significant to some, but that didn't seem right for you. Emerald and diamond was all I could see, and you are like a wildflower, so I asked them for petals. I hope you like it."

Honora exhaled in a rush and stepped into him, wrapping her arms around him and laying her head against his chest.

She said nothing, but her embrace was almost clenching.

"What is it, love?" Gage whispered, encircling her with his arms. "What's wrong?"

"Nothing," she told him, her voice clogged with tears. "Nothing is wrong. Nothing could be wrong. This… is the happiest I have ever been. Ever."

Gage groaned and tightened his hold, resting his chin upon her head. "Darling girl. Hearing that makes me as sad as it does delighted. I want you to be happy. That is all I have ever wanted for you. You deserve to be happy, Nora. But you should always have been happy. It breaks my heart that you weren't."

"I don't care about that anymore." She sniffled and turned her face to rest her chin on his chest, peering up at him. "Just us. Just here. Just you."

He kissed her then, slowly and sweetly, the taste of her tears driving him wild, heightening the sweetness of her and his desire to protect her from any and all hurts.

"I want to make you happy, Nora," Gage confessed, his mouth moving to her brow, dusting against her hairline. "Do I?"

"Yes," she breathed. "So much." She laughed very softly then, surprising him. "And not because you just gave me the most beautiful, perfect ring I have ever seen."

Gage chuckled, kissing her brow quickly. "Cheeky little wife. But the ring didn't hurt my cause, did it?"

"Hmm-mm," Honora agreed. She reached up and cupped his face, forcing him to meet her eyes. "Thank you, my love. Thank you."

Gads, he could have died right then without any regrets. She always called him darling or wretch or something teasing. She had never once called him her love.

Could she love him? Was he really that fortunate? It wasn't a declaration, technically, but suddenly, he hoped as he had never hoped in his entire life. He wanted her love more than he wanted to breathe, not because she was married to him or because he gave her things or because she was grateful for the rescue his proposal had been, but because she could freely give it. Because she felt it. Because it was real.

Because it was true.

And he wanted to give her his love, as soon as he was sure of it. He wanted to love her. He could probably convince himself that he already did, if he worked hard enough, but that wasn't enough. She deserved the real thing. The sure thing. The knowledge.

If he hinted that he might love her or that he was falling in love with her or anything with room to maneuver, she would inhabit the space that remained. She would be consumed by doubts and worries, by insecurities and nerves, and she would never believe that he would get to the full scope. He could not bear to have her thinking that way, let alone living in such a state. She would not expect him to love her, given how their marriage had been entered into, but he could see in her the craving for love. And her great capacity for it.

Someday, they would have enough love to fill their hearts, their lives, their homes... Until he could say the words without doubt or reservation, he would keep the possibility, such as it was, to himself.

"Merry Christmas, Mrs. Trembath," he whispered, touching her fading blush.

She hummed a laugh. "Merry Christmas, Mr. Trembath." With a sigh, she stepped back, wiping at her eyes. "Now, we really need to hurry, or the *ceilidh* will start without us. Are you singing tonight?"

He offered her his arm, and grinned as impishly as he could. "I might be. Are you?"

She lifted a shoulder in an adorable shrug as she looped her arm through his. "I might be. Ironically, no one asked me to sing any Christmas songs."

"What?" he protested without feigning anything at all. "That is a travesty. Can I make an amendment to the evening? I refuse to let Christmas pass without a Christmas song."

"I am quite certain there will be an opportunity for requests," Honora told him as she donned her cloak. "Will you sing a carol on command?"

Gage laughed as he slipped into his greatcoat. "If they can play it, I can sing it. And I don't say that often; only for Christmas."

"Understood." Honora took his arm again as they traipsed outside, walking the cold distance to their barn.

It was interesting, using the barn in the winter. There wasn't snow on the ground, which was fairly typical for Cornwall, but there was the cold bite in the air that spoke of the time of year. It could be cold in the barn, but if they were dancing enough, they would be warm. And there would probably be glasses of mahogany, which could warm the dead. And they could always build a fire outside of the barn and sing around it. There was nothing that said they had to remain inside for the entire *ceilidh*.

At least, he didn't think so.

It had been a long time since he had been to one.

And never as an adult.

The sounds of fiddling filled the air the closer to the barn they got, and Gage grinned at it. "Sounds like it's already well underway."

"Knowing your cousins, I would expect nothing less." Honora gave a little skip, her expression filled with light.

"And to think I once thought you were perfectly sedate," Gage mused, shaking his head in amusement.

"I was then," she retorted. "I didn't know much about myself, but now I do." She smiled up at him proudly.

He returned it, feeling almost smug on her behalf. "And what is it that you know, Nora?"

Honora thought about that for a moment. "I know I like dancing, especially if it's for fun and without restraints. I know I like your singing as much as I like singing myself. I know I feel more at home in Cornwall than I ever did in Bath. I know that life is filled with more joy and hope than I ever thought. I know that I'm not worthless."

Her smile changed, then. It became soft and content, something he wasn't certain he had ever seen on her face before. He wasn't even certain there was a definition to the emotions he was seeing. It wasn't pride, although there were shades of that. It wasn't confidence, though there was a trace. There was satisfaction, understanding, relief, grace, pity, sadness…

It was a lifetime of emotions in one face in a handful of heartbeats.

"I don't know everything about myself," Honora told him in a lower voice, "but I know that I am finding out here in this life with you. Thank you, Gage. For wanting me to be myself, whoever she is. For not asking me to be someone else. For insisting I make decisions for myself. It would have been easier for both of us if I just did and said whatever you asked, whatever you wanted. But you haven't done that, not even once. I just… Thank you. So much."

He had not been prepared for this. It was not something he could laugh off, something he could tease her out of. It was not even something he could kiss her for. This was too deep, too serious, too significant for him to do anything but address it honestly and directly, possibly without much by way of sign of affection. Just taken with the same solemnity with which it was given.

"You don't need to thank me for that, Honora," he told her, choosing to use her full name for this. "Ever. You should have always had the freedom to be yourself. And now you always will. I've never wanted a life with someone who is a glorified servant. I wanted a wife, and to me, that means a partner. A woman, not a puppy. A friend, if I was so fortunate. Whoever she was going to be, I would have wanted her to be herself. And I am and will ever be eternally grateful that she turned out to be you. Whoever you are, whoever you become, whoever you discover yourself to be. Partner, wife, woman, friend. You are all of those things, Nora. All of them."

She was more as well, but he couldn't get into all of that. Not now, not tonight.

Honora smiled gently and leaned into him, her head going to his shoulder, and she said nothing else.

Gage wasn't sure anything else needed to be said, especially not by him. Unless he told her that he loved her, but he couldn't say that yet. He wasn't certain yet.

There would be a perfect time and place and moment when he was certain, and when she would believe him. When she would fully believe that she was actually worth every word.

She might know now that she wasn't worthless, but that didn't mean she would believe the true value of her worth.

Then again, she might never believe that. He would spend his entire life trying to prove that to her, but she might still believe differently.

But when he loved her, when he could say it and mean it, she might believe that.

Believe him.

The barn was alight, just as it had been the night of the harvest supper, and as they approached, Gage could see the festive greenery hung within the place. There was something about it that lightened his heart immediately. Made him eager to dance. Created music in his chest.

Honora stepped into the barn first, the light dancing across her features like fire on ice, her smile the brightest light of all. "Oh, look! Pádraig and Ailís are already playing with the musicians!"

Gage removed his greatcoat and handed it to the footman nearby. "Then hurry out of your cloak, Mrs. Trembath, so we can dance to it before they are done!"

She was quick to do so, all but seizing his hand and yanking him towards the dance floor. There weren't many others in the barn yet, but those who were joined in at once, as did those who arrived shortly thereafter. Pádraig and Ailís grinned at the group as their fingers flew across their violins, their talent somehow blatant and understated at the same time, their joy in the music and the occasion evident.

It was setting the tone for the entire evening, and he was so grateful for it.

That dance was followed by another, and another, and another, Gage trying to make an effort to dance with each of his cousins before moving on to friends and neighbors. Some of the music was festive for the holidays, some was simply festive for dance in Ireland or Cornwall. His cousins Áine and Roisín sang a beautiful and jaunty rendition of "I Saw Three Ships" that everyone else danced to, while Dónal played his bodhrán along with them. It was the sort of evening that his parents would have lived for.

Taking a brief moment of respite with a glass of mahogany in hand, Gage grinned as he saw John and Julia Roskelley enter the barn. He waved them over, delighted to see that Julia looked perfectly well, whole, and strong after the delivery of her boys. One might never know she had done so, looking at her tonight. In fact, if Gage looked around now, seeing those in attendance, he might have thought this scene twenty years old and begun looking for his mother and father among the crowd.

Except Honora wouldn't have been there twenty years ago, and he wouldn't have felt this way twenty years ago.

Details.

"*Nadelik Lowen!*" he greeted as they reached him, handing out two glasses of mahogany to them. "How are the babies?"

"Loud," Julia said with a laugh. "Beautiful. Amazing. Exhausting. Pick a word, and it is apt." She took the glass of mahogany, and as was wise, only sipped it. She made a face, then smacked her lips.

"Every year, I forget that I hate this stuff. But tradition, right?" She took another sip and shuddered.

John barked a laugh and took a drink from his own glass. "Tastes fine to me, darling." He downed the rest, grimaced worse than his wife had, and shook his head. "Strong, though. I see your wife isn't dancing, Gage. May I?"

"Please," he replied, gesturing to the dance floor.

John left with a squeeze to his wife's arm, heading directly for Honora, who grinned in response to his request.

"She looks happy," Julia told Gage with a sigh. "And not just because it is Christmas."

He grunted softly "She is happy. She told me."

Julia looked up at him. "When?"

"Tonight, before we got here." He smiled helplessly, shrugging. "Not too bad for a marriage that made you nervous, eh?"

His friend scoffed a little loudly for his taste. "If you're expecting a sainthood for not being an arse in your marriage, I'm afraid you'll be vastly disappointed."

"What?" he said with a laugh. "Julia, she's happy! You wanted me to make her happy!"

"So congratulations are in order for doing the bare minimum of what a good husband ought to do? Look." She faced him more fully, setting her glass aside and folding her arms. "I love you like a brother, but you are a warm human, and you were going to make any woman happy just because you aren't an arse. And I am happy that my cousin is happy, just as I am happy that you are happy. I can see that you are. I could see it in Honora's eyes when she visited the other day. Do you know what else I could see?"

Slightly worried, Gage shook his head.

"Love," Julia said bluntly, her mouth curving into a slight smile. "My cousin is in love with you, Gage. She might not have said it yet, might not understand it yet, but I can see it. And I know full well that you aren't indifferent to her in that way."

"Far from it," Gage admitted roughly, his eyes moving to his wife at once, as though his heart knew where she was at any given moment.

Julia put a hand on his arm. "Be careful, Gage. Honora is

stronger than she looks, but she is also fragile. She craves love and doesn't realize it. And she'll believe the worst nine times out of ten. With her insecurities, she could read something in nothing faster than a heartbeat."

"Why do you think I haven't told her that I'm falling in love with her?" Gage asked with more harshness than he should have. He swallowed, shaking his head. "I know I need to be all or nothing for her to believe me. I know that she'll never see herself the way she is, let alone the way I do. That kills me, Julia. I want to tell her that it isn't just physical, I want her to know…" He bit his lip, clearing his throat. "But I know her, Jules. I know where her head will take her, and I won't risk it."

"You're a good man, Gage Trembath. And I'm glad my cousin loves you." Julia patted his arm fondly, then turned back to the dancing. "So, the sooner the two of you can give my boys a cousin to play with, the better."

Gage coughed in surprise, choking on laughter after the fact. "Julia Elizabeth Shipley Roskelley, a lady does not speak of such things."

"Blame yourself," Julia quipped, "and the mahogany you provided. Now, if you don't mind, I'm going to ask the musicians to play 'The Holly and the Ivy' and have Honora sing it." She moved away without another word, leaving Gage chuckling behind her.

Did she really think Honora loved him? How could she be sure? How could he? Not that he needed Honora to have the same clarity of her thoughts that he did, but to think that she could… that she would…

That such a woman would give her generous heart to him was more than he deserved.

But now, at least, he had something to hope for.

243

Chapter Twenty-Two

"Last dance! Last dance, ladies and gentlemen!"

Honora smiled at the groan of dismay from the guests. She felt the same way, but she and Gage thought the musicians did not need to spend the entirety of Christmas night entertaining them. Given they had their own musicians with the Dolan cousins, the singing they still wanted to do would be easy enough. Besides, Gage had already sung a traditional Irish carol, *"Dia do Bheatha,"* accompanied by all of his instrument-playing cousins, and Honora had sung "The Holly and the Ivy" and a French carol she adored, *"Noël Nouvelet."* The cousins had sung several other Irish carols that had enchanted the entire gathering and made the dancing even more enjoyable.

"The evening is not ending," Gage laughed, waving down the upset. "The night isn't over. We're only letting our hired musicians go home to be with their families. We have other musicians here, so stay as long as you like!"

That got some cheers from the gathering, and Gage turned to the musicians with a quick gesture.

Honora moved towards him, then stopped as he went to the group of people nearest him. Were they not going to dance this time? It was fine, if that was the case, and the evening was not about to end just because the dancing did. There were many people here, and perhaps he wanted another dance with one of his cousins, as they would likely not have dancing again before they returned to Ireland. And dancing could always take place unexpectedly during music later.

Her heart crashed into her ribs when she saw Gage moving out to the dance floor. With Lady Margaret Hastings.

Honora looked at the group they had come from, and saw Basset, John, and Julia there, still laughing about something or other. The childhood friends who had been so close once, now reunited and reinstating those bonds. All hurts were healed, or healing, and there was nothing to keep them from being just as they had been before.

Except Gage had loved Margaret before.

And now he was dancing with her when he was supposed to be dancing with Honora.

She swallowed and moved back towards the wall, pretending to inspect one of the holly boughs. This was stupid, her husband could dance with whomever he wanted without it meaning something. A dance was not a proposal, and besides, he was married to Honora.

But why, in the last dance of the evening, did he have to dance with her? And why did the entire gathering stare at them as though it meant something?

He had told her that there was nothing to fear from Margaret, and she had done her best to believe that, even to the point of inviting her to various engagements and suppers without reservation. It was easy enough, as Margaret was vibrant, cordial, gracious, effusive… She was as wonderful as she was beautiful, and Honora had to work very hard to not resent her for it.

Seeing how happy she was while dancing with Gage, how entertained that whole group had been together, Honora found resentment and loneliness close at hand.

"Ee be looking like yer in some taking, Honora," came the low, coarse, warm voice of Emblyn suddenly at her elbow. "What troubles ee?"

"Gage," she whispered, turning to face the dancing. "It's stupid, it's nothing."

"But…?"

Honora swallowed. "The last dance is supposed to be mine. He said it would be a tradition. And it would be fine, except…"

"Except the iggit chose her."

"I want to believe it's nothing," Honora hissed between now clenching teeth. "He said she was no threat, but…"

"The heart does not forget as soon as the head," Emblyn told her, something clipped in her tone. "Trus' me."

Something Borrowed

Honora looked at her friend in shock, not at all caring for the pallor in her cheeks and suddenly haunted looks. "Emblyn?"

"I had a love once," she whispered. "And 'e still lives in mine heart, tho' I'd wish 'im gone." She cleared her throat and turned to Honora. "Gage be an honorable man, Honora. Ee knaw this."

"I know," she replied weakly. "I know he is, and he would never hurt me. But our marriage wasn't founded on love. It wasn't even founded on affection—that has only happened since. And as for love…"

"Honora, I heard sommat t'other day and ee need to hear me now."

Honora blinked, the coarse accent and word choice giving her a bit of confusion before she could translate it. "Heard something?" she repeated when she could. "When?"

Emblyn craned her neck, looking away for a moment. Her high cheekbones and pale eyes gave her an almost ethereal appearance, even amidst the simple calico of red, black, and green she wore. Her hair was wrapped about her head like a halo or wreath, rather like Adelaide's, though Emblyn's hair was dark, like her brother's. The similarity in siblings wasn't an obvious one, given they only shared a father, but in this light, with her profile, the family resemblance was plain.

"Emblyn," Honora said firmly. "When?"

"When Gage was recovering from his injury," she finally said, returning her attention to Honora. "I'd been at Helwithin with ee, and he was in the library. Lady Hastings called, and I looked for a book while ee fetched a shawl."

"That was weeks ago," Honora whispered.

Emblyn nodded once. "I thought it was nawthun tearun, but something… tidden sit right. I be close to 'em, but naw close enough for perfect hearin'. Still, seeing how ee be hurting, I be certain ee need to knaw."

Honora didn't want to hear this. Didn't want to know. Didn't want to doubt, fear, speculate, despair…

But she couldn't help herself.

She needed to hear it.

"Tell me," she managed to force out, grinding her teeth.

246

"Lady Hastings told Gage she'd ne'er stopped thinking of 'im that way," Emblyn said in a low voice. "I ain't be certain what way that is, but she said as much. She asked if she could explain herself. She dropped her voice, so I heard nawthun. But then I heard Gage ask her what was wrong with the future they had thought of, and what she really wanted."

It wasn't heartbreaking, but it certainly did lower her spirits. Gage was entitled to know what had caused Margaret to abandon their plans, and he absolutely deserved to know what Margaret wanted, especially if she was trying to bring things from the past into the present. She wanted to ask Emblyn about Gage's tone, his expression, his posture, anything, but she knew that Emblyn probably could not speak to anything related to that, given the situation in the library.

But she knew there was more, and that terrified her.

Emblyn cleared her throat. "I ain't heard what she told 'im, but after whatever she said, Gage said he had held a grudge for far too long and apologized. Sommat else was said, and Lady Hastings said a word about you."

Honora tried to nod, but her head and neck felt frozen. "What was it?"

"That ee are utterly adorable and sommat else, and then she'd be cursed for even thinking it. Afore ee ask, I don't know what she meant." Her pale eyes were locked on Honora's, and there was something in them that held her just as frozen. "Gage then said sommat about a marriage of convenience, sommat too early to tell, and sommat about wanting to. Then ee came in, and all was over."

Honora felt air rush out of her lungs, felt her knees shake, felt her stomach curl into a fist of sorts that just sank among the rest of her organs. She looked out at the dancing again, seeing the laughter rampant on both of their faces as they moved along the patterns. There wasn't blatant adoration among them, but it was not the sort of dance where that would be visible. It was a jaunty, energy-filled dance, not something slow, sedate, and filled with chances to display longing.

If longing was what they felt.

"Honora, I ain't saying such to hurt ee," Emblyn told her, taking her hand. "Ee knaw that. Ee knaw Gage be like a brother to me. I ain't wishing to hurt 'im either. This was weeks afore, and it might be nawthun now."

"I know," Honora breathed, finding some motion in her neck and chin to nod now. "So much has changed since then, and yet…"

"Gage would ne'er hurt ee."

Honora managed to smile, nodding still. "Intentionally. He would hate knowing he hurt me. He would hate knowing he hurt anyone. And I would hate knowing I'd kept him from something he wanted."

Emblyn's brow creased. "Honora, ee can't be saying…"

"I'm not saying anything at the moment," Honora assured her. "I am only speaking. Gage is a wonderful man. It is Christmas. He cares for and about me, and he is trying. That will be enough."

She might have been convincing herself, but there was nothing else to do about it now. She needed to cling to what she knew and not what she feared. She was Mrs. Trembath, not Margaret. She was the one who was married to him, the one who just might be having his child, and the one with whom his future lay.

He had promised not to stray outside of marriage. But she knew all too well what promises could be worth between spouses, if the respect faded. Gage was not the sort to disrespect his wife, but would he have wished that the promise might not have been made? Would he wish for a polite marriage without boundaries instead?

Or was his present desire for and physical attraction to Honora to remain paramount?

The dance ended, and the musicians began to disperse. Gage and Margaret parted without further conversation, and then Gage headed for the side doors of the barn, bringing him closer to Honora. He didn't see her yet, his attention on something outside.

"Rowe! Get that fire going! There's more music to be had!" He laughed almost merrily, then glanced towards Honora and Emblyn. His face immediately changed, going nearly to horror in a flash. He started towards Honora with a determination that was almost frightening. "Nora… I completely forgot about the last dance, I am so sorry."

She could see that he was, and the rawness in her expression went a long way to healing the hurt. "It's all right. Truly."

He took her hands, bringing the one with the new ring to his lips. "No, it isn't. I fell into very old habits."

Honora did her best to shrug. "I can see why. You dance well together. Indeed, everyone seemed to enjoy watching."

Gage's dark eyes narrowed, and he lowered her hand. "Did they stare?"

"Of course they stared," Honora told him, trying for lightness, but certain she was coming off wrong. "A wealthy and beautiful widow returns to the place where she was raised, and dances with her former beau, and you don't think people would stare?"

He exhaled, clearly not believing her attempt at lightness. "I am sorry. I truly did not mean to upset you."

Tears began to form in Honora's eyes, and her throat clogged. "You forgot me."

"I know." He stepped forward and kissed her brow. "It won't happen again. I promise."

"I wish I could be sure of that," she whispered before she could stop herself.

"What was that?" he asked, tilting her chin up.

Honora shook her head, forcing herself to smile. "I wish I could hear Pádraig. More, I mean. Do you think he'll play for us outside?"

Gage cupped her cheek, smiling in a way that made his eyes crinkle. "I am sure he will. He already asked if he could play for you to sing. And we have something special planned ourselves."

Even among her pain, Honora brightened. "Have you? What is it?"

He tapped her nose. "Come out and see, love. You're going to adore it." He laced his fingers with hers and led her outside with some of the other guests. Some chose to remain in the barn, but the bonfire was close enough to provide additional warmth to them. It was designed for the closer family anyway, so those who wanted to leave were perfectly free to do so.

Gage brought her over and pretended to assist her as she sat upon one of the logs that had been placed about the fire. He bowed grandly, then moved over to Pádraig, Dónal, and two of the miners, who pulled out guitars and began tuning them.

Julia came over to sit beside Emblyn on her own log. "What are they doing?"

"They're going to play and sing, I guess," Honora laughed, linking her fingers and looping her hands around her knees. "Gage didn't tell me what."

Her cousin suddenly grabbed her hand, examining her ring. "Oh, Honora, that's gorgeous! Is it new?"

Honora beamed as she wiggled her fingers for her. "Yes! Gage gave it to me tonight."

"Emeralds and diamonds," Julia said on a sigh. "He always said he wanted to give someone emeralds and diamonds. At the time, we thought it would be Margaret, obviously. But I am so glad it's you." She grinned at Honora. "It suits you."

If only her cousin had left the words before that compliment out. If only it hadn't come on this night. If only…

Honora glanced at her ring, keeping her smile in place. Was it tarnished now that she knew it wasn't an original thought? Had he bought this ring for Margaret years ago and simply never given it to her? Had he really bought it just for Honora? Had it anything to do with Honora at all?

She loved her husband. She loved him. Breathed for him. Yearned for him. Utterly adored him.

But now… was he only feeling what he was for her because she was there? Would it have been the same for him with any woman he had married? He was a good man, a physically affectionate man, and a considerate man; none of those things were necessarily specific to Honora. He could have been happy with any woman who was without malice or greed or airs.

Did he mean what she felt she did to him simply because she was his? Her heart was his, and that was something she was free to give, but in the eyes of the law, she actually belonged to him. Did that have something to do with it? He was not the sort of man to view her as a possession to be claimed, but the fact that she was his, did belong to him, might mean that she was safe enough for him to become attached to.

It sounded so distant and aloof, so impersonal and indifferent. Perhaps not indifferent, as Gage would never be indifferent to anyone. But suddenly Honora did not feel as though she was in this marriage—this relationship—at all.

What was real? What was true? Was poor little Honora in love with a man who would never really love her in return? Was he wishing she was someone else? Was he seeing someone else when he was with her?

Would his pretending be enough for Honora's happiness? Or would it grow to curdle her love into resentment? Would she become her mother?

Oh, lands… What if she became her mother and ruined Gage's happiness because she had been foolish enough to fall in love?

She heard the guitars begin to play and managed to focus on the gathered men, illuminated by the light of the fire, her eyes fixing on Gage as though her life depended on it.

He looked thoughtful as he gazed into the flames, something whimsical and youthful in his expression. Something far away and deeply personal, without definition or explanation, but spoke to the depth of his emotions, if not his soul. It was possibly the most captivating he had ever been to Honora, and there was something about that feeling that frightened her.

As though she might lose him.

Pádraig joined the guitars with his violin, and Honora felt her eyes sting with tears at its sweet sound, especially with the slow, comforting strumming of the guitars.

Then Gage began to sing, his voice low, pure, and delicious.

"Bonnie Charlie's gone away,
Safely o'er the friendly main,
Many a heart would break in two,
Should he ne'er come back again."

The other men joined in next, their harmonies clean and haunting.

"Will ye not come back again?
Will ye not come back again?
Better loved ye cannot be.

Will ye not come back again?"'

Honora had never heard this song before, but suddenly, it was the most beautiful thing she had ever heard. The lyrics might have been about the Jacobite rebellion, but the words weren't about them at all, not to her. She was suddenly asking Gage the same question.

Would he not come back again to her? Not that he had ever left, technically, but she wished this day had never happened. That she had never heard of the conversation he'd had with Margaret. That he had never danced the last dance with Margaret. That she had not learned of his lifelong desire to give a woman emeralds and diamonds.

She wanted her ignorant bliss returned to her. The belief that perhaps Gage felt something for her deeper than physical, more sincere than affection, more enduring than respect.

She wanted him back. She wanted everything back.

The song continued, speaking of the Highland men so devoted to the Bonnie Prince, of the bribes they would not take, the hearts turned over to the cause, the complete absence of betrayal, and always asking the question of his returning to them. He would not come back to them in history, but the fervency of the cause, of that love, would still be spoken of for generations. Sung about for ages. Become part of legend and myth.

But the love remained.

Dónal joined in the music now with an Irish flute, piercing the air with its beauty and sweetness, soaring above the guitar and violin like a dove over the Cornish moors.

"Hear the lark's note, sweet and long,
Lilting wildly up the glen;
Yet to me he sings a song,
'Will ye not come back again?'"

Gage's eyes lifted a touch, still on the flames, but Honora found herself looking across the fire to wherever his eyes would have fallen without the blaze between them.

Margaret.

Her heart sank as she saw the serene expression on the woman's face, no less moved by the song than Honora was, and no less reflective.

Suddenly, the words were more painful to hear.

"Will ye not come back again?
Will ye not come back again?
Better loved ye canna be.
Will ye not come back again?"

Was Gage singing to Margaret? Asking her to come back to him? Confessing that she was better loved now than she had ever been, or that he loved her better than her late husband could have? Was she hearing the same thing that Honora feared? That Gage wanted her back with him?

How could a song full of beauty and hope one moment be the source of her anguish the next?

"Will ye not come back again?
Will ye not come back again?
Better loved ye canna be.
Will ye not come back again?"

The music trailed off and applause sounded from the gathering, and belatedly Honora joined in. After all, it had been beautiful and stirring.

That it had also crushed her was besides the fact.

Emblyn surprised her by favoring the group with a bal maiden song, her singing voice rather tremulous but sweet, and the men with guitars knew the song well enough to accompany her. Thus far, no Christmas carols were chosen for the fire, but no one seemed to mind. There was something about music that surpassed occasion or festivities at times, and simply sharing in its loveliness made everything relatable. And sometimes, made nothing relatable.

"Honora," her husband called softly from his position by the fire, his smile as gentle as ever. "Will you sing for us now?"

The request cracked her heart in a deep, resonating tone that only she could hear. She wanted to do anything that Gage asked her.

Anything that would make him happy. Anything that would keep such a smile on his face. Anything that embraced the life they were making together.

But singing while she was in agony would be a new test of her tenuous strength.

Still, she nodded and rose, walking over to Pádraig and the others. "Do you know 'The Lass of Aughrim'?"

The guitarists grinned, nodding, while Pádraig tuned his violin. "I'll be pleased to accompany ye on this one, cousin," he told her with a wink. "And if ye'd like to sing '*Oíche Nollag*' after, I'll be ready for ye."

Honora nodded, smiling at the mention of the song he, Ailís, and Honora had practiced for their own entertainment while they'd been visiting. Perhaps she would need a beautiful Christmas carol to lift her spirits after she sang the most melancholy song she could think of at the moment.

She needed melancholy in order to sing at all right now.

She stood next to the players, clasped her hands before her, and listened for the guitars to start, followed by Pádraig. Then she began to sing, closing her eyes to avoid looking at anyone at all.

Especially her husband.

She'd never get through this song if she looked at him.

The song spoke of longing, love, loss, and the hope of reconnection. Tokens that had passed between lovers, pleading to be reunited with the lost one, for memories to be recalled, and for feelings to be reciprocated, as they once had been. But there was no happy ending to this song, just a continual pleading.

Pleading.

Honora could not do so at this moment for herself, but as this young woman who was separated from her love, she could plead for the world and not be suspected. She could bare her heart and soul for all present and not be Honora Trembath. Not be the woman whose husband didn't love her as much as someone else. Not be the wife who could be bearing a child that could be the only link to keep a husband with her.

Not be a woman suffering heartbreak alone.

Music had always been expression for Honora, especially when she was younger and more restricted by her parents, but this was a new opportunity here. This was a chance to bare her heart and soul without the vulnerability of the real thing. A chance to reveal her pain without suspicion. A chance to send a message to her husband without addressing him. A chance to stop hiding while being perfectly hidden from everyone.

A chance to be Honora without anyone knowing she was being Honora.

Part of her was dying to see if Gage was looking at her in any particular way. If he bore the look of sheer adoration she had always dreamed someone would while she sang. The only romantic ideal she had ever held in her entire life. She wasn't beautiful, lovely, graceful, or charming. But she could sing, and surely that would attract a man someday, somehow. Surely that would give her something in her life.

Her life might not have had the courtship other women wished for, but she had only wanted, just once, to have some aspect of herself that someone could love. Her blush, much as Gage enjoyed it, did not count. She did not intend to blush, had not perfected her blush, wished she could not blush. But her singing… That was something she actually loved about herself, the only thing that she was proud of.

But if she opened her eyes to look at Gage, and he was not looking at her, it would hurt. If he was looking at Margaret, it would destroy her.

So she kept her eyes closed.

Better to be ignorant than wounded.

The song finished, and she mentally kicked herself as her voice wavered on the last note with her tears.

She heard the applause and opened her eyes, noting a pair of tears that leaked out at once, rolling down her cheeks. Gage was on his feet, looking as proud as a man could be, applauding her. Honora smiled and ducked her chin modestly, more for him than anyone else, hoping he would not catch the tears on her cheeks. She sniffed softly and looked up once more, catching the slight wrinkle in her husband's brow as he looked at her now.

She would break if he held her, brushed her tears, or asked her what was wrong, and she could not break.

Clearing her throat, she turned to Pádraig. "Can you and Ailís start up '*Oíche Nollag*?'"

He nodded and waved his sister over, murmuring the song to her. They conferred with the guitar players a moment, then began.

This time, Honora kept her eyes open, thought of Christmas, and smiled as she sang.

It was time to hide again.

Chapter Twenty-Three

Something was wrong with Honora, and Gage hated knowing that. It had been wrong since Christmas and was affecting the last few days his cousins would be at Helwithin. Not that they were complaining, or likely had even noticed, but Gage had noticed. Honora was quiet, far more like the girl he had known before his marriage than the one she had been after. She barely looked at him, though she didn't shy away from him or his touch, and in fact seem to cling to his hand more tightly when he held hers. She always seemed distracted, in her own world, and somehow smaller than her slight frame already made her.

She didn't seem to be there, even when she was there.

She retired early and alone, and when he peered into her rooms at the time he retired, she had been sound asleep. Each and every time. He wouldn't have minded had she talked to him about anything, but she hadn't. They'd had no time alone since Christmas, though there had been plenty of opportunities. Honora avoided being alone with him, of that he was certain.

It made asking for forgiveness for whatever he may have done virtually impossible.

Had it been the dance with Margaret at Christmas? He'd felt horrible about forgetting their tradition and had vowed to himself that he would dance only with her whenever the next occasion arose. But Honora wasn't petty, so he didn't believe she would hold that alone against him, particularly when he had apologized. So the hurt must be deeper, if hurt was indeed the issue at hand. If there was something else, he couldn't see it. Whatever her secret, she was not telling him, and that worried him.

He missed his wife. His friend. His lover, too, but he missed the other parts of her more. He missed her smile, the light in her eyes, the intensity of her attention, the gentle kisses she laid upon his shoulder when she thought he was asleep…

Gage actually ached when he saw Honora now. The distance between them felt immense, and he had no idea how to fix it.

He would give anything to not be going to a dinner party at the Teague home at this moment, but there was no good reason to turn it down. He wished he could have sent his cousins on ahead, as their imminent departure was the reason for this party in the first place. One last evening of the old friendships, they had said.

Gage was more afraid he'd already had his last evening with the wife he adored.

But with Honora not talking to him without others around, he'd not had a chance to ask if they could spend the evening at home alone, and his cousins likely would have felt duty-bound to remain home with them, had they stayed. So here they were in a carriage, rambling off to Chyandour, Grainne and her husband sitting beside Honora, while Máire and her husband sat beside Gage across from them.

Honora looked out of the window the entire time.

The only positive aspect of the situation was that it allowed Gage to stare at his wife blatantly without her scolding him.

She was incomparable, and not just because he missed her. Her gown was some grayish purple, the color of lavender fields on a cloudy day, and it made the color of her eyes stand out like the purest oasis God had ever created. Ribbons, lace, florets, and embroidery decorated the entire expanse of fabric, either in shades of purple or gold, and it only made her seem more impossibly regal in his eyes. Her cheekbones were the most perfectly sculpted piece of art he had ever seen, and it was taking all of his self-control to stop from running his thumb along her full bottom lip, it looked so tempting. Her hair was somehow coiled and curled and pinned as well as loose and flowing, which had him sitting on his hands to keep from tangling his fingers in her tresses.

He was going mad sitting here. Actually and honestly mad. He had never wanted his wife more badly since marrying her, but he truly just wanted to hold her in his arms. Feel her heartbeat against his own. Smell the faint scent of flowers in her hair. Sense the minimal weight of her against his legs as she curled against his chest.

He bit back a groan as he saw Honora bite her lip. How had they grown so far apart so fast?

"Honora," Máire said to the silence, "are you and Ciarán going to sing the song I heard you practicing earlier?"

Honora nodded, lowering her eyes to the floor as she turned to raise them to Máire without having to look at Gage. "I believe so. It's a beautiful song; I am so glad he brought it with him."

Máire grinned across the carriage. "He is the best of us, musically speaking. One of these days, we need to find him a wife. The children adore him, as you've seen. If you have any ideas for him…"

Honora's smile was faint but seemed genuine enough. "You'd want an English bride that might keep him from living in Ireland?"

"Why not?" Máire shot back. "You're English, and we love you. Gage is English, and… Well, we try."

The others in the carriage laughed, and Gage could only shrug for the benefit of the rest. "Half Irish used to be good enough, Máire."

"Aye," she replied, reaching over her husband to pat his knee. "For Auntie Brigid, we try hard. Uncle John tried to be Irish, remember, Grainne?"

Grainne groaned at the reminder, while Gage only laughed. "It was the worst accent, Honora," she said. "Days alive, but 'twas offensive to the ears. Bless his soul, but 'twas."

"You didn't have to hear him practice, girls," Gage pointed out, giving each a significant look. "Torture. Pure torture. Mama begged him to stop, but he only tried harder."

"Oh, but he hugged ye like the day was ending, didn't he?" Máire sighed, leaning her head on her husband's shoulder. "And all was right wi' the world when he did."

"Aye," Grainne agreed, smiling. "Aye, he did. Ne'er did a man love so hard as Uncle John. And ne'er was he afraid to show it." She looked at Gage, winking a little. "Ye take after him thar, Gage. Lovin' hard and huggin' long."

"Well, at least I have that going for me," he mumbled, his cheeks beginning to heat as he looked down at his hands. "Something to live up to, I suppose."

"It's a fortunate inheritance," Honora said softly, making his ears burn. "One to be extremely proud of."

He looked up at her, hardly daring to hope.

But her eyes were also on his hands, not on his face.

"I could only dream of such a legacy," she went on, as though she hadn't noticed his attention. "Such a family."

It broke Gage's heart to hear her say so, knowing exactly what she had endured and from whom. He leaned forward, elbows on his knees, and reached out a hand, praying she wouldn't pull away.

Blessedly, Honora reached out in response, laying her fingers in his and curling them in a secure hold. She might not look at him, but she was touching him.

Gage rubbed his thumb over her fingers gently, just as he had done thousands of times.

She didn't reciprocate, but she didn't let go.

It was something, at least.

"But ye're part of our clan now, Honora," Grainne told her, leaning around her husband to give her an encouraging smile. "And love and affection don't require blood relatives to be inherited."

Gage could have hugged the life out of his cousin for such a sweet statement, but he wasn't about to let go of his wife's hand while she held his. It was as close to a hug as he was going to get, and he was doing his utmost to convey everything he was feeling through the tips of his fingers.

She adjusted her hand, and so did he, now hooking his fingers against hers tightly, forming a spiral between them that could have withstood shocking forces.

Her eyes raised to his, and Gage felt the shock of that connection rocking his entire frame, leaving no fiber or joint untouched by light. He smiled at her, not bothering to hide the relief at seeing her eyes on him. They searched his for a moment, then, impossibly, a corner of her mouth lifted, softening her features just enough to give him hope.

"Aye, Honora," Máire chimed in, reminding Gage of the

conversation at hand. "Like it or not, ye're part Dolan now!"

"Yer a Lynch now, *mo mhuirnín*," her husband pointed out with a chuckle.

She elbowed him hard. "Always a Dolan, no matter what else I am."

The carriage pulled up to the rustic yet majestic edifice of Chyandour, drawing Gage's attention to it. Years of memories flashed through his mind in an instant, and he hadn't set foot in this house since...

Honora's hand was tugged out of his, stopping his thoughts in their tracks and bringing him back to her. She was fidgeting with her gloves, brushing her skirts, adjusting her cloak, all perfectly natural things to be doing as they arrived, and yet...

The timing of those actions with his thoughts was eerie, and the brusqueness of her motions was entirely unlike her.

He flicked his eyes from the house to her again, something not sitting right. Surely she wasn't... surely she didn't think...

But there was no time to ask her anything, as the door to the carriage was opened and the step pulled down. Honora moved for the door before Gage could, using the footman to help her down. His cousins and their husbands followed, and Gage exited last, straightening his jacket as he prepared to enter. Honora didn't wait for him to escort her, just moving along with the rest of them into the house without fanfare or procession.

There was nothing for Gage to do but follow, frowning at his wife's back in confusion. The second Helwithin carriage pulled up as he moved, and the third just behind them. The entire entourage had arrived, which meant even fewer chances to get Honora alone.

Unless he had very good luck.

The Teagues waited inside the entrance hall with Margaret, all coordinated with shades of gold in their gowns and in Mr. Teague's weskit, and all bearing brilliant smiles for them all.

Honora greeted them first, her manner, smile, and voice perfectly warm and cordial, without any sign of strain in her features. She even kissed cheeks with Margaret, which startled Gage, given her reaction to pulling up to the house. If she was mad at Gage, that anger did not extend to Margaret. Or at least, did not prevent her from excellent manners and gracious behavior.

What was going on here, and how could he make it right?

The cousins paid their respects, and Gage stepped up as he heard the other cousins coming in behind him.

"Mr. Teague," he greeted with a nod, holding a hand out to shake. "Mrs. Teague."

"Gage, darling," she replied with a motherly smile while her husband looked beyond him to the next arrivals without any conversation. "Thank you for accepting our invitation. We have so many wonderful memories of your cousins in your younger years."

"I am surprised you still invited us after those memories," Gage told her. He moved his attention to Margaret beside her. "Lady Hastings. How have your boys enjoyed Polmiskin Beach? I understand they were there this week?"

Margaret nodded, her smile bright and perfect as always, her gold ringlets tight and in place. "They were, and David believes it is the best beach he has ever seen. Martin is a touch more reserved, but at two, one must not blame him for holding his opinion back."

"No, indeed." Gage nodded, clasping his hands behind his back. "You look well."

"Thank you, I feel well. Being home has done me a world of good, but I am considering removing to Penzance soon. If you have any connections there for taking a house, I would appreciate a recommendation." She looked down at her gloves, her smile slight. "I find that I am now thinking of Hastings courting me here rather than forgetting how I miss him, so I thought Penzance might suit better. And the boys would enjoy extended time at a beach, if we can manage it."

Gage exhaled in sympathy and took Margaret's hand gently. "The boys will enjoy any place you take them, so long as you are with them. But you cannot escape the memories of Hastings forever, you know."

She dipped her chin in a nod, her throat tightening. "I know. We will return home in the summer, and David will become Lord Hastings in truth, but I am not ready yet." She sniffed and forced a laugh as she removed her hand from his to wipe at her eyes. "Now stop that and go see to your wife. She is absolutely stunning, and you are vastly fortunate that you are already married to her and that the only eligible bachelors here are your cousins. She would be snatched up in a second."

Gage looked towards the sitting room where the others had disappeared to, Honora's figure visible as she spoke with Basset. "Something's wrong, Margaret. I don't know what, but she's... distant. Quiet. Tired. And I don't know what to do."

"Be there," Margaret said quietly, pushing him in that direction. "I have an idea what it could be, but it is not mine to say. Be there. Be with her. Whatever it is, all will work out. You are both too good for it to be otherwise."

He gave her a quick smile over his shoulder and moved to the sitting room with the others.

Adelaide and Julia smiled at him as he entered. He nodded in greeting, looked at Honora, who was still chatting amiably with Basset, then went to the two ladies.

"No Emblyn?" he asked when he reached them.

"Not tonight," Adelaide said with a shake of her head. "She says she's had a little too much refinement lately, but I think it might be something else. Neither Basset nor I could pry anything else out of her, so we've just let her be."

Gage grunted softly. "It seems to be catching." He glanced towards Honora, feeling his shoulders sag as he took in the animation on her features that he couldn't seem to rouse anymore. "Something else that won't be talked about."

"Honora?" Julia asked, rising from her seat. "She seemed fine on Christmas. What happened?"

"I have no idea," Gage admitted, shaking his head. "I have no bloody idea, and it scares the hell out of me."

There wasn't time to discuss it more as the other cousins entered and took over the conversation, followed by the Teagues taking them all to the music room for some entertainment before supper.

"We have a special request for our first number this evening," Mrs. Teague announced as they waved everyone into seats. "Mrs. Trembath, would you sing a duet with Margaret? It has been a long time since we have heard her sing, and she refuses to sing a solo."

"Mama," Margaret protested with some vehemence. "Honora's

voice is far too beautiful to be matched with mine! It is not a fair duet!"

Mrs. Teague gave her daughter a loving but quelling look. "It is one song, Margaret, and it is your father's favorite. If your sister is not here to sing it with you, at least Mrs. Trembath can manage the high notes." She turned her attention to Honora, completely ignorant as to the awkwardness of the situation. "Please, Mrs. Trembath."

Gage looked at Honora, ready to go to her in a moment and tell her she didn't have to if he caught the slightest hint of distress.

But Honora was all serenity as she nodded, rising from her seat. "Of course. Mr. Teague deserves to hear his favorite. I only hope I can do it justice." She moved up to the front, followed by Margaret, who quickly told her what the song was, Gage presumed, for Honora smiled and patted her arm before Margaret asked her mother, "Do you have someone to play?"

Mrs. Teague was already moving to the pianoforte herself. "I will, if you please. It has been a long time since I have played for my daughters, but this song I know." She began to play, and the two other women adjusted their stance before the audience.

Gage stood behind the sofa from which Honora had left, keeping his eyes on her. She had sung plenty recently, and he had been privileged to hear most of it. She had sung with great feeling, even to tears on Christmas, and her power in song had never been stronger. Her gifts had never been more on display. Her majesty never so evident.

And the present distance between them made her more like an untouchable immortal goddess from mythology compared to his hopelessly weak and very fallible mortal form. Something he could dream about, and even worship, but never actually aspire to. But she had been part of him once, had permitted him a taste of her perfection, thus ruining him for anything or anyone else.

Very like those goddesses of old, then.

Was he doomed to always want her from afar now? Was there no hope for them?

Honora began singing first, the formality in her pronunciation reminding Gage of the very few times he had been to the opera in London, and combined with her purity in tone, had him more enraptured than he'd expected. It was so effortless for her, this stirring serenade, and it was impossible to be unmoved. His throat tightened, his eyes burned, and his heart threatened to burst through his ribs and chest just to get closer to her.

Then Margaret began her part of the duet, joining her voice with Honora's, and he suddenly had to blink hard. There was no comparing their voices, though Margaret was a fair enough singer by any accomplished standards. Hers was a lower range, which only added to the beauty of harmonies, but the true talent here was Honora, and everyone would know that.

Gage felt the awkwardness of the situation in a rather raw sense, as though he were Honora, being forced to stand beside the woman her husband had once loved. Forced to share her gift with the woman she felt most threatened by. He hadn't forgotten how worried Honora had been only weeks ago, how she didn't want to like Margaret, how uncomfortable she was about her. And he had assured her there was no threat there. Nothing to fear. The truth was that there wasn't, but that did not mean her fears would be abated.

She had included Margaret in parties and events regardless. She had smiled and talked and laughed, despite whatever she was feeling beneath the surface. She had been a friend and warm neighbor, putting a past she'd had no part in, but every right to fear, behind her.

And he had been idiotic enough to think there was nothing to worry about there. He had believed her act without probing further or seeking to reassure her.

He had no proof that she was concerned about Margaret or what had once been between them, though he and Margaret had settled everything about the truth of the past and the boundaries of the present. Had he even mentioned that to Honora? She knew he wouldn't be unfaithful to her, but was she fearing he might change his mind?

Was this distance even about Margaret? Was it more about Gage? Was there anything he could do about it?

The song was a stunning duet, and the awkwardness that prickled at his mind and throat began to ebb the more Honora sang. There was no doubt as to the skilled one in this duet, and there was no doubt as to the woman with whom he was meant to spend the rest of his life. There was only one voice that called to him, only one heart he hoped to claim, only one pair of arms he wanted wrapped around him.

Everything pointed to Honora. Everything should have been Honora.

Everything.

He closed his eyes as her iridescent voice touched a note so high and pure, it surely resided in heaven itself. He half expected to open his eyes and see the Almighty Himself sitting among them, or at the very least a half-dozen angels who had come down to offer appreciation. Was it possible for masterpieces to be constructed purely by one's voice? How would such a creation be properly appreciated, as artwork hanging in galleries was? Was what he was hearing any less exquisite than what the eye could take in?

The impulse to fall to his knees before his wife and beg her to be his was suddenly overwhelming. If he didn't think she would have been mortified by the publicity of the act, he might have leaned towards giving in, but the respect for her comfort was more important than his needs and desires. If they ever had a moment to themselves, he might be able to tell her just how confused, conflicted, concerned, and contrite he was feeling at this moment.

And how convinced he was that their life together was going to be perfect. Was perfect already. Was perfect because of her. Was worth anything because of her.

Rather like him.

Gage opened his eyes and focused directly on Honora, who was smiling at Mr. Teague as she sang rather than looking anywhere else. It was a sweet idea on her part, having been told it was his favorite song, but it did not give Gage a chance to meet her eyes. Had he been able to do so, perhaps he might have been able to convey the depth of his adoration with a look. Smile at her. Give her some kind of sign. Any sort of communication that she would note that might help his cause against whatever was tormenting her.

Anything.

The song came to an end, and Gage belatedly applauded, trying with difficulty to swallow his disappointment that her voice was now silent, that the experience was ended, that the moment had passed.

Honora and Margaret curtseyed for the group, and then Margaret took Honora's arm and whispered something to her that had Honora smiling, her cheeks turning a trifle pink.

His blush.

How he wanted to touch that blush now, as he had done so many times at home!

Mrs. Teague moved from the pianoforte and held Honora in place while Margaret returned to her seat. "Might I prevail upon you to sing again, Mrs. Trembath?"

Honora smiled, looking tired but pleased, at least to Gage's eyes. "I would be happy to. Ciarán, would you join me? And Áine, would you play?"

Gage smiled as his cousins got up and moved to the front. He'd heard them practicing a few times, but not with any real clarity, and certainly not enough to hear the words. But Ciarán's voice was powerful and pure, a good match for Honora's, and the performance ought to be a better demonstration of what Honora was capable of than any duet with Margaret.

Áine started to play, the notes booming and low, giving no indication of the melody as yet. Then Honora began to sing, a haunting and almost Celtic-sounding melody, perfectly in her range and attuned to her skills. Áine's fingers flew along the pianoforte, now reaching both high and low notes, echoing the haunting tones Honora had begun. The lyrics spoke of a woman begging the stars for answers, though the topic of those answers had yet to be explained, but the fervency in Honora's voice was unmistakable.

Then he heard the question as Áine's playing grew in intensity: Please tell me if he will stay.

Gage's breath caught in his chest as he looked at Honora in agony. Was she singing to him? About him? For him? Or was it just providence that the song spoke of his greatest fears?

Ciarán began singing then, apparently taking on the part of the stars answering her, and the power and gusto with which he did so was striking. The notes soared just as Honora's had, though there was none of the haunting sounds in his melodies. It was majestic and pure, encouraging and hopeful, the pianoforte sounding like a symphony rather than just a single instrument. The words were lost on Gage for the moment, as the response was in another language, likely Italian, but it was doing the trick, in his mind.

Convincing the pleading woman of the beauty of her love and to continue in hope.

At least, that's what he hoped he was saying.

Honora had another verse, back in the darker, more intense melodies that made the hair on the back of his neck stand on end. The notes of pain in her voice, the questions she asked, the desire to know the truth from these stars…

Her eyes met Gage's as she asked, and despite her recent avoidance of them, this time she stayed on him. Connected with him as she sang, and whether she was performing or genuine, he couldn't tell.

He didn't care.

He put a hand over his heart as she sang to him, kept it there as her verse ended and Ciarán began his encouraging response. The anthemic sounds of his cousin's voice spanned between Gage and Honora, swirled about them like some mystic breeze sent down directly from the heavens. As though the song were coming to life before his very eyes.

The roof of Chyandour could have come off, and he wouldn't have removed his gaze from Honora.

He couldn't.

The candles in the room reflected in Honora's brilliant eyes, illuminating them as though they could reach deep into her heart. And as though one searching for answers might find them if only they could look far enough.

Her heart was in her eyes, he realized. Always had been, which was why she had likely avoided his gaze. She would show him what she felt, and she didn't wish to.

His breath caught, and his lips parted as the connection between them took on new meaning, new depth, new power.

Honora and Ciarán sang together then, both in the language of Ciarán's verses, and somehow combining the haunting sound of her parts with the majesty of his. Still Honora stared at Gage, and still he stared back. The music was almost immaterial now, but not quite.

Her words were coming from her heart, regardless of the song, and he saw that.

Knew that.

Felt that.

She wasn't gone from him. Far from it. She was still there, her heart his for the taking, if only he could reach it. Whether that was love, loyalty, or respect, he didn't care. He would take what she could offer, however it would come.

She was still there. No matter what else she felt, how she hurt, or if she was angry, she was still there.

He could still hope.

And hope with all of his might he would.

He smiled at her, pressing his hand more fully against his heart, praying she might understand. She might see. She might also feel.

The last notes of the song trailed off, but Gage did not applaud this time. He kept himself connected to Honora until at last she lowered her eyes, the pink in her cheeks rising once more.

And with the corner of her mouth curving up, his heart skipped two beats, dancing with renewed life he had feared was gone.

She was still there. And so was he.

Chapter Twenty-Four

⁕

There could be no doubt about it now.

Honora was with child.

She was exhausted, she was sick every morning, and her courses had missed a second month. Her joy was mingled with worry, given her fears over Gage's feelings toward Lady Hastings, but there hadn't been any new occasions for her to worry about. Apart from singing beside Lady Hastings for her parents.

Honora never turned down an opportunity to sing, especially not when good manners dictated she do so, but she had been tempted to do so then. A duet with the woman who possibly still owned her husband's heart was more than she ought to have borne. An opportunity for her husband to stare at both of the women in his life without shame or embarrassment, and perhaps to finally choose one.

If he had done so, she couldn't tell.

Then again, with her increasing illness and fatigue, she spent most of her time in her rooms, so she was not exactly spending time in her husband's company. The Dolan cousins had left, so the excuse of guests and company was gone. The house was far too quiet, but she was never disturbed when she was in her rooms. Not even by Gage.

That troubled her.

He could have waited in her rooms for her as he had done weeks ago, and yet he had not. He could have invited her to come to the mine with him, and yet he had not. He could have done any number of things to bring Honora into his company and circle, and yet he had not.

They had meals together, apart from breakfast, unless Gage had gone to the mine. Their conversation was polite, but stilted. That may have been Honora's doing, as she couldn't seem to find the energy to carry on conversation as well as she used to. Her affectionate husband seemed to be continuing to keep the distance she had imposed, and she hated herself for setting it in the first place.

She wanted nothing more than to sit on his lap and curl into his chest, particularly when she was exhausted, weak, and scared.

What if she wasn't capable of being a good mother? What if she was as clueless about raising a child as she was about living her own life? What if her child hated her or couldn't find comfort with her? What if she was too petite or weak to manage childbirth and died before her child could attach to her?

Gage could raise their child with Lady Hastings, if that happened.

Lady Hastings would become Mrs. Trembath, and be the only woman that child knew as a mother.

Honora's eyes filled with tears as she walked the cliffs near Polmiskin, and she made no attempt to stop them. She cried daily now, sometimes multiple times a day, and without any reason half of the time. The day before, she had cried about her toast being cold when she had taken too long to finish it.

She only had small bursts of energy anymore, and she did her best to get out of the house when she had them. A walk out in the fresh air would surely do her and her baby good, so long as she didn't overexert herself. She grew woozy more easily as well, and if she tried to do too much…

She was desperate to ask anyone who would know better than she if any of this was normal or expected, but she dared not let her secret out yet. Adelaide would grow overly excited and tell Basset, who would probably congratulate Gage without thinking. Julia had far too much on her mind with her twins and the upcoming christening. The Grangers hadn't returned to Cornwall yet, and Honora didn't dare ask Lady Hastings.

Emblyn might have had some experience with witnessing this condition in others, but Honora hadn't managed to work up the nerve to commit her thoughts to paper, let alone invite Emblyn into a conversation on the subject.

So today, she would simply walk with her thoughts and her tears. Her fears and her worries, for herself, her child, and her husband. What would he say when he found out she was with child? Would he be delighted that he would become a father? Would he shower Honora with the affection she had been craving but not allowing herself? Would he be pleased and yet wish that someone else was the mother of the child? Would she know if that were the case? Would he feel himself so duty-bound by the child that he cut himself off from the woman he really wanted?

He might never be unfaithful to Honora physically, but that did not mean that he would not be unfaithful in his heart. That he might not wish he had waited longer for the marriage. That he would not resent Honora someday for coming between him and Margaret.

It would crush her. Kill her. Rip her burgeoning heart out and trample upon it.

But she could see it playing out as though it were already in progress. Could see the light in Gage's eyes grow more and more distant as time went on. Could see the letters passing back and forth between the two of them, confessing their true feelings with flowery words and phrases that she would never know and never see. Could feel the emptiness of Helwithin as he stayed there less and less, leaving her and the child alone with the quiet rooms and joyless days.

It would all come to pass, of that she was certain.

She had nothing to hold Gage to her but this child now. The Christmas *ceilidh* and the evening at the Teague residence told her that much. Forgetting Honora once would make it easier the second, third, and fourth time. She didn't look at him while singing the duet with Margaret, more to keep from knowing which of them he was looking at than anything else. But when she sang with Ciarán, Gage had stared at her in a way that made her hope. In a way that made her heart fly.

In a way that made the child within her dance.

But the glow of that song didn't last. The supper had been decent enough, but Honora had been seated by Basset and Roisin, while Gage had been at the far end of the table with Margaret. They had been engaged in deep conversation the entire time, only occasionally talking with Julia or Adelaide. Then there had been more music and dancing after supper, but Gage hadn't danced at all.

Honora hadn't either, but she had been avoiding the occasion by turning pages for whomever was playing the pianoforte. Gage could have come to her to ask her to dance, but he had not. He'd let her keep her distance.

Was he glad for the distance?

Why was she torturing herself with these thoughts? Why was she raking herself across the coals of heartbreak just because she feared it so? She ought to talk with Gage like an adult, not hide herself away and believe the worst. He respected her, had given her independence and strength, and he would listen to her concerns. He would be honest with her and let her know if any of her fears were founded.

But Honora knew, in her heart, that she wouldn't believe him.

Not fully.

Not completely.

She would want to, but she wouldn't.

How could she? Margaret was a stunning woman, warm and vivacious, accomplished and amusing, and well-liked by absolutely everyone who knew her. She might have married Lord Hastings, might have even loved him, but she was still drawn to Gage, that much was clear. After what Emblyn had told Honora about their conversation, there was no reason to believe their feelings had changed.

Now that Margaret had known a marriage, perhaps she knew herself well enough to know she wanted Gage after all.

But she wouldn't want to hurt Honora, she was too kind for that. So they would remain apart, even if they wished to be together.

Why should a couple that loved each other be forced to remain apart? It was Honora's fault that they had to be so. It was Honora who was keeping them from each other. It was Honora's ties to Gage, and Gage's word of honor, that made the situation what it was.

This baby was the only link that Honora could say for certain was for her and Gage alone. Would bind them together. Would ensure they were always connected.

Perhaps the child would heal the division Honora had created out of fear. Perhaps it would erase the feelings for Margaret and give them both the chance to be truly happy. Perhaps it could give them the love that Honora sought from him. Perhaps affection for the child would extend to her.

Perhaps it would compel Gage to come to Honora for more children.

Perhaps it would give Honora the confidence to ask for more.

Perhaps…

Unknowns made her uneasy, and she rubbed at her aching chest as she walked, trying her best to relieve the tension. She paused her step, looking out at the sea. It rolled and rippled gently, looking entirely unthreatening from her point of view. But the sea was powerful, dangerous, and deceptive. It trapped its victims with its gentle appearance and soothing ways until the changes were missed and the threat too great to escape.

She shifted her focus to the sky, the morning light not yet warm. The sun was still rising at this point in the day, but it would soon be behind the clouds and hidden from view. But for now, the rosy colors of the fading sunrise and the dark of looming clouds both reflected near perfectly against the water, adding more light to her present world, if only dimly so. But there was a mist above the reflection that marred perfection, and it was upon that mist she focused now.

She was the mist herself, after all, coming between two bodies of perfection and their equally perfect reflection of each other.

She marred the beauty that could have been.

Would have been.

And that, she feared, was unforgivable.

Honora wiped at the tears as they ran down her cheeks and sank to the ground, her fatigue catching up with her. She had stopped for too long, and now she would need to rest before going back to Helwithin. She hiccupped as she realized she had referred to the place by its name rather than as her home. Was she evicting herself from its presence and its life simply because she was feeling sorry for herself? Deciding her fate before she gave her husband or anyone else a chance to actually inform her as to the reality?

She was sabotaging herself. It ought to be unforgiveable, and Gage would certainly scold her for it, but this was how things always worked. This was how she had been raised. She knew where her flaws were. She knew what her worth was. She knew how she compared against others. She knew she was fortunate to be married at all, especially to Gage. She knew he would have chosen someone else if he could.

She knew he would have married Margaret if he had not decided against love.

These were the truths she knew, and until she had better truths to replace them with, they would remain.

But her child would not know these truths, about her or about itself. Her child would only know love and encouragement and positivity. Would see his or her flaws but not be ashamed of them. Would see potential in themselves, not hopelessness. Would feel loved by both parents, not only tolerated.

Her child wouldn't be like her.

Her child would be more like Gage. Open and engaging, inviting and certain of himself, accepting of love and willing to extend it. Free to be whomever he was without shame or scorn. Willing to work hard because it was right and good. Accepting of himself. Accepting of others.

Proud to let others shine without browbeating himself for whatever he thought he lacked by comparison.

Why in the world would Gage have wanted to marry Honora? If he had known her better, he would not have wished to. If he had thought about love, at the time or in the future, he would not have chosen Honora.

But he had chosen her. And now they would have a child.

Her one chance to make him not regret that choice.

A sudden cramp started in her lower abdomen, and she winced at it, her hand flying there for comfort. She got these twinges on occasion, and every time she thought she had done something wrong. But she was only sitting there now, so she knew all would be well.

She had taken to singing to her child when she got too wrapped up in her mind, and the words she had sung only that morning came back to her and were on her lips before she knew it.

"The water is wide," she began, singing softly as she moved her hand along her abdomen as though caressing her baby. "I cannot cross o'er, and neither have I wings to fly…"

She swallowed, closing her eyes on tears, and imagining that she could teach her child the sound of her voice in this moment alone.

"Give me a boat that can carry two
And both shall row, my love and I.
A ship there is, and she sails the sea
She's loaded deep as deep can be.
But not so deep as the love I'm in
I know not if I sink or swim."

Tears threatened to choke her now, the love for her husband and her child pounding with each fervent heartbeat as though her heart couldn't bear such strength of emotion. The future, the present, and the past all mingled together in her heart and her mind, in the warmth that spread through her arms and legs, in the smile she pictured on Gage's lips when she told him she was pregnant.

She shook her head as she sang the next verse, wishing her baby were old enough to kick against her hand, just to remind her she was not alone here. That she was not alone in life. That she would never be alone again.

A splashing sound brought her eyes open, and she looked around quickly, smiling very faintly as she saw children splashing in the water at Polmiskin Beach. They squealed and laughed, the sounds faint, but reaching her all the same. She couldn't tell who they were, but they were certainly enjoying themselves, despite the cold weather.

A man and a woman stood on the shore watching them, and like the children, Honora could not tell who they were. The distance was too far.

But what if it was Gage? What if Margaret had taken the boys to the beach and Gage had decided to join them? What if they were being a family at this very moment without being a family in truth?

Honora swallowed, staring at the form of the man as though somehow she would be able to know who he was if she continued to watch him. As though he would give her some sign that would tell her if it was her husband or not. As though her heart would bear witness to her of his identity.

But no answers would come. She would only ever wonder. She would only ever fear.

A weak sob escaped her, and she forced herself to sing another verse of the song, for her child if nothing else.

"Oh, love is handsome and love is kind
Bright as a jewel when first it is new.
But love grows old and waxes cold
And fades away like the morning dew."

Her love for Gage would never fade away. That much she knew for certain. But her hopes for him loving her were fading, and there was little she could do about that.

The baby, she reminded herself. The baby would help.

The baby could do wonders for them.

Another cramp hit her abdomen, and this one was fierce and painful. She winced and curled into it, breathing carefully. Had she walked too far, and her body was angry? Was she bringing the pain upon herself with her emotions? Was her baby protesting the despairing, dark thoughts she was engaging in and taking after its father in distracting her from them?

Her back suddenly began throbbing as waves of further cramps hit her stomach, her hips, her deepest parts, stealing her breath and making her moan with its intensity.

This was something new, and her pulse began to pound, her brow began to perspire. What was this? What was happening?

A new sensation hit her, exactly where she feared it might, and frantically, her fingers reached beneath her skirts, found a horrifying sensation, and came back out from the fabric tremulously.

Bright red liquid coated her fingers.

"No," she whispered, her throat clogging with the word. "No, please…"

She wiped her fingers on her skirts and rose unsteadily to her feet, turning for Helwithin and moving as fast as she dared.

"Please, no," she sobbed as she hurried, the pain continuing and moving along her legs. "Please…"

Chapter Twenty-Five

Gage whistled to himself as he entered Helwithin after a good day at Wheal Stout, exhausted and dirty, but eager for supper with Honora, if she was up to it. She had felt unwell last night, according to her maid, so she had taken supper in her room. But if she was feeling better, and dined with him, he was going to be more engaging than he had been of late and tell her everything that had happened at the mine. She would take an interest, and they would be able to talk at last.

He looked at the vase of flowers on the entrance table, noting their freshness and the simple brightness they added to the space. It was something Honora had started doing from almost the first moment she had come to Helwithin, and he loved the innocent touch it was to his home. It made the place their home, not just his. It made Helwithin a home, not just a house.

It made him feel home.

Home.

Honora was home.

Gage's eyes widened as he stared at the flowers. Wildflowers that had been seen upon the moors and glens of Cornwall every day of his life, but here, in a vase at his house, they were a reminder of his wife and warmed his heart like the touch of her lips. Without even seeing her, he was thinking of her, feeling for her, loving her...

He loved Honora. Wholly, entirely, completely. The touch of flowers in his home. The feeling of her hand in his. The smell of her hair as he held her at night. The taste of her mouth. The sweetness of her laughter. The blush upon her cheeks. The determination in her eyes. The tone of her voice.

The sound of his name from her lips.

He stumbled into the table, gripping it for strength and stability. He loved Honora. But of course he did! He knew he would, knew he could, knew that someday…

But someday was today.

Someday was probably yesterday, the day before, or three weeks ago, but what mattered was that today he knew.

He knew.

He laughed and darted towards the stairs, needing to tell Honora now. She was probably resting, as she seemed to be doing frequently of late, but he was determined. He would burst into her room and crawl upon the bed to whisper his love into her ear if he had to.

Shouting it from the rooftops was better, but probably ill-advised.

"Honora!" he shouted before he could stop himself, laughing like a madman.

There was no answer, but he didn't expect her to answer.

"Mr. Trembath, pardon me…"

"Not now, Murray," he said, waving him off as he reached the stairs.

"Gage, we found a house!" came a new voice that had him skidding.

He looked towards the drawing room, frowning a little. "Margaret? What house?"

She appeared from the room, rolling her eyes. "Honestly, Gage. In Penzance! Your contact says there is one available right now that has direct paths to the beach! I had to tell you right away. I've already written him back to ask that he begin the proceedings for us to let it for the spring."

Gage grinned, nodding in approval. "Excellent, I'm glad you found one. I need to speak with Honora, so if you'll excuse me…"

Margaret cocked her head a little. "Honora? I was told she was not at home when I arrived."

That was odd. Honora had been looking thin and frail of late and was always exhausted. As far as he knew, she wasn't going anywhere, apart from daily walks. Where would she go?

"Murray," Gage said slowly, looking at his butler and smiling. "Did Mrs. Trembath go to her cousin's?"

"The carriage is here, sir," Murray told him with a shake of his head. "I know nothing about her leaving."

"Mrs. Crane told me she was not at home," Margaret offered, her brow creasing. "When I arrived and asked, I mean."

Gage wet his lips, something nagging at him. "Let me go check her rooms. Just in case." He turned and jogged up the steps, something sharp and hot beginning to pound through his veins. "Honora? Honora! Mrs. Crane!"

"Sir?" Mrs. Crane replied, sticking her head out from one of the rooms, looking bewildered. "Do you need something?"

Gage nodded once. "Where is Honora? Murray says she's out, but the carriage isn't gone."

Mrs. Crane's eyes widened. "What? I was told she was gone when I sought her out for Lady Hastings. Bess told me she was out." Her brows snapped down and she whirled on her heel, marching for the family rooms. "Bess!"

"What's going on?" Margaret asked as she came up behind Gage, her voice clipped. "What's wrong?"

"I don't know," he replied shortly, following his housekeeper without looking at her. "But I don't like it."

They all reached Honora's rooms to find Bess in the process of stripping the bed, her countenance drawn as she faced them all.

"Where is the mistress?" Mrs. Crane demanded, folding her arms.

"Out," Bess replied in a small voice.

Gage barged forward, not apologizing when he jostled Mrs. Crane. "Out where, Bess?" he demanded. "The carriage is here, how is she out?"

Bess whimpered softly, balling up the linens anxiously. "She... she left this morning. After dawn. Packed a single valise and left the rest. Said I wasn't to tell a soul, thanked me for being her friend. Told me the carriage would be sent back before it was missed. Sir had already left for the mine, so no one would miss it."

"Where did she go?" Mrs. Crane barked before Gage could.

"I don't know," Bess whispered, shaking her head. "She

wouldn't say. But I'm so afeared. She was so unwell yesterday with the loss and the bleeding, and she didn't sleep a wink with the pain."

"Loss?" Gage repeated sharply. "Unwell? Speak plainly. What is wrong with my wife and why the hell is she gone?"

Bess clenched her teeth, still shaking her head. "The mistress was with child, sir. She lost it yesterday and kept saying that was it. Said she must away for everyone's happiness, and when I inquired... She pretended she'd said nothing. Sir, I don't know no more, but I'm so afeared she doesn't mean to come back."

It wasn't possible. Wasn't happening. Honora wouldn't leave him. She couldn't. He loved her, and he had reason to believe she loved him. How could she leave?

"Gage." Margaret grabbed his arm hard, forcing him to turn and look at her. Her fair eyes were ice cold. "Gage. If she suffered a loss only yesterday, she is in great danger. She wouldn't know it, but she is. She could continue to bleed, and badly so. She could take fever. She will be weak and overwrought and in no condition to travel, let alone by herself. The risks of her going anywhere in her condition..."

He was already moving, wrenching himself out of her hold and bolting down the hall. "Send word to Basset! Have him meet me at Truro, or on the road to it! If she's running, she'll go there for a stage!"

He wasn't certain how he got to the stables, let alone mounted his horse, but suddenly, he was on the road to Truro, galloping hard and barely aware of the wind whipping against his clothes, his face, his hair. The roaring against his ears could have been from the same, but it also could have been his own rage and panic.

How could she leave? Without a word to anyone about her plans, her destination, her reason. How could she be so selfish?

That was wrong, he corrected at once. Honora did not have a selfish bone in her body; she would never have done this for herself. If she was leaving without a word, she had a good reason for it, at least in her own mind. It would help someone or do some good. Either there was a plan in place, or she was sacrificing herself for some cause.

Whatever it was, he wasn't about to let it happen. However good or noble her intentions, this was wrong, and he would tell her so. He would tell her how ardently he loved her, how precious she was to him, how crucial she was to his happiness and success, how desperately he wanted a future with her…

A child. She had been with child. Had that been why she had been distant and exhausted? Had she not known how to tell him what she herself was going through? Could he have helped her if he had known? Or was this something only another woman would comprehend?

She had lost their child. Knowing how pure, true, and generous her heart was, that would have been a cruel blow. He wanted to hold her while she cried for their loss. Wanted to cry with her for their loss. Wanted to know everything about every moment of their child. Wanted the child to be as real to him as it had been to her, though now it was gone from them both.

Child or not, he needed Honora. For happiness, for clarity, for sanity, he needed Honora. Whether or not she needed him was not for him to decide, but he would try to be needed by her. To be useful to her. To be anything to her.

But he needed her in order to be anything.

He heard another set of hoofs over the sound of his own galloping against the wind and glanced over his shoulder. Basset was not far behind him and pushing hard to catch up. They met eyes only for a moment, but Gage saw the same determination in his friend as he felt in his chest.

No matter what they found in Truro, they would find Honora. They would track her down, wherever she had gone and however long it would take. He would finally talk with her, try to understand, and do what he could to bring her home.

But what if she did not want to? What if the life he had offered her was not what she wanted and that was why she had left? What if, in encouraging her to find herself and her own strength, he had provided a way for her to realize that she did not want him at all?

Was that possible? Was Honora leaving him because she wished to? He couldn't believe it, but what if…?

His mind whirled with possibilities as he rode, time having no meaning and distance fading fast. Only when he began to see signs and indications of nearing Truro did his thoughts begin to clear and his focus return. The wildness had to be tamped down just enough that reason and sense could prevail. Though he would be wild regardless of either.

Basset rode up beside him as the galloping had to slow as they entered the town. "Try the coaching inn first," his friend said briskly. "It will be the best option if she is trying to get away. We can spread out from there, if we don't find her."

Gage nodded but hated that possibility. If she wasn't there. If they couldn't find her. She had to be there.

She had to.

The coaching inn was before them moments later, and Gage nearly threw himself from his horse as he rode up. Somehow, he landed on his feet, tossed the reins towards Basset, and bolted into the building, heart pounding so furiously, he could barely breathe.

Please don't let me lose her!

He shoved the thought out of his head the moment it was complete. He would not lose her.

He couldn't.

The room was about half-filled with patrons, he noted as he scanned it frantically. It shouldn't take too much to find his wife in here.

Assuming she hadn't departed already.

"No," he muttered softly. She was here. She was going to be here.

He took a few steps farther into the room and cleared his throat as Basset appeared at his shoulder. No one really paid attention or moved at all.

Except for one.

As those beautiful, blessed green eyes hit him from the back of the room, his stomach dropped to his toes and his breath hitched. He couldn't even say her name, yet he could feel his lips form it. But the moment was broken all too soon as he noticed that she looked petrified, her grip on her reticule white-knuckled and clenching, her eyes red-rimmed and swollen, her skin paler than was normal, almost deathly.

He saw the tears fall in the same instant that a heartbroken, pained cry was ripped from Honora's throat as she jumped from her seat, racing across the room, knocking her chair aside.

Before he knew what was happening, he was running. "No! No, Nora, no!" he bellowed, upending a table in front of him in his desperation. He leapt over chairs and probably some patrons, but his wife was running away from him, damn it! "Nora!"

She skirted around tables and chairs, but her steps were unsteady, and her speed limited.

He'd never been so grateful for her limitations in his life.

"Stop, Nora, stop!" he roared, shoving another table out of the way, and in the next moment, he was on top of a table, then propelling himself off of it towards Honora. Luck was with him, for suddenly, he found himself holding both of her wrists and thrusting her back against the wall.

"Let me go, Gage," she sobbed weakly, struggling in his hold. "Please, please, let me go."

"Not on your life, Nora," he choked out, wishing he could erase all of his life that had brought her to this. Tears threatened him now, relief and agony colliding within him. "You are never going anywhere ever again, do you hear me?"

A whimper escaped from her lips, and she wrenched her wrists against his hands, trying to free them.

"Nora, stop. Stop," he groaned, swallowing back his emotions. "Nora, please, stop. Sweetheart…"

With that endearment, she crumpled completely and looked away, sagging against the wall behind them. "Oh, please," she whispered. "Please, Gage, don't. I can't…"

"Nora," he murmured, resting his forehead against the wall beside hers. "Oh, Nora, why didn't you tell me? Our baby, Nora…" His voice broke, and he touched his lips to her hair softly.

She shook her head. "Our baby is gone, and it is better for everyone if I am gone as well…" Her fingers splayed, and then she was sinking, her eyes rolling back, all color fading from her face.

"Nora!" He scooped her up into his arms, her limp frame weighing almost nothing even in this state. "Get a doctor!"

No one seemed to move, though eyes were on him now.

Basset slammed a fist down on a table. "Get a doctor for the lady! Now!"

That got people moving, a few bowing and scraping in their haste to either be of assistance or simply get out of the way.

Basset strode to the innkeeper behind a counter. "A room. Any room. Now."

"Yes, sir," came the quick reply from the man, who waved at Gage. "This way, sir. There's a room upstairs all ready."

Cradling his beloved Honora, Gage hurried over and started up the stairs behind him.

"How is she?" Basset asked from his back.

"Out cold," he ground out. "I don't... I don't know..."

Basset put a hand on his shoulder as they reached the landing. "She's strong, Gage. She'll be all right, I am sure of it."

Gage nodded and turned into the second room on his left, following the innkeeper and laying Honora on the small bed in the room. He began working at her traveling cloak and nudged at Basset. "Get her bonnet off. Her boots, too. Innkeeper, a basin of water and some rags. Tea. Madeira. Anything."

"Yes, sir. Right away." He vanished, leaving the two men to their work.

Gage tugged the cloak from under Honora as Basset flung the bonnet across the room and moved to her shoes. Together they untied the laces and cast the shoes aside. Gage moved up to the head of the bed, cupping Honora's face in his hands.

Basset cleared his throat. "I'll go down and bring the doctor up when he arrives."

Gage barely acknowledged him as he left, his entire being and attention focused on his wife.

What had she said? It would be better if she were gone? That could not be further from the truth. It would have been hell. Could she really not see it? How much he needed her? How incomparable she was? How incredible? How perfect for him?

But he had not lived in her heart and mind, and before their marriage, she had never once had a voice of her own. A positive thing to say or think about herself. Had he not done enough to improve such things for her?

No one would be better with Honora gone. No one.

He moved his hands to hers, feeling for the pulse at her wrist, grateful to find it throbbing steadily, even if it wasn't as strong as he would have liked.

Basset returned with the innkeeper and the doctor a few minutes later, and Gage remained in his place as the doctor examined her. Checked for fever, felt her pulse, pressed on her stomach, examined her limbs. Basset answered his questions as best as he could, and Gage chimed in for details he would not be privy to. But only Honora could answer the more intimate questions, and she had not come around yet.

Gage took the rags from the innkeeper, soaked them in water, and dabbed them along Honora's brow and face. She stirred and moaned weakly, her eyes cracking open and fixing on Gage. They widened as she looked at him, nothing in their depths giving him comfort.

He couldn't bear this. He took the hand he held and brought it to his lips, kissing softly before taking another rag to set at her brow.

Honora swallowed, and turned her head away, but left her hand where it was.

That was something, at least.

The doctor said something about watching her closely and returning when she was more awake. He left the room with Basset, and the door was shut behind them.

Alone in the room, Gage set the rag back in the basin, adjusted his hold on Honora's hand, and sighed. "Honora... what did you mean when you said it would be better if you were gone?"

She did not make any motions towards him, and her hand felt cold and limp in his hold. "Just that," she told him in a very soft voice. "If I were gone, your life would be better. You would be happier. Free."

Gage squeezed his eyes shut, his throat tightening, "If you believe that, then I have truly failed you."

He heard a rustling on the bed, felt her shift slightly, but couldn't move himself. He could only sit there, eyes closed, and fight for the words of his heart.

"I love you," he said in a low voice, emphasizing each word carefully. "With a consuming, indescribable depth I am still struggling to comprehend. In a way I have never known before and didn't know was possible. I love you. And I have never… There's only you, Nora. There only ever will be you."

"Gage…"

He opened his eyes and turned to face her, covering her hand with both of his and holding it in his lap. "I need you to tell me something. I know how generous your heart is, and I know it is not in you to injure a single creature. I know that you would give yourself up to make someone else happy. But what I need to know is this: What is it that you want? Forget about me, forget about anyone else. Just you. What do you want?"

Her brilliant green eyes filled with tears, which flowed down her cheeks as she stared up at him in anguish. "All I wanted was to run back home and beg you to love me."

His heart shattered into a thousand tiny pieces, somehow filling him with as much warmth as it did pain. "Oh, my love…" He dropped her hand and leaned down to kiss her. She reached for his face, her fingers scratching along the stubble at his jaw. He cupped her jaw and explored her mouth fervently, reveling in her hold on him, as if she would never let go, and knowing he never could. "I do love you," he whispered against her soft lips, tugging them gently. "Almost from the start. And every day I have found myself loving you more."

Honora began to cry in earnest, her fingers falling to his shirt and gripping hard. "I love you," she rasped, her tears making the words pitch in tone. "I didn't want to leave you, but I thought… I thought…"

"What did you think?" he asked gently, pulling back and brushing her hair back from her damp skin, cupping one cheek and stroking it with his thumb. "Tell me, what?"

She shook her head slightly. "I just thought… with Margaret…" She took a would-be controlling breath. "She is beautiful and lovely… and you deserve… I wanted you to be happy, both of you, and I was…" She blinked hard and a few tears leaked out. "And then I lost the baby, and it broke the only thing I thought could bind you to me."

"Nora," Gage murmured softly. "Sweetheart, I am bound to you. Not by our vows, but by my heart. By my choice. By my love, my

287

devotion, my complete adoration. It took me long enough to realize it, but once I did, I understood just how long I have felt this way. If you ever leave me, Nora, you had better take me with you. I am nothing without you."

Honora shuddered, soft, tired sobs racking her. "I'm sorry. I'm so sorry."

"Don't be sorry," he whispered, leaning close and pressing his lips to her brow. "Be mine. Be my wife, my lover, my friend, my morning and evening... Be my everything, Nora. God knows, I want to be yours."

"Hold me, Gage," Honora suddenly pleaded, her fingers practically clawing against his shirt. "Please, please, just hold me."

He kissed her brow again, rising from his seat. "I will, love. As long as you like, as long as you need. Come here." He lay down beside her and pulled her into his embrace, cradling her against him.

She immediately tucked her legs between his, burrowing her face into his chest, her arms reaching around his body and latching on to him as though they were in some tossing sea, and he would keep her safe.

Exhaling slowly and softly, Gage ran his fingers through her hair, dismantling whatever style or hold had been placed on it. He simply ran his hand over her scalp and into her tresses over and over, trailing down her back from time to time, comforting himself with the feel of her in his arms, and hopefully comforting her by the reminder that she was not alone.

Neither of them was.

"Will ye not come back again?" he whispered against her hair. "Better loved ye cannot be. Will ye not come back again?"

"Yes. Forever. Always," she told him. Then she shook her head, her tears dampening his shirt. "I wanted this baby so much, Gage. So much. I wanted to tell you, but I wanted to be sure, and then when I was... I told myself lies that I believed. And perhaps as punishment, I lost our baby before I could tell you. I thought it was a sign that the lies were true, and that I should leave. With my pain as mine alone, and not yours."

Gage tightened his hold on her, resting his mouth against her scalp. "I want your pain to be my pain. I want to share any pain, any hurt, any trial. I want to share everything with you, and I will, if you will let me."

"This is hard to explain," she managed, clearing her throat. "It feels as though I have lost part of myself. Perhaps six or eight weeks in existence, and its loss has shattered what I knew of myself. What I knew of life. What I thought about the future. I have lost something that cannot be replaced, and it is terrifying. My emotions do not belong to me, my body feels foreign, and I could sleep for weeks. But I am afraid to sleep, for fear that when I wake, it will be as if this child had never been. But it was real, Gage. It was so real." She buried her face against his chest, her tears renewed.

His own tears were falling now, and he let them fall. Let them shower her hair and mingle with her own. He had known of his child for mere hours, and already it was gone. He was only at the beginning of his pain, but she had been feeling it for a lifetime longer. One day, but a lifetime within its bounds.

A hole was forming in his heart, and it was going to grow and expand, but he would share that pain with Honora. Help her carry it. "I wish I had answers for you," he managed around his tightening throat. "For us. I wish there was something that could be done, some healing to extend. But I have nothing. I just ache for you, and I ache for our child. That… will never go away. But I offer you what strength I have, and I ask for yours in return. We can get through this. Now… are you all right?"

He felt Honora nod against him, then shake her head after a moment of hesitation. "Everything hurts," she murmured. "Physically and emotionally. I am dizzy, and I could not sleep last night for pain and agony. I almost came to your rooms."

"I wish you had." He nuzzled softly, then tilted her face up to kiss her lips tenderly, stroking her cheeks. "I am so relieved I've found you, and that you were strong enough to endure this so far. Where were you going to go?"

"Ireland. You once told me it gave one a sense of home as soon as one stood on the shores."

"A sense, yes," he confirmed. "But do you know what I realized today? When I discovered you were gone?"

She looked up at him, her eyes wide and filled with hope and dread. "What?"

Gage smiled, his thumb rubbing across her too-pale cheek. "Whether I am in Ireland, Cornwall, or anywhere else in the world, no place will be home without you. You are my home, Nora. You are all I need. Everything I need."

She smiled faintly, her eyes fluttering at his touch. "What if I cannot have another child?" she whispered, covering his hand on her cheek. "What if I cannot bear you an heir and the estate falls from your family line?"

"Well..." Gage thought about that, leaning his head on the pillow and gazing down at his wife. "Then it falls to some distant cousin, or our godson, who will undoubtedly take better care of it than I can. I'm not at all concerned about the estate. I can live without that. But I cannot live without you. I will not."

"You could," Honora told him as she pressed a kiss into his palm. "I know you could."

Gage folded her into his embrace again, resting his mouth at her ear. "I could," he murmured as his lips dusted the tender surface. "But I would not want to. And that is the difference."

Honora sniffled, her kiss pressing into his neck. "I love you, Gage," she said softly, her lips branding the words into his skin.

"I love you, my love," he returned, his fingers resuming running through her hair. "And now it is my turn to be the stubborn nursemaid to you. Revenge will be sweet, and you will do everything I say. There will be no sneaking out of bed to scamper about the house. There will be no begging to go downstairs by yourself. I will carry you everywhere until I am satisfied you can walk, and when you can, you will only walk with my assistance. You will have a warm bath every day, even if only to soothe your aching, and only I will tend you. There will be no chance for nighttime wanderings, as I will be lying beside you on guard..."

Honora's laughter reached his ears, and it was sweeter than any music he had ever heard, even from her. It was the song of his heart, though it came from her lips, and it began what would be a slow, painful process of healing for them. But it was a beginning together, and that was what mattered.

"And I will sing to you," he went on, enjoying how her laughter rippled through her frame and into him. "I've been practicing my Christmas gifts, and know a few others, and I will make up songs if I run out of them…"

Epilogue

"Another push, mistress. One more. All of your might."

Honora took in a pair of panting breaths, nodding amidst the sweat and the pain, her left hand gripping the linens beneath her while her right hand gripped that of her husband.

Sitting up, she bore down with all of her might, a harrowing cry ripping from her chest and likely from the depths of her soul, the pressure unlike any pain she had ever known in her entire life.

And then there was a release.

Her heart stopped and her lungs deflated, then both started functioning properly again as she lay back against the pillows, gasping for air while her entire body pounded with her pulse.

A shrill wailing filled the air, and at the same time filled Honora's body with light.

"It's a girl!" Gage shouted from beside her, kissing her hand repeatedly. "My love, you've done it! We have a daughter!"

Honora managed a laugh that was so choked with tears, it hardly qualified. "A daughter?" She raised her head, her legs shaking in their propped-up position. "Let me see her."

The doctor grinned and held up the still-crying baby, her dark hair already curling like her father's.

She was the most beautiful sight Honora had ever seen.

"Oh, Gage," she whispered, still laughing. "Look at her!"

He rose and sat beside her on the bed, pulling her gently into him, his arms going around her. "Yes, my love. Look at her."

Honora gripped his arms, watching as the doctor cleaned the baby and handed her to Julia, who had been standing nearby to help.

"Oh, little lamb," Julia cooed, tucking the blankets more securely around her. "Auntie Julia is going to spoil you so terribly. And Auntie Addie will be just as bad."

Gage laughed, kissing Honora's head. "Does Adelaide know you're telling our daughter to call her Addie?"

"I'm doing my best to be a bad influence early," Julia said, though her words were directed to the baby in playful tones rather than looking at Gage at all. "Now, love, let's take you to Mama and Papa, shall we?" She walked around to Honora's side and handed the precious bundle off, not bothering to hide her tears.

Honora cradled her daughter in her arms, the tiny eyes closed and perfect little mouth gaping with the smallest breaths, the distress of moments before gone now. Her daughter's fingers curled into fists, one of them moving to her mouth, and she settled in Honora's hold as though she had always belonged there.

"Good morning, darling one," Honora whispered, drawing a finger down the soft, perfectly pink cheek. "You were in a hurry, weren't you?"

"Takes after her papa in that," Gage murmured as he reached out to press his finger against his daughter's fingers. They opened up and encased his finger securely, making Gage chuckle. "Already, she has a hold on me."

Honora leaned into her husband, overwhelmed by love. Love for him, love for their daughter, love for their life… Everything before now had been worth it, and whatever came after would be fine. She had worried about losing this baby every step of the way, as she had lost their first, but blessedly, here they were. A healthy, plump baby girl with her father's hair and charm, alive and well, and theirs.

Perfectly theirs.

"And with the way she cried, she probably has her mother's powerful voice," Julia pointed out from Honora's other side, wiping at her eyes.

"Only when I sing," she said. "And her father has a beautiful voice."

Gage kissed her cheek, laying his head against hers. "Not even remotely beautiful compared with yours."

Honora tsked at him in a hint of a scold, but it was not in her to argue right now. The only thing she wanted to do was hold her daughter and remain in her husband's arms.

This was the happiest place she had ever been.

"I want to call her Bridget," Honora announced quietly. "After your mother, Gage."

She heard his slight choking sound and tore her gaze from their daughter to look up at him.

His eyes were filled with tears, and his throat bobbed several times.

Honora laid a hand on his cheek, smiling gently. "I never met her," she whispered for him alone, "but I feel her here. I feel her in this house, and I know her through you. I want our daughter to adore her grandmother and to become just like her."

Gage shook his head and kissed her, his lips fervent and sweet. "I want our daughter to become just like you," he rasped, taking her mouth again with surprising depth and intensity. "I love you so much."

"So," Honora managed, when he let her, "that's a yes?"

He laughed and gave her another quick kiss. "Less of the cheek, you. But yes, I would love to name her after my mother." He touched his brow to hers, then looked down at their daughter. "Good day, Miss Bridget Trembath. It is a joy to meet you in person at last."

Julia sniffled loudly. "And what about her middle name? Another lovely Irish name?"

Honora shook her head. "I don't think so. How about Grace?"

"How about Honora?" Gage answered before she finished.

They exchanged bemused looks, and Honora smiled at him, her cheeks coloring. "She's already going to have to cope with being my daughter. Surely, bearing my name is a bit much."

"Nothing about you is a bit much," Gage assured her. "Everything about you is perfection."

Honora rolled her eyes and looked at her cousin for help. "Julia?"

She only shrugged. "I agree, your name is lovely and would be perfect for her. But I like your choice as well."

That was not exactly helpful, but Honora looked down at her little girl all the same. "Such a marvelous girl could probably endure a marvelous name. Bridget Honora Grace Trembath."

"Perfection," Gage murmured. He leaned past her to kiss his daughter's brow. "What do you think, *hwegen*? Will it do?"

"What does *hwegen* mean?" Honora asked, looking at him with a curious smile.

Gage smiled back. "'Darling' or 'pet.' I am certain she will give me something else to call her someday, but *hwegen* will suit for now."

Honora suddenly wanted to cry again, overcome by joy, by love, by disbelief that this was her life. That she had found such an existence with a man who adored her and whom she adored. That they had grown closer to each other in the days following their loss than she thought possible. That mere months later, they had conceived again, this time with no secrets or doubts. That now there was physical proof of their mutual adoration, and a new light in their future.

Who knew how many other lights there would be as time went on, but of one thing she was certain: that future was brighter than she could ever have dreamed it would be.

"Sing to her, Gage," Honora managed around fresh tears. "Sing to our little girl for me."

Carefully, he took the baby from her, but secured Honora to his side with his other arm as they lay back against the pillows. He kissed Honora's brow, then looked down at their precious Bridget with all the love in the world. "My love is like a red, red rose," he sang softly, "that's newly sprung in June…"

Coming Soon

Something Blue

Cornwall Brides
Book Four

"In prosperity and adversity…"

by

REBECCA CONNOLLY

Printed in the USA
CPSIA information can be obtained
at www.ICGtesting.com
LVHW010805061223
765353LV00067B/1105